THEY DON'T MAKE THEM LIKE HUMPHREY BOGART ANYMORE AND I'M NO EXCEPTION.

This is why I chose to go to my room and lie down instead of getting right into my car and driving off to confront Marisa's pursuers. But the longer I lay there, fully dressed on my motel bed and staring at the ceiling, the more I realized that I had almost no other choice. Eventually, I knew, they would begin to look for me too. I stood a better chance of confronting them successfully at a time and in a place of my own choosing than just sitting back and waiting for them to find me. That was my rational brain at work, but I had more urgent concerns. My main one in all of this was coming out intact. It would be just like Mellini to want to break my fingers. And Castle, Emile's hired playmate, would also welcome the opportunity to even his score with me by beating a rattling tattoo on my helpless carcass. As I lay there, paralyzed by my fear and wondering how in the hell I had gotten myself into this mess, I could almost hear my bones snapping like dried celery stalks. . . .

"FAST, FUNNY AND FURIOUS. . . . Murray brings uncommon literary flair to his tangy evocation of lowlife."—*Publishers Weekly*

"ENGAGINGLY SLEAZY AND ENGROSSING. . . . Murray is at least a length and a half in front of the literary tough guys, and closing in fast on Leonard."
—*Kirkus Reviews*

Bantam Books by William Murray

WHEN THE FAT MAN SINGS
THE KING OF THE NIGHTCAP

THE KING
OF THE NIGHTCAP

William Murray

BANTAM BOOKS
NEW YORK · TORONTO · LONDON · SYDNEY · AUCKLAND

THE KING OF THE NIGHTCAP

A Bantam Book
Bantam hardcover edition / August 1989
Bantam paperback edition / August 1990

ISBN 0-553-28426-6

Published simultaneously in the United States and Canada

Bantam Books are published by Bantam Books, a division of Bantam
Doubleday Dell Publishing Group, Inc. Its trademark, consisting of
the words "Bantam Books" and the portrayal of a rooster, is
Registered in U.S. Patent and Trademark Office and in other
countries. Marca Registrada. Bantam Books, 666 Fifth Avenue, New
York, New York 10103.

PRINTED IN THE UNITED STATES OF AMERICA

O   0 9 8 7 6 5 4 3 2 1

This book is dedicated to the memory of Jack Glass, who died at Santa Anita one afternoon with a winning ticket in his pocket. He left behind a lot of memories of good times and took the love of his friends with him.

"Nobody ever committed suicide who had a good two-year-old in the barn."

—OLD RACETRACK PROVERB

"Never knock a horse until he's dead."

—CHARLIE WHITTINGHAM, HORSE TRAINER

One

MONEY

"I ain't old, Walter, I just been around too long," the old man said. "Like some of these goddamn horses I bet on."

"Yeah, I know what you mean," Walter agreed, nodding his head in commiseration. The two men were sitting side by side at the bar. "They have their good days and their bad days."

"Mostly bad, I figure."

"Well, shit, Harry, they're only human."

I sat down at the end of the bar and listened, but my mind wasn't really on this conversation. It was bad enough that I had lost eighty dollars of my own betting on animals I knew nothing about, but I still hadn't been able to find Fingers. In fact, I couldn't be sure he was even around. All I had to go on, after all, was a rumor Jay had insisted I track down. Fingers had to be somewhere, we had reasoned, and he might as well be down here, in Tijuana, where perhaps he thought he could hide from us. By that time I didn't think we stood much of a chance of getting our money back, but we had to try. Fifteen thousand dollars is a healthy little sum, especially to a dedicated horseplayer like me.

"I guess I'm not good for much but talk," Harry said. "Them goddamn horses sure can take the juice out of a man."

"They can kill you, Harry," his friend said.

"I ain't about to die just yet," Harry informed him. "My father lived to be ninety-six."

"How'd he die, Harry?"

"In a goddamn car accident," Harry said. "Some damn woman ran a stop sign and hit him. There wasn't a damn thing wrong with him, except he couldn't see too good out of one eye."

"And he was driving?"

"Sure, that's what he did all his life. He was a goddamn bologna fetcher."

"A what?"

"He sold meat for a company out of Illinois."

A small, plump, blond woman, who had been sitting a few stools away from him, got up and went over to him. She moved in close and ran her hand up his back. "I really like you, Harry," she said in a Spanish accent. "Why don't you and me, we go dancing?"

"Not now, honey," Harry answered without even looking at her. "I want a couple of damn drinks first."

"Sure, that's all right," she said, smiling and hanging on to his arm. "You drink and then we go dancing." She turned to address the rest of us, as if she had made a discovery it was important to share. "You know, Harry is very good looking, when he puts his teeth in."

"And I ain't that old," Harry said, his jaw set and his elbows resting on the bar. He had a full head of white hair that seemed to perch on his head like a beret, and his pink face glowed in the darkness. "Not so old I don't know what I'm doin'."

"Here's to you, Harry," Walter said, raising his glass to toast him and then turning to confront the room at large. "Let's hear it for old Harry here. He knows what he's doing, which is more than I can say for the rest of us on this planet."

There must have been fourteen or fifteen of us in the room by that time, and we all raised our glasses to him. Surely there was no reason not to, especially since the only woman in the room was hanging all over him. I couldn't really tell in the dim light, but I had a feeling she was at least fifty years old herself and blond was not her natural color. Still, the only man among us who seemed to interest her at all was Harry, and that had to count in his favor. We drank to his health.

I had an odd feeling that I'd been in this place for days, even though I knew with absolute certainty that it couldn't have been more than twenty minutes. The room was small and dark, with a tightly curved bar and tables packed between it and the door. There were bullfight posters on the walls and a huge velvet painting over the bar of a kneeling Aztec maiden with breasts like small bongo drums. The light came mainly from a single neon strip mounted over a counter holding several rows of bottles and glasses within easy reach of the bartender, a short, skinny Mexican with a tiny mustache and black curly hair plastered to his skull by some sort of sweet-smelling cream. He stood there, arms folded against his stomach, between quick forays to replenish our drinks, and he seemed entirely uninterested in the conversation I had been listening to, probably because he had heard it, or something very much like it, too many times before. His name was Pancho, or at least that was what all the gringos in the place called him. I felt as if I'd blundered into a reunion of survivors.

I ordered another Dos Equis and watched the woman work on Harry, while the talk flowed on, harmless and inconsequential, around me. I had tomorrow's *Racing Form* tucked into a side pocket and I was planning to get back to my room at the Conquistador early enough to do a little homework. I was convinced I had embarked on a futile quest and I was annoyed not only at myself, but also at my old sidekick Jay Fox for having persuaded me to come down here in the first place. We had nothing to go on except a rumor that Fingers had been spotted in the Caliente clubhouse, but racetracks are notorious for being small, self-contained worlds awash in tattle. I didn't really believe I'd find him, but I thought I'd give it one more day before heading back to L.A.

"Hey, Dan the Man!" a voice called out in the darkness. "How's it going?"

"How should it go? It went great," the new arrival answered as he moved toward the bar.

"Have a drink," Harry said. "Hell, have two."

The newcomer settled into a seat beside me and ordered a Corona, then turned and nodded affably to me. "Haven't seen you before," he said.

"Lou Anderson. My friends call me Shifty." We shook hands.

"Just visiting?"

"Came down for the racing," I explained. "I don't go to Hollywood Park if I can help it."

"You live up in L.A.?"

"West Hollywood. You?"

"Chula Vista. That's just a few miles from the border."

"I gather everybody in here is a horse degenerate."

"Why else would anybody come to Tijuana?"

"To shop?"

"I guess. Me, it's the horses."

"I figured maybe, with the off-track wagering now at Del Mar all year around, nobody'd be coming here anymore," I suggested.

Dan the Man laughed. "A lot of people don't come, like you say," he agreed, "but if you want to bet a lot of different tracks, you still got to come here. You can bet tracks all over the country here, starting at nine o'clock in the morning. Where else can you get this much action?"

"Las Vegas."

"Too far to go and too expensive. And anyway, I'm strictly a horseplayer."

"Me too."

He leaned in close to me. "I got a program that's going to earn me a minimum of a hundred thousand a year," he confided, suddenly looking solemn and conspiratorial. "I just put it into action two weeks ago."

I love stories like this; in fact, it's one of the reasons I'm hooked on the races, apart from the horses themselves and the betting, of course. I looked more closely at my new friend, and I could tell that he was absolutely serious and that he was waiting, a little tensely, for my reaction. "A hundred thousand a year?" I echoed. "That sounds like a good program. What is it?"

He told me, but not so loudly that the news would permeate the room. Anyway, he needn't have worried on that score; the action in the place was centered on Harry and the woman, who was still hanging on to his arm and trying to coax him out into the night. She had a gold front tooth that gleamed like a small beacon in the darkness whenever the light from the bar caught it just right. Dan the Man had my almost undivided attention.

He was planning to enrich himself, he revealed, by betting two hundred dollars to show on fast horses in sprint races. He didn't need to buy a *Racing Form* or even a program, because he could glance at other people's or simply look at the past-performance sheets from a copy of the *Form* that the management of the Foreign Book at Caliente obligingly pasted up on the wall for bettors too cheap or too broke to buy their own paper. "I don't need to stand there a long time," Dan the Man explained, "because it only takes me about five minutes. I only need to look at a horse's last three races and total up the speed ratings."

"No kidding?" I said, feigning amazement. "It's that easy?"

"You bet it is, and I can prove it."

"Then why are you telling me?" I asked.

"Because nobody believes me and people think they can make a killing at the track, that's why. You aren't going to play my system, are you?"

"Probably not," I confessed with a smile. "I usually don't like to risk that much on a single race. And I like to vary my bets."

"Sure, I understand," Dan the Man said, motioning

to Pancho for another beer. "That's why I can tell you or anyone about it. Now, that is." He took a long, last swig of his first Corona and pushed it away from him as Pancho arrived with his refill. "After a while, when I've established myself, I'll stop talking about it. If we all do it, the tracks will change the rules on us. I know they'll cut me off here. Hell, in Mexico they can do anything they want. Eventually I'll have to move to Vegas, probably. But it'll be a while before they catch on to me."

"A horse's last three races, huh?"

"Yep, that's it. I've been testing the system for two years on a computer and it works."

"Sounds good," I lied.

"Remember, now, only to show and on sprint races," he reminded me. "Money in the bank."

He was in his mid-thirties, a round-faced innocent. He sported a mustache and was wearing dark gray polyester slacks, a white short-sleeved sport shirt with scarlet flamingos cavorting across his chest, and a red baseball cap tilted high up off his forehead. He owned a hardware store in Chula Vista, he told me, and he'd been coming to Caliente once or twice a week over the years, betting only small amounts, winning some and losing some. From now on, however, he was planning to come down every Friday night and spend the weekend at the motel next to the bar we were in, directly across the street from the track. This would be a little hard on his wife and two kids, he conceded, but they'd understand, once the money really started to roll in.

"So how are you doing so far?" I asked.

"I'm only ahead a hundred and eighty dollars," he confessed. "I got a couple of dumb rides last week and another one today, so I only broke even. But it's just a matter of time. I have to win; no way I can lose. And this is money you can hide from the tax man."

"Sounds promising, Dan."

"Yeah. What did you say your name was? Swifty?"

"Shifty, Shifty Lou Anderson."

"That's a funny name."

"I'm a close-up magician," I explained. "I deal cards a lot. A shift is a way of dealing."

"That's wild," Dan the Man said. "A magician, huh? Ever hear the one about the Polish magician who tried to saw his wife in half with a spoon?"

I admitted that I hadn't heard that one, so Dan the Man proceeded to tell it to me. I missed the punch line, but I laughed when he did, after which I asked him if he knew Fingers.

"Who?"

"Tall, thin guy about forty-five. He has these long knobby fingers he kind of snaps and wiggles all the time. You couldn't miss him if you ever saw him. He's always in motion."

"So what's his real name?"

"Pendleton. I don't know his first one," I said. "He's just a guy you see at the track. He's always at Santa Anita or Hollywood."

"And you think he's down here now?"

"Somebody saw him and told a friend of mine."

"So you came down to look for him."

I abruptly decided to be cautious. "Well, yeah. I'd like to see him, if he's here. I don't know anybody in Tijuana, and he's a lot of laughs."

"Let me ask," Dan the Man said, picking up his drink. "Somebody in here might know him." He moved along the length of the bar, leaning in from time to time to ask about Fingers, but nobody had ever heard of him. "Sorry," he said, settling in his seat again.

"What the hell kind of a name is that?" Harry called out.

"It's a nickname," I explained. "You'd understand, if you ever saw him in action."

"I knew a guy named Knuckles once," somebody else volunteered. "Maybe they're related."

"Come on, Harry," the woman said, tugging at the old man's arm again, "we go dancing now."

"Look out, Harry," Dan the Man warned him. "That isn't all she wants."

"That she can't have anymore," Harry said. "I used it too much when I was young."

"What'd it do, Harry, fall off?"

"Well, you know where I live, don't you? Limp-Dick Acres, we call it."

I paid for my drinks and was about to say good night to Dan the Man, when Pancho came back with my change and leaned across the counter. "*Señor?*"

"Yes?"

"This man you are looking for, I think I know him."

"Fingers?"

"I think he is the one. I see him at the track."

"When?"

"Two days ago, at the dogs. He is with another man I know, not a good man."

"American?"

"*Sí, señor.*" Pancho glanced quickly around the room, then leaned in very close to my ear. "At the dog races, tomorrow night."

"Thanks."

"*Señor,* this other man, he is *violento.* He is a friend of yours?"

"No, only Fingers."

"Good. *Buenas noches, señor.*"

"See you at the races, Dan," I said, heading out toward the parking lot and my car.

I couldn't sleep. My room at the Conquistador was on a corner of the second floor, overlooking a central courtyard, and it was quiet enough, but my mind had begun to race. Not even a quick perusal of the *Form* had managed to distract me. The past-performance stats seemed to blur before my eyes into a jumble of meaningless statistics; I couldn't discern a pattern or a trend in any of it. I dropped the paper on the floor and lay on my back, staring up at the blank ceiling.

How could Fingers have just disappeared with our money? I knew as well as Jay that he was not to be relied on in most areas of human endeavor and that he was a dubious character at best, but by vanishing with our loot he had broken every rule of the track and put himself hopelessly beyond the pale of horseplaying respectability. Terminal losers like Fingers could stay in action in his world only by executing the routine little chores and errands the big players and the professionals like Jay demanded of him. By running away he had made it impossible for himself to keep showing up, at least on the premises of the Southern California racing emporiums we frequented.

It had been about ten days now since Jay had hit his big ticket, on the next-to-last card of the Oak Tree fall meet at Santa Anita. The Pick-Six combination ticket was worth exactly fifteen thousand forty-two dollars, a nice coup, especially when you consider it had only cost two hundred and eighty-eight dollars, about ten percent of it put up by me. Forty percent of the ticket had been bought by two members of Jay's betting syndicate, both of whom had been in the box with us when the last winner in the sequence had come bounding home down the hillside turf course, at odds of better than four to one. We had all begun jumping up and down, hugging and congratulating each other on our coup. All except Jay, of course. He had long ago trained himself not to show too much emotion at the track, so he had simply sat there, grinning contentedly, while the rest of us had made fools of ourselves.

"Come on, Jay," I had urged him. "Loosen up a little."

But he had continued merely to sit there, a placid island in a turbulent sea, surrounded by his charts and notebooks and workout sheets, as serene in his success as if it had been preordained in the zodiac. "We're going to need somebody to sign for this one," he said. "I'm over my limit this year."

That was when Fingers had suddenly appeared among us, as abruptly as if he had been summoned out of a bottle. He was a tall, gangly, scruffy-looking man in his mid-forties who had the eyes of an ancient; he had crawled out of so many holes that he looked as if he had been buried alive and dug up a little too late. "You had that?" he asked, standing just outside our boxful of celebrants. "You had that, Jay? Hey, nice hit!" And he snapped and waggled his long fingers in excitement, fluttering them about his head as if spanking gnats. "Hey, Jay, you need me on this one?"

"I think so, Fingers. Hold on, okay?"

"Sure, sure," Fingers answered, nodding and twitching and letting those long, bony appendages of his execute their mesmerizing little dance. "Hey, nice hit! That's great, guys! Nice hit, no kidding!"

After the race had been declared official and the payoff blinked dazzlingly at us from the tote board, Jay turned to Fingers and handed him our ticket. "We'll be right here, Fingers," he said. "Come right back."

"You bet, Jay. Nice hit. I'll take care of it." And he rushed away through the crowd, moving toward the mutuel windows like a gerbil scurrying toward its burrow.

His departure alarmed one of our associates, a dark-haired ex–football player who owned a 7-Eleven franchise in Monrovia. "Hey, where's he going?" he asked, watching Fingers disappear with our winning ticket. "Who is that guy?"

"Don't worry about it, Bud," Jay reassured him. "It's okay. I've used Fingers before."

"Yeah? Well, I don't know," Bud said. "I'm going to follow him."

"Suit yourself," Jay answered, unconcerned. "He usually goes to the grandstand Special window, but if the line's too long, you'll find him downstairs."

Bud took off after Fingers, but by then Jay's chosen gofer had long since vanished in the crowd. I wasn't worried, but I could understand why Bud and Emile, our other partner in the ticket, might be nervous about dispatching some total stranger on such a potentially lucrative mission. "You are certain he will come back?" Emile asked. "What if he just takes off? It is our money."

"He'll come back," Jay said.

"He had better," Emile said. "That *is* my money."

I looked at him. His full name was Emile Legrand, a French-born producer of pornographic movies. He was short, paunchy, with a mean-looking mouth, small eyes, and the reputation of tough man in a deal. He was about sixty and had been around the track forever, always a loser until he had latched onto Jay. "Take it easy, Emile," I said. "We'll get our money."

"I don't like the look of this man Fingers," the producer said.

Jay sighed, realizing that once again he'd have to explain the facts of track life to this parasite. Bud and Emile were Jay's bread and butter, the sort of people who wanted to gamble on horses but didn't know how to win, so they had entrusted several thousand dollars to my friend Jay Fox to bet for them. Jay did all the handicapping, took a twenty percent commission on any winnings, charged nothing if they lost. So far at the meet they had just about broken even, but then Jay had come up with this winning Pick-Six ticket, a so-called exotic wager in which the bettor has to select the winners of six consecutive races, no simple task, and now they stood to show a handsome profit. (I had come in on this coup by luck, having stopped by Jay's box at the start of the day, glanced approvingly at his selections, and tossed thirty dollars into the kitty.) "Maybe you don't mind putting yourselves on the line with the Feds," Jay now said, "but I'm not going to do it."

"We would have to pay taxes anyway," Emile said with a shrug. "What is the big deal?"

Jay told him what the big deal was. "If you hit a
ticket like this, where the payoff is three hundred to one
or better, the IRS makes you sign a tax form and deducts
twenty percent at the window. Then, at the end of the
year, you have to declare it and pay more taxes on it, if
you're in a high enough bracket. You like that, Emile?"

"No, I do not."

"That's on top of the house vigorish, where they cut
a minimum of fifteen percent out of every dollar you bet
and more on the exotic wagers," Jay continued. "I call
that triple jeopardy. You beat it by getting some floater
like Fingers to cash the ticket for you."

"We have to pay him for this?" Emile asked.

"Fingers has no income," Jay said. "At the end of
the year, when he files his tax return, he sends in his
form along with programs and losing tickets proving that
he's a loser. The government then sends the money it's
withheld back to him."

"It sounds insane to me."

"It is insane, but that's how it works."

"How dumb can the government be?"

Jay pondered that one briefly. "I would say, Emile,
that it would be impossible to underestimate the intel-
ligence of the government."

"What a bizarre way to make a living," the producer
observed. "This Fingers person must do splendidly."

"Splendidly? I'd guess Fingers picks up maybe
thirty grand a year," Jay volunteered. "It's better than
stooping."

"What is that?"

"Stooping? That's when you go around picking up
discarded tickets, hoping that someone threw away a
winning one," Jay said. "You go from that to being a geek
in a carnival."

"He certainly doesn't look like a man who makes
thirty thousand a year," Emile declared.

Jay laughed. "Fingers is a horse degenerate," he
said. "He could be earning a million a year and it

wouldn't carry him through a season at the track. He makes just enough this way to keep himself in action."

Our winning ticket had come in on the last race of the day and the stands had begun to empty when Bud reappeared. "I can't find him," he said. "He's gone."

"He'll be back," Jay assured him. "Give him a few minutes. It takes a little while."

Half an hour later, we were still sitting there, the last occupied box in our section of the grandstand. Bud was in real distress and Emile was angry, even though Jay continued to maintain a cool front. "It's not possible that he would just take off," he said. "It can't happen."

"But it has happened," Emile pointed out. "And I would like to stress that it is our money."

"Maybe he got into some kind of trouble," I ventured. "Maybe he got himself arrested."

"What for?" Jay asked.

"I don't know. Guys like Fingers, they're always skirting the outer fringes. Maybe the cops picked him up."

"Or maybe somebody hit him over the head," Bud suggested.

"Not likely," Jay said, "in this crowd."

"I find this very unpleasant," Emile observed, standing up. "It seems to me, Fox, that you are responsible for our money."

"We're all losers, not just you, Emile."

"Quite true, but it was your decision to entrust the ticket to this person," the producer argued. "I do not remember being consulted about the matter."

"Hey, yeah, that's right," Bud said. "You owe us."

Jay sighed, stood up, and began to assemble his papers for departure. "I still think he'll show up," he said, "but if he doesn't, we'll find him."

"How?" the producer asked.

"Fifteen thousand dollars doesn't take you very far at the track, not the way Fingers bets," I observed.

"Oh, terrific," Bud commented. "Terrific. He's going to blow our money at the windows."

"I don't think so," Jay said. "I think Shifty's got the answer. He's probably been picked up on some charge or other. I know for a fact that Fingers doesn't pay his parking tickets. He must have all kinds of outstanding violations. I'm sure he'll show up eventually." He moved toward the exits. "I'll see you both here tomorrow." And he walked calmly out of the box, leaving his dismayed and angry partners behind.

"I think you two are in this together," Emile said as I started to follow him out. "You will not get away with it. I have friends."

"Really, Emile? It can't be anyone who ever worked for you." And I quickly left him there, bubbling quietly in his own vinegary juices.

I dozed off at about four, then woke up at seven-thirty, feeling as unrefreshed as a wilted head of lettuce. A pale gray light slanted into my room through the half-drawn curtains, and I could hear cars moving along the Boulevard Agua Caliente. Tijuana is a town that never seems to go to sleep; at any hour of the night there is traffic in the streets, a feeling of hustle and bustle emanating from the very stones and the pink dust that seems to hang over the downtown area like an ozone layer. The potential for fun and games is high here, and the air seems to throb with possibilities, making it as difficult a place to relax as Las Vegas.

I stood under a hot shower for ten minutes, wondering what the hell I was going to do about Fingers if I did find him. "Just talk to him," Jay had instructed me. "There must be some reason for this. Tell him he can't get away with it, that we'll get him in real trouble if he tries to come back to the tracks in L.A. Tell him we'll turn him in to the IRS. Most important of all, Shifty, find out what's happened to the money. Maybe we can get part of it back and that might take my two idiot partners off my case. Do what you can."

Fingers had not materialized in the days after his disappearance, and both Emile and Bud had turned nasty, especially as Jay seemed suddenly to have lost his handicapping touch. He hadn't been able to pick a winner since Fingers had vanished, thus putting more pressure on himself. The only ray of hope had come on Wednesday, when Bet-a-Million had stopped by our box before the third race. He was a slight, anxious-looking man of about forty with a large nose like a tapir's, who spent most of his time sniffing out horses that couldn't lose, mainly odds-on favorites, and plunging heavily on them. He was sustained in this ruinous enterprise by a family-controlled trust fund that doled out enough money for him to stay alive while keeping himself in action. "Jay, I hear you're looking for Fingers," he now said, sniffing around our box as if trying to detect the scent of a potential killing. "I saw him last Sunday, in Caliente. I went down there to bet on a horse I knew about, and there he was."

"What was he doing?"

"Nothing. Betting horses, I guess. I didn't talk to him. You got anything live today?"

"Why would I tell you if I had? You'd knock the price down."

Bet-a-Million grinned sheepishly. "Aw, come on, I promise. Didn't I just tell you about Fingers?"

Jay sighed. "Okay," he said, "you can bet the four horse in the feature to place. He won't run worse than second, even if he falls down out of the gate."

"That's what they told me about that pig in Tijuana. I bet a grand on him, the gate opens, and the jockey jumps off. He's one to nine and he doesn't even finish. The little crook just jumped off him."

"It wasn't his turn," Jay said. "You knocked the price down too low."

"Yeah, it's so crooked down there," Bet-a-Million said. "I don't know why I went down there."

"Bet-a-Million, there are no sure things in life or in racing."

"Tell me about it," he mumbled, moving away from us on the trail of still another monster coup.

"An incorrigible," Jay observed. "But it's the guys like Bet-a-Million who keep me in action."

That's how I had been persuaded to come down here, but I felt very strongly that I'd been dispatched on a fool's errand. Jay couldn't have believed very much in the move himself or he would have joined me. I had found his excuse about the importance of having to be present during the opening days of the Hollywood Park meet inadequate, even if I did understand his method of operation. "Seeing a race is five times as important as reading about it in the *Form*," he explained, as if I'd never heard it before. "If you find him and you need me, I'll come down. Meanwhile, Shifty, it's only a couple of days. Either he's there or he isn't. Caliente's a small track. There's no way Fingers can disappear down there."

The shower made me feel slightly more human. I got dressed and went down to the coffee shop, where, to my amazement, I found Harry slumped over a table in one corner, his hand around a large glass of fresh orange juice. He looked exactly as I had seen him the night before, with every white hair in place, except for his eyes, which were bloodshot. I sat down at the next table and ordered coffee and a roll. "How'd the dancing go?" I asked.

The old man looked at me blankly, then shook his head. "That woman didn't want to dance," he said. "She just wanted to get into my goddamn pants. Got me drunker than a boiled owl and kept me up half the goddamn night arguing. I finally gave her twenty bucks to get her the hell out of my room." He reached into the side pocket of his jacket, pulled out a small bottle of tequila, and poured some into his juice. "Damn women are all the same. I come down here every weekend to get away from the widder women in the park where I'm at. All they want to do is picnic. You going to the races?"

I nodded. "Sure."

"You drivin'?"

"Yeah."

"I'll ride over with you, if you don't mind. We'll leave about eleven?"

"Okay."

"I want to make the double." He put both hands on the table and pushed himself to his feet. "I'll have a snooze for a couple of hours. Meet you by the front desk at eleven."

"Fine."

"My name's Harry," he said, sticking out his hand, "Harry Dundee."

"Lou Anderson." His grip was firm, like that of a much younger man. "I have to hand it to you, Harry. You must have led a good life."

"No, I didn't. I've just always had me a good time." He headed for the door. "I might live to be a thousand, if the goddamn women don't kill me."

Two

TRACKING

Harry was waiting for me when I showed up at the front desk at eleven and we walked out to the car together. The sleep had done him some good; he looked pink and healthy and ready to go, with a large pair of battered binoculars draped around his wrinkled neck like a leper's bell. When he saw my car, the old Datsun, which by now looked as if it might have been used to slow down the German advance on Paris in 1914, he grinned at me. "You ain't been hittin' too many winners lately," he said.

I smiled back. "Harry, there's only a hundred and thirty thousand miles on it and I've never had a major engine repair job. Who cares what the body looks like?"

"You wouldn't say that about them widder women," he answered, climbing in beside me. "Sure would save me money and trouble."

The car started up immediately, of course, and I eased it out of the parking lot toward the avenue. The Conquistador is a two-story motel built in the style of a Spanish hacienda, around a central courtyard used as a parking lot. The exit debouches into the Boulevard Agua Caliente, opposite the modern glass-and-steel twin towers of the new Fiesta Americana Hotel, about half a mile from the track. "Convenient place to stay," I observed as I turned left into the flow of traffic.

"And cheap," Harry agreed. "Say, you know what you can do with this pitiful thing? You can sell it down here. It already looks like a Mexican car."

"You're sounding a little racist to me, Harry."

"Aw goddammit, it don't matter none to me," the old man said. "Mexicans is okay. Except for that damn mariachi music they play. It'll like to deafen you. And they'll steal you blind."

"I've noticed that about the human race in general."

"Goddamn, but you're a thinker," Harry said. "With your brains you ought to be able to pick some horses."

"I intend to try, Harry."

"Well, down here it don't do much good to handicap. You got to look at the damn board. These horses is all a bunch of pigs that you don't know how they're going to run. They kind of take turns, so you got to watch the betting action, if you know what I mean."

"I think I do, Harry. I guess you don't play the Foreign Book."

"Oh, sometimes I'll bet a few dollars on Santa Anita or Hollywood Park, but mainly I like the live racing," he said, "even if the horses I bet on is sometimes dead. Goddamn, but it's a tough way to make a livin'!"

"What time do the dogs run?"

"Oh, an hour or so after the horses, I guess," Harry said, "but you think horses is hard, wait'll you try the dogs."

I turned up the slope of a small hill and into the track parking lot, tipped the Mexican attendant a dollar to keep an eye on the Datsun, then followed Harry into the Foreign Book to buy programs and check the scratches. "This goddamn place pays the freight for the whole operation and it's a sinkhole," Harry said. "They got crabs in the men's room that can jump ten feet."

The Foreign Book is a rectangular stone building in front of the main entrance to the grandstand and it was already swarming with the several hundred regulars, many of them Americans, who come every day and who haven't seen a live horse race in twenty years. Entries and results from all the tracks in action were posted on a huge blackboard running the full length of the back wall. The bettors, mostly shabbily dressed middle-aged men,

sat at tables facing this wall, milled about the floor under
the TV monitors strategically placed all over the establishment, or were gathered around a bar and refreshment stand at one end. The scene was not reminiscent of
the royal enclosure at Ascot. In fact, with the day only a
third over, it had already achieved a truly Hogarthian
level of sordidness, with the bettors shuffling glumly to
and from the windows over a toxic carpet of losing
tickets.

This depraved spectacle was not for us. Once we
picked up our programs for both Caliente and Hollywood Park, I suggested we sit in the clubhouse, where I
could keep an eye out for Fingers. Harry expressed a
preference for the more gracious surroundings of La
Cupula, a large sunken area inside the main emporium
that is bathed in comforting gloom and has padded seats
and hordes of accommodating waiters. From the outside
it looks like a miniature cathedral dome tucked up
against the orange-colored bulk of the main grandstand,
which reminded me of an Aztec temple. The original
structure, a much homier affair, had been destroyed by
fire in 1971 and had been rebuilt as a massive, four-story
concrete paean to grandiosity.

"I thought you said you came for the live racing," I
ventured as we headed for the main escalator. "You can't
see the races live in there, can you?"

"Hell, no," Harry answered, "but after last night I
need someplace to relax. In La Cupula I can catch a
snooze between races."

"You don't handicap?"

"No, I just watch the board," he explained. "I see a
horse get knocked down the last few minutes, I go and
bet on him. You listen to me, Lou—it's the only
goddamn way to go here."

I told him I'd catch up to him later and left him. I
had decided I'd also take a look around the Turf and
Jockey clubs, just in case, and I walked into the main
entrance for the richer punters, up the steps of a palatial

doorway beyond which several glass-enclosed floor-to-ceiling cages contained a collection of about a hundred exotic birds, all swooping about and chattering noisily to one another. In one corner enclosure, a couple of enormous pythons basked, quietly digesting. "Hey, Myrtle, look at them snakes," someone behind me observed as we made for the elevators. "Wonder what they feed them monsters."

"Favorite-players," I said, but I don't think the man heard me.

"I hope everything's locked up in here," Myrtle said. "Oh, Georgie, look at the birds! Aren't they gorgeous?"

"Sweetheart, we'll miss the double. I didn't come here to look at no birds," Georgie told her as she tugged him toward the exhibits.

I had no intention of betting on any of the early races on the card, a bunch of meaningless gallops for maidens and established losers, so I spent the first hour touring the premises looking for Fingers, as I had the day before. He was nowhere to be found. The Jockey Club was occupied only by a couple of dozen elegantly dressed young Mexicans eating elaborate meals in a formal setting high above the finish line, while the Turf Club, on the floor below, contained a scattering of middle-class Americans studying *Racing Forms* and tout sheets. It wasn't crowded and I could tell that the attendance was off, due undoubtedly to the newly created betting parlors north of the border. It made me a little sad, because I liked Caliente and I hoped it would survive. Where else could people come to race their cheap horses, now that the purses in Southern California had become so large that they had begun to attract the top racing stables from all over the country? Besides, several thousand Mexicans depended on the track for their livelihood; it was one of Tijuana's principal industries.

In the clubhouse, I found a seat about fifty yards

beyond the finish line, high above the action, and
bought myself a Coke and a Mexican hot dog, a spicy
sausage tucked under a mound of onion slices and chili
peppers that can cause internal bleeding. As I munched
away, periodically dousing the flames in my mouth with
swallows of Coke, I kept an eye out for Fingers, while
simultaneously trying my best to isolate a winner from
the mass of losing statistics in my *Form*. I wasn't
planning to blow another eighty dollars, and I was
determined not to bet at all until something jumped out
at me from the available information. But race after race
went off without me; these were animals only a degenerate could love, horses either of no ability or crippled
old platers long past their prime, running on memories.

It was sad, I thought, especially since racing in
Tijuana had such a colorful history. The first track had
been built here in 1916 by a plunger named Sunny Jim
Coffroth from San Francisco, who gave his name to a
handicap offering a fifty-thousand-dollar purse back in
the nineteen-twenties, when that kind of money was
unheard of in racing. In 1932, a great Australian horse
named Phar Lap won the hundred-thousand-dollar Caliente Handicap, the largest prize in racing history. In
1941, women jockeys got their first chance to ride here,
and Caliente had also been the first track to have an
announcer call the races, to build fireproof stables, to
develop helmets and goggles for jockeys, and to offer
daily doubles and other forms of combination bets,
including the Pick-Six, still called the 5-10 here because
it began with the fifth contest and ran through the tenth
on the normal twelve-race card. "About as easy as
pogo-sticking across the Mojave," Jay had once defined
the Pick-Six, even though it hadn't kept us from playing
it over the years.

The glory days were clearly over. The proliferation
of racing in the richer economies north of the border had
reduced Caliente to the status of a bush track. The
purses were small, which meant also that no one could

make a living just from the racing itself; you had to set up your animal to make an occasional betting coup, which makes it pretty hard to risk a wager merely on your handicapping skills. I decided I'd sit on my money all day, if I had to. The atmosphere was relaxed and congenial, and all I had to do was keep an alert eye out for Fingers. Not a bad way to spend a few hours in the sunshine. Anyway, I was planning to return to L.A. no later than the following morning.

That afternoon a man Jay had never seen before stopped him as he was heading back to his seat after cashing a small ticket on the fifth at Hollywood. He was a tall blond hulk dressed in a dark gray pinstriped suit and a red silk tie nailed to his shirt by a diamond clip. He was in his forties and had a beard that partly covered a long, thin scar slicing his left cheek from the corner of his eye to his chin. When he smiled, that side of his face didn't move, which made it seem as if he were leering at some obscene spectacle. The atmosphere he exuded, Jay felt immediately, was not restful. "Is your name Jay Fox?" the man asked, confronting Jay under one of the monitors in the grandstand area.

"Yeah."

"You're handling some investments here for Emile Legrand?"

"I wouldn't call them investments, exactly."

"You've been handling some money for him."

"I don't know. Who are you?"

"Just call me Bert."

"Sorry, but that's not really enough to go on. You a friend of Emile's?"

"I have a rooting interest in Emile's affairs."

"Is that so? That's nice. Well, it's been enlightening." And Jay started to move past him toward his box.

Bert put out a hand and grabbed Jay's arm at shoulder height. He had a grip like an ice tong. "We haven't finished our conversation," he said with that leering smile.

"Hey, get your hands off me," Jay said.

Bert relaxed his grip. "Sorry," he said, "I didn't want to get physical. But we have to finish our conversation."

"I'm not sure I'm up to it," Jay said, not smiling back. "Look, I don't know you, I've never seen you before, and if Emile wants to talk to me, he knows where I sit. Oh, yeah—and anytime he wants the rest of his money back, all he has to do is ask for it. In person."

"Emile is very busy this week," Bert explained. "He's in pre-production in Long Beach. He asked me to speak to you."

"What about?"

"This money you owe him."

"Let me explain something to you, Bert," Jay said. "When Emile asked me to pick his horses for him, it wasn't quite like investing in treasury bonds, okay? I don't owe Emile a dime. We're both losers on what happened to our Pick-Six ticket, which I assume is what you've been sent here to discuss. And I'm doing my best to track that problem down."

Bert smiled again. "Not good enough, fella. Our assumption is you owe us the money."

"Yeah? That's a dumb assumption."

Jay again started for his seat and again the hulk grabbed his arm, iron fingers clamped on flesh. "I'm not through talking to you," Bert said.

Jay is an ex-athlete and in good shape. He weighs about a hundred and eighty pounds, fifteen over his best playing weight, when he was terrifying the public tennis courts in L.A. as a teaching pro and all-around hustler, but he runs at least five times a week and also works out in a gym from time to time. He decided he didn't want Bert's hand clamped to him, and reacted. His left arm swept upward and knocked the man's grip aside, then he stepped back, bouncing lightly on his feet and ready to move in any direction.

Bert merely stood there, a pair of pale blue eyes focused unblinkingly on the handicapper. "Not too smart, pal," he said. "You don't walk away from me when I'm talking to you."

"Wrong," Jay told him. "I told you to keep your hands off me."

Bert took a step toward him and leaned slightly forward so that he could keep his voice low but not be misunderstood. "I don't like you, fella," he said. "You're the kind of punk that would rip a guy off. I know you. You and this other character are in this together. Emile knows it and now I know it. So I'll tell you what's going to happen. You're going to pay us the money, see, or sometime, somewhere, when you least expect it, I'm going to catch up to you and I'm going to start out by breaking both your kneecaps and a few ribs. And if that doesn't work, I've got fancier things I can do to you. The hospital bill alone could cost you a lot more than you owe us, fella. So I'd think about that, if I were you."

"You got a last name, Bert?"

"Sure." He reached into his pocket and produced a business card. "Here." He held it out and Jay took it. "When you're ready, you just give me a call. And it better be soon."

Jay glanced at the card. It read "Wilberton Castle, Consulting Services." Below that was a local phone number. Jay put the card in his pocket. "Thanks," he said. "You know I'm going to report you for this."

Bert smiled. "Aw shit, go ahead. I don't give a damn what you do, fella. It doesn't change a thing."

Out of the corner of his eye, Jay noticed a uniformed security cop he knew standing about thirty feet away, at the corner of a refreshment stand, and beckoned him over. "Charlie," he said, "how come the track allows these professional hoods in here?"

Charlie was old and fat and his stomach bulged

alarmingly over the brown belt holding up his gun, but he wasn't awed in the least by the presence of the ominous-looking Bert Castle. Also, he liked Jay, who occasionally put him onto live horses during the course of the year. He looked up at Bert out of narrowed, hostile eyes. "What's going on?" he asked.

"He's making threats," Jay said. "He thinks I touted him onto a loser. I've never seen him before, so he's obviously got me confused with somebody else."

"You want to make a report in the security office?"

"I think I may do just that."

"Do you have some identification, sir?" Charlie asked the hulk.

Bert stared at Jay and said nothing.

"I'll bet he has a gun on him," Jay observed. "I wonder if he's got a permit for it."

"Would you come along with me, sir," Charlie said, taking Bert's arm and steering him toward the ground-floor security office.

Bert never took his eyes off Jay. "I won't forget this, fella," he said, then turned and allowed Charlie to lead him away, the guard walking one wary step behind him through the bettors on their rounds to and from the windows.

Jay didn't see Bert again that day, but after the ninth, on his way out to the parking lot, he stopped by the security office and spoke to Charlie. "Yeah, the guy had a .38 automatic, a Beretta, in a shoulder holster," the guard said. "He didn't have no license either. So we booked him and turned him over to the Inglewood police. Who is he?"

"I don't know, Charlie," Jay answered. "Some guy I've never seen before, like I told you. He's going to have my kneecaps and ribs broken."

"What for?"

"You got me. Maybe it's because I can't pick winners all the time and somebody told him to bet on some loser I liked. The paranoia factor is high at the track, Charlie, and there are a lot of nuts running around."

"You said it," Charlie agreed, "but watch yourself, Jay. You don't want to go touting people."

"I never tout, Charlie, you know that."

Charlie nodded. "He sure is a big sonbitch," he said. "Watch yourself, Jay. I don't think they'll put the guy in the slammer, not for more than a day or two, unless he's got a record and there's a warrant out for him."

"That's okay. I just want the cops to know where to look, in case anything does happen to me."

"Good thinking," Charlie said. "Say, how about that filly of Whittingham's in the feature? Can she run?"

"Like the wind, Charlie," Jay said, "if you like betting on one to two shots with Shoemaker up."

I didn't see anything I liked until the last race, a gallop at a mile and a sixteenth for eight ancient platers running for a claiming tag of four thousand dollars. The horse on the rail was a five-year-old gelding named Digby, who had once competed with some success on the Southern California circuit. Obviously sore-legged, he had never managed to put together more than six or seven races a year, but in twenty lifetime starts he'd won five of them and run second three times to much better animals than those he was up against today. As far as I knew, he'd never run farther than seven furlongs, and in his previous race, two weeks earlier, he had tired badly at six, after showing a high turn of speed for half a mile, and finished fifth. But there were positive factors to be considered. His last race had been run after a layoff, probably for some injury or other, of nearly seven months, and he had had to run very fast to get the lead, thus using himself up. The race had to have done him some good, and now he was competing in a field utterly devoid of speed; his seven rivals were all plodders who came from far out of it, if they ran at all. I figured that the horse could easily open up at least six lengths on this field without expending himself, gallop along in front during the middle part of the race, and have enough left to hold off the plodders in the stretch. Just to be sure, however, I decided to check my figures with Harry.

The old man was asleep, head slumped forward on his chest, in an easy chair facing one of the big screens in La Cupula. I sat down beside him and gently shook him awake. "Harry, how are you doing?"

His light blue eyes focused quickly on me. "Is it post time?" he asked, groping for his program.

"Not yet. I want to ask you about a horse." I thrust my *Form* under his nose and gave him my analysis of the race.

Harry listened, nodding thoughtfully, then said, "What are you going to do about the goddamn girl?"

"What girl?"

"The girl ridin' him."

I looked at my program and sure enough, there she was. The jockey's name was Jill Thorne. "Can she ride?" I asked.

"I don't bet no goddamn girl jockeys," Harry said.

"Some of them can ride, Harry."

"Maybe, but they ain't strong enough to hold a race horse together. She rode him last time, didn't she? He ran like a goddamn quarter horse."

"Maybe it was a workout."

"And maybe it wasn't."

"Anyway, how are you doing, Harry?"

"Made two bets, cashed them both," he said, glancing up at the tote board. "I ain't bettin' this race. I'll see you at the car, if I can remember where the hell we parked." And he sank back in his chair and closed his eyes.

I returned to my seat as the horses were coming out on the track and focused my binoculars on Digby, who was leading the post parade. He looked a little sore and a bit washy behind, but he was on his toes, ears cocked

forward, and his appearance confirmed my feeling that
he was going to be hard to beat. Jill Thorne, whom I'd
never seen ride before, looked good on his back. She had
long legs tucked up into the stirrups and long, dark-
blond hair that she wore in a ponytail. As the horses
broke one by one into their warm-up gallops and began
to head for the starting gate, I noted how Jill stood up in
the irons while keeping a firm hold on the reins, letting
the animal know that he was about to compete, but not
letting him get away from her prematurely. She looked
like a competent, professional rider and I wondered
where she had come from. It was unusual to find a
female jockey riding the California circuits these days,
especially at Caliente, a haven of Mexican machismo.

The distrust that most bettors, the majority of
whom are men, feel for female jocks was being reflected
in the odds. Digby had opened at four to one and, in my
opinion, should have been favored, but five minutes
before post time he was at seven to one. I walked back to
the windows, stood in line for three minutes, watched
the odds go up another notch, and bet thirty dollars to
win on the animal. By the time I was back in my seat and
the horses were at the starting gate, he had gone to nine
to one.

To my horror, Digby did not break on top. He must
have swerved in his stall or something when the gate
opened, and by the time the field hit the first turn he
was in the middle of the pack, tucked in along the rail
four or five lengths off the lead. I kissed my thirty dollars
good-bye and sank back in my seat to watch the disaster
unfold. That's the trouble with betting these goddamn
speed horses, I told myself. If they don't break alertly,
you're sitting on a loser. And that's also the trouble with
betting on girl jockeys.

Although I'd given up any hope of winning my bet,
I kept my glasses focused on the race and so began to
notice how well my horse was now being ridden. Instead
of rushing her mount up into contention and then forcing

him to expend all his speed in the effort, as many journeymen jocks would have, Jill Thorne kept a firm grip on the reins and allowed Digby to settle into stride, while saving ground all the way around. As the field swung into the final turn, she moved him up until he was only two lengths back, but still behind the three leaders, a small wall of horses. Then, at the head of the stretch, a hole opened as the horse on the rail began to tire and drift out. Digby suddenly shot through it, practically scraping the fence and with the jockey flat on his back, pumping hard and occasionally shaking her whip at him, so he could see it. I stood up and began to cheer.

At the sixteenth pole Digby was four lengths in front, but obviously tiring badly. The favorite was making a big run on the outside and the two animals hit the finish line together, but I knew who had won. My Amazon had stolen the race and brought in a winner by the margin of somewhere between a nose and a head. The man in back of me didn't think so and was already congratulating himself on having bet a bad six-to-five shot, but he abruptly quieted down when Digby's number went up as the winner and the race was declared official. "These fuckin' crooks here," this prince declared, "they want to let the fuckin' girl win one. Jesus, what a bunch of fuckin' crooks."

Digby paid $9.60 for every two-dollar ticket, another surprise. Somebody must have pumped several hundred dollars at least through the windows on him at the last second to knock the odds down that much. But I didn't care. The win had more than bailed me out of my previous day's losses, and I got up to go and cash.

As I was standing in line, Dan the Man shuffled past me. He was humming tunelessly to himself, with his red hat perched far back on his head. "Dan, how are you?" I asked.

He stopped and looked at me; his eyes had a stunned, faraway look. Three of his first four horses had run out of the money, he informed me, and he had found himself down five hundred and forty dollars, an impossible hole to climb out of with show bets. Since then he'd gone back to combination wagering in an unsuccessful effort to get out. "I don't understand it," he said. "It always worked on paper."

"You know what I'd do, Dan?"

"What?"

"I'd quit coming here for a while and I'd keep the store open nights." It was a cruel thing to say, but I guess I've become intolerant of stupidity over the years.

Harry was waiting for me out in the parking lot. He seemed cheerful enough, even though he hadn't bet on the last race. "They gave it to the damn girl," he said. "They opened up the rail for her. It was like a goddamn benefit race."

I didn't contest this analysis, even though I knew it was a false one. "The dogs get under way at seven-thirty," I said. "You want to come back with me?"

"No, sir," Harry said. "I'm goin' home tonight. Got to keep the widder women happy. You gonna be here next weekend?"

"I hope not. If I don't find Fingers tonight, I'm leaving myself."

"The border will be easier if you wait till after midnight."

"Thanks. Good suggestion."

We said good-bye in the courtyard of the Conquistador. "Here's my address," the old man volunteered, handing me a card, "if you're ever down my way." We shook hands. "But listen"—and the light blue eyes sparkled with mischief—"if the trailer's rockin', don't bother knockin'."

As I opened the door of my room, the telephone rang. It was Jay and he filled me in on the encounter with Wilberton Castle. "I think I may come down and join you," he said. "It might be a good idea to get out of town for a few days."

"Don't do that, Jay. If I don't find Fingers tonight, I'm out of here."

Jay thought that over. "I don't know," he said. "I think this guy really intends to do some damage."

"Have you called Emile?"

"Yeah, but I can't reach him."

"Maybe it's all bullshit, Jay. Big talk."

"Maybe, only . . ."

"Only what?"

"When I got to my car, on the way out—"

"Yes?"

"Somebody kicked out my headlights."

"Some sore loser."

"Maybe a preview of coming attractions."

"Well, watch yourself. I'll call you, okay? Either later tonight or tomorrow morning. Just sit tight till then."

"Okay, Shifty." I started to hang up, but he added, "How'd you do?"

"I won a few dollars on a horse ridden by a girl jockey."

"We're both living dangerously," Jay said.

Three

DOGGING IT

I spotted Fingers as the dogs were being led to their little boxes a few minutes before the first race of the evening. He was sitting about ten rows in front of me, nervously clutching a thick program and talking to a fat Mexican with a walrus mustache. Fingers's head on its long neck was bobbing up and down, as if overly eager to agree with what it was hearing, while the fat Mexican sat stolidly in place, his gaze concentrated on the bone-thin four-legged competitors below. I guessed that he must have touted Fingers onto some sort of sure thing in the race, because the American's movements were clearly those of a man with a rooting interest in the proceedings.

The dog track, which looked to be about a quarter of a mile in circumference, lay directly below us. It was illuminated in the surrounding darkness by overhead lamps and looked tawdrily cheerful. A sound of yapping canines punctuated the murmurs of the small crowd of two or three hundred people in the stands around me. Suddenly, the mechanical rabbit flashed past as the doors of the boxes popped open and the hungry greyhounds set off in disorderly pursuit. I paid little attention to the race, because I've always considered the sport a frivolity and it held no charms for me at all. I watched Fingers. During the twenty or so seconds it took to run this affair, his body movements registered a gamut of emotions ranging from initial elation to extreme disappointment at the outcome, not a good portent for our first meeting since his disappearance from Santa Anita.

The Mexican said something to him, shrugged, got up, and moved away. Fingers glanced at his program, folded it, stuffed it angrily into his jacket pocket, and slumped back into his seat.

After the result of the contest had been declared official and the dogs had been rounded up by their handlers to be returned to their kennels, I moved down and sat directly behind my quarry, whose eyes were still scanning the floodlit scene below us and who was oblivious of my presence. I gave him another few seconds, while I tried to figure out how to keep him from bolting, then decided that I had no choice but to risk it. "Hello, Fingers," I said, "we've been wondering what happened to you."

His head spun around to look at me, alarm etched on his features. "Oh, Christ," he said. "Shifty, you won't believe this, but I was just going to get in touch with you guys." His hands began to move.

"We've been a little worried, Fingers."

"I know you have. Jeez, I'm real sorry." *Snap snap*.

"You want to tell me about it?"

"Yeah, sure, of course." And he spun out his tale of woe. He had left our box that afternoon, he told me, and gone downstairs to cash the ticket. On his way he had bumped into an acquaintance of his named Mellini. "You know Bones?" he asked.

I shook my head.

"You'd know him if you saw him. I mean, he's been around. He's like a little stocky guy with not much hair on him and he—"

"Fingers—"

"Yeah, well, okay, so like I was saying, see"—*snap snap*—"I owed Bones some money."

"How much money?"

Fingers's entire body was in motion by this time, as if he were trying to unfold himself inside his skin. The joints of his hands crackled like tiny castanets. "Well—uh—about ten grand."

"So you used our money to pay your debt to him."

"Uh—not exactly." His eyes roved wildly about the stands.

"Then please tell me, exactly."

It took about fifteen minutes to pull it out of him, in bits and pieces. During all that time he never stopped looking around and I guessed he was either waiting for the fat Mexican to return or for the appearance of the mysterious Mellini, nicknamed Bones. The essence of his story, however, was simple enough and drearily familiar. Mellini was evidently some sort of loan shark, of the sort that hangs around racetracks. Fingers had borrowed money from him during a particularly lean period some months earlier, at a usurious rate of interest compounded daily. He'd been unable to repay it, and the sum owed had mounted catastrophically week by week until it had reached ten thousand dollars. He'd been intending to put off settling this obligation until after the first of the year, when the IRS would presumably begin to repay him the money deducted from the tickets he'd been cashing for others, including us. "I mean, I got maybe twenty-five, thirty grand coming in," he said.

"So what happened?"

"Bones wouldn't wait," he explained. "I mean, like he saw me in the sign-up line and he came over to tell me he wanted the money right away."

"He probably figured that if it got any higher, you'd never be able to pay it back."

"He saw me in line there, you know."

I sighed. "Okay, Fingers, so what happened to the rest of it?"

"The rest of it?"

"Yes, the difference between the ten thousand you owed Bones and the fifteen thousand you owe us."

"Oh, well, yeah"—*snap snap snap*—"you see, it ain't quite like that."

"What isn't?"

"The deal."

"What deal?"

"The deal with Bones."

"I thought you said you owed him ten thousand."

"Right, right."

"So where's the other two?"

"The other two?"

"Come on, Fingers, don't play dumb, please," I said. "The difference between the ten grand you gave Bones Mellini and the balance of the payoff after the tax had been deducted. That should be about two thousand, maybe a little more."

"Oh, yeah, sure." *Snap snap, jiggle jiggle*.

"I mean, if Bones couldn't wait, maybe we could," I continued. "We'd take the two thousand now and you could pay us the balance after the first of the year, when the IRS comes through for you."

"Yeah, that's right," he agreed, but with a regretful tenor to his voice, as if he were sorry, genuinely grieved, in fact, that that solution hadn't occurred to him earlier. "Only it's like this, Shifty, see," he continued, swinging around in his seat now to impose the full weight of his sincerity upon me, "Bones had this horse—"

"Oh, God, Fingers," I interrupted him. "Has it got four legs?"

And so at last he told me about the horse. It was a seven-year-old named Fred's Folly. Imported a couple of years earlier from Ireland, it had been running in San Francisco. Bones had been tipped off that the horse was a good buy and could be had for twelve thousand dollars. The trainer in San Francisco was short of cash and needed to sell the horse, but the transaction had to be carried out in a big hurry, within twenty-four hours. That was why Bones hadn't been able to wait for his money.

"This story is making me sad," I said.

"Sad? Why sad, Shifty?" Fingers looked mildly alarmed. He leaned in to peer closely at me, as if he could find the source of my grief somewhere below the surface of my skin. "I mean, what's sad? I'll give you your money."

"When, Fingers?"

"When? When it comes in, Shifty. I mean, I'll send in the forms on New Year's Day. I mean, I wouldn't wait even a day or two, you know?" He let out some air and it seemed to deflate him. He slumped into his chair, looking defeated and suddenly old.

I thought I had figured out the end of the story, or most of it, so I prodded him with my guess about it. "You went in with Bones, right? You bought a piece of this beast with the last two grand, our two grand."

He nodded and said nothing more. Even his hands had stopped moving; they lay on his lap like dying birds, twitching spasmodically from time to time.

I waited for him to say something, but he remained silent, his eyes now focused on some spot beyond the tote board below and the darkened infield behind it. Before I could think of anything else to say, the fat Mexican came back and sat down beside him. He thrust a pudgy finger at the program in his hand. "This one," he said. "He win for sure."

Fingers looked at him, the weariness of ages of losses etched into his face. "You sure, Luis?" he asked.

"*Sí*, I am sure," the Mexican said. "He win easy. We take him with the one and the seven. Is winning bet, John."

Fingers reached into his pocket and produced a crumpled ten-dollar bill. "Okay. Luis, you bet it for me." He handed the Mexican the money. The man got up and headed for the windows.

"So that's your real name."

"What?"

"John. I never knew."

"Oh, yeah. These guys down here, they don't know me from anywhere."

"I looked for you at the races today. You given up horses?"

"For now. Bones don't want me to bet. Not till we run the horse." Fingers began to snap into motion again, as if the mere mention of horses and the prospect of being able to resume betting on them had served to revive him.

"Why won't Bones let you bet?"

"He says I can't handle it, Shifty. He says I make a spectacle of myself, see. He wants us to kind of lay low."

"He's going to put one over, isn't he?"

Fingers looked around again, obviously alarmed at the possibility he might be seen with me. "I can't talk about it, Shifty," he said. "Honest, you got to trust me."

"Trust you? How can we trust you, Fingers?"

He saw the Mexican heading toward us as the dogs for the next race passed below us, on their way to the starting boxes. "Here comes Luis," he said. "Don't say anything about—you know. . . ."

"Who's Luis?"

"He works for Bones. I'll tell you all about it later."

"He win easy, you watch," the Mexican said, sitting down beside Fingers.

I leaned forward. "How do you know he'll win?" I asked.

The Mexican smiled. "He get a little moose juice," he said. "You know, with dogs is not like with horses, señor."

"Moose juice."

"To run fast, yes. But not to run slow. That one is easy."

"In what way?"

"You give him a little chorizo, a little sausage. You give him a nice big drink of water. He don't run so fast. You want him to run real slow, you cut his nails short."

"Interesting," I said, looking at the board. "I guess a lot of people know about this."

"Señor?"

"Your animal is even money."

The Mexican smiled again. "*Sí, señor*, but we have him in the Exactas on top of the one and the seven."

A few seconds later, the dogs popped out of their boxes again in pursuit of the ridiculous mechanical rabbit. Just as Luis had predicted, their dog ran as if he had a battery up his behind and won easily. Unfortunately, neither the one nor the seven finished in the money behind him. "Look at them dumb fuckin' things," Fingers said, vastly disgusted. "They should shoot 'em all."

"Fingers, maybe you better go back to horses," I said. "You don't win here either."

The Mexican turned around to look at me with more than casual interest. "This is Shifty," Fingers said quickly. "He's a friend of mine from up north. Shifty, this is Luis."

"Sanchez Gomez," the Mexican said. His grasp was warm, flabby, and moist; it felt uncomfortable. I withdrew my hand quickly but smiled as innocently as I could manage to. His eyes were small and very black, all but buried behind his fat cheeks and low brow, and they did not seem excessively friendly, even though he did smile back. His teeth were as white as piano keys beneath the hair. "You know each other long?" he asked.

"We see each other around," I answered. "At the races."

Luis nodded, then stood up. "We go now," he said. "Come on, John."

"John and I have to talk," I said before Fingers could get out of his seat. "I need some information about all of this." I gestured toward the dog track below. "I've never been to the dogs before, and there's three more races."

Luis hesitated, then shrugged. "I don't like nothing else tonight," he said. "I wait for you at the car, John. You don't be late."

"No, no, I won't be long," Fingers said. "Two minutes, that's all."

I watched the Mexican leave. He moved ponderously but gracefully, like a small float in a parade. "Who's your friend?" I asked.

"I told you, he works for Bones," Fingers said. "I mean, like, he works for Sandy."

"Sandy who?"

"Hatch, he's a trainer down here. Look, Shifty, I got to go." He stood up, shivering like a sacrificial goat.

"Where are you staying?"

"Right here, in the stable area."

"Where?"

"Barn fifteen, why?"

"Because I'm coming around to see you in the morning, that's why." I put a hand on his forearm to steady him, perhaps keep him from bolting. "We have to talk a little more, Fingers. I mean, you owe us all this money—"

"I know, I know, I told you I'd make good. But in a couple of months, after the first of the year."

"I'm not sure that's good enough. I'm going to call Jay tonight and then we're going to talk again tomorrow morning, all right?"

"I don't know, Shifty—" He looked genuinely distressed, and I guessed that there had to be more to his story than what he had told me so far.

"I know you're in a bind," I said, "and I guess I have to believe you, Fingers, when you tell us you're going to pay us. But we have problems of our own. Jay has his group to worry about. And one of them is threatening a little mayhem if he doesn't get his money. You understand, Fingers? We've got to thrash all this out after I talk to Jay."

"You ain't the only one with problems," he said.

"I guess I know that. Mellini?"

He nodded in abject misery. "You know why they call him Bones?"

"No."

"He breaks 'em."

"A lot of people are going around doing that these days."

"He don't always do it himself," Fingers explained. "He's also got people who do it for him. He's got specialists."

"He sounds like a charming fellow."

"I wouldn't mess with him, Shifty, if I was you."

Jay Fox lived in a small, ramshackle ground-floor apartment half a block from the beach in Santa Monica. He had moved there a few weeks earlier from a place he'd lived in for years, a bachelor pad a couple of blocks above Sunset in Hollywood, because he liked to run on the flat sand at low tide. He'd heard about the place from an interior decorator he knew whose friend, a studio hairdresser, owned the property. The interior decorator was a diseased horseplayer who occasionally picked Jay's brains for winners, a technique Jay allowed him to get away with because he was amused by him; the interior decorator was a bitchy gossip and well-known Hollywood wit. In any case, nothing Jay told the man could help him, because, like many losers at the track, he had a genius for taking good information and betting it incorrectly. To repay Jay for the favors he'd received, however, he had told the handicapper about the apartment, which had been recently vacated by a gay male couple who had lived in it for years. Thanks to Santa Monica's rent-control law, the price was reasonable and Jay had been able to move in right away. He hadn't taken down the magenta drapes or even unpacked all his boxes, and he had yet to put any of his posters up on the walls, but he'd reported to me that he was ecstatic about his new location. "The beach is right there, Shifty, just like at Del Mar," he told me two days after taking possession of it. "I can run in either direction, up under the pier and the bluffs or south toward Venice. It's great. Once I get it fixed up."

I was reminded of all this that night, when I phoned from the Conquistador to tell him about finding Fingers, because Jay was so upset. He had come home from the track by taxi, leaving his car with its shattered headlights in the track parking lot, and come in to find that his house had been broken into. Someone had entered through a side window into the kitchen and trashed the premises.

"What did they take?" I asked.

"Nothing, that's the weird part," Jay said. "They just tore everything up. Slashed the bed, the curtains, threw the furniture around, dumped everything in the drawers on the floor, and took a crap in the middle of it."

"The local Visigoths. Probably teenagers looking for dope or something to sell for it."

"Yeah? Then how come they didn't take the stereo or the TV or my typewriter?"

"They didn't?"

"No, nothing. They spray-painted swastikas on the walls."

"Sounds like a gang just having a little fun."

"Goddammit," Jay said. "And the people upstairs say they were home all day and they didn't hear a thing. Of course, they're pretty old."

"Did you call the cops?"

"Oh, sure, but what do they know? They think it was kids. But I don't think so."

"Why not?"

"It could have been one person. On the mirrors in the bathroom somebody scrawled 'Pay up!' surrounded by more swastikas and some iron crosses."

"Jay, it can't be that guy at the track. He could have smashed up your car, maybe, but he wouldn't have had time to get into your apartment."

"He could have done it this morning, when I went out. But I know one thing."

"What?"

"I've got to get hold of Emile."

"And the other guy, what about him?"

"Who? Oh, Bud."

"Yeah."

"He's just a lout."

"He was pretty sore about what happened."

Jay thought that one over. "You know, you're right," he said, after a moment's rumination. "He was more upset than Emile was, except that it was Emile who sicced this guy Castle onto me."

"Maybe they're both after you."

"Terrific. Just what I need, Shifty. Goddammit!"

"Maybe you better talk to Bud too."

"What can I tell these guys I haven't already told them?"

"Stall them. Get them off your back. I'm going to see Fingers again tomorrow morning."

"You said he has no money."

"At least we know where he is," I tried to reassure him. "And maybe we can get in on this horse. Do you know this guy Mellini?"

"I know who he is. He's a bloodsucker."

"He also breaks people's bones. Maybe he and Bert Castle could get together on you."

"This isn't funny, Shifty."

"No, I guess not."

"Listen, I'm going to lie low tomorrow. I'm going to pick up my car and come home. I'm going to straighten up the apartment and wait to hear from you. I want you to call me right after you return from the backside."

"Listen, Jay, about all of this, I don't mind doing it—it's partly my money—but I can't stay here. I've got a job."

"When?"

"I've got a three-day convention of toy manufacturers, in Anaheim."

"So you've got time, Shifty. This is important."

After this conversation I found myself in a state of mild anxiety. What *was* going on? I sat back against the bunched-up pillows of my king-size bed in the Conquistador and stared at the blank wall while I tried to figure it all out, but I couldn't make much sense of it. We clearly were not going to be able to get any money out of Fingers, at least for a couple of months, so we'd have to find a way to stall Jay's angry partners. Unfortunately at least one of them obviously had no intention of waiting. I told myself that it was really Jay's problem, not mine, but I couldn't very well turn my back on him. He was my best friend, and we had been helping each other out of jams for years. I wasn't sure at this point what exactly I hoped to achieve by involving myself in Fingers's dubious affairs either, but I reasoned that I had to play the string out all the way and at least have a closer look at what was going on. If Bones Mellini and his associates were planning a little coup, maybe we could get in on it. Fingers owed us that much, at least.

I couldn't sleep, so I got up, took some decks of cards out of my overnight bag, and sat down at the table by the window overlooking the motel courtyard. I began to deal, then to run through some of my better moves. I hadn't practiced in a couple of days and I could use the work, especially with a job coming up. I may not be the best close-up magician in the world, but I'm a good one and with cards I'm probably one of the two or three top guys. My friend Vince Michaels, who lives and works mostly in Las Vegas and who's the finest prestidigitator I know, says I'm the best with cards and that I could be the best at everything if I'd take it as seriously as he does. But that would mean having to give up the horses and I can't do that. Vince is a fanatic; I'm not. He only gets off on magic and lives like a hermit. I love magic, too, especially what I can do with a deck of pasteboards, but I also like horses and women and opera and good food and drink, not necessarily in that order. What the hell, I'm an all-around player, that's all, one of life's happier dilettantes. Isn't that how my agent, Happy Hal Mancuso, would put it? No, that's not how he would put it. "You're a fuckup, Shifty," he once told me. "You got a lot of talent and you waste it on shit that isn't going to earn you a dime. And the fucking horses, they'll break you in the long run. You wait and see. I don't know why I'm wasting my time on you."

He loved me, that's why. His own life was so boring, so totally dedicated to making deals and earning big money for clients he despised, he couldn't do without me. I kept him honest, I made him feel a little cleaner at the end of his working day, which he spent hustling for comedians, rock bands, actors, and other overpaid talents in what he called the Age of Trash. He loved me and he needed me, the one client he represented who couldn't make him enough in commissions to pay his weekly phone bills. Or maybe I was just comedy relief, the curmudgeon's clown, a confirmation of his sour view of the whole human race.

I sat there and dealt myself hands for over an hour. I palmed, sleeved, crimped, jogged, blind-dealt, faked-cut, fanned, did everything I could think of to do and it all felt right. I ran through nearly every move I had in my repertoire, after which I fished out the rest of my tools—my coins and sponges and bits of string—and I worked them all, swiftly and cleanly and not bungling any of it and not missing a single move. And at the end of it all, I suddenly realized I'd been emptied. I felt drained and calm, as peacefully in love with life as if I'd just sung one of Verdi's great love duets or seen a good ten-to-one shot loop the field to win going away, and I got up from the table and went to bed.

I fell asleep so fast I didn't even have time to turn the light out.

Four

FINGERINGS

Jill Thorne was sitting on a bale of hay between Barn 15 and its neighbor when I showed up there, at about eight o'clock the next morning. I recognized her right away, even though she wasn't exactly dressed like a working rider. She was attired in scuffed boots, blue jeans, and a man's white shirt open at the neck. Her long blond hair was again pulled back into a ponytail, but this time under a white cowboy hat with a long black feather stuck into the band. She was wearing big gold hoop earrings and lipstick and looked more like a model pretending to be a horsewoman than the genuine article. It wasn't until she opened her mouth that I began to think differently. "Howdy," she said. "You lookin' for someone?" She had a flat southwestern accent that sounded like a small wind blowing across a prairie.

"Fingers."

"Who?"

"Pendleton, John Pendleton. Tall, thin guy who snaps his fingers a lot."

"That what they call him?" She smiled, revealing a row of even white teeth that seemed to glow in her tanned countenance. "Damn if that ain't just perfect for him. He'll be comin' back in a few minutes, 'case you want to wait."

"Where is he?"

"He and Luis went over to the quarantine barn." She cocked a thumb backward, over her shoulder. "They got a two-year-old they're shippin' north."

"Fingers? I didn't realize he was running this operation."

"He ain't." She laughed. The sound of it was surprisingly soft and mellow, deep in her throat, a contrast to the hard, nasal twang of her conversation. "I guess he ain't much of anything, right?"

"He's a survivor, and that's about it."

"Friend of yours?"

"Not exactly. We know each other."

"I guess he owes you money, then."

"I guess you're a pretty sharp guesser."

"He must owe everybody money, right?"

"No comment. My name's Lou Anderson."

"Nice to meet you," she said, sticking out her hand. I shook it. It was small, callused, and hard. "That was a hell of a ride you gave that horse in the nightcap," I said. "I cashed a nice ticket on you."

"That so?" Her face brightened at the compliment, then suddenly turned solemn. "Damn, I hate what they did to him."

"Who?"

"He broke down after the race."

"I didn't know."

"I had to jump off of him, 'cause he nearly went down."

"What did you mean by 'did to him'? Who did what?"

"Aw shit, it's no secret. And anyway, I'm always shootin' my mouth off." She plucked a bit of straw off her pants legs and flicked it away, her eyes lost in regret. "They shot him so full of cortisone in his knees, he didn't even know how bad he was feelin'. That's how come he run so good."

"You're lucky he didn't break down during the race," I said. "You could have been hurt."

"Yeah, well, it wouldn't have been the first time. I guess I done broke about every bone in my body at least once by now. You a horseman?"

"No, not me." I smiled. "I just bet on them."

"You sure don't look like no horseman. I guess I knew that."

"Is Mr. Hatch around?"

"Naw, he don't generally get here this early. Round about nine usually, if he makes it at all."

"Isn't he in the horse-training business?"

She grinned. "You could say that," she answered. "I guess you could say that. Aw hell, Sandy's a good horseman, one of the best, when he ain't on the bottle." She cocked her hat forward over her eyes, leaned back, and stretched. She had small, knobby little breasts, unfettered by a bra, that pushed up against the tight cotton of her shirt. I felt a twinge of desire for her. "Got to get to work, I guess," she added, springing lightly to her feet.

"You riding something?"

"Just kind of makin' the rounds. I ain't got an agent," she explained. "If I don't come around, nobody gives me nothin' to get on. I guess maybe Sandy ain't goin' to show up today, or else maybe later."

"Who takes care of the horses?"

"Luis. You know him?"

"Yeah, I met him last night with Fingers."

"It don't do no good to talk to him."

"Why not?"

"He's Mexican. He ain't goin' to ride no girl on his horses."

"Are they his?"

"If Sandy ain't around, he makes the decisions." She clicked her tongue disapprovingly against the roof of her mouth. "I can ride just about anything, but it don't cut the mustard with these Latinos. They only got one place for a woman and that's in the hay."

"Or the kitchen."

"Yeah, honey, and I don't cook worth a shit." She started to move away. "I'll see you around, hear?"

"I'd like to talk to you some more, Jill," I said.

She turned back briefly. "Hell, I don't mind. I'll probably be back. I got to go see a couple of guys about a horse."

"You ever heard of one called Fred's Folly?"

"Oh, sure," she said, and laughed. "Wait'll you see him. He's down at the end over there, by the tack room. He looks like an old country blues singer I once knew back in Texas, but don't let that fool you. He can run some. I wouldn't mind ridin' him neither." And she moved away in long, loping strides toward an adjacent stable, her ponytail swishing to and fro like a Thoroughbred's. I smiled as I watched her go, because something about her made me want to. She was open and friendly and full of life.

I walked over to the barn. It was a long, low, whitewashed building with a red-tiled roof, one in a long series separated by open areas where the grooms and other stablehands were tending to their charges. It was a familiar sight to me. I've been hanging around racetracks since I was sixteen, and I like the feel of them, the quiet, purposeful hustle and bustle of a routine as repetitive and familiar as that of an army camp. I figured that if magic ever failed me, I'd take refuge back here, disappear into this locked-in world of beginnings and endings and irrational hopes.

"Señor?"

I turned around. A thin little man with a worn, copper-brown face and wiry arms had come up behind me. He had a rake in one hand and his features, under a battered-looking straw cowboy hat, were seamed by years of sun and hard work. "Señor, you are looking for someone?"

"Yes, I'm waiting for Luis and Fingers."

"Qué?"

"Señor Pendleton."

"Ah, sí, muy bien, señor." He smiled, touched the fingers of his free hand respectfully to the brim of his hat, and went back to raking up the area around the shedrow.

"*Donde está el caballo* Fred's Folly?" I asked in my finest L.A. Spanish.

The little Mexican grinned and pointed to the stall I'd been heading for. "*Está un caballo extraordinario,*" he said, "*un fenómeno.*" And he laughed, chuckling softly to himself as he worked.

El fenómeno was standing with his back to me, and at first I couldn't really see him. I clucked to him and he turned around so that he could cast a wary eye in my direction. I understood immediately both what Jill had meant and why the Mexican was laughing. Fred's Folly was a chunky, barrel-chested chestnut with a white blaze along the full length of his nose, but what was outstanding about him was his belly. It was so large I thought he was in foal, even though I knew he was a full horse. "Jesus Christ," I muttered to myself. I couldn't imagine this animal galloping around the track, much less actually competing in a race. I clucked at him again, hoping that he'd move so I could get an even better look at him, but he turned back to his original position, presenting me with a full rear view of powerful hindquarters that at least looked like those of a professional race horse. But with that belly on him, he had to be at least two or three months away from a race.

"Who the fuck are you?"

I turned around and at first I thought I was hearing things; I couldn't see anyone. Then I looked down. I was being confronted by a gnome dressed in tennis sneakers, baggy gray pants, a checked short-sleeved sport shirt and a blue cat cap with a long brim that hid his eyes. His face was bright red and the spent stub of a cheap cigar protruded from the corner of his mouth. While waiting for my answer, he removed it just long enough to spit a stream of brown juice into the dirt at my feet.

"My name's Lou Anderson. I'm waiting for Pendleton," I said. "He told me I could come and see him."

"Fingers? You ain't a friend of his. He don't have friends. He owe you money?"

"As a matter of record, yes."

"How much?"

"Enough."

"That asshole Mellini ain't going to like that."

"I'm not here to make trouble," I assured him. "It's just that Fingers ducked out on us. I'm trying to come to some arrangement with him."

"What do you mean, arrangement?"

"I don't know. Some of what he owes us is tied up here." I cocked a thumb over my shoulder in the direction of the horse's stall.

"Old Fred?" The gnome snorted and shifted the cigar stub from one corner of his mouth to the other. "Good luck."

"When are you going to begin working him?"

"Working him?"

"Sure. You are Sandy Hatch, aren't you?"

The gnome grunted. "You can't work him."

"Why not?"

"The sonofabitch is bowed twice. He ain't got that many races left in him. All I can do is gallop him."

"He can't run with that belly on him, can he?"

"He's always had it," the trainer said, "even before, when he was sound. Least that's what they tell me."

"When's he going to run?"

He shrugged. "How the hell do I know? When I think I can get a race or two out of him."

"What does Mellini say?"

The gnome didn't answer. Instead, he spat again, turned on his heel, and walked away from me. He disappeared around the corner of the barn, and a few seconds later I heard an angry stream of Spanish punctuated by American epithets. A yellow-faced groom came running back, heading for the tack room, where he grabbed a bundle of bandages and a bottle of liniment, then hurried off in the direction of the trainer's voice.

The high-decibel diatribe continued and I noticed that it had a galvanizing effect on the Mexican hands around the barn. People appeared and disappeared on various tasks, moving quickly and not talking to each other. The wiry little man with the rake worked at a furious pace now, amid clouds of dust and bits of hay and straw. I sat down on an upended bucket outside the tack room and waited.

A few minutes later, the gnome returned and stormed past me into the tack room. "Goddamn fucking lazy spics," I heard him say. "You can't fucking count on them to do one fucking thing right."

I stuck my head into the room. "You certainly have a way with words," I observed, smiling, trying to keep it light. "You must be greatly loved by your men."

"What? What the fuck are you talking about?"

"I haven't come across such an inspirational address to the troops since General Patton."

The gnome glared at me. He was perched on a corner of a battered wooden desk strewn with papers, racing charts, and old programs. He had been trying to pour himself a mug of coffee from an electric machine plugged into a cord hanging from the ceiling, but he was having trouble. His hands were shaking so badly that he couldn't manage it. "Goddammit," he mumbled.

I got up and took the cup from him, filled it, and handed it to him. He steadied it with both hands and managed to raise it to his lips. He took several swallows, gasped a bit, then very carefully, still using both hands, set the container down on the floor so that he wouldn't spill any of it on the desk. Then he looked up at me and I could see his eyes under the brim of the cap. They were as red as his cheeks. "Get the fuck out of here," he said quietly.

"If you insist," I answered, "but I am going to talk to Fingers."

"I don't give a shit what you do. Just don't let Mellini catch you hanging around. By the way, how'd you get in here?"

"I got press credentials, Mr. Hatch."

"Press? You're a fucking reporter?"

"No, don't worry. It's just that I know how to get into racetracks. It offends me to have to pay for the privilege."

"Beat it."

I walked out into the sunshine. Jill Thorne was heading toward me and she smiled. "Hatch is here," I said, "only I wouldn't go near him this morning."

"I'm used to it," she said. "He's got a couple of horses I can get on. He's one of the few back here who'll let me ride."

"I guess he knows a good thing when he sees it. What's his basic problem?"

"Tequila and hookers," Jill said, "and in that order." She smiled at me and again I felt an impulse toward her.

"Where can I find you, Jill?" I asked.

"I'll be around," she said. "You won't have no trouble." She brushed past me before I could get up the courage to ask her for a date. "Hi, Sandy," I heard her say as she walked into the tack room, "you look like shit."

Jay picked up his car that morning from the Hollywood Park lot and had the headlights replaced at a gas station on Century Boulevard. He had intended to drive home to finish tidying up his apartment, but, on impulse, he drove all the way out to Monrovia to confront Bud Jackson, the other disgruntled member of his betting syndicate. "I figured I'd get nowhere if I just called him," Jay later explained to me. "Whereas if I just showed up, I might surprise him and learn something."

The tactic worked. Bud Jackson was standing behind the counter of his store, which was located in a corner mini-mall about a block and a half away from the Holiday Inn in Monrovia. When Jay came through the door, he paled visibly and took a step away from the counter, as if about to reach under it for a gun or some other weapon.

"Hey, wait, Bud," Jay said, forcing himself to smile. "I just want to talk to you."

"What about?"

"About you or some friends of yours tearing up my place yesterday."

Bud expressed no surprise. "You're full of it," he said calmly.

"Am I? I don't think so. The people above me were home and they saw you leave," he lied.

"I wasn't there. You're lying."

Jay looked at him. "Somebody was, Bud, and I think you put him or them up to it."

Two customers came into the store, and Jay pretended to scan the magazine and newspaper rack while Bud waited on them, then he approached the counter again. "Look, whatever it is you think you're accomplishing with this kind of crap—"

"You don't seem to get it, Jay," Bud said, interrupting him. "We gave you our money in good faith. We put up with the losses. We put up with you taking a big percentage of the winnings. Then, when we do hit, you run off with our money."

"Don't be a jerk," Jay snapped. "Why in hell would I do that? Does it make any sense to you?"

"Sure. You've been losing and you needed the money."

"I haven't been losing and I don't need your money. Anyway, I think I've found Fingers."

"Yeah? Where?"

"He may be in Tijuana. Shifty's down there. We've been looking for him and Shifty got a tip he might be in TJ."

"What's he done with the money?"

"I don't know yet. We're in the process of finding out. In the meantime, I want you to lay off."

Bud didn't reply. He folded his arms and leaned back against the wall behind his cash register. "You got some nerve coming in here and threatening me," he said after a moment or two, during which his tiny football mind must have been ponderously reviewing the evidence and his options. "I ought to call the police."

"Okay, Bud, why don't you?" Jay asked with a smile. "We can let those dummies sort it all out. Are you and Emile in this together?"

"What do you mean?"

"I mean, are you working as a team, or what? One of you sics a professional goon on me, the other one trashes my apartment—"

"Oh, get out of here!" Bud barked at him. "Just get out and get me my money! Get out before I do call the cops!"

Before Jay could answer him or figure out what else he could do to impress this fool, the door swung open and two young toughs walked into the store. They were in their teens, but seemed to be dressed for Halloween. They were all in black—black boots, black pants, black shirts—and festooned with Nazi paraphernalia, including swastikas and large iron crosses dangling from chains around their necks. Their heads were shaved and their eyes were blank. "Hey, Pops," one of them said, "I need a twenty. For gas."

Bud opened the register and came up with a twenty-dollar bill. "Where are you going?"

"We're makin' a run to Berdoo, okay?"

"Okay, but be back here by six. Terry's off tonight and I need you in here."

"Sure, Pops." The boy took the twenty, grabbed two Hershey bars from the counter, and went back out to the lot, his idiot twin shadowing him. Jay watched them clamber onto a Japanese motorcycle and roar out into the road toward a Texaco station two blocks away. "Your son?" Jay asked. "Nice boy."

Bud didn't answer, but simply stared blankly at him. He looked about as innocent as Dr. Frankenstein reassuring the villagers that they had nothing to fear from the big guy in the cellar. "Okay," Jay said, "now I know who did it. You sicced your moronic kid and his skinhead playmates on me. What a jerk you are! If I catch them hanging around my place, Bud, I'll grab your kid and make him eat what he dumped on my stuff. You got that?"

"You get out of here," Bud said. "You get out right now."

"And you let that creep wait on your customers? What are you selling in here, human skin?"

Bud glared at him but said nothing more. Jay turned and walked out to his car. "I didn't know what else to do," he told me on the phone. "I felt like a jerk, but at least I found out who trashed my place."

"So what can you do about it?" I asked. I was lying on my bed at the Conquistador, trying to put the small pieces of my own day together in my head.

"Nothing yet, Shifty. It depends on what's happening at your end."

I told him. "So I waited in my car for Fingers and this fat Mexican to come back and they didn't," I concluded. "When I asked Hatch about them, he told me he didn't know anything either. And, of course, he told me to get lost again. He's not an affable sort."

"I know about Hatch," Jay said. "He used to be a good trainer. He had a string up in San Francisco for years and occasionally he'd ship one of his better horses to Santa Anita or Hollywood Park. He was never high up in the standings, but he won his share and had a good winning percentage. Then I sort of lost track of him. I guess I knew he was in Mexico, but I didn't know why. Some of the top trainers used to send their young horses to him and then later they sent him their bums. I mean, Shifty, this guy could train. I guess it was the booze that got to him."

"Good guess," I said.

"So now, what about Fingers?"

"Well, when he didn't show up," I told him, "I took a walk up to the quarantine barn, figuring I might meet him on the way. Nothing. The building was empty, except for the horses in some of the stalls there, and a couple of guys hanging around. Nobody knew Fingers and nobody had seen Luis either."

"What's the quarantine barn?"

"It's the place where they hold the horses for twenty-four hours before they ship them over the border or after they've been sent down here," I explained. "I asked one of these guys. The horses cross the border around eight-thirty or nine A.M., after they've been cleared medically and by the customs people. It's a routine procedure. Mellini must have had a horse coming in or out. But I guess I missed them."

"So what do we do, Shifty?"

"I don't know, Jay. I guess I'll hang around one more day and try to find Fingers again. I'll check the dog races tonight and I'll go by the barn again tomorrow morning. After that I have to head up to Anaheim till the weekend."

"Maybe I'll come down there. I can help you, and it wouldn't hurt to get out of town for a couple of weeks. And maybe we can get in on this coup Mellini's planning. Also, we can keep tabs on Fingers and maybe get some of our money back."

"I have doubts on both counts."

"You want to call me again in the morning? Make it around noon. I have a dental appointment."

"You call me, Jay. It's a hell of a lot cheaper. You're not going to the track at all?"

"Shifty, it's Tuesday, remember?"

"I'm in Tijuana. You tend to lose track of time down here."

"Yeah, well, on Tuesdays the track is closed. But since I have to go to a window every day, I'm planning to stop by a bank and stick my card into one of those machines."

"What for?"

"It's a sure payoff, Shifty, the only one I know about."

Five

POSSIBILITIES

Fingers did not show up at the dogs that night. I hung around the grandstand for three races without risking a dime, but I found the action boring and decided to go back to my motel. On the way out, however, I changed my mind and backtracked upstairs to the Jockey Club, where I found some sort of private wingding in progress. Heedless of the canine action going on in the bright circle of light below them, a large party of well-dressed young Mexicans was celebrating somebody's birthday. An enormous rectangular cake festooned with candles graced one end of a long buffet table that seemed about to buckle under the weight of masses of shrimp, guacamole, enchiladas, burritos, chilis, nachos, tamales, carnitas, tortillas, salads, and other local delicacies. Just looking at this feast was threatening to clog my arteries, but I suddenly realized I was very hungry; I hadn't eaten anything since breakfast.

Even though I looked respectable enough, I wasn't exactly dressed for the occasion. I was wearing khaki slacks, an open-necked yellow shirt, and a dark brown sport jacket, but the other guests were resplendent in expensive dark suits or evening dress. Some of the women were wearing furs and all were heavily bejeweled. It was mostly a young crowd, I noted, in their twenties and thirties, and a cheerful one. Loud talk and laughter filled the room, all but drowning out a trio of two guitarists and a singer entertaining in one corner. Nobody paid any attention to me or questioned my presence, so I quietly joined the chow line and began loading up. I couldn't tell from the inscription on the cake whose birthday it was, but by that time I had a full plate and I didn't care anyway. I picked up a glass of champagne from a tray beside the cake and then looked around for someplace to sit down.

I had just spotted an empty chair at the end of a long table against the far wall when I was accosted by the maître d'. "Señor, you are with someone?" he asked. His tone was affable enough, but the smile on his face seemed forced and his dark eyes were cold.

"Well, actually, I was looking for someone."

"Truly? You see, señor, this is a private affair."

"I guess I knew that."

"Who is it you were looking for, señor?"

I pondered trying to snatch a mouthful of the goodies on my plate before allowing myself to be ejected, but before I could do so or come up with some sort of delaying tactic, I heard a familiar nasal twang behind me. "Hey, how you doin'?" the voice said. "It's okay, Julio, he's lookin' for me."

"Ah, muy bien, señorita," Julio said. He nodded coldly to me and walked away.

I turned around. "Thanks, Jill," I said. "I thought I was going to have to eat and run or maybe do both at the same time."

"I saw you in the line and I waved to you, but you didn't see me," she said.

She looked dazzling. She was wearing a tight-fitting black silk cocktail dress cut just above the knees, black spiky-heeled pumps, a single strand of pearls around her neck, and long pearl earrings. Her shoulders were bare, and she seemed to have been moulded into her dress, which showed off every line and curve of her slender frame. Her arms were strong, but not out of proportion to the rest of her, and the muscles she had developed from her years on horseback were long and flat, not hard and knotted, as is the case with many riders. Her legs looked fine, too, with strong calves tapering down to slender ankles and feet. Her eyes, I noticed for the first time, were a disturbing blend of gray and green, and her long blond hair lay piled on top of her head.

"How could I have missed you?" I asked. "You look fantastic."

"You look hungry." She smiled. "Gettin' enough to eat?"

"Barely. Where are we sitting?"

"Over there." She pointed to a table for two in one corner and I followed her over. Hatch popped up out of his chair like a gopher from his hole, then abruptly sat down again when he recognized me. A bright orange toupée sat on his skull like a pie plate and he was wearing white slacks and a magenta sports jacket that probably glowed in the dark. He did not seem delighted to see me.

"Hello, Sandy, you're looking very dapper," I said, extending my hand. He did not shake it.

"Sit down," Jill instructed me. "Don't pay him no mind. He's hopin' to get into my pants tonight, and he's scared you'll screw it up for him."

"I thought he only liked hookers."

Jill laughed. "He's going to make an exception for me."

"I hope you're kidding."

"Stick around and find out."

I pulled up an empty chair and sank into it. Hatch glared at me out of his red eyes. "This is a crock of shit," he said. He suddenly bolted out of his chair and headed for the elevators.

"Where's he going?" I asked. "Not more than ten or twenty miles, I hope. And maybe he'll get lost or ambushed on his way back."

"He's headin' for the bar," she informed me. "Ain't no way Sandy can make it through the night on wine and bubbles."

"Does he get even more charming when he's drunk, or is he always such a sweetheart?"

"Aw, you don't mind him, Lou. He's just an old geezer whose whole life has turned sour, that's all. He ain't really mean. He just acts mean."

"Odd you should say that. I mistook him for a lecherous gnome with the manners of a Renaissance buffoon and a heart as big as a shriveled walnut."

"How you talk, mister," she said. "What are you, some kind of writer or somethin'?"

I reached into my pocket, pulled out a small deck of cards, and went into my routine. Ten minutes later, after I'd snaked a missing jack out of her hair and showed her a couple of fine-tuned variations on the Erdnase Shift, I had her gasping with pleasure. "Hell," she said, "this is better than a good lay."

"I wouldn't say that," I countered, "but it'll do until the real thing comes along. And speaking of which, here comes your charming escort." I had spotted the orange toupée, now slightly askew, bobbing toward us through the crowd.

"He ain't my boyfriend, if that's what's botherin' you," she said. "He's tried, all right, but he ain't. He'd sure like to."

"I think that's probably the only thing we have in common. Who is?"

"What?"

"Your boyfriend."

"Ain't goin' with anyone right now," she said, only the hint of a smile on her face. "I been hit pretty hard a couple of times, mister."

"I guess you have. You don't have to tell me."

"I'm just down here to ride horses. Sandy's got a couple of decent animals he says he'll let me up on."

"So you string him along."

"It's a man's world, 'case you ain't noticed."

Hatch rejoined us. He was holding a tumbler two thirds full of either whiskey or tequila and his face was dark with displeasure at my continued presence. I had a strong feeling, however, that Jill was using me to keep him from launching a major assault on her, so I determined to ignore his hostility and stick around, as long as I sensed that she wanted me to.

"What's the occasion?" I asked, forcing myself to smile.

"It's Lupe's birthday," Jill explained. "Lupe Camacho, he's the leadin' rider down here. That's him, see?" She pointed to a big table in the center of the room where Camacho, a short, broad-shouldered elf with the face of an Aztec god, sat surrounded by taller men and half a dozen slick-looking women. "He can really ride."

I knew about him. Years ago he'd established a reputation as a top rider in Panama, Mexico City, and Caliente, then gone north to make it on the California circuits. Unfortunately he'd been caught halfway through his second season using a buzzer, a battery-charged electrical goad, to help a tiring front-runner along and had been suspended for a year. He had come back to Mexico and remained, riding year after year among the top two or three in the standings south of the border. To the locals he was a hero, even though he also had a reputation for managing to lose a lot of races on odds-on favorites.

"Who's giving the party?" I asked.

"Management," Jill said. "He's ridden more winners here than anyone. I guess they figured the publicity— "

"Let's get out of here," Hatch interrupted. He stood up.

"Hold on, Sandy, we're partyin', ain't we?" Jill answered. "And it's free."

"Too many fuckin' Mexicans," the trainer said. "I'm going to take you home."

"No, you ain't," Jill said. "Me and Lou here, we're havin' a ball, ain't we, honey?"

"You bet." I smiled at Sandy, then looked alarmed.

"Wow, don't move!" I commanded, then reached over and plucked a small rubber duck out of his wig. "Wonder how that got there. Oh!" And I fluttered both hands over him to produce a cascade of little rubber animals from his pockets and out of his ears. "My God, Sandy, you're carrying a zoo around with you! What have you been up to?"

Jill squealed with delight and clapped her hands together like a child. "You're crazy," she said, gasping with pleasure.

The trainer stood up in a fury. "What is this shit?" he snarled. "What the fuck are you doing?"

Looking suddenly very serious, I got up with him. "Uh-oh," I muttered, "I missed one." I reached out, grabbed his toupée and lifted. With a small snapping sound, it came loose, revealing the presence of a tiny mouse sitting squarely in the middle of his pale, naked head.

Jill shrieked. Hatch clutched his skull, grabbed the mouse, and stared dumbly at it.

"Here," I said, handing him his wig. "You don't want to let rodents make a nest up there, Sandy. It could get uncomfortable and it's not very sanitary."

The trainer suddenly took a wild swing at me. Luckily, he missed, but the force of his effort sent him spinning past me and into a passing waiter carrying a trayful of loaded wineglasses. They both went down in a tangle of flailing limbs and spraying liquid. A woman screamed. Several men rushed over to help, but Hatch, now in a blind rage, lashed out and caught one of his would-be rescuers flush on the nose. Blood squirted over his fingers and onto his shirt. The victim retreated, howling and holding both hands to his face. A small army of agitated Latins now closed in on the scene and Hatch disappeared behind a wall of legs and bodies, though I could hear him in full and obscene cry.

I turned to Jill, who was gazing on the developing

carnage with amazement. "I think it's time to make a nimble but graceful exit, don't you?"

"Jesus, you better get out of here," she said.

"Well, come on, then."

She shook her head. "You go. I got to stay and get him calmed down. That Mexican he hit is the nephew of a big politico down here. He could go to jail."

"Why doesn't that distress me?" I asked.

"Come on now, you go." And she literally pushed me away from the table.

On my way out, I skirted the agitated group around the fallen trainer. He was being restrained by two of the waiters and the maître d', while the Mexican with the bloody nose was being tended to by his friends, one of whom had clamped a napkin full of ice cubes to his face. I saw Jill push her way through the men toward Hatch, then I stepped into an elevator and left.

Outside, the air was clean and cold. The orange grandstand glowed in the soft evening light like a stranded spaceship and faint sounds of music came from within. I walked toward my car feeling increasingly depressed. I had a dismal conviction I couldn't shake that this tough, talented, good-looking woman I had just met was going to give her body up to that foul-mouthed gnome in order to keep her career going. So it is still a man's world, I reflected as I got into the Datsun and gunned it angrily out of the parking lot. But did it have to be quite so corrupt?

I didn't want to go back to my motel, so I drove past the Conquistador and kept on going toward downtown Tijuana. I knew that I was in a dangerously reckless mood, but I didn't care. I hoped Hatch would go to jail, mainly because I wanted to shut my mind to the spectacle of him pulling Jill Thorne into his bed. I didn't think he would be arrested, however, if only because I was sure she would prevent it from happening. Also, I reasoned, Hatch himself had to be at least fairly well

connected after all these years on the local racing scene;
somebody would keep him out of the hands of the law,
even if he had slugged the son of the president himself.
And Jill had to be more than a little annoyed at me over
the incident. I've really done it this time, I thought. I
felt like getting drunk, disappearing all the way into my
own personal little black night of the soul.

I drove slowly, idly eyeing my surroundings. Tijuana may be, as some people claim, merely an extension of San Diego, its American twin just across the
border, but it is clearly a foreign country. It's a vast
sprawl of mostly small, low-lying, multihued buildings of
all shapes, tumbled together seemingly at hazard and
with no apparent regard to function. The rich live in the
hills west of downtown, their villas basking in isolated
splendor behind high walls and iron gates, while the vast
majority of the population resides in the squalid neighborhoods, most of them consisting of small adobe huts,
on the gently undulating land that stretches for miles
toward the south. The really poor survive in shacks and
improvised shelters, some of them made out of cardboard, in colonies of squatters, fugitives from the even
more dismal poverty in the interior. This is the Tijuana
the tourists only glimpse from their cars as they stream
across the border toward the heart of the old city along
streets lined by tile factories, car emporiums, liquor
stores, and the other enterprises catering mainly to
gringos. It's not pretty, but it's alive and throbbing with
possibilities, especially for anyone intent on making a
deal or simply having a good time.

The main fun zone consists of a stretch of several
blocks of Avenida Revolución, a broad avenue lined by
curiosity shops, strip clubs, cafés, restaurants, and cheap
hotels, dominated by the imposing, faintly Moorish bulk
of the Frontón Palace. I drove past the latter, then
turned right up a side street toward a parking lot. I
didn't think even the most desperate thief in Mexico
would want to break into my Datsun, but in Tijuana it's

safer to leave any car with a foreign plate in a guarded lot. As I got out and looked up, I saw Fingers pass along the sidewalk toward Revolución. I started to call out to him, but noted that he was not alone. He was flanked by two men I had never seen before, one of them short and heavily built, the other also short, but ferretlike, with a small head thrust forward on its neck, as if nosing for prey. They moved quickly up the street, and by the time I reached the sidewalk they were crossing the avenue.

From the corner I watched them enter a restaurant halfway up the next block called the Encanto. I gave them a few minutes to get settled, then followed them inside.

"*Señor,* a table for dinner?"

Over the maître d's shoulder and through a beaded curtain I could see Fingers and his two friends sitting at a corner table. The fat man was looking at a menu while the ferret was sniffing the room. Fingers looked miserable, his head seeming to vibrate on its long stem like a ball mounted on a spring. I had a disquieting feeling that he was terrified.

"*Señor?*"

"It's okay, I'm not sure I'm going to eat," I said. "I'll have a drink."

"*Muy bien, señor.*"

The bar was on my right. It was small and comfortingly dark, with an angled view of the dining room. I sat down at the far end of the short counter, from where I couldn't see or be seen by Fingers and his friends, but which provided me with a good view of the entrance foyer. I needed a drink and the time to evolve a course of action. Why was Fingers so frightened?

I ordered a margarita over the rocks, with no salt, and barely had time for one sip before I was accosted by a dark-haired beauty who looked naked in her clothes. "You do not want to drink alone, darling," she said, throwing an arm around my neck and thrusting a well-endowed bosom in my face.

"Well, actually, I do," I said.

"No, that is sad. Why do you not buy me a bottle of *champagne*?" she asked, pronouncing it in the French fashion.

"Because that would be too expensive," I said. "But I will buy you a drink, if you'll be a nice girl and leave me alone."

She shrugged and looked at the bartender. "A Scotch, Victor," she said, then rattled off a stream of Spanish that made him laugh and shake his head.

"I have a feeling you're making fun of me," I observed.

"No, I don't do that," she said. "I just tell him a yoke about *chilangos*. You know *chilangos*?"

I shook my head. "No, sorry."

"They are the people from Mexico City," she explained. "We don't like them in Tijuana. We make the yokes about them."

"I learn something every day down here."

The bartender served the girl her drink and she raised it in a small, ironic toast to me, peering at me over the glass with large, lustrous black eyes framed by an excess of mascara. "You are sure you wish to be alone?"

"Right now, yes. But thanks."

"That is fine." She sipped her drink, then leaned over to whisper in my ear. "I can do wonderful things for you," she said. "I think you are very nice." Her tongue flicked against my eardrum.

"No, really," I said. "Maybe later." I could peer down her dress all the way to her waist, and it was not a displeasing view. "Really."

"Really," she echoed, and stood up. "My name is Marisa. I wait for you." And she retreated to a corner table, where she sat down with two other working girls. Within a couple of minutes all three of them were laughing, and I wondered again whether I had become an object of humor or whether Marisa had told her friends her "yoke" about the *chilangos*. Well, it didn't matter, did it? And anyway, I was the only man in the bar then, this being a relatively slow night in Tijuana.

I finished my drink, ordered another one, paid up, then, glass in hand, I walked into the dining room. Smiling, I headed for the corner table. Fingers saw me coming and stood up; he looked genuinely delighted to see me. "Hey, Shifty, how are you doing?" he said. "I sure am glad to see you. Did you get my message?"

"No, I didn't."

"I left it at the motel. These fucking Mexicans, they can't do anything right." Without waiting for a reply, he introduced me to his companions. "This is Rico Mellini," he said, indicating the heavyset man. "And Larry Youkoumian. I'm surprised you guys don't know each other. Hey, Shifty, come on, sit down." And he hastily pulled out a chair, practically pushing me into it. "What are you drinking?"

"I'm all right, Fingers, I've got a drink," I said. "So what did your message say?"

"About the horse, Shifty, you know . . . About me giving you your share of the horse . . ."

"Oh."

His whole body was in action now, his fingers snapping in manic rhythm. He turned to Mellini. "Shifty owns my share of Fred now," he informed the loan shark. "That's my fifteen percent, right?" *Snap snap.* "Right?" He looked straight at me and I could see the terror in his eyes. *Please,* they were saying, *please* . . .

"That's right," I said, keeping it casual and matter-of-fact. "I guess I need to know about the paperwork. I'm not licensed."

"Oh, that's no problem," Fingers said. "Right, Rico? No problem at all. You can do that in the morning, Shifty. Larry here knows how all that works. You can take care of it, right, Larry?"

"Yeah, I can take care of it," Larry said. "Okay, Rico?"

Mellini nodded. So far he had said nothing. He

merely sat there, shoveling some sort of heavy pasta into his mouth, seemingly indifferent to this surprising development. From time to time his small black eyes would glance back and forth from Fingers to me, but he remained inscrutable during all of Fingers's agitated dialogue. He reminded me of a Gila monster, a slow-moving, dangerous reptile of the sort that avoids the light and remains quietly hidden in dark places, waiting to clamp his poisonous jaws on anything unaware enough to approach him. I had no idea what Fingers was up to, but I understood that this man was the source of his fear and that somehow he was trying to remove himself permanently from any involvement with him. I also had the disquieting feeling that Fingers's very safety somehow depended upon my acquiescence to his scheme, whatever it was. I didn't think I was in any danger of my own, but I was definitely on the alert by this time, although I didn't exactly know against what.

Fingers suddenly stood up. "Okay, well, I'm going," he said. "I'll see you guys."

"Listen, Fingers—" I began.

He cut me off. "Don't worry about the rest of your money," he said. "You tell Jay he'll get it after the first of the year, okay? Meanwhile, you got the horse, right? That's two grand's worth, like you said, okay? Okay?"

I nodded. "But listen—"

"I ain't going to be around for a while," he said, "but don't you guys worry, okay? I'm going up to Oakland. I got a brother there who's in the used car business. I'm going in with him for a while."

"You're going to get a job?" I asked. I couldn't have been more surprised if he'd told me he was planning to be an astronaut. "You, Fingers?"

He smiled sheepishly and rocked back and forth like an inflated rubber doll. "Yeah, well, I guess I got to," he said. "I've kind of fucked things up recently." He glanced nervously at Mellini. "I'm going to get out of this, at least for a while." He hesitated, as if waiting to be dismissed.

Nobody said anything. And with one last wave, one final knuckle-cracking flutter of those strange hands, he was gone.

Mellini looked up at Youkoumian. "Take care of it," he said.

"Sure," the ferret answered, nodding. "Sure thing."

"The same as with Rivers, remember?"

"Sure, sure."

"Who's Rivers?" I asked.

"Another guy in the horse business," Youkoumian explained without telling me anything. "And you," he added, now pointing at me, "you come by the stable office, okay? We'll fix you up with the papers. Only one thing . . ."

"Yeah?"

"You stay out of our way," he said. "You don't question nothin', you don't ask no questions about nothin'."

"Is it okay if I ask when the horse is going to run?"

"Just look it up in the papers. We don't want no dumb minority owners askin' dumb questions and wasting our time, you got that? Once a month you get a statement, and if there's money owed, you pay it."

"To whom?"

"To the stable account. You got that?"

"Yeah."

Mellini shoved one last huge forkful of pasta into his mouth; tomato sauce ran down his chin. "Now beat it," he mumbled. "Larry and I got things to talk about."

"Is it okay if I occasionally go by the stable to have a look at old Fred?" I asked. "I mean, it *is* my money."

"Suit yourself," Mellini said. "Only don't come botherin' no one. Now beat it."

"Well, it's been charming," I said, standing up. "By the way, which fifteen percent of the horse do I own?"

Nobody thought this remark was even faintly amusing, so I left. On my way out, I glanced into the bar. Marisa was sitting at the far end of the counter with a

couple of American sailors. One of them had his hand on
her leg, about halfway up her thigh, and was leaning in
very close to her, his chin almost resting on her naked
bosom. I waved and she smiled. "You come back," she
said, "you come back another time, all right?"

Why not, I thought as I let myself out into the
night, why not? In Tijuana anything seemed possible. I
now had fifteen percent of a broken-down old horse
owned by a couple of thugs and trained by an alcoholic
lecher who hated my guts. I couldn't wait to tell Jay. The
way his luck had been running recently, he could hardly
be surprised.

Six

PLEASURE
FACTORS

"You what?" Jay asked, as if I had told him we had invested our money in a bubble-gum mine. "You what?"

"I didn't know what else to do," I explained.

"So you put our money into a broken-down seven-year-old plater owned by a loan shark."

"Something like that."

"Shifty, have you gone nuts?"

I proceeded to explain to him that I didn't think I'd had any choice. "Fingers wanted out in the worst way," I concluded my account of my night's work. "He's going up to San Francisco to get into the used car business with his brother. He says he'll pay us the balance after the first of the year, when the IRS refund check comes in."

There was a long silence at the other end of the line.

"Jay?"

"Yeah."

"It's only fifteen percent, and I'm telling you, these guys are getting ready to pull one off down here," I insisted. "We may be able to cash a big ticket. All we have to do is stay on top of what's happening."

"So how do we do that?"

"One of us has to be here pretty much all the time," I said. "They're not going to tell us anything, so we have to act on our own. And it's not going to be too long."

"What makes you think so?"

"Mellini's here with his pilot fish."

"Who?"

"Some guy named Larry Youkoumian."

"I know him," Jay said. "He's a walking plague."

"He speaks very highly of you."

"Bullshit. You know what one of his scams is?"

"What?"

"He cuts himself and Mellini in on other people's big tickets. He finds guys with two out of three in the triples or five out of six in the Pick-Six and buys up percentages of their tickets. They also get to cash those tickets, so they can knock off the IRS later for the refunds. You know what? I'll bet that's what they did to Fingers."

I thought that one over and, of course, it made perfect sense. If they had spotted Fingers waiting to cash our ticket, they could easily have pressured him into handing it over to them. "So I guess Fingers is lying," I finally observed. "We'll never see our money from him."

"Now you're beginning to understand, Shifty."

"Okay, then our only chance is to bail out on whatever they're planning to do down here," I said. "Our little investment in Fred's Folly is beginning to look better."

"I'm coming down there."

"Good idea, especially as I've got to head north in the morning. I'll be back by the weekend. And you obviously need to get out of town for a while."

"Yes. My precious bodily fluids are in some danger of being drained. What kind of shape is Hatch in?"

"The usual, I suppose. He's a great fan of mine."

"Really, Shifty?"

"No, not really. Actually, he hates my guts. Look up this girl jock, Jill Thorne, when you get down here," I suggested. "She's okay, she knows a lot and she can also ride."

"I'll do a little homework tomorrow morning and

drive down in the evening," Jay said. "Where are you staying in Anaheim?"

"Some motel near the trade fair. If I don't hear from you, count on my being back in Tijuana late Friday night," I said. "I'll get you a room here. It's cheap and nice enough. Unless you want to double up and save some money."

"No way. One of us might fall in love."

"Yeah, I suppose. I don't know about love, Jay, but there's a great-looking working girl at the bar of the Encanto. That's a restaurant downtown, across from the Frontón Palace."

"A working girl? In the age of AIDS?"

"She's fun to talk to, if you get lonely."

"What's her name?"

"Marisa. I'll see you Friday night."

Again I had a hard time sleeping, but I made it to the stable area by seven the next morning. I didn't see either Jill or Hatch, but Youkoumian was waiting for me. He was slumped behind the wheel of a gray Lincoln Continental parked beside the barn. When he saw me, he stuck his head out the window. "Hey, let's go," he said.

"How long is this going to take?" I asked.

"Not long."

"I'll follow you over," I said. "I have to go north right after we finish."

We drove around to the frontside and I followed him into the racing office. He seemed to be well known there and nobody questioned my credentials. It was evidently enough for me to have been presented as an associate of Larry Youkoumian. Somebody took my California driver's license, typed up the information on it on a form, and motioned me over to a counter, where I had my picture taken. Within twenty minutes, I found myself holding a piece of paper identifying me as a member in good standing of the Jockey Club Mexicano, signed by me and the stewards, none of whom I'd met.

"Okay, that's it," Youkoumian said as we headed back to our cars.

"They don't ask any questions about your background?"

"Don't worry about it. All they want is the *dinero*." And he rubbed his thumb and forefinger together.

"When's the horse going to run?" I asked.

He shrugged. "I don't know. Maybe next week. Check with Hatch." He climbed into his car. "Hey, by the way," he called back, "the horse is going to run in your name."

"My name only?"

"You got it."

"Why?"

"We got our reasons."

"Hey, wait a minute—"

But before I could pursue this interesting development any further, he had swung the big Lincoln out into the aisle and was speeding away from me. I stood there for a moment, trying to figure out exactly what this development might portend and whether it could pose any threat to my future welfare, then I decided I didn't have the time to deal with it just then and opted to let it go. I promised myself that I'd look into the matter over the weekend, when I got back. If I had to, I told myself, I'd go to the Mexican stewards or the Racing Commission to clarify the matter. I wanted them, at least, to be aware that I was not the only owner of Fred's Folly. I was reasonably certain that Mellini and Youkoumian were planning something a little out of the ordinary for our horse and, though I was eager to be in on what I assumed would be a betting coup, I didn't want to be the only one implicated, if anything went wrong.

In fact, as I pulled into one of the dozen or so long lines of cars inching toward the border crossing, with its booths of uniformed U.S. Customs and INS officers, all toting guns and looking suddenly unfriendly, I began to entertain some second thoughts about what Jay and I were becoming involved in. I had a feeling that security at the Agua Caliente track might not be quite up to the standards maintained north of the border and that Mellini was planning to take advantage of that fact, probably by doping old Fred's Folly to win. It wouldn't be the first time that had been tried, and not only in Mexico, but I didn't want to be part of it.

Actually, I then began to think, I was being more than slightly hypocritical. I *did* want to be part of it, at least to the extent of cashing a big ticket, but I didn't want to be involved in doing the deed itself. I was a typical horseplayer, all right, always looking for an angle, no different really from Fingers and the other degenerates. But then, I reasoned, we were in trouble. Or at least Jay was. Somehow we had to get back the money they'd cheated us out of, or Jay risked being physically maimed, maybe even killed. *Killed? Ye gods, what have we gotten into down here?* Mellini was not exactly cast appropriately in this role I'd assigned to him—the rescuer of our frail fortunes. Maybe I was losing my mind, as Jay had suspected.

But then an odd thing happened to me as I sat there in the hot, dusty, early-morning haze of Tijuana, waiting to get across the line. I began to feel a strange sense of euphoria. My God, I had actually become part owner of a race horse! The concept dazzled me. I had been betting on horses ever since the age of sixteen, when I was first whisked out to the races at Aqueduct in New York by an older cousin who went regularly. He was considered a hopeless degenerate by my parents because he had squandered his life on horses, crap games, and slot machines, but he opened up a whole new world to me. From the moment I first saw the animals come out onto the track, with the jockeys in their brightly colored silks parked like elves high up on their backs, I fell in love with them. When I went down to the paddock before the next race to have a closer look, my relationship to them was confirmed for life. I had never seen anything as beautiful as a Thoroughbred before. And the fact that you could actually make money by wagering on such an aesthetic experience proved to be mind-boggling to me.

We had a big winning day, one of the rare occasions when my cousin got lucky, but it truly wasn't the money that hooked me. I knew even then that betting on anything for a living had to be a tough proposition. No, it was the spectacle itself. I remember coming home that night in a daze. All I could see was the way the horses looked in the post parade and the way they exploded out of the starting gate and the awe-inspiring moves of the winners as they turned for home, either on the lead, kicking up dirt behind them, or coming on in full majestic stride to mow down the tiring front-runners. In my whole life I've only fallen in love at first sight once, and it was with horses that first day at Aqueduct, so many years ago now. As far as I'm concerned, no more significant meeting of lovers has ever taken place than at my introduction to the Thoroughbred, an encounter compared to which the convergence of Abelard and Eloise qualifies as a mere flirtation. And now, at last, I actually owned one of these marvels and my name would appear on a racing program as the possessor of it. I had never expected to find myself in such a position, if only because in my profession the best one can hope for financially is survival.

I could understand Jay's amazement and I could sympathize with his doubts, especially about becoming too deeply involved with Mellini and his noxious associate. Jay was a pragmatist. His moves at the track were dictated by the numbers, the ones that appeared in the *Form* and in his charts and in the detailed notations he made daily in his big black notebooks. He had stripped the game of sentimentality and as many of the other emotions as he could eliminate from his careful calculations. To him, the running of a horse race, its outcome, and whether he would risk his money on it or not were simply factors to be considered as precisely and thoroughly as possible. He was playing a complicated numbers game for which he had devised an unwavering set of rules and by which he was prepared to live or die. There was no room in the game for sentiment, most certainly not love. And who is to say he was wrong? I had my magic to fall back on, the practice of which ennobled me; it was my small contribution to the pursuit not of happiness, which is largely unattainable, but of meaning. For Jay that question was totally irrelevant; his life was wrapped up in whether he won or lost. Handicapping winners had nothing to do with aesthetics, but only with survival. If he failed at it, what else could justify his existence?

When I finally drove up beside the little booth at the border checkpoint nearly an hour later, I was still feeling pretty cheerful. I even managed a smile for the corpulent young officer who first checked my license plate number on his computer screen, just in case I happened to be wanted for some misdemeanor or other, then leaned down to peer at me. "Where are you coming from?" he asked.

"The racetrack," I said.

"Are they running on weekdays now?"

"No, I have a horse there."

"Oh. Bringing anything back?"

"Dreams."

He looked mildly disgusted, but waved me on through. I picked up the freeway heading north.

Jay arrived in Tijuana that night. Instead of checking into the Conquistador, he chose to stay at the Country Club, a somewhat seedier establishment that lacked even a semblance of charm but had the advantage of being located directly across the street from the track. That way, Jay reasoned, he'd be able simply to stroll over to the Foreign Book at any time of the morning, in case he found a horse to bet on at one of the half dozen or so tracks whose races were beamed by satellite onto the monitors in the room. "Ordinarily, I wouldn't do that," he explained to me the next day, "but I may be here for a while, and you never know. Anyway, I can take a break from handicapping Hollywood Park by just crossing the street, watching a race or two while having a cup of coffee, and come back. And I might see something. We ship horses all over the country to run now, and the California animals tend to go off at good odds in the East, where they don't know them. You know me, Shifty, I'm always looking for the edge."

He rented one of the cheaper rooms in the old section of the motel, a long, low building fronting on its parking lot. The room was on the ground floor and comfortable enough, with a king-size bed, a TV set that broadcast one Mexican channel clearly, and a bathroom that smelled of cleaning fluid and disinfectant. When Jay drove downtown for dinner, he left nothing of value, not even his old binoculars, in the room. He had brought a thousand dollars in cash and wore it around his waist in a money belt.

He ate at the Encanto, then, remembering my tip, he stopped at the bar for an after-dinner drink. He ordered a beer and looked around the room. It was empty. "Excuse me," he asked the bartender, "but a friend of mine said there was a nice girl in here called Marisa. Is she around?"

"Not tonight, señor," the bartender told him. "She is entertaining at a private party."

"Entertaining?"

"Singing, señor."

"Ah. Sounds like it might be fun. Where is it?"

"It is private, señor."

"But where?"

The bartender shrugged, then he grinned. "It is the chief of police's birthday, señor."

"That could be the blowout of the year. What's your name?"

"Victor, *señor*." He leaned over the bar. "Not all the girls are taken, *señor*. There are places—"

"Oh, I know about those, Victor," Jay said. "My friend was here for dinner the other night. He said Marisa was a lot of fun. I thought I'd buy her a drink."

"She may come later if the party finishes early."

"Do you think it will, Victor?"

"No, I do not think so."

"Is Marisa a good singer?"

"She sing the mariachi music very good, yes." He dried a couple of glasses and put them away, then looked closely at Jay. "You know about Marisa, *señor*?"

"Know about her? Only what my friend told me."

"Ah," Victor exclaimed, nodding thoughtfully, then looked away, humming softly to himself.

"What's to know, Victor?"

"Nothing, *señor*. Like your friend say, she is much fun. I tell her you ask for her."

"Yeah, do that. I might be back. If not tonight, maybe tomorrow."

He left and walked across the street to the Frontón Palace, where he spent the next hour or so watching the jai alai games. The young men in their colored uniforms, with curved baskets attached to their arms, gracefully caught balls ricocheting off the walls of the long, rectangular court and sent them spinning back, either in looping throws or vicious slams or floating little dunks, all aimed at earning them points. They played singly and in teams under a tote board blinking the changing odds on various kinds of bets, just as at a racetrack. Jay bought himself another beer and sat halfway up in the cheap seats, listening to the ping of the hard ball in play and the cavernous slap-slap of the players' shoes as they maneuvered for position on the court. He found it restful and the spectacle pleasing, even though he hadn't the slightest intention of making a wager. I asked him about that the next day, when I called him. "When I first started gambling," he answered, "the first rule I learned,

Shifty, was never to risk a dime on any endeavor depending exclusively upon the skills of human beings. It's bad enough you got to have jockeys on horses and trainers to train them. But imagine risking money on the honesty of an underpaid athlete whose only visible source of income is what happens when he and his friends, who share locker room space and see each other every day, catch and throw the ball at one another. The possibilities for larceny are mind-boggling."

He became aware, however, of a small group of middle-aged Mexican men who seemed to be cashing tickets. There were four or five of them, and they were sitting a few rows below him. From time to time, one of them would get up and amble toward the parimutuel windows. He would come back, distribute tickets and bundles of greenbacks, and sit down. The men never became excited at any point of the game and they didn't bet on every contest either. After about twenty minutes Jay moved down so that he was sitting only a couple of rows behind them. He became more interested in their action than in the games themselves. "The ringleader was a guy named Luis," he said. "He made all the ultimate decisions. I don't think they ever missed."

"What did he look like?" I asked.

"Big, fat guy, dark, a big mustache, mid-forties."

"I think you just met Luis Sanchez Gomez, Hatch's foreman."

"Yeah? You sure? He wasn't around this morning, when I went by the barn."

"Who was?"

"Nobody, except a couple of the hands. But I didn't hang around very long."

"Did you see the horse?"

"Yeah. Shifty, if that sucker can even break into a gallop, it'll be a miracle."

"So who else did you see?"

"No one, really. I had to get over to the Foreign Book. I had a couple of bets to make."

I should have known. The whole idea of Jay in Tijuana was to keep an eye on things while I was making big magic for the toy people in Anaheim. I figured he should have hung around a little longer, gotten to know Hatch, picked up a few tidbits of information, sniffed the prevailing winds. But not Jay. He had come to Tijuana primarily to remove himself from the local scene, but he wasn't going to allow it to interfere with his betting action.

"I don't think you really believe we can bail out on old Fred, do you, Jay?"

"What do you want me to say, Shifty? The horse is a cripple."

"He's bowed, that's all."

"Where's Fingers now?"

"Gone, I'm pretty sure. Up in Oakland, with his brother."

"What can we do here, except buy a little time?"

"Your job, Jay, is to keep an eye on what's going on when I'm not around."

"I know that, Shifty, and I'll do it. But there was this horse running in New Jersey . . ."

"Okay, how'd you do?"

"It should have won, but it got shuffled back on the turn and had to check twice at the sixteenth pole. It ran third. But the Philadelphia bets both came in. I made a couple of hundred. You want to hear about Hollywood Park?"

"No, not really."

"Shifty, this isn't a racetrack down here, it's an orgy."

That's the whole point about racing, I thought as I hung up the phone, the pleasure factor. Here was Jay, with two guys convinced he'd cheated them out of thousands of dollars, both ready to commit violence in order to get their money, and all he could think about was picking winners. The man was incorrigible, I told myself as I lay back on the bed in my motel room, turned on my reading light and snapped the *Form* open.

Seven

TOYING

I've never really enjoyed working conventions and trade shows, mainly because the sort of magic you're expected to perform at these functions has so little to do with real close-up. As a magician, you've been hired essentially to help hustle somebody's product. Nobody cares whether you're a real artist or not, and the atmosphere isn't conducive to producing the best work you can do. These people have all been brought together to sell goods; when they stop selling, they want to play, and their idea of play usually has little to do with being entertained by someone who is as delicately skilled at his craft as a concert pianist tickling a little Mozart. Still, I get through these engagements by thinking of them simply as jobs of work—get in, get it over with, make them laugh, if you can, and get out. And keep your eye fixed firmly on the money, because the money is always good. In this case, I was being paid fifteen hundred dollars for what amounted to eight or nine hours of work over a period of two and a half days. All I had to do, as I understood it, was work the aisles and keep the potential customers entertained. Not an onerous task, and I'd be able to earn a little commission for Happy Hal Mancuso too. He doesn't ever expect to make money off me, so I'm always delighted to be able to mail him a check. He hadn't found me this job; I usually pick up the trade shows and conventions on my own, either through pals in Las Vegas or the Magic Castle in L.A. A friend of

Vince's in Vegas had put me on to this gig. Magicians are good people; they help each other out quite a bit.

This particular show was billed as the Western Toy Fair and it was being sponsored by an organization of California manufacturers. They had taken over the Moreland, a big hotel a couple of blocks from Disneyland, and brought in all sorts of booths and displays designed to whip up some pre-holiday buying frenzies for their products. I had no idea exactly what sort of toys I'd find on sale, but I thought I'd better have a look around before the doors opened to the public that Wednesday afternoon, so I drove over from my modest Ramada Inn digs about a mile east of the place and walked in to get acquainted.

"The association is going to do at least a hundred million dollars this year," Jeff Regan, the marketing executive I was introduced to, informed me as he gave me a quick tour of the premises. "Not bad, huh?" He whisked me into a main showroom full of tables and banners and displays. People were running around popping open cartons and boxes full of toys and games and costumes in all kinds of shapes and colors and sizes. Somewhere I could hear tinkly music being piped in, and one aisle over from us two men were setting up a huge sort of moonscape populated by plastic dinosaurs and space-age creatures of every variety. Beyond them, I caught a glimpse of a mountain of naked, sexless dolls piled up in front of stacked boxes of costumes and accessories. "Those are the Lovelettes," Jeff Regan said. "They're dolls you dress up. The costumes come separate. Sells like crazy, better than Barbie this year. Then look here, kid." He pointed to an end display featuring a bristling array of realistic-looking rocket launchers and space vehicles. "*Star Wars*, right? Only this is Space Combat. It's going be big this year. We got laser beams that look like the real thing. Knocks your eyeballs out. And it's all going to sell, kid. It's all going to sell like crazy."

It was strange to hear him call me kid. Jeff Regan was in his late thirties or early forties, dressed in trendy designer jeans to look younger and with a sculpted hairdo that made him look like the host of a teenage TV disco. He was a contemporary, but I guessed his manner had to do with establishing a pecking order. I was just another association hired hand, employed to promote products and create a cheerful selling atmosphere. "Now look over here," he said to me, hurrying me up the aisle by his side, like a carnival barker hustling a rube, "look at this, kid." We stopped in front of a display of horrific-looking head masks and makeup kits. "'Monster Mash,'" he said. "Remember that song? Well, this is the song brought to life, kid. You buy all this shit, complete with the putty and the fake scars and crap, and you can make yourself up to look like any kind of monster you want."

"Like Nixon or Meese?" I asked.

"What?" He looked startled, then slapped me on the back. "I get it! Hey, that's funny, kid, that's funny! We're going to sell a ton of these. The kids'll scare the shit out of each other at Christmas, right? Right! Okay, now—"

"Hey, Jeff, can I see you a minute?" a man's voice called out from somewhere behind us. "We got a problem with Desert Doozies. You want to take a look at this?"

"Sure thing," Regan called out, then turned to me and smiled. "You got the picture now?"

"I think so, Jeff."

"You work the aisles tonight, tomorrow, and Friday morning," he continued, looking beyond me and signaling his imminent arrival to the beleaguered Desert Doozies, whatever they were. "You keep 'em laughing, right? Keep 'em happy, kid. We want them in here full of wonder and joy and bucks, got that? And remember about the party and dinner tomorrow night, okay? That about it?"

"I get the picture, Jeff."

"Good, good. I'll see you, kid. Look around, have a good time. You got any problems, you talk to Marian, my secretary. She's in Room 214, right? The blond broad with the big bazongas, but hey, can she type!" And he shot away from me on his rescue mission for Desert Doozies, which turned out to be, I later found out, an electrically animated display of motorcycle warriors inhabiting the ruins of a civilization apparently destroyed by some sort of modern holocaust. Where, I wondered, had Mary Poppins gone, and what was the Wizard of Oz up to these days?

I spent a couple of hours that afternoon putting together a little act I thought might be appropriate, then showed up at the fair at four. I worked the aisles until dinnertime, threading through the exhibits and pausing here and there to entertain. I'd brought along a lot of basically simple comedy effects—the Clatter Box, the Egg Bag, 'Round the Block, Rigid Rope, Lectric Laff, Zipper Banana—stuff for kids, all moves any amateur could get away with. I had decided that what the show needed, especially in this age of the super-realistic terror toy, was comedy relief, and I turned out to be right. The kids, especially, loved me. In fact, everywhere I stopped I was gathering such large knots of viewers that Jeff Regan pulled me aside. "Listen, kid," he said, "you're doing terrific, I'm getting great feedback on your act, but don't block the aisles. We want the people moving past all the displays, you know what I mean? We're here to sell all these products and we don't want gridlock in the aisles. Do your act, but not more than a couple of minutes anywhere, and keep moving. We're selling here, know what I mean?"

"I know what you mean, Jeff."

"Good, good," he said, and he slapped me lightly on the back. "If you think of it, work around the Lovelette display a little more. If we can get the kids over there, we'll sell a million of those dolls." And he bounced away from me again, always on the move, hustling, hustling.

I took an hour break at seven o'clock and went into the hotel coffee shop to have a bowl of soup and a salad. I can never eat much when I'm working, but you have to put something in your stomach. When I'm doing my best stuff, I can lose as much as two or three pounds a night. This was easy, child's play compared to real close-up, but it was physically punishing. I was constantly on my feet and always on the move, keeping it bright and cheery and minimally phony, even though nothing I was doing gave me any real aesthetic satisfaction.

I was on my second cup of coffee and getting ready to go back to work when I spotted Emile Legrand. He was sitting with a couple of men I'd never seen before in a corner of the room, diagonally across from me. I was certain he hadn't seen me and, even if he had looked my way, he might have failed to recognize me. I was wearing dark shades and a dark blue blazer, about as close as I ever get to a formal outfit of any sort, but not my usual track attire of khaki slacks, sneakers, and a windbreaker. Also, I was clearly out of context, as far as he was concerned. I decided I'd see if I could wait him out, get some idea what he was up to before trying to speak to him, especially as he was not alone. I reasoned that he was probably shooting somewhere in the area, a surmise that seemed plausible from the look of his two tablemates. They were both men in their thirties who looked as if they'd been working; they were dressed informally in slacks and sweaters, with comfortable walking or running shoes on their feet. I sipped my coffee and waited.

Nothing happened. After another ten minutes, I glanced at my watch and got up to go back to work. Emile never looked in my direction, so I paid my check at the cashier's stand and left. On my way out, I stopped at the front desk and asked for Mr. Legrand's room, only to be told that no one by that name was registered there.

Just a hunch, but I decided that it didn't matter and went back to the main showroom.

Half an hour later, I saw Emile again. He was alone, strolling idly along the main aisle and examining the displays. I was in the middle of a routine with a mildly amused quartet of middle-aged, motherly women by the pyramid of Lovelettes, so I temporarily lost him from view. I produced a beautiful feather flower out of my jacket pocket and pretended to smell it, but it wilted and drooped. I looked appalled and the women laughed. Then, to my astonishment and theirs, the blossom slowly righted itself. One of the women squealed with delight and clapped her hands. I smiled, bowed, and silently handed her the flower, which this time turned out to be a real one, a large chrysanthemum. "How did you do that?" the woman asked. "My kids would love this."

"Magic, madam, magic," I said, looking around for Emile.

"Do they sell those here?"

"I don't think so," I said. "They're not lethal."

"Not lethal?"

"War toys, madam, war toys. We want today's kids to be able to kill, don't we, when the time comes?"

"What does he mean, Daisy?" one of the group asked the woman with the flower clutched uncomprehendingly in her hand.

A small telephone rang in my pocket. "Excuse me," I said, "I'm being called." And with another quick little smiling nod, I danced away from them up the aisle and around Take-Over, a new board-game display that had something to do with corporate mergers. It was another attempt, I guessed, to displace Monopoly as the nation's favorite game, but I don't remember it now and I paid little attention to it then. I was looking for Emile, who seemed to have vanished.

I couldn't find him at first and I thought he must have left, but then, just as I was about to get back to work with my Fantastic Multiplying Bottles, I spotted him. He was at the Monster Mash, looking over the head masks. I left my effect under one of the corner stands, figuring I'd pick it up in a few minutes, and watched.

Emile picked up several of the heads, hefted them in his hands, then pulled out a credit card and handed it to the girl behind the counter. She looked surprised and pleased, then picked up a phone and spoke into it, after which she wrote out an order. Emile signed for it and then walked rapidly out of the showroom. On his way out, he paused to look around, but again failed to see me. I was trying to decide whether to speak to him, when he was rejoined by the two men who had been in the coffee shop with him. The three of them went out through the hotel lobby.

I strolled over to Monster Mash. The clerk who had taken Emile's order was a dark, pretty brunette of about twenty, dressed in a long black satin gown and made up to look like a vampire. "Where are your fangs?" I asked.

"Oh, hi," she said with a laugh. "Hey, I've been watching you. You're fantastic."

"Thanks, but you really haven't seen anything. How are *you* doing?"

"I'm pooped. I've been on my feet since nine this morning." She reached down and picked up the face of one of the Walking Dead. "Do I look as bad as this guy?"

"Hardly." I smiled. "You sold a lot of these?"

"Not too many. Frankenstein's always big. And Dracula, of course. And then there's Mr. Zombie, this guy over here." She pointed to a livid green head hanging from the end of the table. "Want to try one on?"

"No, thanks. Listen, that guy who was just here—"

"The man with the accent?"

"Yeah. What did he buy?"

"Hey, that was my best sale of the day."

"Really?"

"You bet. Twenty gorilla masks and twenty black capes."

"Twenty of each?"

"You got it. He said he was making a movie. I asked him if there was a part for me." She giggled.

"You an actress?"

"No way. I'm a communications major at UC Irvine. This is just a three-day job. There are two of us on this booth. What the hell, five bucks an hour and ten percent commission. I can use the bread."

"Did he offer you a job?"

"No, he said I was too young."

"How old are you?"

"Nineteen. What kind of movies does he make?"

"Dirty movies."

"You're not serious?"

"Sure I am. He's probably shooting a porn horror flick."

"You're not serious?"

"Do I look like I'm joking?"

"How do you know?"

"I know him."

"Gee, you must be right," she said, a faint line of thought suddenly creasing her smooth forehead, like a breeze ruffling the undisturbed surface of a small pond. "Oh, wow! He wants these delivered by eleven tomorrow morning."

"Where?"

"Just south of here." She glanced at the sales slip. "Laguna Nigel."

"Let's see," I said, taking the slip from her and memorizing the address. "Yes, that's it all right." I handed the slip back to her and smiled. "So you don't want to be a porn star?"

She blushed through her vampire makeup. "God, my boyfriend would kill me." She paused, as if seriously thinking it over. "What do they pay?" she asked.

"More than you're making here."

"Well, I guess I could, if I didn't have to *really* do it."

"I think you'd probably have to really do it."

"Well, I don't know . . ."

"Hey, Anderson," a now-familiar male voice sang out behind me, "let's go to work, buddy."

I turned around. "Oh, hi, Jeff," I said. "I've been working."

"You've been shooting the shit here for ten minutes," he said. "Let's get with it. We got toys to sell here."

I waved good-bye to the girl, who looked a little flustered, and went to retrieve my props. Two hours to go, I figured. Time to charm the suckers. Maybe I'd even give them one or two legitimate good moves before quitting time.

"Okay, Shifty, I met the kid," Jay said to me that night when I called him in Tijuana. "She's terrific. I really like her."

"Who's that?"

"Jill. You know, Jill Thorne. The girl jock."

"Oh, you did? How did that come about?"

He had gone by the barn in the late afternoon, after the fifth at Hollywood, the only race on the card that interested him at all. It was already growing dark and he hadn't really expected to find out anything about our horse, but he hadn't felt like going back to his dreary motel room yet and so he had simply driven around to the stable gate and over to Barn 15. "She'd been out galloping our horse over the training track," he said, "and she was just coming back when I got there."

"That's a funny time to be galloping him, isn't it?"

"That's what I thought, so I asked her about it."

Jill had told him that Hatch wanted it that way. The trainer was hiding the horse, in effect, while trying to get some of the excess weight off him with a series of long, slow two- and three-mile gallops. No one was around the training track at that hour and it had been easy to keep old Fred pretty much out of sight.

"Was Hatch around?" I asked.

"Oh, yeah. Apparently he always goes over there with her when the horse is out," Jay said. "You're right, Shifty, they are planning to put one over."

"I told you. Did you talk to Hatch?"

He had introduced himself to the trainer and been given much the same boorish treatment I'd received. Jay, of course, had been indifferent to what Hatch thought of him. Besides, he had been really taken with Jill and had focused pretty much on her. After she'd dismounted and turned the horse over to a groom, he had persuaded her to join him for a cup of coffee in the track kitchen, a couple of hundred yards away. There he had quietly pumped a bit of her life story out of her, but for some reason he was reluctant to share it with me. "She's had quite a life" was all he told me. I gathered that he might have something going with her, and I felt a sudden strong twinge of jealousy, which surprised me again. It was amazing, the effect this woman was having on me, even though I hardly knew her.

"You know the horse is gay, don't you?" Jay said.

"What are you talking about?"

"Jill told me," he explained. "You can't use a pony with this horse. He'll try to mount it."

"You mean the comfort horse?"

"You got it. You can't pony this beast to the track. He goes crazy. Jill's got a real touch with him, so Hatch has been using her exclusively to gallop him."

"This must have just happened. Now, listen, Jay, I've got some news for you." And I told him about seeing Emile at the toy fair.

"You didn't say anything to him?"

"No. But I found out he's shooting a movie near here."

"Stay away from him, Shifty. The last thing we need is him finding out where I am. Was that big goon with him?"

"No, just a couple of his crew."

"Watch yourself. Emile's a mean little prick and you don't want to run into this guy Castle."

"He's got no argument with me."

"Maybe he doesn't know that," Jay said. "Emile thinks the two of us are in this together. Castle could break you in half."

"Jay, you haven't been hanging around with the right sort of people lately," I said. "You've got to become a little more discriminating."

He laughed. "I knew Emile for years before he bought into my action this fall," he said. "He used to pick my brains for free. And I thought he was just another harmless loser I could help out."

"So you don't want me to talk to him if I do see him again?"

"Well, I wouldn't push it, if you know what I mean," Jay answered a little hesitantly. "I mean, watch yourself, Shifty."

"You know, when I first met him, he certainly seemed affable enough," I commented. "You never know, do you?"

"About people like Emile? No. He's definitely an acquired distaste."

Eight

SHOOTING

The house in Laguna Nigel, a bedroom community just north of San Juan Capistrano, turned out to be the largest of four models built to launch a new development called Whispering Glen, high up in the hills about halfway between the San Diego Freeway and the ocean. None of the houses for sale in this project had yet been completed, and their skeletal wooden frames crouched on the barren, terraced land like large insects. The bulldozers had scraped the terrain flat, and the area, all white sand peppered by clumps of weeds and surrounded by low hills of scrub and small, twisted pine trees, looked as empty of possibilities as the surface of the moon. Even the models had an unfinished look; the land around them was unlandscaped and as desolate-looking as the rest. No welcoming banners advertising the advent of this new residential community flapped in the breeze, and the only sign of occupation was the presence of a dozen cars and two rental trucks parked along the street beside the largest of the models, a two-story white stucco house at the very end of a circular dead-end court. The developer must have run out of money.

I parked halfway down the block and walked up to the front door, where several men were busy unloading battered-looking Victorian furniture from one of the trucks and carrying it inside. Nobody questioned my presence, so I merely nodded to them and walked in.

"You're late," a young man holding a clipboard said

to me as I stepped into the hallway. I recognized him as one of the two men I'd seen with Emile at the toy fair. "You atmosphere?"

"Yeah," I answered. "Sorry. The traffic— "

"Skip it," the man said. "I know about traffic. Anyway, the trucks with the sets and props were late too. You better get upstairs and get changed. The dressing room is at the end of the hall, on your right. What's your name?"

"Oh. Stoker," I said, improvising, "Bram Stoker. You the A.D.?"

"Yeah. Stoker? I don't see any Stoker here." He was gazing at a typewritten list of names, but it was dark in the hallway and he obviously thought he must have overlooked me. He leaned over his clipboard, running an index finger along the column.

"I'm probably not on there," I said. "Is Emile here?"

"No, not yet. He may get here later. You a friend of his?"

"He told me about this."

"Oh, well, it's okay then, especially since we got two guys who haven't showed up yet." The man lowered the clipboard and glanced unhappily toward the living room, where the movers with the furniture were arranging it under the direction of a chunky, middle-aged man wearing a black jump suit and a baseball cap. Beyond him, a movie camera had been mounted on a platform about five feet above the floor, while klieg lights were being set up to illuminate the action. "Max is going to have a stroke, if we don't get this scene shot today." He looked back at his list and wrote my name down. "Stoker? Okay. Get upstairs and into costume."

"What scene is this?"

"Where Justine is brought to the castle and meets the Marquis for the first time," the A.D. said. "It's tricky because it's such a big deal. I told Max we could shoot with four actors, but no, he's got to have a big scene here. I don't know why. The audience only wants to see her get it anyway. Go change. If these other two guys show up, I'll tell 'em we're not going to use 'em. One more, one less, who cares? Max thinks he's Bernardo Bertolucci, for Christ's sake!"

"This is supposed to be a castle?"

"Who'll know? We're only shooting interiors."

"What about the gorillas?"

"What gorillas? Who needs gorillas? We're shooting mild SM, not animal sex. We got weirdos, we need apes too?"

"I was around when Emile bought these gorilla masks."

"I don't know anything about gorilla masks. Maybe he figures we'll use them in the outdoor orgy, I don't know." Two men carrying a large dark red settee began to inch toward us along the narrow corridor. "You better get upstairs," he said. "We should be under way here in about twenty minutes."

I went up a flight of stairs and came upon a group of eight or nine actors lounging about the hall and a dressing room in ragged-looking eighteenth-century costumes. The men were fully dressed, with great powdered wigs on their heads, but the four women were bare-breasted and also naked behind, where their skirts had been cut away. Everybody seemed relaxed to the point of boredom, as if the day were a routine one, and no one seemed at all surprised to see me. "You get stuck on the freeway too?" one of the men asked me.

"Yeah."

He pointed to the dressing room. "The costumes are hanging up in there. The wigs are in a box on the table. Just find something that fits you."

"What scene is this? Anybody seen a script?"

"Script?" one of the women echoed with a short, harsh laugh. "Max says he's going to talk us through it. Rocco's the only one with any lines, except for Ellen saying, 'Yes, sir,' 'No, sir,' all the time."

I went into the dressing room, wondering what kind

of loony scene I had maneuvered myself into this time. I had no idea what would happen if Emile did show up and the A.D. told him that his friend Bram Stoker, the author of *Dracula*, had appeared. Would he recognize me? What would he think I was up to? A good question, since I wasn't sure myself. It had seemed so odd to find the horseplaying pornographer at my toy fair that I hadn't been able to resist following him here. I expected I'd have an opportunity to speak to him about Jay, if I decided to chance it, and maybe get him to call off his goon, but I hadn't considered that he might sic the man onto me as well. I thought it might not be a bad idea at all to get into costume, so I picked out the only one of the three still hanging on the clothes rack that came close to fitting me and slapped a big white wig on my head. I was ready to improvise. I pinned my wallet and my car keys into the inside of my pants, just in case I had to make a fast getaway, and rejoined my fellow Thespians in the hallway.

"What are you guys, anyway?" the woman with the harsh laugh asked as I appeared.

"Courtiers, I guess," a man answered. "We're buddies with the Marquis."

"And what are you?" I asked.

She laughed the harsh laugh again. "Sluts, what did you think?"

"That I knew," the man said. "You got a great chest."

"Yeah? Well, keep your hands off 'em. We're doin' bits, but for a hundred bucks a day I ain't lettin' no one touch me."

"You ain't supposed to be touched, honey," another one of the courtiers observed. "You just bring Ellen in and the Marquis gets to do her. He's the only one in this scene."

"That's lucky," I said.

"Max says we get to do a big torture-Lesbo number on her later in the picture," the woman said. "For that we get decent bread."

"I don't know, Norma," a thin, mousy-looking blonde behind her piped up. "I don't know about this. Stripping is easier."

"What do you know, Addie?" Norma snapped. "You don't know shit. If I get to do my fertility dance in the garden *and* the torture scene, we can pick up maybe a grand in two days. That's like a week in Long Beach."

"Yeah, I guess," Addie agreed plaintively, "but I don't know. I mean, I thought this was going to be real classy and artistic and all and look at this costume."

"On you it looks good," one of the courtiers said. "You a stripper? Where do you work?"

"The Body Shop, in Long Beach," Norma said, glaring at him. "And don't get any ideas. Addie's with me, got that?"

"Sure, sure," the man said. "What do I care? I'm an actor."

"Yeah, I'll bet you are," Norma said, putting an arm protectively around the blonde, "I'll bet you're some actor."

"Okay, places, everybody!" the A.D. called out from the foot of the stairs. "Let's hurry it up now! We're running late!"

We trooped dutifully downstairs and the A.D., whose name turned out to be Lester, positioned us about the room. A fire was blazing in the fireplace and we were asked to sit around a large purple cushion that had been placed directly in front of the hearth. The white walls of the room had been hung with patently phony-looking tapestries to try to make it look authentically continental, and black curtains had been drawn across the windows. "Okay, Rocco stands here, at the end of the mantelpiece," Lester said. "Ellen comes in from over there. She's brought in by the servant girls of the Marquis. You got that?"

Nobody said anything.

"Max?" Lester called out. "Max, we're all set here!"

The fat man in the jump suit emerged from the back

of the house with a cup of something in his hand and gazed distastefully around the room. "Rocco? Ellen? Come on out here! We'll talk this through once."

Rocco and Ellen, who were apparently the stars of the picture, now appeared, also from somewhere at the rear of the house. Rocco was a muscular, low-browed, curly-haired kid in his twenties, obviously of Italian origin. He was dressed in a shiny black costume with white silk stockings, buckled high-heeled shoes and a white shirt with a ruffled front, and he was holding a riding crop. Ellen was wearing a long black cloak that covered her from head to toe. She was barefoot and had a thick mop of dyed red hair that framed a round, petulant little face with thin lips and a weak, dimpled chin. She looked like a Lovelette brought to life.

"All right, let me explain this scene," Max began. "You guys are all friends of the Marquis, right? He's invited you here for the weekend from Paris to enjoy his latest captive, the beautiful and innocent Justine. That's Ellen here. You have been waiting for her, you see? So you will show some anticipation, some real interest, some excitement, please. The Marquis is going to display her for you, you see? Now Justine, that's Ellen, she has been in her dungeon quarters upstairs. You women, you're the permanent sex slaves and servant girls at the château. You're—"

"Château? What's a château?" Addie asked.

"A château is a castle, for Christ's sake," Lester said.

Max glared at her, his cup trembling slightly in his hand.

"Addie, just do what I do," Norma whispered. "And shut up."

"Okay, I was just asking—"

"As I was saying," Max resumed, ignoring Addie, "you women have been preparing Justine for her introduction to the Marquis and his band of roués."

"His what?" Addie asked.

"Whoremongers," Lester snapped.

"She has been stripped and anointed with aphrodi-
siacal oils that will make her even more alluring—"

"What kind of oils?"

"To make the Marquis horny," Lester explained.

"I'm always horny," Rocco said, grinning at Ellen.

"I hope you washed this time," Ellen said. "You
stank like a goat last week."

"I was supposed to, you dumb cunt, I was playing a
gardener."

"Not for real, you asshole."

"What are they talking about?" Addie asked.

"This is their third movie together," Norma whispered. "The last one was *Lady Chatterley's Cherries*.
Don't you remember? We saw it."

"Are you all quite finished here?" Max inquired,
setting his cup down on the camera platform and turning
to confront his bickering cast. "Are we all quite, quite
finished now?"

"Quiet, everybody!" Lester shouted. "I want quiet
now! *Quiet!* We're making a movie here, for Christ's
sake!"

"Thank you, Lester," the director said. "Now,
Ellen, Rocco, let's see if we can run through this one and
then we'll shoot it."

"You want the whole scene in one take?" Rocco
asked. "I'd better have a couple of minutes, after the
rehearsal."

"No, no, up to the point of the sex scene," Max
explained. "Then we'll do the post-sex scene, where the
girls lead Ellen off again and the Marquis toasts the affair
with his friends." He turned to Lester. "The champagne?"

"It's ready. In the kitchen, Max."

"Good. And don't forget, it's drunk out of her
slippers."

"Right, right. It's all set."

"Then we can let atmosphere go and shoot the sex
scene."

"Is he going to use a condom this time?" Ellen asked.

"You bet, babe," Rocco told her. "That's why I need a couple of minutes."

"We're going to shoot it so we hardly notice it," Max explained.

"So did they have condoms then?" Addie asked.

"You, shut up!" Lester barked.

"I'm sorry," she said, "I'm sorry."

Max glared at her and I thought he might actually fire her, but he turned away and finished leading us through the scene, which he was planning to shoot in one take, up to the point where the Marquis approaches Justine, reaches up with his riding crop, and flicks the robe open, causing it to drop around her feet and to reveal his naked victim to his cronies from Paris. "And at that point, gentlemen," Max said to us, "I want you all to react. You've never seen anything so desirable, you want her, and you realize that soon you will all have her, that this is the beginning of a great weekend of fantasy and lust. Got that?"

No one answered him, but he seemed satisfied that we had understood, because he clapped his hands together and said, "Fine, let's run it once."

"Okay, places, everybody!" Lester called out. "And quiet, please! This is a run-through now! Quiet!"

The scene began well enough, with Norma, Addie, and the other two servant girls leading Ellen in from the pantry, while we all gazed appreciatively at her. "A little more lust, please!" Max called out as Ellen mounted the cushion and the women sank humbly to the floor at her feet. I did my best to drool, but without much success. The courtier next to me was picking his nose.

"All right now," Max said. "Rocco, deliver your line and then you show her off to your friends."

Rocco sneered. "Her name is Justine," he said, flicking his riding crop against his shoulder and knocking his wig slightly askew. "Shit," he said.

"It's okay, Rocco, just get on with it," Max said. "It's only a rehearsal."

"What a jerk," Ellen said, with a little giggle.

"Please, Ellen, we have a time problem," Max warned.

"Sorry, Max."

Rocco tightened his wig and again picked up his cue. "Her name is Justine," he said, pointing at her with the crop. "She is a virgin."

"React, guys, react!" Lester shouted. "A virgin, for Christ's sake!"

The courtier next to me took his finger out of his nose and dropped his jaw. I leaned eagerly forward in my chair and so caught a glimpse of Emile, standing inside the darkened front hall. He seemed to be alone.

Still sneering, Rocco now walked up to Ellen and caressed her chin with his riding crop, then lowered it to the clasp holding her robe together and tried to unsnap it. Nothing happened. "Fucking thing is stuck," Rocco said.

"Ellen, why don't you leave it open for him?" Max asked.

"Because the robe won't stay on," she explained. "It's a heavy bugger."

"What kind of dialogue is this?" Addie asked.

"Okay then," Max said, "here's what we do. Rocco, instead of flipping the robe off her, just point your crop at her, okay? Now, you girls, you get up, all four of you, and you take the robe off her, then back subserviently out of the room."

"Back sub-what?" Addie asked.

"Just watch me," Norma said. She looked at Max. "I'll unclasp it, okay?"

"Fine, fine." Max turned to Rocco. "Okay, now once the robe is off her, you walk around her and show her off to your friends, right? You caress her with the crop, you make love to her with it, you understand? And guys, when he does that, it drives you crazy. I mean, you can't

wait to get at her, but you can't touch her. Not until the
Marquis enjoys her and deflowers her. After that, it's
sauve qui peut."

"No shit," Ellen said, "and what the fuck am I
supposed to be doing?"

"You're terrified, see? You don't really know what's
going to happen to you, but you suspect the worst, see?"

"Suspect? I'm naked in a roomful of horny frogs and
all I do is suspect?"

"Ellen," Max reassured her, "just don't think too
much about it, okay? This isn't *Gone With the Wind*
we're shooting here, see? I'll do the thinking. You just
look real sexy and terrified, okay?"

"Okay, okay. Let's get on with it."

"All right, places, everybody! Let's run it one more
time!" Lester called out. "Then we'll shoot it, right,
Max?"

"Right."

Max mounted the camera platform and took a look
at the scene through his lens as we ran it again, this time
without a hitch, thanks to Norma. At Rocco's signal, she
unclasped the robe and crawled away with it, her buns in
the air, followed by the rest of the women. Even Addie
kept her mouth shut and Max seemed satisfied. "Great!"
he said. "All right, this one's a take!"

"Did you see the bazongas on this chick?" the
courtier next to me murmured. "Like fuckin' torpedoes,
man!"

"Very impressive," I admitted. "It's a miracle what
silicone can do."

"Yeah, they don't exactly move a lot, do they? Do
you think anybody'll believe she's a virgin?"

"No one in the entire universe," I said, "but then,
credibility is not the issue here."

It took only forty minutes to shoot not merely this
scene, but the next one, in which, after the Marquis has
done his number on Justine and the sluts have led her
away somewhere, presumably to a dungeon, we all toast

the event by drinking what turned out to be ginger ale from her shoes. I wasn't sure what the significance of the event was, but then, I wasn't really caught up in the evolution of what I had no doubt would turn out to be a porn classic, a masterwork of sleaze on the order of *Deep Throat* or *Behind the Green Door*. Who was I to judge?

As we were changing back into our clothes, Lester came upstairs and handed all of us envelopes, each containing a fifty-dollar bill. "The call is ten o'clock tomorrow," he said. "Two hundred apiece for the garden orgy. If it rains, we'll shoot some of the torture sequences. A hundred for those. It's mostly foreplay stuff, with the women doing her. Any problems?"

I looked at my watch; I had less than an hour to get back to the toy fair and to get ready for the evening party as well. "Emile still around?" I asked.

"Yeah, somewhere," the A.D. said, hurrying back downstairs. "Be real quiet leaving, guys," he called back. "We may be shooting the fuck festival with Ellen and Rocco. Go out the back, through the kitchen."

When I came down a few minutes later, they were shooting and I caught a glimpse of Rocco, his wig once more askew, about to pounce on his helpless victim. "Okay, now, grab her!" Max ordered. "We're rolling here!"

I let myself out through the kitchen, where Norma, Addie, and the other château sluts were sipping soft drinks and smoking, then walked around the side of the darkened house toward the street. Emile was sitting in his car, parked directly in front, and talking into the telephone. He didn't see me, and I could easily have left without being noticed, but, after all, I had sacrificed a lot for my art that afternoon and I had come up there with the idea of speaking to him. So I waited until he finished his conversation and then smilingly walked up to him. "Hello, Emile."

He did one of the finest double takes I've ever seen. "Anderson?" he asked. "What are you doing here?"

"I worked in your movie this afternoon," I said. "A couple of your extras failed to show, so I filled in."

"How extraordinary. Who told you we were shooting here?"

"I'm working at the Western Toy Fair," I explained. "I got the address from the salesgirl where you bought the capes and stuff."

"I see. And you wished to talk to me, I gather."

"I thought I might, yes. I didn't count on making fifty bucks just for sitting around in my tights and a white wig. But I can parlay the loot into a few Exactas."

"What did you wish to speak to me about?"

"I just wanted to tell you that Jay didn't steal your money. He told me you had some goon accost him at the track the other day."

"A goon? You mean Castle? He is my business associate. It was his idea. Wilberton reacts poorly to being cheated."

"Nobody's cheating you, Emile. Jay's doing his best to get your money back, but it may take a while. We've located Fingers."

"Indeed? And where is he?"

"Never mind, it doesn't matter. He doesn't have the money. He was strong-armed out of it by a loan shark he owed. He's promised to pay off after the first of the year."

"What sort of credence can we put in this promise?"

"Not much, I grant you, but we haven't got a choice."

"It is difficult to explain such reasoning to a man of Wilberton's impetuous temperament."

"So I gather, but you could help."

"Why should I? For all I know, you are in it with him."

"You don't really believe that, Emile. If you thought about it for even thirty seconds, you'd realize how silly that is."

"So you wish me simply to accept this fact of our missing money, is that it?"

"I'm saying that you should give Jay a chance to make good, that's all. We know where Fingers is, we know that he has to wait until after the first of the year to get his money back from the IRS. You don't help matters any by siccing your strong-arm onto Jay. He's a loser, too, in this deal. We both are. He tried to get hold of you, by the way."

"Did he? This is the first I have heard of it. All I know is that he has disappeared."

"So did you. We heard you were making a movie somewhere."

He smiled faintly. "Well, of course, I am always in production somewhere."

"Anyway, Emile, I guess that's all I had to say. Call off your dogs."

"I do not think Wilberton would relish being referred to in such cavalier terms."

"Nothing personal, Emile. Just a figure of speech."

He opened the car door and stepped out onto the sidewalk. "I suppose I should see what they are doing inside."

"What's the name of this turkey, by the way?"

"Turkey?"

"Flick. Movie."

"Ah. *Justine's Ordeal*. It is based on the Marquis de Sade's novel. Very loosely, of course. We cannot show *everything*, you know."

"It was an easy fifty bucks. Thanks."

"If you come back tomorrow, it will not be so easy. Have you performed in sex scenes?"

"Not in public, Emile, and not for money. No, I think this is the beginning and the end of my X-rated career."

"Will you be speaking to Fox?"

"Sure."

"Then please tell him that we still expect to be paid in full."

"I think he got the message, Emile."

"Good. I am not a man who forgets such things." He started to walk toward the house.

"Emile, what are the masks for?"

He turned back. "Masks?"

"Didn't you buy some masks at the toy fair?"

"Ah, yes. For the horror movie I am shooting next week."

"You churn these out pretty fast."

"One a week, my friend."

"All X-rated."

"*Naturellement, mon cher. Au revoir.*"

I got into my car and drove away. A waste of time, I remember thinking as I nosed down through the barren hills of Whispering Glen toward the freeway. Unless we got real lucky, I figured Jay might have to remain in Tijuana, or at least out of sight, until mid-January.

Nine

NIGHT REVELS

I got back to Tijuana by nine o'clock Friday night and checked into the Conquistador again. Jay had left me a note at the front desk. "Jill and I have gone to the jai alai," it said. "After ten, we'll be at Tia Juana Tillie's, on Revolución. Or I'll see you early tomorrow morning at the barn. Fred is running."

That was a lot of information for me to assimilate from one brief note and I sat on my bed in my room to chew on it for a while before leaving for downtown. It was a few minutes before ten, but I stopped by Tia Juana Tillie's before heading for the jai alai and found Jay and Jill sitting at an outdoor table, checking the street action. "Hey, Shifty, sit down," Jay said. "Have a margarita. They're fantastic here."

"How you doin'?" Jill asked. "Just get here?"

"Yes. Make any money?" I answered, pulling out a chair and joining them.

"Luis wasn't there tonight," Jill said. "Jay didn't know who to bet, so we came on over here early."

"Yeah, I had kind of a slow day," Jay explained, "so I wasn't about to blow any more money on the little thieves with the baskets on their arms."

"You lost?"

"A hundred dollars, on a horse in New York," Jay said. "That was pretty dumb, Shifty."

"I guess." I smiled at Jill. "How'd you do?"

"Me? I don't usually bet on horses," she said. "I just ride 'em."

She looked wonderful, bare-legged, in sandals, a short white denim skirt and a light blue blouse open at the neck. She had just enough makeup on to highlight her strong, even features, and her tanned skin glowed in the soft night light from the street. It was an unseasonably warm evening, with a hot desert breeze blowing, and dozens of American kids, out on the town for a good time, packed the outdoor tables or moved in chattering, laughing groups in and out of the noisy bar area. Tillie's was a local tradition, the headquarters in Tijuana for visiting gringos, especially the military. "This town turns me on," Jay commented. "The air here is electric with action."

"Tell me what's going on," I said. "I can't believe the horse is running. He can't be ready."

"He ain't," Jill answered, "but Sandy wants to put a race into him."

"Are you up on him?"

"Camacho's riding him," Jay said.

"How come?"

"He's got a real live horse for Sandy in the feature," Jill explained. "I'm hoping to get up on somethin' of his fairly soon, but he ain't ridin' me yet."

"Why not? I thought you had an understanding with him."

"Not really," she said. "Ever since that ruckus at the party he's been kind of cool, if you know what I mean."

"I'm sorry about that."

"Yeah, well, hell . . ." She laughed. "It kind of took the wind out of Sandy's sails. He'd been pushin' pretty hard, but I don't jump into the hay with no one just for a job."

"Integrity," Jay said. "You'd know about that, right, Shifty?"

"I guess."

Something about this conversation was depressing me, but at first I couldn't figure out exactly what it was. Some minutes passed before I realized that Jay and Jill were holding hands under the table. I'd been gone for only three days and these two seemed to have become an item in my absence. I looked at Jay. He sat there, just as he did at the track, serenely confident, calm, and vastly pleased with himself. I had to resist a momentary impulse to kick his chair out from under him. The fact is I was jealous. What did the handicapper have that I didn't? And I'd been deluding myself that this girl was attracted to me too. It made me want to lose myself somewhere.

". . . So what do you think they're up to, Shifty?"

"Who?"

"You haven't been listening."

"Sorry," I said, "my mind was on something else."

"They're using the race to set the horse up," Jay continued. "Wouldn't you say?"

I looked at Jill. "What do you think?"

She nodded. "Sandy's put him in where he can't do nothin'," she said. "It's a sprint for five-thousand-dollar claimers, the seventh. Old Fred'll just be startin' to run when the race is over."

"What if somebody claims him?"

"Ain't nobody goin' to take him," she answered, "not lookin' like he does and double bowed and all. You'd have to be crazy."

"Let's hope he doesn't break down again."

Jay grinned. "Hell, Shifty, Hatch'll have Camacho primed. He won't do more than jog around the track. I've seen that jock jump off one to two shots out of the starting gate. They do things down here they don't even think about trying at the major tracks anymore."

"Lupe uses a buzzer too," Jill said, leaning forward and keeping her voice low, even though no one could possibly overhear us through the noise of the revelers on the sidewalk and the traffic in the street. "This horse he's ridin' tomorrow for Sandy has a ton of speed, but he spits it out usually at the eighth pole. He ain't goin' to do that tomorrow."

"I figure Lupe'll hit the horse with enough juice to short-circuit the tote board," Jay said. "Here, take a look." He reached into his pocket and produced a copy of the Caliente *Form*.

I opened the paper first to the seventh race, where I found Fred's Folly listed at odds of twenty to one against a field of eight other horses going six furlongs, then I took a look at the ninth. Hatch's horse, a five-year-old gelding named El Gato, was the third choice of the newspaper's handicappers. He had more early speed than anyone else in the race, but, as Jay had indicated, he displayed a distressing tendency in most of his efforts to stop running in the stretch.

"Take a look at the race in September at Pomona and the one in November at Los Alamitos," Jay instructed me.

"Okay, he won those two," I said. "They're both bullrings with short stretches. He didn't have to run that far on the straightaway."

Jay laughed. "That isn't it. See who rode him?"

"Camacho. He rides him in most of his races."

"And he pops with him when the odds are right."

"Seems to me it wouldn't take a genius to figure that out. What odds will he go off at?"

"I figure three to one, five to two," Jay guessed. "There are a couple of other fast nags in the race, and sometimes the horse doesn't fire, even when he's bet on. We'll cash a nice ticket, Shifty."

"And, of course, somebody will bet for Camacho."

"You are overstating the obvious."

"Hey, I got to go," Jill said, suddenly standing up. "It's late."

"Really?"

"I got to be at the track at dawn, mister," she said, "or ain't nobody goin' to give me nothin' to ride." She leaned over and gave Jay a peck on the top of his skull. "See you at the races, guys, hear me?" And she walked briskly away toward the parking lot where she'd left her car.

"You can give me a ride back, right?" Jay asked. "Jill drove us here."

"Sure." I slumped into my chair, toying unhappily with the stem of my empty margarita glass. Jay seemed disinclined to say anything, but simply sat there, staring benignly out at the passing scene like the monarch of a small kingdom reviewing the palace guard. When I had had about as much of his low-keyed lese majesty as I could stomach, I decided to confront him head-on. "So what did you promise her?" I asked. "A fabulous Hollywood career?"

He looked at me, mildly surprised, as if I had dribbled pabulum down my shirtfront. "Oh-oh," he said, "you were going to make a move on her yourself, right?"

I didn't answer. I knew I was making a fool of myself and I was having a hard time understanding why, but I couldn't help it. I felt as if somebody had hit me in the stomach and left me to nurse the dull ache there that might take some time to heal.

"Shifty, you didn't tell me," Jay said. "I just asked her out and things sort of happened from there."

"It's okay," I made myself say. "Obviously, there's something about you, Jay."

"Chemistry, I guess," he said. "We just sort of hit it off right away."

He had taken her out to dinner and she had finished telling him her life story. She still didn't want to say too much about her childhood growing up on a ranch in West Texas, but he did learn that her mother had died young and she'd been raised by a hard-drinking father who had let her down in a lot of ways. "About the only thing he liked to do was run cattle and drink," she said. "And he brought these women home he'd picked up in bars someplace." She began hanging around horses to take herself away from him and ran off at sixteen with a rodeo rider. That didn't last, but she kept moving, through Texas and Oklahoma and up to New Mexico. She went to work as a hot-walker and began riding in races at half-mile tracks, in what they called bullrings, in dusty little towns where they rode right down to the bone and nobody cared how old you were or what sex you were and people bet on the races with each other and not through the parimutuel machines. She'd ridden quarter horses, Appaloosas, Indian ponies, Thoroughbreds, mules, just about anything that neighed and had four legs. "If they can run, I can ride 'em," she said.

It hadn't been easy and she'd taken some bad spills. She broke her back once and cracked several ribs and punctured a lung and fought off a tick fever that nearly killed her. It hadn't discouraged her or diminished her enthusiasm for the animals or the racing, but Jay thought she had the oldest-looking eyes he'd ever seen on a woman still in her twenties. "She got married at sixteen to a jockey she met in Elko, Nevada, and they rode the fair circuits together up there one summer," he said. "Then he got drunk and beat her up one night. She said it reminded her of the way it had been with her father, so she left him. She was pregnant at the time and she was going to have the baby, but she miscarried."

She hadn't been seeing anyone and she hadn't dated anybody for a long time, she told Jay. She had to be up at dawn nearly every morning to gallop or to work horses for anybody who'd use her. "No trainer's goin' to put you up on anythin' in the afternoon 'less you get your ass out of bed in the mornin'," she explained. Her whole life had become the track. She'd have gone out with guys, but she had a tough-minded outlook on her situation. "Maybe if I was just some dumb little bar-hoppin' gal I'd do better," she said, "but there ain't nothin' I can do except ride and you can't do that if you hang around bars or get yourself in too deep with some guy." The men would see her at the races and they'd write her letters. They'd want to do things to her or they'd want to dance real close with her and some of them even proposed marriage. She read all of their letters but never answered them. And she only very rarely went out, even for a drink, with anyone. The track was her world, the only one she wanted just then, and she was determined to make it as a race rider. "Some gals, like Julie Krone and Karen Rogers, they made it back East," she said. "I thought about goin' back there, but I don't know anyone. I got to get me on some good horses down here. I'll win with 'em and then I can ride wherever I want to." Jay had taken her to Reno's, an elegant restaurant downtown, where they'd had a couple of drinks, a quiet dinner, listened to a good guitar player sing some romantic Spanish ballads, and then she had asked him to take her to his motel room and make love to her. "I did better than that," Jay said. "I got us a room at the Fiesta Americana, up high, with a view over the lights of the city, and I bought us a bottle of champagne and made a big romantic evening of it."

I wanted to ask him how it had been, but I also didn't want to hear the answer, so I contented myself with merely eyeing the passing parade, which at the moment consisted mainly of the noisy crowd pouring out of the Frontón Palace after the last match of the night.

"She was fantastic, Shifty," Jay volunteered. "She makes love like a leopard in heat."

"I don't think I want to hear this, Jay," I said.

"She told me she hadn't been with anyone for six months," he said. "She also told me she liked me, but not to get any wrong ideas."

"What kind of wrong ideas?"

"About a permanent relationship, I guess," he explained. "She's absolutely determined not to be owned by anyone."

"She couldn't have picked a likelier partner than you," I had to concede with just a hint of rancor. "It must be a case of natural selection."

"I never thought I'd find myself in bed with a jockey," he said, smiling broadly. "Literally, that is."

"I wonder if it will affect your handicapping."

"No way, Shifty," he said as he paid the check and we got up to leave. "I just look at the numbers. Anyway, it's the horse that does the running. The rest of us are just along for the ride."

On the way back to the motel, I finally told Jay about my odd encounter with Emile during the shooting of his porn epic. I made the story as entertaining as I could and Jay laughed a lot, but he seemed neither too concerned nor overly curious about the situation. Most of his questions had to do with working in the movie rather than with the dilemma in which he still found himself. "I guess you're going to have to stay down here for a while," I observed.

"The way things are going," he answered, "that might not be too much of a hardship. I've been holding my own at the races and now there's Jill."

"You're not exactly out of reach down here," I pointed out. "Emile could find you, if he really sets his mind to it."

"I suppose so," Jay said, "but I have a feeling this is all going to work out in the end. We'll just keep a low profile, Shifty, and go about our business."

I dropped him off at the Country Club and drove back downtown. I was too agitated to sleep and I decided that what I needed was a quiet drink by myself and a little time to sort out my thoughts. That's what I told myself, but obviously I must have been lying, because I could have done that simply by dropping into the bar of the Conquistador or by walking across the boulevard to the Fiesta Americana. Instead, I went back to the Encanto and I would like to be able to say that I didn't have anything special in mind.

Victor, the bartender, recognized me and nodded affably to me as I entered. The small room was full, mostly of middle-aged Mexican men, either grouped at the bar or sitting at the tables with the half dozen or so working girls who apparently frequented the place regularly. The atmosphere was cheerful enough but subdued, the faces blurred by the cigarette smoke that hung in the air against the dim lights and the voices indistinct through the noise of guitar music and singing from inside the restaurant. I found an open spot at the far end of the counter, settled myself on a stool, and ordered a brandy and soda, after which I took another look around the room. "Is Marisa here?" I asked when Victor returned with my drink.

"*Sí, señor,*" he said, nodding toward the dining room. "You do not hear her?"

I picked up my drink and went inside. Marisa and a trio of guitarists were entertaining at a large table of elderly American couples against the far wall. She was in the middle of some sort of happy mariachi song full of yips and laughs and long, dark-sounding notes that celebrated the triumph of love and matrimony over betrayal and death. It was terrific. Her voice wasn't pretty at all—it was frayed, with a quick vibrato and a tendency to flatten out on long, held notes—but it was heavy with passion and a lust for living. I was amazed. When she had finished, on one last dark note and a chorus of accompanying yelps from her patrons, I put my drink down on the corner of the nearest table and applauded, along with most of the other diners. One of the Americans in the dinner party gave her a ten-dollar bill, and she stuffed it into her bosom, then leaned over, took his head between her hands, and kissed him loudly on the forehead. Everyone clapped again and cheered. Smiling and blowing kisses, she began to walk across the room toward me.

"This your drink, fella?"

"Oh, sure. Sorry," I said, picking it up. I didn't even look to see who had spoken; I assumed it was some other American having dinner, whose space I had temporarily invaded. I kept my eyes fixed on Marisa. "You were great," I said as she came up to me. "Can I buy you a drink?"

"Ah, it is you!" She laughed. "Sure. You have more time now, eh?"

"I have lots of time."

We went back to my corner of the bar and Marisa ordered a Scotch and soda. As usual, she looked incredibly available, in the same sort of clinging, low-cut blouse she had worn a few nights earlier. "*Salud*," she said, raising her glass to me before drinking.

"You're a wonderful singer," I said. "I had no idea."

"You think I am just here for the men, huh?"

I started to deny it, but she cut me off with a big, dark laugh, followed by a hand pressing on the back of my neck. "You are right, baby," she said. "You want to make love?"

"Let's have a drink. Unless you're in a hurry?"

"I am not in a hurry," she said.

"Listen, you sing really well," I said. "Don't they pay you?"

She laughed. "Pay me? I starve, *amigo*, on what I am paid to sing. I have a family."

"You married?"

"No, no. But I am from Los Mochis," she said. "It is poor. My parents, they have ten children, I am the young one. I send money." She moved in very close to me again. "But this is sad talk. I don't wish to be sad. What is your name?"

"Shifty."

"*Cómo?*"

"That's what my friends call me. My real name is Lou."

"Okay, Shifty. That is a funny name."

"I'm a magician. *Un mago.*"

"*Sí?*" Her eyes opened wide and she leaned back to look up at me. "Is true?"

"Watch." I took a quarter out of my pocket, set it spinning on the bar, then quickly placed my hand over it and made it vanish. "See?" She laughed, so I followed it with a couple of other simple moves and got her to clap her hands with delight. I was about to try my Ring-on-a-Stick with her when suddenly I saw her expression change abruptly. She looked frightened.

I turned around and saw Larry Youkoumian standing in the entrance. He was gazing straight at us, but gave not the slightest flicker of recognition. After a few seconds, he turned around and walked out again. I looked at Marisa. "What was that all about?"

She shook her head. "He is not a nice man," she said.

"I guess I knew that. That's old Larry Youkoumian, my partner in the horse business."

She stared at me in amazement. "Your partner?"

"We own a horse together."

She backed a couple of steps away from me, looking at me as if I had begun to grow hair between my eyes. "Is not possible," she said.

"It's just a business arrangement, Marisa," I explained. "I sort of inherited a small piece of a race horse he and a couple of other guys have down here. One of the owners owed me money. It's nothing complicated, Marisa. Really. I hardly know good old Larry. What's so terrible about him?"

"You don't know nothing?"

"Nothing, honest."

She shook her head and looked briefly away from me. "Is better you don't know," she said, now coming in close to me again. "You take me home, Shifty, all right?"

"Marisa, I'm not used to paying—"

"Is all right," she said. "You take me with you. If he come back for me, I have to go. . . ." She let the explanation trail away into an indistinct whisper, but I gathered she was truly alarmed at the prospect.

I put Larry down for a sadist of some sort, another high mark for him, and decided to act out my newly assigned role of Lochinvar, rescuer of tarnished damsels.

"Come on," I said. I paid up, took her arm, and we headed out toward the street. Larry Youkoumian was waiting for us by the beaded curtains leading into the restaurant. "Marisa," he said, "Rico would like you to join us."

She didn't answer, but she stopped walking and I could feel her tremble beside me. "Well, hello, Larry," I said. "I'm sorry, but Marisa's with me this evening."

The ferret looked expressionlessly at me. "Beat it," he said.

"I'm sorry, Larry, but I don't think I want to do that. That's why I made a date with Marisa."

Youkoumian stared at me. "What's the matter with you?" he asked.

"I don't know. Is my fly open? I like to make jokes. Actually, since you ask, I'm in wonderful form. I wish I had time to show you some of my better moves." I took Marisa's hand and tugged her toward the exit. "Say hello to Rico and tell him I'll see him at the races."

"Hey, you," the ferret snapped, "you need a road map or something?"

"I don't think so, Larry, thank you. I know where I am almost all the time."

One of the aging American diners Marisa had been serenading earlier suddenly came through the dangling beads on his way to the men's room and, as the curtains parted briefly, I caught a glimpse of Bones. He was sitting at the table where I had put my glass down. Next to him, turned three quarters away from me, sat a very large blond man I had never seen before. He was wearing a dark blue, pin-striped business suit, but I didn't have time to note anything else about him.

"Honey," the older man said as he recognized Marisa, "you were great, *muy fantastico!*"

"Thank you," Marisa answered, but her face looked pasty under her makeup, as if she had become suddenly ill.

"Come on, sweetheart," I said, falsely jovial, "let's

go party." I wanted to play my role well, because I didn't want Larry Youkoumian to take me too seriously. I whisked Marisa out into the street. "Where to now?" I asked as we headed back toward Revolución and the lot where I'd left my car.

"Is not good," she said. "They follow you. Come on, we go to a place I know."

"Marisa, they're not going to follow us. You've been seeing too many bad TV shows."

"Ah, TV. You don't know nothing," she said.

"About old Larry and Bones?"

"About nothing."

That was true enough, I guessed, so I allowed her to lead me up the avenue a block and a half and then down a long flight of filthy carpeted steps into a dark, smoky room calling itself the Rinoceronte. The atmosphere in the place was pink with lust. There was a long bar on the right crowded with flashy-looking hookers and potential johns and the noise was deafening. A three-piece band was playing very loudly, while a naked girl was dancing clumsily but provocatively on a tiny platform surrounded by tables of customers, mostly men, who tossed coins and crumpled dollar bills at her feet every time she performed some particularly obscene movement. "What is this place?" I shouted. "What are we doing here?"

Marisa didn't answer. She pulled me across the room until she found a free table against the far wall and we sat down. A waiter appeared, I ordered two beers, and then I turned to look at her. Her features were indistinct in the dim light, but she was gazing at me with large, lustrous eyes that seemed oddly blank, as if she had suddenly withdrawn into herself. I leaned toward her so I wouldn't have to shout. "Marisa, what's going on?" I asked.

"I was here, in this place, last year," she said.

"You mean you worked here?"

"Sí."

"You sang here?"

"You are *un inocente*, Shifty. There . . ." And she waved toward the bar, where a sailor was in the process of massaging the naked breasts of a tall, serene-looking girl, who continued impassively to sip her drink and to chat with one of her colleagues on the stool next to her as he worked.

"Well, I suppose it's one way to pay the bills," I said. "I didn't think you were in the Encanto bar every night because you enjoyed it."

"*Estupido*, you understand nothing."

"Marisa, I've been in these places before. Really."

"You don't see nothing."

"What's to see? It's just show-and-tell time at the playground, isn't it?"

"*Cómo?*"

"Never mind. But listen, what I want to know is, what's so terrible about old Larry Youkoumian and Mellini? What do they do? Beat you up or something?"

"You don't ask," she said. "Is better you don't know, okay? They are not nice."

"That's not news to me, Marisa."

"I tell you something," she said, leaning in toward me. "They do bad things. You do not know them for sure. You don't do business with them, Shifty."

"Horse business, that's all. We own one horse together."

She shook her head. "There is other business, Shifty."

"What is it, Marisa? Drugs?"

She didn't answer, but looked unhappily away from me again. On the stage, a young, muscular American, dressed in sneakers, khaki pants, and a short-sleeved sports shirt, was now dancing clumsily with the naked girl, both hands on her buttocks. A security guard in a brown uniform and two waiters were trying to persuade him to step down, but he was too engrossed to pay any attention to them. The audience was clapping and cheering him on. Then, without warning, the girl sud-

denly put both hands against his chest and pushed him
very hard. He fell back into the arms of the waiters, wh
caught him and returned him quickly to his table. Th
boy, who was clearly drunk, did not resist, and th
incident did not lead to violence, as I'd been afraid
might. His friends, all young studs like himself, probabl
either marines or sailors from the military bases north o
the border, cheered and clapped him on the back. On
of them rose to his feet, perhaps to replace him onstage
but he was blocked by the guard, who smilingly bu
firmly pushed him back to his seat. The girl, meanwhile
finished her dance, scooped up her money, and ra
offstage, to more cheering and clapping and whistling.

"You want to go now?" Marisa asked.

"Yes. I've got to get up early."

"I make love to you, all right?"

"Marisa, I like you a lot, but I don't pay for—"

"I know. Is all right. Come on."

As we passed the bar on our way out, the sailor ha
his face against the serene-looking girl's breasts and hi
arms wrapped around her waist, but she still seemed t
be paying no attention to him. She said somethin
jokingly to Marisa in Spanish as we left, in a surprisingl
dark, masculine voice, but I didn't understand it.

Marisa said nothing else to me until we were insid
my room at the Conquistador, then she turned an
kissed me. It was a warm and loving kiss and I reache
out for her, but she pushed herself away from me. "No,
she said, "is I who make love to you. You understand?"

"I didn't know there were ground rules. I have
condom."

"No," she said, shaking her head. "You do nothing
Shifty. I do everything, okay? Or I go."

"Are you sick, Marisa?"

"No. But I want to do it this way, okay?"

I wasn't sure what to say to her at this point, bu
before I could pursue the conversation she began t
undress me. She did it swiftly, expertly, and lovingly, s

that by the time she led me to the bed I was aroused and ready to abide by any rules she wanted to impose. She kissed me again and allowed me to caress her breasts, which were lovely and firm, with large, dark nipples the size of poker chips, but she refused to strip completely. "Is that time, you know?" she said. I didn't care what time it was by then. She had begun to make love to me with her mouth and I was helpless.

I don't know how long Marisa made love to me, but every second of the time was exquisite. I had expected her to be an expert, but not to be as careful and subtle and committed to providing pleasure as she was. And when it was all over, she held me in her arms for a while before preparing to leave. She was being thoroughly professional, like any good working girl, I realized, but not callously indifferent. I was touched.

"Marisa, let me drive you home," I said, sitting up. "It'll only take me a minute to get dressed."

"No, I take a taxi," she said, leaning over and kissing me again, but on the cheek this time. "Is all right, Shifty. So long."

"Marisa, wait." I got up, went to my pants pocket, and took out some money. "Let me—"

"Now you make me angry," she said, opening the door and flashing me a quick smile. *"Un inocente, pero muy simpático."* And she left, her high heels clicking loudly on the terrace outside my door until they faded away down the steps of the courtyard below.

I called the front desk and left a wake-up call for six o'clock, then fell back against my pillows. I slept like a stone.

Ten

RUNNING

Fred's Folly was standing outside his stall when I arrived at Barn 15 the next morning. The little Mexican with the copper-colored face was on his knees in front of him, adjusting the protective front wraps the horse would wear during the race, partly to keep the animal all in one piece, partly to prevent outsiders from ascertaining exactly what kind of shape he was in. Jill was leaning against the side of the barn, watching the groom work, and she waved to me as I stepped out of the Datsun and headed toward them. The other hands were all busy with one chore or another, and a couple of horses were being hot-walked after coming back from the track, but neither Hatch nor Luis seemed to be around. The sky was already a deep, very bright blue overhead and it promised to be another hot day, with the desert winds kicking up dust in the surrounding hills. I felt relaxed and happy with myself and the feeling must have been reflected on my face. "You're lookin' good," Jill said as I came up to her.

"I'm feeling great."

"Jay ain't comin'?"

I laughed. "You don't know him well enough," I said. "Jay doesn't need to look at the horses, he just adds up his numbers." I glanced at my watch. "It's about seven-thirty, which means he's finished his preliminary calculations, having to do with trouble lines, past performances, speed ratings, all that basic stuff, and now he begins to assemble it all into a significant configuration of statistical probabilities. If the patterns of numbers click into shape, a bet emerges."

"How you talk, Shifty," she said. "You got a mouth on you to stop the wind blowin'. I never heard the like."

"Well, that's Jay for you. It's the new alchemy."

"What's that?"

"In the old days, alchemists were people who turned lead into gold," I explained. "Jay does it with numbers."

"Beats me," she said with a laugh. "Come on, let me get you a cup of coffee. You about ready?"

"You read my mind." I indicated old Fred, who was standing quietly in place, but who was looking at me now with mild curiosity, his ears cocked alertly toward me. "How's he doing?"

"Miguel says great."

The little groom looked up at me and grinned. "*Si sente bien,*" he said, patting the horse affectionately on the chest. "*Es un auténtico caballo de carrera.*"

"Miguel says he's a real race horse," Jill explained. "He always wants to run, that's for sure."

"Yeah, well, tell him not to bet even one peso on him today."

"I think he knows," she said. "Miguel's been around. He used to be a rider, till he got too old."

"I figured. The horse does look better. Still fat as hell, though."

She laughed. "He sure is goin' to fool people when Sandy puts him in to run some."

"I guess. I hope I'm not one of them."

We started to head for the track kitchen, but Jill suddenly snapped her fingers in irritation. "Shit, I damn near forgot," she said.

"What?"

"This guy Cervantes, he's a trainer here, I promised him I'd take this two-year-old through the starting gate for him," she explained. "I got to go."

"You coming back?"

"No, I guess not, 'cause I got a couple of horses I got to take over to the trainin' track for Romero."

"Who's he?"

"Another guy back here." She started to run off toward some other barn. "I'll see you at the races, after the fourth. I got a mount in the fourth."

"I saw that," I called after her. "The horse can't run, can it?"

"Not a step," she shouted back, "but I'm payin' my dues." She disappeared around the corner of the next stable.

I kept on going until I found the track kitchen, an old adobe hut that had been converted into a sort of cafeteria after the original establishment had burned down a couple of years earlier, and I picked up a plastic cup full of black, bitter coffee, then went outside to drink it. About fifty yards away from where I was standing between two shedrows, I could see a corner of the quarantine barn, with a couple of large horse vans backed up to the entrance. I watched two skittish fillies being unloaded and then I saw Luis Sanchez Gomez lead a horse into the van, followed by two other grooms leading their own animals. From the stream of instructions, delivered in Spanish, that Luis yelled toward the van, I gathered that all three horses belonged to him or to the connections he worked for. When he'd finished, someone inside the van shouted something back and he nodded sullenly before turning away. The two grooms returned and another man I'd seen around the barn now appeared, carrying a couple of racing saddles. He vanished inside with the horses. Luis did not wait for him. He and the first two grooms left and I heard the roar of a pickup truck driving away. I waited, sipping my coffee out there in the sunshine, but the third man remained inside the van with the horses. Ten minutes later, as I was sipping the last of my coffee, the big truck roared into life and began to move slowly away.

By the time I got back to the stable, Miguel had

returned our champion to his stall, all ready for his race that afternoon, and the grooms who had been with Luis were standing outside the tack room, talking to each other. I didn't see Sanchez, but Hatch came out, looking more and more like the picture of Dorian Gray. "Get the fuck out of here," he said the minute he saw me.

"I don't know why I'm so unpopular," I said, smiling. "I'm sorry about the other night, Sandy, but you were out of line."

"You damn near got me arrested, you son of a bitch."

"You have a terrible temper, Sandy," I said, trying to be as pleasant as I could. "How did I know you'd take a swing at me? I was just showing you a few moves."

"You're a fuckin' menace. You're—"

"I shouldn't have messed up your rug," I admitted. "I'm sorry about that."

I thought he might take another swing at me, but Youkoumian's big gray Lincoln Continental pulled up at the end of the barn and Larry stepped out of the car. He didn't seem delighted to see me either, but his arrival did have the effect of at least shutting Hatch up.

"Just thought I'd come by and see our horse," I said as cheerfully as I could manage it. "You're looking dapper, Larry."

Youkoumian did not answer. He shut the car door, then leaned back against it and gazed at me as if he'd suddenly identified me as the source of a minor plague. "You," he said at last, "come here."

Hatch began screaming in Spanish at something going on behind me, and I heard a scurrying about around one of the stalls. Miguel, his face yellow with fear, shot past me toward the tack room, while Hatch moved toward the source of the trouble. The ferret never took his eyes off me. "Come here," he said again.

His attitude was not reassuring, but I did as he asked. When I came up to him, he leaned his pointed face up into mine, close enough so I could smell his breakfast. He apparently began the day on garlic and olive oil. "You," he said softly, "you don't do that again."

"Do what again, Larry?"

"When Rico wants to see somebody," he explained, "he wants to see somebody, you understand me?"

"She didn't want to see *him*, Larry. She was with me."

"What's that got to do with it, dummy? You stupid or something?"

"Actually, I have a pretty high IQ. I didn't think it would matter that much to Rico."

"You thought wrong. You ain't too quick."

"Larry, what do you eat in the morning?"

"Huh?"

"Do you put garlic powder on your cornflakes?"

"A comedian," he said. "You're a comedian."

"I do like to make people laugh. Now, listen—"

"No, it's you who listens," he said. "This ain't funny. Rico's real pissed off."

"What about, for God's sake? The town's full of hookers. Rico can have any girl he wants."

"What's the matter with you? You think there's that much good stick-pussy around? Where you been?"

"What kind of pussy?"

He stared at me, evidently unable to grasp the enormity of my ignorance. "What'd you get?" he asked. "A good blow job?"

"I think perhaps I'll spare you the details of our courtship," I said. "I have pretensions to being a gentleman."

"You got pretensions to being an asshole," Larry said, his dark, beady eyes alive with malice. "You got pretensions about living. Just keep this shit up and see what happens."

"Keep what up?" I answered, doing my best to appear calmer than I felt. "I had a date with her. She decided to come with me instead of with Rico. What's the big to-do? Rico can see her some other night."

"You're dumb. You're real stupid. You made Rico look bad, you know that?"

"He's not a glorious view at any time," I said. "But tell him I'm sorry. He can see Marisa tonight, if he wants. That is, if she wants to see him."

"If she wants . . ." he began, then actually smiled at me. "I don't believe you."

"I don't think Marisa cares all that much for Rico, if you want to know the truth. I would guess he's probably rude to her and she doesn't like it."

I was relieved to see that I had apparently at last succeeded in disarming him; he simply couldn't deal anymore with the scope of my abysmal obtuseness. His jaw had dropped open and he was speechless. "Are you all right, Larry?" I asked. "You look odd. Is it something I said?"

"Go away," he finally whispered, "just go away. You're too dumb to be breathing. Take off."

"Sure," I said cheerfully. "I just came by to check out the horse. I'll see you guys at the races. Tell Rico I'm sorry. She's a nice kid. We had a good time."

I sauntered nonchalantly toward my car and never looked back. I wasn't at all sure I had gotten away with my act, but I fervently hoped I had. Dissembling and misdirection are two of the most valuable tools a magician needs to disguise his better moves, especially when you're playing to an audience of one and the consequences of being found out could be unpleasant. Maybe I had succeeded in fooling Youkoumian and maybe I hadn't, I told myself as I drove out of the track, but I hoped I had and that at least he'd cool Mellini down. I didn't want my bones broken at any time and I couldn't count on Mellini's gift of tolerance, I was certain of that much.

I didn't know what to think about Marisa at that point. I had a very uncomfortable feeling about what we had done the night before, but I told myself it didn't matter. The act of love, at least, had been genuine.

* * *

I found Jay, about half an hour before post time for the first race, sitting at a table in the Foreign Book, his papers and charts spread out before him, his eyes glued to a contest in New Jersey. The horse he had wagered twenty dollars to win on ran second, but as usual he didn't allow that minor misfortune to depress him unduly. "If you have a real opinion at a racetrack," he was fond of saying, "there are going to be a lot of days when your horses run well but not well enough. You have to suffer through them, that's all."

I sat down and brought him up-to-date on recent events, but without telling him anything crucial about my evening with Marisa. "And I suppose you know that Jill picked up a mount in the fourth," I concluded.

"It has no chance, but it'll keep her in action," Jay said, jotting down notations in one of his notebooks. "So the horse looked okay?"

"Still fat, but pretty good," I volunteered. "You coming upstairs?"

"Not yet. I have another bet going in New York," he explained. "I'll see you in the paddock before the seventh."

I started to leave, but then decided I'd better ask him what I was afraid to find out. "Have you ever heard the opprobrious term 'stick-pussy'?" I inquired.

"Sure, it's prison talk. It means a guy the cons use for a woman," Jay said. "Where'd you hear it?"

"Oh, Mellini and Youkoumian were talking about somebody last night," I said. "They used it."

"They've both been in the slammer, I'm sure, so they'd know."

"Where'd you hear it?"

"Around the track, I forget where. Graphic, huh?"

"Yes," I agreed, feeling a little sick to my stomach. "I'll see you later."

"Shifty, I wouldn't risk a dime here until the ninth,

and even then we'd better be careful unless the price is right on Camacho's speedball in the feature."

"I hear you, Jay."

I left him to his notebooks and his numbers and went upstairs to the bar of La Cupula, where I had a beer and did a lot of heavy thinking. Evidently, Marisa and I had a little talking to do. I confess that I was still clinging to a ragged hope that I had somehow misinterpreted the ferret's remark about her, but I knew I was fooling myself. I was not only what Marisa had called me, *un inocente*, but just about as obtuse as Youkoumian thought I was. I morosely nursed my beer through the first two races, a couple of unbettable contests for cheap maidens, then went upstairs to look for a seat somewhere over the finish line.

"Well, how you doin'?" Harry Dundee called out as I passed him in the aisle. He was sitting with another man in an outdoor box two rows down from the top. "Come on in here. You alone?"

"For now. You got room?"

"Hell yes." He indicated an empty seat behind him. "You remember Walter," he said. "He knows everything. He even knows who the Unknown Soldier is."

Walter nodded to me and allowed me to shake his hand, which felt soft and boneless, like a small pillow. I recognized him from my first encounter with Harry. He was a short, plump old man with spiky, iron-gray hair and dark brown eyes. He was dressed in a food-stained gray jump suit and looked about as benevolent as a moulting buzzard. He didn't bother to answer my cheerful hello.

"Shifty here's a magician," Harry told him. "He can do a whole bunch of tricks."

"Yeah?" Walter said, uninterested. "Well, don't do them today."

"Don't pay him no mind," Harry declared. "He's got a personality that's just pitiful."

"We're here to play horses, aren't we?" Walter sai
"If I want tricks, I'll go to a show."

"Walter's like we are, Shifty," Harry explaine
"He's a serious player."

"I promise not to show you a single move," I assur
Walter. "Who do you like in the third?"

"No one can win the third," Walter answered. "]
one in this race can run. The one that doesn't fall dov
will win."

"Pitiful, just pitiful," Harry said. "Shifty, the fo
horse will win this race. He's got the best time, the be
post position, and the best jockey. Only he ain't goin'
pay much."

"Don't listen to him," Walter said. "The only part
a horse he knows is the rear end, because it's like looki
in the mirror."

"It occurs to me," I said to Walter, "that if you tri
hard enough, you could bring on an eclipse of the su

Harry laughed. "Got you there, Walter," he sa
standing up. "I'm goin' to make a small bet here."

"On the four?" I asked.

"Sure. I can use the money." And he headed fo
betting window.

Walter snorted contemptuously. "He never learn:
he said. "Harry still thinks he can beat this game playi
favorites."

"He's a pretty smart bettor," I said. "I'd guess
does all right."

Walter seemed pained by my observation. "Y
know what he said to me last week?"

"What?"

"He said this jockey Camacho out here was a sm
rider."

"I guess he is, if he decides to try."

"You think a jockey can be smart?" Walter asked, l
eyes widening in dismay. "Smart? If jockeys had a
brains, they wouldn't be wearing size-one hats."

It was hard to argue against such fierce logic, so

smiled and nodded agreement. Harry came back, having bet ten dollars to win on the four horse, which promptly came romping easily home by five lengths and paid $3.60 for every two-dollar ticket. "That takes care of lunch," Harry said.

"I guess you don't eat much," Walter commented. He had watched the race without a flicker of emotion and seemed actually disappointed by Harry's win.

"Do you ever make a bet?" I asked him.

"When I see something I like and at the right price."

"You don't want to hold your breath till that happens," Harry said. "Old Walter can sit out here for weeks before he'll risk a dollar on anything. It's pitiful, just pitiful."

"Harry, you're old, you're going blind, and most of the time you're drunk," Walter said. "Shut up, why don't you?" Having evidently been goaded beyond endurance, he now rose from his seat and shuffled morosely away from us.

"Where'd you meet Mr. Sunshine?" I asked.

Harry laughed. "Ain't he a pisser? He lives in the park," he explained. "He ain't got but about a million dollars, but you can't get him to spend a goddamn dime. He makes about one bet a week, if that."

"Does he win them all?"

"Not more than the rest of us, but he won't never admit it. He can't stand the idea anyone could get the best of him, see? So every bet's got to be a winner. If you listen to him, he ain't never had a losing day. Oh, old Walter's a card, all right. But he ain't such a bad guy underneath all that."

"Is he married?"

"Hell no. What woman would put up with that? He don't even mingle with the singles, and there's plenty of them widder women would like to play bridge or go to the dances with him, only he says no one knows how to play but him and the women keep steppin' on his feet. He's a character."

Jill's only mount of the day, in the fourth, turned out to be an unimpressive professional maiden that finished somewhere in the middle of the pack, his twenty-third consecutive failure to win. Walter informed us that the horse's inability to run was due entirely to the presence on his back of a weak girl jockey. "What about the other twenty-two times he lost?" I asked.

"Don't argue with Walter," Harry advised me. "He's got an answer for everythin'. Hell, if the horse had won, he'd have said it was in spite of the rider."

"I'd have been right too," Walter snapped.

"Walter, you just don't like women," Harry said. "That's how it is and you know it."

"All cunts are pricks," Walter said.

"Pitiful, just pitiful," Harry observed.

I thought about Marisa and winced.

Jill and Jay showed up at the paddock for the seventh, but neither Youkoumian nor Mellini appeared, which was all right with me. "I saw them in the Turf Club," Jay informed me. "I guess they don't see any reason to come down. They're waiting for the ninth."

We stood out on the grassy circle of the walking ring and watched Hatch supervise the saddling of our champion. Miguel did most of the work, but the trainer kept a close watch over him and it was he who made sure the cinch was tight enough, adjusted the bit and the blinkers, checked the bandages on the horse's front legs, while never taking his eyes off the preparations for even a second. It was the first solid indication I'd had that, whatever else he might be, Hatch was at least a genuine horseman. He emanated a nervous but thorough competence that I found reassuring, and I began to believe he would bring old Fred up to a race for us.

When it came time for Miguel to lead the horse out into the ring, Luis Sanchez Gomez appeared, sweaty and huge under a straw-colored sombrero. He stood off by himself, looking bored, and I figured he'd been dispatched to the scene to keep an eye on things by Mellini and the ferret. Fred's Folly moved stolidly about behind the other horses with his head hung low, seeming not in the least interested in the proceedings around him. "He looks like a cow," Jay observed.

Jill giggled. "He does, don't he? He's a smart old horse. He knows it ain't his day, so he ain't much interested. He's just goin' to go out there and get through it."

"How are we going to tell him when it is his day?" Jay asked.

"He'll know," Jill assured us. "This old horse is real smart. You'll see."

The only flicker of interest old Fred displayed occurred when he caught a glimpse in front of him of the honey-colored pony being used to escort another horse onto the track. His head came up and he snorted, suddenly bouncing up on his toes. "*Darse prisa!* Move it!" Hatch called out to the rider on the pony, who quickly spurred his mount just out of reach of old Fred's bobbing head.

"He does go for ponies," Jay said.

"That's why Sandy keeps the blinkers on him," Jill explained. "He'd try and mount all them ponies otherwise."

"We got us a gay horse," Jay said. "Shifty, you got us into this."

"No, I didn't," I retorted. "You and Fingers did."

Lupe Camacho now came out, looking like a chunk of Swiss chocolate in our dark brown silks, and Hatch gave him a leg up without bothering to talk to him. "Isn't he going to say anything to him?" Jay asked.

"Ain't nothin' to tell him," Jill said. "He knows it ain't a go, honey."

We stood there silently and watched Fred's Folly jog out onto the track. He looked almost like a draft horse, but once on the course he put his head down, arched his thick neck against the tight hold Camacho maintained on the reins, and broke into a lumbering gallop past the stands. He was the only unescorted entry in the contest, and suddenly he looked, despite his avoirdupois, like a real race horse. The betting crowd, however, didn't seem to think he looked like much of anything, because he was thirty to one on the board at the time and eventually went off at twenty-five to one.

We didn't bother to go back upstairs, but watched the race from down below, by the rail. Camacho allowed Fred's Folly to break alertly enough, but then took him back until he was twenty lengths behind the leaders. He remained there, moving at his own pace, and came in last, though I noticed with interest that he lost no more ground from the half-mile pole to the finish and came galloping past us at the end, looking as fresh as if he'd been out for a promenade on somebody's sun deck. "He sure needed that one," Jill commented. "Next time he'll know what it's all about. He ain't been in a race in about a year, ain't that so?"

As we headed back upstairs, Jay seemed lost in thought. He said nothing more, but sat down over his papers at a table he had commandeered in the Turf Club, his arms folded and a pensive expression on his face. Jill, always hustling, spotted a trainer she'd been looking for and went off to have a cup of coffee with him, while I went back to the box to say good-bye to Harry and Walter.

"Was that your horse?" Harry wanted to know. "That is you in the program, ain't it?"

I admitted that it was. "But I only own a small piece of him," I said. "I don't know why it's only my name they're using."

Walter cackled grimly. "I think I can guess what piece of him you own," he said.

"He's not a sprinter," I said. "We gave him the race. He needed it."

"I guess he did," Walter observed, "but did we?"

"He's in training to go long," I explained.

"Oh, I thought it was to be a float in the Rose Bowl parade."

"Pitiful," Harry said, "just pitiful, Walter. A man's horse loses a race and you got to spit on his shoes. You're one miserable human bein', you know that?"

I didn't hang around to hear Walter's reply, but I guessed it would be appropriately acidic. When I got back to Jay's table in the Turf Club, I found him in a mildly agitated mood, an unusual state for him. "Shifty, we're not betting on El Gato," he announced.

"Why not?"

"Because I don't think he's going to win, that's why. It's too obvious."

"Things are pretty crude down here."

Jay shook his head. "It's wrong, all wrong," he said. "I've been thinking about it very hard. There are a thousand players out here who can read the *Form,* and they're all going to see what we see. El Gato is such a setup, it jumps off the page at you. Even if it is a go, they'll knock the price down to where you can't play him. Trust me. Where's Mellini?"

"Probably upstairs, in the Jockey Club. He's sort of mad at me, so I'm not going to look for him."

"Mad? What about?"

"Never mind, it isn't important. Anyway, he needs me right now."

"For what?"

"Fred's Folly is running in my name only. Didn't you notice?"

"I'd be a little nervous about that."

"I am, but there's not much I can do about it. He and Youkoumian seem to have the Mexican Jockey Club wired."

"I think I'm beginning to worry about you, Shifty," Jay said. "You may have gotten yourself in a little deep here. Maybe you ought to get out now, while you can."

"How do I do that?"

"You could give up your interest in the horse."

"One more race," I said. "After that, we'll see. How else are we going to get some of our money back and get these other guys off our backs? We can't exactly count on Fingers."

Jay's prediction about the ninth turned out to be accurate. El Gato went off an odds-on favorite in the race, at three to five. He looked terrible, too, all lathered up and switching his tail wildly about as Camacho took him to the post. When the starting gate opened, he exploded out of it to grab a four-length lead. Halfway around the turn, he had stretched it to six, but then he began to tire. The two other speed horses in the race drew abreast of him at the head of the lane, but they had all been running much too fast. The timer showed the half mile in 43.4 seconds and the five-eighths in fifty-seven flat. A rangy old mare named Mombi came from at least fifteen lengths out of it half a mile from home to win going away, while El Gato dropped back to last. She paid $12.60.

"They put one over," Jay said.

"What makes you think so?" I asked.

"That mare should have been at least twenty to one. She didn't belong in this field."

"Well, it'll cheer Walter up," I said. "He thinks every race is fixed."

"Who's Walter?"

"An old guy I met here."

Jill came back to our table looking stunned. "Golly," she said, "I can't figure El Gato, can you?"

"Honey, you didn't bet on him, did you?" Jay asked.

"Only a couple of Exactas," she admitted. "Sandy told me he'd win easy."

"Sandy stiffed you."

"He wouldn't do that," she said. "I know he wouldn't. And I just saw him. He's madder than hell. Lupe wasn't supposed to burn him up like that. He was supposed to use him a bit to get the lead and open up a length or two, then maybe hit him with the buzzer at the eighth pole to keep him goin'. They done that to him before and it works."

"So what went wrong?"

"I don't know," she said, "but the horse sure wasn't himself. And Sandy ain't fakin' it. He's madder than a wet turkey."

"Let's get out of here," Jay said, beginning to gather up his paraphernalia. "There's nothing else to bet on today. Jill, you coming with me?"

"I guess," she said. "Ain't much to do around here."

"Shifty?"

"No, I'll catch up with you guys later, maybe. Where will you be?"

"We'll have drinks at the bar in the Fiesta Americana," Jay told me. "Meet us there by eight o'clock and we'll figure out a place to have dinner." He took Jill's hand and started to leave.

She looked back at me over her shoulder. "The man thinks he owns me," she said, smiling. "You come with us, hear? I'm tryin' to get this dude to take me dancin'. You dance, Shifty?"

"I move around to the beat," I said. "I thought you had to get up early in the morning."

"I do, but tomorrow I'm takin' it easy. If we ain't at the bar or you're late, look for us at La Pulga. It's a dance place on Revolución, near First, okay?"

"You better show up, Shifty, because I can't dance," Jay called back as they left.

I walked upstairs to the Jockey Club and found it nearly empty, with only a scattering of bettors still seated at the tables. Mellini and the ferret didn't seem to be around, but I sat down at an empty table near the entrance and ordered an iced tea. I didn't know exactly what I was looking for and I had no idea what I would have done if Bones Mellini and Youkoumian had been present. I suppose I would have put on my innocent act again and asked about El Gato, but I didn't imagine that that approach would have worked very well. No, I think that what I really wanted was a sense of the events, a confirmation of a rooted feeling I was nurturing about the race I had just seen. I believed Jill about Hatch, but I couldn't believe that the outcome of the contest had been a surprise to the men he worked for. And so I sat there and sipped my tea and waited as the horses went to the post for the tenth race, an uninteresting competition for cheap three-year-old colts and geldings going a mile and a sixteenth.

After the race was over, as the animals came back toward the unsaddling area below me, the elevator doors opened, disgorging Luis Sanchez Gomez into the lobby. The Mexican foreman went straight to the alcove containing the betting windows, lingered inside for three or four minutes, then emerged, stuffing a bulky envelope into the side pocket of his jacket. He went back to the elevator landing, punched the down button, and waited, fidgeting impatiently. When the elevator finally arrived, he stepped quickly into it and disappeared from view. The whole process had taken less than five minutes.

I glanced at the *Form* and found a horse in the eleventh and final race on the card I thought had a chance, then got up and went to the windows. I found myself alone in the alcove, with only one bored young clerk on duty, leaning back, arms folded, against the rear of his booth. He roused himself when he saw me and leaned over his machine, smiling. "Yes, sir," he said.

"Ah, you speak English, good," I said, pointing to my program. "You like this horse in here?" I indicated my selection in the nightcap, a five-year-old mare named Secret Bride. "I don't know much about these horses."

"Yes, she can run good," the clerk said. "That is a good horse."

"Well, all right," I answered. "I guess I'll bet ten dollars to win on her."

"Very good, sir," the clerk said, taking my money and punching out my ticket.

"I've been real lucky with fillies and mares today," I volunteered. "I bet that Mombi, you know, in the feature."

The clerk grinned. "Good, sir, very good. That was a smart bet."

I laughed. "I don't know about smart," I said. "I just liked her name. I couldn't believe it. I guess she's a good horse."

"Oh, yes, she's a good horse," the clerk said.

"I saw this big fat guy with the mustache bet a bundle on her. Boy, I guess he made a killing!"

The clerk winked at me. "You know him?"

"No, I've just seen him around."

"He and Camacho, they are like this." The clerk put his hands together.

"Camacho didn't ride her, did he?"

The clerk grinned. "No, sir. But his brother, he own and he train the other horse."

"The winner?"

"Yes, sir." The clerk shrugged and smiled again, as if to tell me that this was the way of the world, was it not? Before I could ask him anything else, however, two other players came into the alcove. I favored the clerk with my sappiest dumb-gringo grin and waved good-bye, then went back to my table and sat down.

I opened my program and looked back at the ninth race. The owner of Mombi was listed as Quadra Esmeralda, a stable name. I searched for it elsewhere on the program but didn't find it, then leaned back in my chair and tried to think the matter through. My main concern was trying to figure out exactly how the boys had managed to put their little coup over without involving Hatch and why they would have cut him out of it.

I was thinking so hard that I forgot to pay any attention to the race I had bet on, until the horses were being loaded into the starting gate. To my amazement,

Secret Bride broke on top and went wire to wire for an easy win, at odds of better than eleven to one. I walked out of the track with a hundred-dollar profit for the day. It sometimes doesn't pay to study too hard at the races.

Eleven

DIRTY DANCING

It was dark when I drove into the stable area. I parked the car along the side of the road, by a big water tank near the stable office, and walked back toward Barn 15, mainly because I didn't want to advertise my arrival. I don't know why I was being so cautious, but I had a strong feeling that something during the day had gone seriously wrong. It was confirmed when I turned a corner by the backside recreation center and started up between the rows of stables. A flatbed truck was parked at the end of Barn 15 and three men, one of whom was Miguel, were engaged, with the aid of a winch, in loading the carcass of a horse into it. I stopped some yards away and watched. No sooner had the animal been hauled up than the other two men got inside and drove off. Miguel watched them go, then walked dejectedly away down the shedrow.

I caught up to him outside an empty stall that he had begun to sweep out. It smelled bad, as if something had already begun to decompose in it. "Miguel?" I said softly. *"Buenas noches."*

He was surprised to see me, but nodded. *"Señor."*

"Fred's Folly okay?"

"Oh, *sí.*" He waved in the direction of our champion's stall and rattled off something in Spanish that I didn't understand, though I caught the words *enfermedad, caballo,* and *muerto.* He was obviously upset and now began to sweep vigorously.

I walked past him down to old Fred's stall and found

him, as usual, facing backward, his head down and h
enormous haunches turned toward me. I called softly
him, but he took no notice of me. The old pro wa
asleep, I guessed, exhausted from his recent outing, h
first race in over eight months. His front legs wer
wrapped in heavy bandages, as if he were being he
together by them, and I wondered if he'd stay soun
One bow was bad enough, but two? In my years at tl
track I'd learned to recognize bowed tendons, tl
inflammation, caused mainly by hemorrhaging, th
afflicts the big flexor tendon along the back of a horse
front leg, from the knee to the hock. Not all horses c
come back from such a serious injury. We were going
have to be lucky, and I found myself wondering abo
Hatch. I had to take Jill's word for it that he was
competent horseman, but his luck did not seem to be
flower.

"Miguel," I called out to the little groom as I walke
back past his stall, "*el caballo muerto es* El Gato?"

"*Sí, un fallo cardiaco, señor,*" he answered befo
rattling off a further explanation I couldn't decipher wi
my racetrack Spanish.

"*Gracias,*" I said, "*me da lástima*. I'm sorry."

I walked down to the end of the shedrow and saw
light under the tack-room door. I knocked. No answe
so I banged on it a second time, then pushed the do
open. Sandy Hatch was sitting in a chair tilted ba
against the wall, his head slumped forward on his che
His hat had fallen to the floor, and his pale, bald dor
glowed like a faint full moon in the dim light of the sing
bulb suspended above him. A half-empty bottle
tequila sat on the desk by his hand. He was breathing,
I knew he was alive, but, as I stood there, uncerta
about what to do, he suddenly slid off the chair to t
floor. He lay there on his back, snoring, his mouth op
and his eyes staring blindly at the ceiling. I thought
might be in danger of choking to death on his own von
if he became sick, so I went down on my knees a

rolled him over onto his side. He never woke up, but simply lay there, his snores now filling the night.

I stood up and looked around. The room was a mess. There were dirty clothes and rags piled in one corner and on the metal cot against the wall opposite the desk. Trash had spilled out of the wastebasket onto the floor, and the desktop was covered with papers—old *Racing Forms*, condition books, programs, bills, and the sports sections of several Mexican newspapers. On a set of shelves by the door reposed several bottles of liniment, various medications, pills, creams, and a big pink container of Pepto-Bismol. On a corner of the desk I spotted some white grains that looked like sugar. I emptied one of the smaller pill bottles, which contained what I assumed were Actifed capsules, and carefully scraped the white grains into it, then dropped it into my pocket. I took one last look around, then started out, only to find the doorway suddenly filled by the bulk of Luis Sanchez Gomez.

"Hello, Luis," I said, "I'm glad you're here. Your boss has passed out."

."What you want?" the Mexican asked, making no effort to get out of my way. "What you doing here?"

"I came by to see if our horse was all right," I explained, "and I found El Gato dead and Sandy passed out in his chair. He fell down and I rolled him over so he wouldn't choke to death if he throws up. Why don't you help me get him on the bed?"

Luis thought all this information over, then grunted, and between the two of us we were able to hoist him onto the cot, where he lay breathing like an asthmatic seal. I maneuvered myself between Luis and the door, so that when he once again turned to me I could risk telling him a bit of what I knew. "Nice hit," I said.

He blinked uncomprehendingly at me. *"Qué?"*

"I said nice hit," I repeated, smiling at him. "I saw you cash the ticket on the mare. Were you all in on it?"

"You stupid," the Mexican said. "You are stup
man."

"Hey, Luis, I don't give a shit what you guys do,"
said. "I just want to be in on the action. Did you have
kill the horse or what?"

"We don't kill no horse," he said. "The horse dr
dead in the stall after we get him back."

"A heart attack, is that it?"

"Sí. Why you ask so many questions? Is not good
ask so many questions."

"One more. Why didn't you tell Sandy you a
Camacho were going to cook El Gato on the front e
and fix it for the mare Lupe's brother trains to come i
I hear he was real sore about what happened."

The Mexican shrugged. "He talk a lot, just like yo
He drink too much and he talk a lot." He took a st
toward me and I prudently backed away so that I w
standing in the doorway, one hand casually up agai
the frame but ready to move quickly. "What about yo
Why you talk so much?"

"Calm down, Luis," I said, keeping the tone re
lutely light. "I'm just a little annoyed I wasn't in on
that's all. I'm supposed to be in a partnership here.
like to know what's going on. I hope you guys are
planning some kind of nonsense with Fred's Folly, tha
all. I want to cash a ticket on that sucker."

"What you scared of?" the Mexican suddenly aske
"You think I'm going to hurt you, gringo?"

"I don't know what to think, Luis. I really do
know what's going on," I admitted, quite truthfully. "Y
play a lot of funny games with the horses down here a
I know why. It's because the purses are so small y
have to play some games to survive. Okay, I can b
that. Only I've never seen an operation like this o
where you don't even tell the trainer of your own ho
what kind of shit you're pulling. No wonder Sandy's
a drunk. How much did he lose on El Gato?"

"He don't bet. I tell him not to bet."

"So why was he so angry, then, if he was in on it?"

The Mexican didn't answer. I thought he might be measuring the distance between us, so I stayed on the alert. "It's because you did something to El Gato, right? You did something you weren't supposed to do," I continued. "That's what pissed Sandy off. You killed his horse."

"Mister, you got stupid ideas, you know that? You got a mouth on you."

"Look, I told you I don't give a damn what you guys do," I said, "so long as I'm in on the action. And remember, my name's the only one listed as the owner of Fred's Folly. Anything happens to me, Luis, and you might have some explaining to do, right?"

The silence danced in the air between us like a suspended blade. The fat Mexican stared at me out of his little pig eyes and then he shrugged again, affecting a vast nonchalance I was sure he didn't feel. "I don't give a fuck," he said. "You go now. You stop asking questions. Mellini, he don't like all these questions, man. You understand?"

"Sure. Anyway, Luis, it's always a pleasure to chat with you," I said. "Please remember, I like to be kept well informed. It's too bad about El Gato, but what the hell, it's only a horse, right?"

"He was one broken-down sonbitch," Luis said. "You go now."

"Sure. I'll see you at the races, Luis." I started to turn away just as the trainer suddenly propped himself up on one elbow and heaved his insides out all over the Mexican's lower trousers and expensive leather boots, then he collapsed again with a groan. Luis swore loudly and reached for a rag to wipe himself off. I left them there, two people obviously just made for each other.

Harry Dundee could dance a mean tango. The old man was the first person I saw when I walked into the bar on the ground floor of the Fiesta Americana. A small

orchestra was playing and several couples were out o
the floor, but it was Harry who immediately caught m
eye. His partner was a bone-thin woman in her seventi
who was dressed like a prom queen in a frilly purp
gown with a bouquet of orchids pinned to one shoulde
She had a skull-like face, her skin pulled tight from o
too many lifts, and her hair had been dyed black, but s
could dance. Actually, what she could do was follc
Harry, who had more moves out there than Ru
Valentino. He swerved and dipped and twirled I
partner with a reckless abandon that eventually su
ceeded in banishing everyone else back to their table
When they had finished, with one last whirling flash
spindly, varicosed legs and a backward dip that end
with the lady no more than six inches off the floor, h
back braced by Harry's right arm, I found mys
applauding, along with many of the other people in t
room.

Harry saw me and waved, then, when the orchest
launched into some soft rock, he led his partner off t
floor toward where I was standing. He was breathing
little hard, but seemed vastly pleased with hims€
"Well, hello there," he said as they came up to me,
want you to meet Marge. This gal's one hell of a dance

"I can see that," I said. "You guys ought to ente
contest."

"Aw, we don't do that anymore," Harry answere
"We just like to dance for the hell of it."

"Well, Harry, it was a revelation seeing you c
there."

"It took me a long time to get him to bring
here," Marge said. She had a high-pitched little vo
that seemed to be focused somewhere up inside I
sinuses. "He never wants to take me anywhere."

"That ain't true," Harry said. "Only women a
horses don't mix, and I come down here to play t
horses. Marge here lives at the park. Hey, Shifty, co
have a drink with us."

"I'm looking for a friend of mine and his lady, but they've probably left already," I explained. "Anyway, go ahead. I'll join you in a minute."

They made their way to a corner table, near the main lobby, and I took a look around the room. I didn't find Jay and Jill, so I came back and sat down with Fred and Ginger, intending to have one drink with them before pushing off for La Pulga and the hard-rock scene. "Well, how'd you do today?" Harry asked as I joined them.

I told him, though I left out of my account any reference to the El Gato fiasco. "The last race made me a winner," I said. "I'm having a lot of luck with it these days."

Harry laughed. "You're the king of the nightcap, Shifty," he declared. "Maybe you ought to pass all the other races and just wait for it."

"I've been thinking about that, Harry. How'd you do today?"

"Pretty good, pretty good." And he launched into a detailed account of his afternoon, which included an analysis of what he thought had gone amiss in the feature, his only losing wager of the day. He had it all wrong, but I let him ramble on because being able to talk about your action to a fellow horseplayer is one of the peripheral pleasures the game affords. Even if I hadn't been entertained by it, I'd have let him continue, because, as he talked, I saw Marisa and Mellini enter the hotel. The loan shark went to the front desk and picked up a room key, then they stepped into an elevator and disappeared from view.

"Harry, honey, why don't you order us a drink?" Marge suggested. "We're just sitting here, about to perish from thirst."

Harry beckoned a waiter over and ordered two beers for us and an Orange Blossom for Marge. "This damn woman can drink the both of us under the table," he said. "See them bones she's got on her? They're all hollow. It helps her to float pretty good too."

Marge giggled. "Harry picked me up at the pool one day, when I was with the Aquabelles."

"What's that?"

"A bunch of damn women get in the pool and do all these routines," Harry explained. "Like them old Esther Williams movies. Aw hell, it gives 'em somethin' to do."

"It's good exercise," Marge said. "This dirty old man used to come over and watch us and one day he just picks me up."

"Well, you don't want to go in the pool when them Aquabelles has been in there for a while," Harry said. "Godamighty, but the water ain't safe, with all them gals pissin' in it."

"Harry!" Marge exclaimed. "That's just terrible!"

"You know it's true," he continued. "They're in there a couple of hours and don't none of 'em ever come out to take a leak or nothin.' You do better just watchin' 'em or you could catch some disease."

"So you singled Marge out," I prodded him, while I kept an eye on the lobby.

"Not exactly," he said. "She saw me there and just threw them bones at me."

"He kept asking me to go to one of the dances with him," Marge said. "Finally, just to shut him up, I said I would."

"Well, you sure can dance together," I told them.

"Marge is about the best in the park," Harry said. "I already seen her dance there, so I knew what I was doin' when I asked her to come with me."

"We have a dance every Saturday night, with a live band," Marge said. "Only this old fool would rather come down here and spend his money at the races, so even if he comes home on Saturday night, he's too tired to go. So I had to get him to bring me down here."

"Well, you're both terrific. What do you do, Marge?"

"Me? Nothing. My husband passed away two years ago. He was a better dancer than Harry was even."

"Not likely," I said, "unless he was Fred Astaire."

"Aw, she's always sayin' I ain't as good as her husband was," Harry declared. "Ain't you noticed about women, how they's always makin' out how much better it was or it could have been if you hadn't of come along? Hell, she probably killed the poor son of a bitch by makin' him dance when he ought to have been lyin' down. Just livin' with a woman can kill a man. You notice how it's these women that live forever? They kill all the men off and get their money."

"I sure couldn't kill you off, you old fool," Marge said. "You're too darned ornery to die."

The orchestra began to play a samba, and Harry stood up. "Come on, honey, let's go fool some people," he said.

"I hear you."

They went out on the floor and began to dance again. If anything, they were even better at the samba than the tango, and they soon cleared the area of competitors. Old Harry danced like a man possessed, and Marge never failed to keep up with him and match his every move. I was so mesmerized by them that I failed to note the arrival of Larry Youkoumian, but when I glanced again toward the lobby, he was in the act of hanging up one of the house phones, after which he went over to a chair and sat down facing the elevator bank. Five minutes later, as Harry and Marge were heading back to our table, an elevator door opened and Mellini stepped out. Youkoumian got up and the two of them then headed toward the exit to the garage.

I stood up as Harry and Marge rejoined me. "I have to go, Harry," I said, dropping a couple of dollar bills on the table. "Thanks for your company."

"You goin' to the races tomorrow?" Harry asked.

"Is the Pope Catholic?"

"I guess that means you're goin'."

"You need a ride?"

"Naw, I'll go over with Walter. Come and sit with us."

"I'm going too," Marge said brightly. "They're going to let me go with them."

"*I* am," Harry corrected her. "Walter don't know nothin' about it and I ain't goin' to tell him. He'd raise holy hell with me."

"I'm going to be very good," Marge said. "I'm going to bet exactly what Harry tells me and I'm not going to ask any questions."

"If you don't keep quiet, honey, Walter's liable to pitch you over the railin' and I wouldn't want to see you get hurt."

I left them there, discussing the next day's arrangements, and went to the front desk. I asked for Mellini's room number and was told that it was 1102, then I went to one of the house phones. No one answered, so I got into an elevator and went up to the eleventh floor. I paused outside the door to 1102 and listened. At first I heard nothing, but then I thought I made out a sort of soft moaning. I rang the bell and the moaning stopped. I rang again and then knocked. Nothing. "Marisa," I said in a low but urgent voice, "Marisa, it's me, Shifty. Open up."

Nothing.

I went downstairs and waited until a party of half a dozen Mexicans came in carrying suitcases and headed, chattering, for the front desk. I joined them, as they were registering and talking, and got the attention of the youngest of the room clerks, a young woman I didn't think had noticed me earlier. "Eleven oh two, please," I said. She gave me the key without a moment's hesitation and I went back upstairs.

Ten minutes or so had passed, so I stopped to listen again, heard nothing, and rang. No answer, so I rang a second time and also knocked. Still no answer. I inserted the key in the lock and opened the door.

Marisa was lying facedown on the bed. She was naked and her hands had been bound with clothesline to the springs. I came up beside her and leaned down. Her face was bruised and swollen and one eye was nearly shut. "Marisa? It's me, Shifty."

At first I thought she hadn't heard me, but then she actually smiled. "You go, Shifty," she whispered. "He come back."

"What's he going to do, kill you?"

She laughed, but the sound of it was harsh and ugly in this room. "Is what he does," she said. "You go now, okay?"

"No, it's not okay." I went to my knees and began to untie her.

"Is a game for him, Shifty," she mumbled. "He don't know nothing else."

"Sure it's a game," I said, freeing one wrist and moving over to the other side of the bed to undo the other one. "To Mellini maybe it's all a game and killing people is foreplay. Does he pay you for this?"

"What you think?" she asked. "I tell him no, but he don't listen. Go away, Shifty."

I finished untying her, but she continued to lie there on her stomach. I took her by the shoulders and tried to help her up. To my surprise, she held on to the mattress and wouldn't let me. "Marisa, sex for money is one thing, but you want to get beaten up?" I said. "You don't have to do this. Come on, I'll take you home."

She turned her head away from me and continued to lie there, so I sat down on the bed beside her and put my hand on her shoulder. "Listen, it's okay," I said. "I know about you. I didn't know the other night, but I know now, okay? And I'm not angry at you. Really."

She lay there for a moment longer, then, with a groan, she pulled herself up on one elbow, swung her legs over the side of the bed, and sat up, leaning forward on her arms. I couldn't see the full extent of her injuries, but I could tell that she had been really worked over.

Her neck was also bruised and there were several small cuts on her breasts and stomach, as if inflicted by a very sharp razor blade. She was too dizzy to stand up and it was hurting her even to sit. The sheet where she had been lying was bloodstained.

"Jesus," I whispered. "Come on, let me help you." I looked around the room and found her clothes. They had apparently been torn off her and were lying scattered about the floor. I retrieved them and brought them to her. "Come on, Marisa."

"No," she said. "You go, Shifty. You go now, quick."

"I'm going to get you out of here. Let's go." I went into the bathroom, found a washcloth, soaked it in cold water, and came back to the bed. I sat down next to her. "Here, this will help. Then we're going to get dressed and get out of here."

She pressed the cloth to her face and groaned, then put it to her swollen lips and peered over it at me. "I'm sorry," she said, "I'm sorry. I don't want to fool you. You nice to me." She began to cry.

I picked up her panties and handed them to her. "Come on, Marisa, before he comes back. Where'd he go?"

She shook her head. "I don't know," she said. "The phone ring and he go downstairs. He say he come back."

"Get dressed, let's go. Can I help you?"

"No, is okay. I'm okay."

The tears continued to run down her face, but she slowly eased her legs into her panties and began to pull them up. She was having a tough time, so I helped her. And as I did so, I had to accept the irrefutable evidence of her residual masculinity; she had the tiny, limp penis of an adolescent boy.

"You make love to a man, huh, Shifty," she mumbled. "Is first time, huh?"

"No, Marisa, you made love to me," I said. "I wouldn't have let you if I'd known."

"You sorry, huh?"

"No. Anyway, you're not a man, are you? You want to be a woman and you are, except in a technical sense. I understand now what you were doing with me at that nightclub. You could have told me directly, couldn't you?"

"Sure, sure," she whispered, "but I like you. I want to make love to you. You don't let me, if you know. Right, Shifty?"

"Right. It's nothing personal, Marisa."

She laughed. "No, nothing personal," she said. "You funny, Shifty."

I finally got her to her feet and helped her into the bathroom, where she washed herself off. It took another ten minutes to finish getting her dressed, then, with her leaning heavily on my arm, we made our way downstairs and across the street to the Conquistador. "Does he know where you live, Marisa?" I asked her once we were inside the courtyard. "You want to stay here tonight?"

"No, is all right," she said. "I go home."

"I'll drive you."

"No, is all right. You call a taxi."

"I'll drive you. Is it far?"

She shook her head, so I helped her into my car and got in beside her. "Where to?"

"*La Zona Norte*," she said. "Is not far."

We drove back toward the center of town, then, following Marisa's instructions, I took an avenue paralleling Revolución, heading north toward the border. The road was off the tourist beat, through a dingy-looking neighborhood of small stores, cafés, nightclubs, and tumbledown apartment houses. At First Street, or Calle 1, I turned left and up several blocks to Avenida Gonzalez Ortega. "I get out here," she said. "Is right there."

"You sure? I don't want to leave you in the street."

"I'm sure. I'm okay."

I pulled over and helped her out of the car. She leaned against it for a moment, as if to get her balance.

Her face looked puffy and blue. "Come on, I'll take you inside," I said.

"Shifty, you stay, *testarudo*. Is right there." She smiled, her white teeth gleaming in the darkness. "One day I be a real woman for you, Shifty. I get the money and I become a woman for you."

"I guess I'd like that, Marisa, but I'm not sure I can wait for you."

"That's why I come here, you know," she said. "In Tijuana there is many of us. Is one place to make money."

"Meanwhile, you better stay away from the bad guys."

"Oh, Rico, he's a sick man. You be careful, Shifty." She put a hand up to my face. "You be careful. He can be so bad."

"You should know."

"He pay me much money, but I tell him no more, only he don't listen. Is like with the horses, he do what he wants. Is like everything. And now there is this other thing."

"What other thing, Marisa?"

She shook her head violently. "No, I don't tell you. You don't ask, Shifty, please."

"And what does he do with the horses, Marisa? He seems to move them around a lot. Is it drugs?"

"I don't know, Shifty. He don't tell me and is better you don't ask, okay? He kill us both." She pushed herself away from the car and began to walk shakily toward a small, whitewashed two-story building about a third of the way up the block. There were no streetlights, but there was a three-quarter moon and I could follow her progress. I waited until I saw her open a gate and disappear into an interior courtyard before I got back into my car and drove away toward Revolución.

La Pulga turned out to be a narrow three-story building that literally seemed to be throbbing to the sound of a decibel count high enough to drown out an artillery barrage. At least a couple of hundred people, mostly teenagers, were pressed against one another under a whirling kaleidoscope of multicolored lights and bobbing up and down on dance floors that were too small to give them any room to do anything but move perpendicularly, while several hundred others packed the bars or lined the walls, waiting for an opening to find their own jumping space. It took me about ten minutes to push my way in and another ten or so to find my friends. Jay and Jill had commandeered a corner of their own on the top floor, where Jay mostly stood stolidly in place as Jill shook. The handicapper looked relieved to see me, as if I had arrived barely in time to rescue him. He took Jill's hand and pulled her off the floor toward me.

"Having fun?" I shouted.

"No!" Jay yelled back. "Let's get the hell out of here!"

"Hey, what's the matter with you guys?" Jill screamed. "It's early!"

"You want to go to deaf?" Jay bellowed. "Come on!"

We pushed our way out into the street and found a relatively quiet bar a couple of doors away, where we settled into a booth and ordered beers.

"You guys," Jill said, "what a bunch of deadheads! I was just workin' up a good sweat."

She looked incredibly desirable, her skin glowing from the exercise, making her seem almost naked in her blouse and miniskirt. I tried to think pure thoughts; after all, she was with my closest friend.

"Jay don't even dance," Jill said. "He just stands there."

"I do what I can," the handicapper declared. "You can't move in there. It's like the Black Hole of Calcutta. And my ears are full of stones now."

"What?" I asked. "What did you say?"

"See what I mean?"

"Oh, you guys," Jill grumbled, "if it ain't somethin'

to do with horses and bettin' and all like that, you ain't even interested."

"What took you so long, Shifty?" Jay asked. "Another five minutes and both my eardrums would have ruptured."

I told them what I'd been up to, though I left out the bloodier details and the delicate matter of Marisa's sexual status, and it changed the tenor of the conversation. "I don't think I want to be partners with these people, Jay," I concluded my account of the evening's festivities. "Not only are they a couple of scumsuckers, but they're surely up to something really illegal. I'm talking about fixing races, I'm talking about dope."

"I can't believe they killed that horse," Jill said. "Sandy wouldn't do that. He wasn't too sound, so Miguel's probably right."

"What makes you think they're running drugs?" Jay asked.

"Why are they spending so much time down here? Just to cash a big ticket?"

"Sure. We know they're playing games," Jay agreed. "That's what we're doing here too. We're trying to get in on it so we can recoup what Fingers owes us. Isn't that what we're doing?"

"And get Emile and his bullyboy and Bud and his rotten kid off your case, right. But this is heavy stuff, Jay, and it's my name that's listed as the owner of the horse."

"So what? What do you know? Nothing. Anyway, what makes you think they're into drugs?"

"I've got a long nose," I said. "And there's a lot of movement back and forth."

"What do you mean?"

"Across the border, Jay. These guys are moving two and three horses a week, maybe more, over and back."

"What about it? It happens all the time, Shifty. Everybody moves horses around. If you got a cheap horse, it costs a lot less to stay down here and ship up and back to Hollywood Park or Santa Anita."

"And with them kind of horses," Jill cut in, "you can't even get stall space at Hollywood or Santa Anita. You ain't got no choice. You got to ship up and back."

The explanation made sense, but it didn't convince me. "I'm going to do a little checking," I said. "I just don't like the smell of it."

"Just hang on," Jay urged me. "Jill's been telling me Hatch is sure to run Fred's Folly in a week or at most two. He'll be going for it then."

"How do you know?"

"He'll have to," Jill said. "The horse ain't got but one or two races in him. And he ain't goin' to sprint him again. It wouldn't make no sense. He'll run him long and try to get one big move out of him."

"And that's where we bail out," Jay said. "Once we get our money out, Shifty, we can walk away from this."

"And if Hatch puts Camacho up, we don't even know if we'll get an honest race out of him. Jesus Christ, Jay."

"They'll pay him to ride honest," Jay assured me.

"Say, you better get me home," Jill said. "I ain't workin' horses tomorrow, but I *am* ridin'."

"Yeah? What race?"

"The nightcap," she said. "He ain't much, but I can maybe pick up a piece of the purse with him."

We finished our beers and left. I told Jay I'd meet him the next day in the Foreign Book, an hour or so before post time, and headed off down a side street toward my car. The nearest lots on Revolución had all been full, so I'd had to park a couple of streets away, at the corner of a small shopping center full of little stores catering mostly to middle-class Mexican customers. I had figured the car would be safe there, at least for a couple of hours, since the action was all up on Revolución and no one would be expecting an American to wander away from the hub at that hour of the night.

It was a serious miscalculation. I had just inserted the key into the door lock when I heard someone coming rapidly toward me, apparently from one of the shadowy storefronts. I started to turn my head to see who it was, but realized immediately that I was under attack and had no time. As the man approached me, I stepped to one side, bent down on my left leg, and lashed out with my right one. I was lucky. The kick caught him at knee height from the side and took his legs out from under him. He fell heavily, striking his head against the metal fender of a battered pickup truck parked directly behind me. It was dark and I couldn't see him clearly, but he was a large man and obviously very strong. Despite the fact that he was stunned from the blow, he immediately began to push himself up. He was on his knees when I hit him a second time, this kick catching him just behind the ear and sending him crashing into the hood of the truck. He grunted and fell forward on his face.

I briefly contemplated giving him one more shot to the head, but decided against it. The most prudent course of action was to remove myself from the scene, so I scrambled into my car, started up the engine, and gunned out into the street. As I drove away, I glanced up into my rearview mirror. My assailant had hauled himself to his feet and was leaning heavily over the hood of the pickup. I couldn't see his face, but his hair, I realized with a start, was blond.

Twelve

NUMBERS

I love the smell of a racetrack in the early morning. It's a scent compounded of warm horseflesh, hay and straw, manure, the barnyard blends of small animals— chickens, goats, dogs, cats—the occasional elusive whiff of hot coffee, the aromas of grass and earth, of dust hanging in the air. It's an atmosphere in which I can bask for hours, preferably leaning against a rail, with the spectacle of the horses before me and the sun warm on my back. Time spent in this manner, I've discovered, can help to banish the ugliness of recent events, soften the effects of even the most catastrophic failures. It puts me in touch with a primal source inside myself, as if by blending into such an uncomplicated scene I can recapture my own lost innocence. There is, too, the near mystical beauty of the animal itself, serene within the simplicity of its being, existing in the small, self-contained world it ennobles by its presence, incorruptible, impervious even to human chicanery. Hanging out at racetracks in the morning has become a form of therapy for me, an odd one, I admit, but one that seems to work.

At least it did that Sunday morning. By the time Jill came by where I was standing, at the gap through which the horses come onto the main track from the stable area, I was feeling at peace with myself, unworried even by my involvement as a horse owner with such an unsavory duo as Mellini and Youkoumian. Anyway, I had formulated a plan of action. All I needed was a couple of more pieces of information, though I wasn't sure at that point who could tell me what I needed to know.

"Hi there," Jill called out as she came trotting up beside me. Dressed in jeans, riding boots, a sleeveless T-shirt, and a protective helmet, she looked not only adorable, as always, but every inch the professional horsewoman. She was mounted on a lean, skittish bay colt who kept tossing his head up and down, fighting the tight hold she had on him, as we talked. "You're up early."

"I like to get up early," I said. "You working this horse?"

"I just breezed him," she said. "He's about a month away."

"Two-year-old?"

"Yeah, soon turnin' three, on January one. He don't know what this is all about yet." She patted the animal's neck, trying to settle him down. "He's pretty green still. Wants to run all out all the time, gets himself all worked up, burns himself up. They may have to cut him."

"Who is he?"

"Name's Collin's Gem. He ain't much, but he could be a useful sort, if he ever settles down."

"So how's old Fred?"

"Doin' good. Went nice and easy this mornin'. He's gettin' the message, Shifty. Sure is too bad he's bowed."

"What message?"

"About racin'. These old studs, they get kind of lazy, but he's goin' to be ready."

"Was Hatch there?"

"Yeah, lookin' like death. I asked him why he ain't puttin' me up on nothin'."

"What did he say?"

"He ain't talkin' much today," she said. "He must have really tied one on last night."

"I guess he did."

"You know that horse I'm on today, Troubador?"

"Yeah?"

"I've decided I'm goin' to win with that sucker. You can bet on it."

"I may just do that, Jill."

"See you, Shifty." And she moved away from me, standing high in the stirrups, her tight little body poised above the animal like an emblem of grace in action.

I lingered at my post for another ten minutes or so, then pushed myself away and headed back toward my car, which I had parked up behind the stable office. I didn't want to go by our barn, because I had had just about enough of my sleazy partners for this particular weekend, so I made a long loop around by the pony track, then back along by the test barn and the detention enclosure. Another group of horses was being loaded into a van for the trip north. I didn't see anyone I recognized, but as I nosed the Datsun along the dirt road I caught a glimpse of Youkoumian's big gray Continental parked by the feed store.

Jay seemed only mildly interested in what I had to say about my morning activities. He had his charts and his notebooks spread out on a table facing a TV monitor in the Foreign Book, and his eyes were on the screen showing horses being loaded into a starting gate in Philadelphia. "I got a nice double going, Shifty," he said. "If the five horse wins, I'm looking at a five-hundred-dollar payoff."

The five horse popped the gate and had the lead all the way to the sixteenth pole, but got caught by the favorite in the race and finished second. Jay grunted his displeasure, but decided to make the best of it. He'd had a saver bet on the winner, which brought him a small profit, so he had not too much to complain about. "Get us some coffee, will you, Shifty," he asked. "I've got to make some notes."

"I liked it better when we were racing in L.A.," I told him. "Down here the only gofer you've got is me."

"I'm the statistician, I keep my finger on the

numbers," he said. "An onerous task, but somebody's got to do it."

When I came back with two plastic containers full of weak but hot liquid, he was hunched over one of his books, scanning a long column of figures for the answer to who knows what arcane horse riddle. I set his cup in front of him and sat down beside him. "Emile's bullyboy tried to nail me last night," I said.

"What?" He looked up at me, startled. "Emile's what?"

I told him about being attacked as I was getting into my car. "I think it may have been this guy Castle."

"Couldn't be."

"No? Big guy, well dressed, blond hair."

"Did he have a scar?"

"I couldn't tell."

"It can't be him."

"Why not? Emile probably figured out we were down here."

"There are lots of big guys with blond hair, Shifty. It was probably some dude trying to rip you off."

"What was he doing in that part of town?" I asked. "He had to have followed me. Do I look like I carry a lot of money on me? Does the Datsun convey an impression of wealth on the loose?"

"I don't get it," he said, looking suddenly very preoccupied. "What would he accomplish by beating you up?"

"Or maybe killing me."

"Yeah, it doesn't make any sense. I'd have recognized this guy if he showed up at the track, which is the first place he'd look for us." He took a long sip from his coffee, then shook his head. "No, it can't be Castle," he said. "It must be some guy who saw us at La Pulga, saw us leave, saw you go off alone toward a fairly deserted part of town and figured he could knock you over for a few hundred bucks. Nothing else makes any sense, Shifty."

"I'm inclined to agree with you," I answered, "but I still think it may have been Castle. I think he may also have been at the Encanto the other night with Mellini, when I went to hear Marisa sing. There was a big blond guy at their table. I didn't pay much attention, but it could have been him."

"This is incredible," Jay said. "You better be careful. We'll keep an eye out today at the track. If he's around, we'll see him."

"Unless he's hurting too much."

"Yeah, what about that?" Jay looked at me in amazement. "Where'd you learn to defend yourself like that, Shifty?"

"I bought a book on self-defense. I've been in a lot of action the last couple of years, and I thought I ought to know something."

"You studied martial arts?"

"No. I read this book and I took a course. It was taught by the woman who wrote the book," I said. "She's a little blond lady who could probably break you in half. I was the only guy in her class."

"It was a course for women?"

"Yes."

"But why?"

"Because I'm not a jock and I'm not exactly physically overwhelming," I said. "Women's self-defense stresses avoidance, indirection, escape, the oblique attack, all techniques I use in magic. I thought it was the right course for me. But I never thought I'd have to use it."

"It seems you did pretty well."

"I was surprised," I admitted. "But I wouldn't want this guy to catch up to me again. Watch yourself, Jay."

He folded his arms against his chest and sat back in his chair. "I don't like it, Shifty," he said. "I don't like it at all. But I still maintain it doesn't make any sense. It can't be Castle. He'd have come after *me*."

"You weren't alone and you didn't stray from a

crowded area. I did," I argued. "Who knows what's going on in Emile's head? But you know what I find really strange about all this?"

"No, what?"

"Emile seems to be going to an awful lot of trouble for what amounts to a few thousand bucks," I said. "I mean, he must make a lot more than that with his porn movies and whatever else he's into. Why all this vindictiveness, if that's what it is, over being stiffed for a few bucks?"

"Good question, Shifty, but you don't know Emile. He's a mean prick who doesn't like to be taken, even for small change. He's got the personality of a cobra."

"Nice business associates you picked, Jay. Very nice."

"I didn't pick them. They picked me."

"Next thing you know, Bud's kid and his motorcycle punkers will come down here after us." I stood up. "Anyway, I'm probably going up to L.A. tonight or tomorrow."

"Good idea. Stay up there if you want. I can take care of things down here. But why are you going?"

"Oh, I've got things to take care of. And I want to check with Hal to see if there's any work in the offing. I forgot to leave a number or to activate my answering machine. I'll be back by the weekend, if not sooner."

"Don't worry about anything," Jay assured me. "I'll let you know if the horse is entered."

"Okay." I started out toward the parking lot. "See you at the races. By the way, did Jill tell you? She thinks she can win the nightcap with Troubador."

Jay shook his head sadly, like a Pope being informed that one of his cardinals can walk on water. "No chance," he said. "That pig is one for thirty-seven lifetime. All the other horses would have to fall down for him to win."

"You still don't believe in miracles, do you?"

"Numbers, Shifty, I believe in numbers."

* * *

"Yeah, and if a frog had wings, he wouldn't have to wear his ass out hopping," Walter said as the horses for the first race jogged past us on their way to the post.

"What's agitating your friend?" I asked, sitting down behind them in the box. "And where's Marge?"

"I told Walter here the four horse could win if he could somehow get himself out of the gate on time," Harry explained.

"Of course he hasn't been able to do that in fourteen tries," Walter observed, "but Harry doesn't let facts stand in the way of hope."

"That's one of the things I like about Harry," I said. "Did Marge come along today?"

"Oh, hell yes," Harry answered. "She's over there gettin' us some stuff. Been waitin' on us hand and foot all mornin'. She don't want old Walter here to get mad at her."

"She's a nice woman," Walter said, "very pleasant to have around."

"I thought you wouldn't mind, Walter."

"Just don't bring her again."

"Who am I going to root for?" I asked. "Anybody make a bet here?"

"Ain't nothin' to bet," Harry said. "This is a bunch of professional maidens."

"Dogs," Walter added, "every one of them."

Marge came back to the box carrying coffee and pastries just before the race went off and sat demurely behind her men, next to me, while the animals did their thing. The four horse broke last, as usual, and made a belated run down the lane that brought him in third, only two lengths behind the winner. "See?" Harry said. "If he could only get out of the gate. Maybe he needs to go long."

Walter snorted contemptuously and jabbed at the horse's record in his *Racing Form*. "They tried stretching him out to a mile twice already and he dies," he said.

"This is your classic bad closing sprinter. He's never going to break his maiden."

"That's so sad," Marge said. "Can't something be done about helping him? Perhaps find a race just fifty yards longer for him?"

Walter grabbed his coffee and stood up. He shot Marge a savage glance, as if she had suggested he perform some unspeakable act in public, and stormed out of the box. Harry turned to look at her. "Honey, I told you not to say nothin'. Now you got him all riled up."

"But what did I say?" she asked.

"If there's one thing Walter can't stand at the races, it's damn fool questions."

"Perfectly sensible observation, I thought," I said. "They ought to write special races for the very worst horses."

"Like the Special Olympics for disadvantaged people," Marge added brightly. "That way everyone gets a chance to win."

"Marge, don't say nothin' to Walter about that when he comes back," Harry told her. "He might jump off the roof of the grandstand."

Walter returned to the box just before the next race, but left again the minute it was over. He repeated this tactic for the next several races, and it became clear to us that he intended to spend the day as far away from Marge as possible. He would consent to sit with us only during the running of the race itself, when he could be reasonably certain that Marge would not give in to the temptation to make an observation. "He don't want his mind contaminated," Harry explained as Walter bolted for the fourth time. "He says he can't think right if the people around him is sayin' dumb things."

"Honestly, that's ridiculous," Marge commented. "A person has a right to ask something if she don't know it, don't she?"

"Well, that's the way Walter is. You got to take him as he is or just forget about him."

"But where does he go?" I asked.

"Oh, he's got friends he can sit with."

"Walter has friends?" Marge asked. "Who'd put up with the old coot except for you?"

"Most times he sits by himself, all right," Harry said. "He tolerates me, but sometimes I make him mad, too, and he just goes off somewhere, disappears till he gets it all straightened out in his head. He's a character, Walter is. I don't mind him. He's a good handicapper."

"But not such a great human being," Marge observed. "Well, I'm going to make a bet." She pointed toward the track, where a line of horses was again filing past us out of the paddock. "See that one with the cute face and the jockey all in yellow? I'm betting on that one. It's seven, my lucky number." And she left, presumably to wager two dollars on a lightly raced three-year-old named Briarpatch ridden by Lupe Camacho.

"You know, I kind of like that horse," I said, looking at my *Racing Form.* "He's got some speed and I think he's coming up to a good one. He was a little short last time. He'll be tighter today and maybe Camacho can hold him together."

"By God, I think you got somethin'," Harry agreed. He glanced up at the board, where Briarpatch was showing odds of eight to one. "Price is right, but let's wait. With Camacho up on him, the odds'll drop, if he's live."

"Good suggestion," I said. "Shall we tell Walter, when he comes back?"

"I wouldn't if I was you. If he ain't thought of it himself, it'll just piss him off if the horse wins."

No sooner had Marge come back with her ticket than the odds on Briarpatch began to drop. With two minutes left, he was listed at nine to two. Harry and I both got up to go and bet on him just as Walter came back. "Where you going?" he asked.

"We're going to bet a little money on Briarpatch," I said. "He looks live."

"Maybe," Walter agreed grudgingly, "but you aren't going to get a price. He'll be favored by post time."

"Maybe not, Walter," Harry said. "There's a couple of solid horses in here. Anyway, if he drops below five to two, I ain't bettin' him."

Briarpatch went off at seven to two, the third choice in the race, at a flat mile, and Harry and I both wagered on him to win and place. When we returned to our seats, Walter informed us that we had made a dumb bet. "One of the favorites is going to run first or second for sure and place isn't going to pay anything," he declared. "You should have bet him straight or passed the race, like I did."

"Oh, that's so boring," Marge declared. "I bet two dollars on him to win and also an Exacta with that other cute horse, the gray one. Three is my other lucky number, three and seven. I took both of them in the Exacta, so I win if they finish first and second to each other, right?"

"That's right, honey," Harry said. "So you spent six dollars? That's a lot for you, Marge. That's like a thousand dollars for old Walter here."

"I just loved the way they looked and those *are* my lucky numbers," Marge said. "I just know I'm going to win."

Walter sat there like a stone, his arms folded firmly across his chest and his eyes focused on the starting gate, where the horses were now being loaded into their stalls and stood poised against the barriers, ready to burst out into the clear. I knew that Walter was looking forward to enjoying our loss, so I turned to Marge. "Now, come on, Marge," I instructed her, "we have to root our horse in. If we don't root, he may not run."

"Oh, really? Golly, I'm so excited!" She was holding her ticket with both hands clasped in front of her, as if it were a crucifix, and she sat straight up in her chair, her face aglow with excitement. She suddenly looked twenty years younger and I saw the beautiful woman she had once been.

We turned out to be right about Briarpatch. Camacho broke him alertly out of the gate and took the lead around the first turn, while saving ground along the rail and not allowing his mount to run too fast too early, thus using himself up on the pace. On the far turn, however, he asked Briarpatch for his speed and the horse opened up three lengths on the field by the head of the stretch. Marge was screaming with excitement, jumping up and down in her seat, and exhorting her favorite to bestir himself. "Come on, Patchy, come on!" she shrieked. "You can do it! Come on, baby! Come on, sweetie! Patchy! Patchy! Patchy!"

I thought Walter might have a stroke. He sat there like a statue, refusing even to look at the race through his binoculars, his face a frozen mask of disapproval. He perked up briefly when Harry announced that Briarpatch, now halfway down the lane, had begun to tire, but relapsed into a state of near shock when he realized that the horse closing determinedly on the outside was not one of the two favorites but Marge's lightly regarded gray, a longshot named Furious Billy. "Get up there, Billy!" Marge screamed. "Come on now, you can do it! Come on, Patchy! Hang in there! Come on, my honeys, come on! Oh, Lordy, Lordy, come on home to Mommy!"

Furious Billy caught Briarpatch in the last jump, beating him by a head. There was an official photo called for to make sure, but we all knew who had won. The longshot had gone off at sixteen to one, which meant that our place bets on Briarpatch would pay a little better than even money to compensate for our losses on the win bet, but Marge's two-dollar Exacta figured to return a payoff of about a hundred and fifty dollars. Walter did not stick around to find out. He rose to his feet, shot Marge a single grim look of pure disgust, and again left the box. "What's the matter with him?" she asked. "It ain't his money, is it?"

"No, honey, but Walter can't stand it when things don't go the way he thinks they ought to go," Harry explained. "It's just pitiful, ain't it?"

"I think what happened is that the horses heard Marge rooting for them," I observed. "They never would have run this well otherwise. You're a terrific rooter, Marge."

She smiled sweetly, then shrieked and clapped her hands with joy as the tote board first flashed the official order of finish, then, a couple of minutes later, the payoffs showing that her Exacta was worth $147.60, while the place on Briarpatch paid $4.80. "Oh, my gosh," Marge exclaimed, "isn't that wonderful? Oh, honey, I can buy that new dress I wanted so bad! Oh, my gosh!" And she jumped to her feet and rushed out of the box to cash her ticket.

"Take it easy, Marge!" Harry called after her. "They ain't goin' to run out of money to pay you!"

Walter did not come back to the box until just before the feature. He reappeared this time with a copy of the *San Diego Union* under his arm and sat down in his seat to read it, as if completely indifferent to the outcome of the races. He had even discarded his *Form*, I noticed, and was paying little or no attention to anything having to do with the movement of money. Marge prudently kept her mouth shut and Harry, grinning hugely, simply turned around in his chair and winked at us. I smiled back, but I couldn't resist the temptation. "Cashing any tickets, Walter?" I asked.

"Nothing to bet," he said. "On days like this I just pass them by."

"Really? We've cashed a couple of little tickets here, haven't we, Harry?"

"Oh, sure," Harry said, "but Walter's right, there ain't much to bet on."

"I just pick them by looks or their numbers," Marge

said, "but I'm not betting anything else today. I want that dress, Harry."

"How about the last race?" I asked. "You like Troubador?"

Walter snorted derisively. "A horse that has won one race in thirty-seven starts and ridden by a girl? You think that's a good bet?"

"She thinks she's going to win it."

"They all think they're going to win," Walter said. "You might as well start digging a hole in the ground and hope to reach China by morning as try to win a race with that kind of logic. I'm here to win money."

"How can you do that, if you never make a bet?" Marge asked.

"Walter ain't never lost any bet he ever made," Harry said. "That's how come he's always in such a good humor."

I thought Walter might bolt again under this on-slaught, but this time he decided to affect a vast indifference to our struggles with the parimutuel machines. He sat quietly in place, humming tunelessly to himself, as Harry and I turned our attention to the feature race and tried to come up with a winner. We settled on the favorite this time, but decided to pass the race because the odds on him were sure to be too low. It was the only decision we'd made all day that Walter approved of. When the horse came in a badly beaten third, he turned to us and said, "See? You can't play those kinds of horses. You never know whose turn it is. I'm just sitting here now because Harry wants to stay. He doesn't know any better." And he calmly went back to reading his paper.

I spent the next couple of races with Jay in the Turf Club, where he had settled himself at a front-row table directly over the finish line. The handicapper was not too pleased with the way the day had turned out for him and, like Walter, he had decided to wrap it up for the afternoon. He wasn't planning to risk even a token bet on Jill's plodder in the nightcap, but was hanging around merely to please her. "After which we are going to have a quiet dinner somewhere and I'm going to let her have the old diamond cutter," he announced.

I winced. "I don't think I want to hear about you and Jill, thank you."

"Oh, sorry about that, Shifty. I keep forgetting you have designs on her yourself."

"Had, old buddy, had. But I really do like her."

"So do I. By the way, whatever happened to that Mexican working girl—"

"A brief romance," I cut in, "and all too one-sided."

"Too bad."

"Any sign of Castle?" I was eager to change the subject.

"No. You?"

I shook my head and ordered a margarita from a passing waiter. Ordinarily, I don't drink at the track, because booze clouds the mind and you have to stay alert to win, but I felt the need. Something about the way the day was turning out, or perhaps it was Jay's casually carnal attitude toward this woman I liked, was bothering me. Why would she have selected him, when he obviously cared so little for her? All right, he had these macho good looks, all those muscles garnered from years of hustling suckers on public tennis courts, but I fancied myself as a man of vast and worldly charm. I could make cards dance, coins change denominations, pluck objects out of the air, dazzle the world with misdirection, illusion, and smart patter. Why him? Why not me? I sipped my drink glumly for two races, while Jay calmly went about his tedious routine of constructing towers of logic out of an ephemera of small, seemingly unrelated facts. In his own idiosyncratic way he was more of a magician than I was.

Twenty minutes before post time for the nightcap, I stood up. "Are you coming?" I asked.

"No," he answered. "The horse has almost no

chance and I have some work still to do. I'll see you later. Want to join us for dinner?"

"I'm going to pack up and head north," I said. "I'll be back Thursday or Friday. Watch yourself. I still think that was Castle last night."

"Yeah, I will, Shifty. Take care," he said. "Stay up there if you want to. I'll call you if I hear anything."

I left him to his numbers and went down to the paddock. By the time I got there, the horses were already out in the ring and the jockeys were drifting in by twos and threes from their nearby quarters. Jill was standing by her mount, a big, bony five-year-old chestnut with an ugly mulish head and what appeared to be the disposition of a duckbilled platypus. I couldn't imagine him winning anything, an impression shared evidently by everyone else, because his odds were thirty to one. I decided not to risk more than two dollars on him, and then only because Jill was riding him. There has to be some room, but not much, for sentiment in racing.

She saw me standing by the rail and waved smilingly to me, then turned to confer with the trainer, an ancient Anglo man wearing an old gray overcoat that came nearly down to his ankles and a battered old brown cap tilted forward over his eyes. He leaned over Jill and patted her lightly on the shoulder, then stood calmly beside his horse, waiting for the paddock judge to call out, "Riders up!"

I looked at my program. His name was Jim Felton and he had been around for years, an old Gypsy horseman of the kind that has spent a lifetime chasing small pots at the end of tinsel rainbows with animals that can't run. Once, about twenty years earlier, I remembered, he had had a good horse, a fragile speedball that had won a couple of stakes before breaking down, and he had survived since then on dreams, tight-fisted owners, and small purses. I decided I'd bet five dollars on Troubador across the board, just because I'm ornery

enough to want the Jim Feltons of this world to win one
every now and then. And also because I had an indefen-
sible hunch; Jill, in her tight white pants, black boots,
dark green checked silks, with her long blond hair pulled
back into a golden ponytail, looked every inch a winner
to me. I told myself I was betting on her, not the horse.

When the animals headed out onto the track, Jill
leaned over Troubador's neck and gave him a big,
affectionate pat, then waved her stick at me and rode out
onto the main oval. I looked at Felton. Hands thrust into
his overcoat pockets, he was shambling back toward the
stands. I fell into step beside him. "Mr. Felton? I'm Lou
Anderson, friend of Jill's."

The old man glanced sideways at me, his small
brown eyes shadowed by the visor of his cap. "How are
you?" he answered.

"Pretty good, thanks. Jill thinks you're going to win
this one."

The old man grinned, revealing the yellowed last
survivors of a lifelong struggle against the ravages of
nicotine and alcohol. "She say that? I'll be darned," he
said. "She sure is a nice kid."

"I'm glad you're using her," I said. "She can really
ride."

"I guess she can," Felton said. "Leastways I can
count on her to give me an honest one. Had a fella last
week, he pulls my horse out of the gate, darn near
strangles him, then he comes around to the barn the
next morning and he says to me, 'Mr. Felton, I'd like to
take your horse back.' You know what I said to him?"

"I can guess."

"I asked him, 'How far back do you want to take
him?'"

I laughed. "I just wanted to wish you luck," I said.

"We'll need it," the old man answered. "This old
sucker's just another horse. Can't run much, but he
keeps on coming. He pays his stable bills and that's
about it. I wouldn't bet much on him."

We parted and I went back to the box to find that my friends had left. There was a note on Harry's seat. "Walter wanted to beat the traffic and Marge didn't bet, so we'll see you next weekend. Harry." I glanced up at the board. Troubador was forty to one. I went to the betting window, bought my ticket, came back and sat down, feeling more than a little foolish. I couldn't remember ever having bet more than five dollars on any horse at forty to one.

In fact, I began to waver. Twice I rose up out of my seat, intending to go and turn my ticket in for a smaller one, but each time I made myself sit down again. What the hell, I reasoned, I was fourteen dollars ahead on the day, so I might as well go home a one-dollar loser. Three minutes before the race I decided to switch chairs, for luck, and I moved into the front row of the box, into Harry's seat. And, as I sat down, I happened to glance at the Sunday papers Walter had left behind. Right there, on the front cover of something called "The Arts" section, was a photograph of Emile Legrand.

He was not alone in the picture, but he was the central figure in it. A serious-looking young man holding a pamphlet or a program of some sort stood on his left, and a beaming, middle-aged couple, apparently local patrons of the arts, lounged on his right. Emile, unsmiling but obviously very satisfied with himself, was staring straight ahead into the lens. Everyone was elegantly attired, the men in dinner jackets, the lady in a long white dress with a mink stole casually draped around her patrician neck. The caption identified Emile as an independent movie producer and the owner of a number of the important pre-Columbian artifacts on display at the Ferrara Gallery, in downtown San Diego. "Here, with Mimsy and Lane Dark, and Neal Brown, curator of the exhibit, Mr. Legrand discusses the cultural significance of the collection, which will be on view through the Christmas holidays." I riffled quickly through the section to see if there was an accompanying story, but

couldn't find one. I reread the caption again, then tore
the picture out and stuffed it into my pocket.

"They're off!" the track announcer suddenly barked
as a bell rang and the starting gate popped open. "And
it's Wiseguy going to the front, with Pablo's Boy and
Nerone on the outside, Two Cities on the rail and Mr.
Collier also right there. Into the turn they go . . ."

It wasn't hard to find Troubador. As usual, he was
lagging early and Jill had moved him over to the inside
as the animals went around the clubhouse turn. He was
last in the ten-horse field, at least fifteen lengths behind
the leaders, when the horses reached the straightaway. I
didn't even bother to raise my glasses, because I had no
trouble seeing exactly where he was—already hopelessly
out of it and galloping clumsily along all by himself. I
wrote off my fifteen dollars.

I did note, however, that the pace was pretty fast for
such cheapos, with the leaders locked into a three-horse
duel, going all out. Someone would win the race from off
the pace. At the three-eighths pole, several of the
trailers began to close some ground, including Troubador. Jill kept her nag on the rail, still saving real estate,
but eight or nine lengths out of it as the field moved
around the second turn. I picked up my binoculars when
I realized I had a chance, perhaps, to finish in the
money.

At the California tracks, the jockeys ride tight
around the turns. You can't afford to lose ground on the
outside at these mile ovals, but in Mexico the fields tend
to spread out, because the riders aren't as skilled and
because, with the small purses, there's less of an incen-
tive always to do your best. Also, bad horses are harder
to ride and don't do anything, including changing leads,
as readily as good ones. This race was proving to be no
exception. The tiring leaders swung out into the middle
of the track. Two of the horses making a run at them on
the turn were carried even wider, leaving an enormous
gap on the inside. Troubador, lumbering along on the

rail, suddenly found himself only four lengths behind with an eighth of a mile to go and clear sailing the rest of the way.

I rose to my feet. It isn't often I find myself rooting home a forty-to-one shot and I thought this called for a little vocal encouragement. "Come on, baby!" I shouted, more to Jill than to the horse. "Come on, sweetheart! Bring him home to me! You can do it! Come on, Jillie!"

The horse, of course, didn't have it in him to make any kind of real run. Even with Jill up on his back, whipping and slashing to get him to put out his best effort, he just kept bumbling along, head down, like an arthritic old commuter running along a station platform to catch his last train home. At the sixteenth pole he was still two lengths off in fourth place.

Fifty yards from the wire I got lucky. One of the tiring leaders suddenly swerved out, perhaps from an injury, and bumped both the horses outside of him, causing them to check momentarily and their riders to steady their mounts. It was enough to make the difference. Troubador came bumbling and shambling along unimpeded and hit the wire half a length in front.

I threw my *Form* into the air and dashed down to the winner's circle. I was standing there when Jill came back, Troubador still lumbering along beneath her, still looking less like a winner than Mister Ed, the talking horse. Jill was grinning from ear to ear, and I caught her in my arms as she jumped out of the saddle. "Great ride, Jill!" I said, hugging her tightly. "That was great!" And I kissed her on the cheek.

"He just done his thing," Jill said. "We got real lucky."

Four of us had our picture taken with Troubador in the winner's circle, including Jill, Felton, and the stocky Mexican groom who worked for the trainer and who muttered angrily to himself throughout in Spanish because he had neglected to make a bet. "That was a fine ride, young lady," Felton said after it was over and the horse was being led away. "Too bad the owner wasn't here to see it. He's up in L.A. and he didn't think this horse could ever win another race. And maybe he never will." The old man smiled. "Darn, and I didn't have a nickel on him neither."

Troubador paid $84.60, $32.40, and $8.40 across the board, giving me a net profit of just under three hundred dollars for the race.

Jay joined us as Jill and I were walking back toward the jockeys' room. "I'm going to have to start paying some attention to you," he said to her, smiling.

"Yeah, and less to them damn numbers of yours," she said. "It ain't numbers that win horse races, mister."

"I can't argue that point today," Jay admitted. "Nice hit, Shifty. What'd you have on him?"

I told him.

He laughed. "The king of the nightcap strikes again," he said.

Thirteen

CROSSING

I had already checked out of my motel, but I hung around until after ten o'clock that night before trying to cross the border. There are always long waits on Sunday nights, with all the traffic heading back from weekends in Baja, and I didn't want to sit in my car inhaling exhaust fumes for several hours while inching toward the control booths. Unfortunately, it's impossible to predict exactly what will happen, because from time to time the U.S. authorities, obsessed with their losing war on drugs, decide to conduct car-by-car checks. Sometimes the INS and the Customs people, ever jockeying for additional public funding and jealous of their little prerogatives, will go to war on each other by conducting unheralded slowdowns, usually by failing to staff their quota of checkpoints. On such occasions the long lines of waiting cars will back up for miles, all the way into downtown Tijuana. The public inevitably pays for all such bureaucratic fandangos and the level of foolishness at the border, protected (if that's the word) by a handful of conflicting federal and state agencies, is high, sometimes achieving true lunacy. Nevertheless, the chances of being trapped for an eon in one of these farcical operations are less if you cross late at night or in the very early morning, so I killed several hours by treating myself to a tremendous lobster dinner at a restaurant with the improbable name of Mr. Fish, then dropped into the Encanto for a getaway *cerveza*.

The place was nearly empty, with only one working

girl sitting by herself in the far corner of the bar and a couple of older Mexican men talking quietly at the counter. Victor, at his usual post, looked tired and drawn, drained of energy, I guessed, by the weekend's festivities. He nodded affably to me when I came in, however, and poured me a Dos Equis. "How goes it, Victor?" I asked.

"Good, *señor*," he said. "Your friends was here."

"My friends? A couple?"

"No, no, the ones who eat here. They know you, no?"

"Mellini? Youkoumian?"

"Three men. They was here ten minutes ago. They ask for Marisa."

"Was she here?"

"No. We have not seen her."

"Did they say anything else?" I casually put a ten-dollar bill on the bar. "Do they know where she lives?"

"I don't know, *señor*. It's important?"

"Maybe. Marisa is sick, Victor. She doesn't want to see anyone."

"Ah." He seemed to be thinking the whole matter over very carefully, then he picked up my ten-dollar bill, punched it into his cash register, and returned nine dollars in change.

"Keep it, Victor," I said. "I had a very good day."

He smiled and scooped the bills off the counter into his vest pocket. "*Gracias, señor*," he said. "I don't think they were staying, *señor*."

"Where? In Tijuana?"

"*Sí*. One of the men, the big one, he asked when they were leaving, *señor*."

"To cross?"

Victor nodded. "I think yes, *señor*. But the short one, with the dark face . . ."

"Mellini."

"Yes. He was angry and upset about something. He

is the one who ask about Marisa. The others, they wish to go."

"Thank you, Victor." I took one more swallow of the beer and stood up to depart. "Did this big man have blond hair?"

"Yes, I believe so, *señor*. He have a bandage on his head. *Y una cicatriz.*"

"A scar?"

"*Sí, señor.*"

"Victor, you haven't seen me."

"No, *señor*, I see no one. You come back?"

"Next weekend, maybe."

"Go safely, *señor*."

I drove into the Zona Norte and turned down Avenida Gonzalez Ortega. A big gray Lincoln Continental was parked across the street from Marisa's apartment building. I pulled over to the curb behind it, about half a block away, and sat in my car in the darkness, waiting. I had a clear view of the house, but I couldn't tell if anyone was in the Lincoln or not. I knew it would be foolhardy on my part to go inside, but I had a hard time just sitting there. I even contemplated going to the police, but I couldn't imagine what I would tell them. That several men were having violent sex with a transvestite? Big deal, who cares? And then what I had heard about the Mexican police itself was not reassuring. They were reportedly both corrupt and sadistic, or at least a number of them were, and celebrated for torturing suspects to obtain confessions. They might arrest Marisa and not her gringo johns. Or they might arrest me on some charge or other, perhaps for having inconvenienced them, who knows? Mellini and Youkoumian had connections here, they were known in town, and they would know whom to grease, *la mordida*. And everything I'd heard about Mexican jails made me want to stay right where I was, behind the wheel of my immortal Datsun, ever ready for a quick disappearing act.

I sat there for nearly an hour, with only an occasional car passing, and I had just about decided to give it up, when two men suddenly appeared out of the shadows of the house and rapidly crossed the street. I recognized Mellini and the big blond hulk who had attacked me the night before. I shrank into my seat, my hand on the car key in the ignition. But they didn't notice me, parked there in the darkness and behind a line of other cars. Larry Youkoumian now stepped out of the Lincoln and opened the back door of the sedan for his boss, while the big blond man got in on the other side. They were moving quickly and it was a matter of a minute or two before they pulled noiselessly away from the curb and left.

I waited a couple of minutes, then got out of my car and walked across the street. The entrance to the two-story structure led directly into a walled courtyard shaded by a couple of large jacaranda trees. It was dark, with only a single lighted window on the second floor casting a dim glow along a covered balcony that ran the full length of the building. The place contained no more than five or six flats, I guessed, but I had no idea which one was Marisa's. I stood under one of the trees and listened, but heard only the distant sound of a radio playing Mexican rock and the passing of cars in the street outside. I contemplated walking up the staircase and then along the balcony to look for Marisa's place, but I was afraid of being seen or heard by one of her neighbors. Mellini and his blond thug had to have made some noise, I reasoned, and I began to wonder if anyone had checked to see what was going on or bothered to call the police, who might, in fact, be on their way at that very moment. The thought struck terror into my soul and spurred me into action. I started for the stairs, intending to make a quick check of the outside doors to see if I could locate Marisa's apartment. I was afraid of what I might find, but I forced myself to proceed.

By the time I stepped out from under my tree, however, my eyes had adjusted to the darkness and I noticed a small adobe hut at the rear of the yard; it was shielded by a tall, ragged hedgerow that had not been trimmed in months. If Marisa lived back there, then that would account for the silence of the neighbors, since the little structure was isolated from the main building, about thirty yards away. I walked slowly and cautiously toward it, slipping sideways through a narrow gap in the hedge leading straight to the front door.

I paused at the single step before the entrance and listened. The house was dark and silent. I walked up to the entry, listened again, then gently turned the handle. It came off in my hand and the door swung open. "Marisa?" I whispered. "Marisa, it's me, Shifty. You okay?"

Nothing.

I stepped inside, pushed the broken door shut, and groped along the nearby walls for a light switch. I couldn't find one, so I eased myself cautiously around the perimeter of the room, feeling my way past a low table, then two overturned armchairs, finally to the edge of a bed with a nightstand, beside which lay a table lamp that, I assumed, must have been knocked to the floor during some sort of heavy action, perhaps a struggle. Sick with fear at what I might find, I leaned over, picked the lamp up, made sure it had an unbroken bulb in place and was apparently still plugged in, then forced myself to turn it on.

My immediate reaction, when I could see my surroundings, was one of mingled shock and relief. I had more than half expected to find Marisa on the premises, either dead or in terrible shape, but the single square room was empty. It had, however, been totally trashed. Every piece of furniture had been overturned and broken, the padding on the chairs slashed, the double bed torn up, the mattress eviscerated. All the drawers in the bedside tables and in a large dresser against the far wall had been removed, and their contents, mostly clothes and personal objects such as costume jewelry, dumped on the floor. A row of dresses, slacks, and blouses had been pulled off its rack and the clothes lay in heaps, slashed and torn. Every one of the dozen or so pictures, mostly of clowns, wide-eyed infants, and some crude landscapes, that had been hanging on the walls, had been taken down and ripped from their frames. Even a set of family photographs, one of which showed a willowy young man of about fourteen, whom I recognized as Marisa, surrounded by his hugely grinning parents and half a dozen other relatives back in Los Mochis, had been knocked to the floor. In one corner, where Marisa had improvised a tiny kitchen around a portable gas range, all the plates, glasses, pots, and pans had been thrown about, into a corner or against the wall or dropped into the single sink that also obviously served as a washbasin. Just beyond it was a tiny bathroom, containing only a toilet and a narrow, uncurtained stall shower, with a medicine cabinet that had been pulled out of the wall, emptied, then flung aside. The whole place looked as if a gang of Hell's Angels had moved through it, determined not to leave one stick standing, one item intact, one object uncontaminated by their presence.

The most obscene depredations had been carried out against what I imagined had been Marisa's little collection of dolls and stuffed animals, about thirty of them in all. Each one had been torn apart and dismembered, then scattered around the room. As I gingerly stepped through this rubble heap that had once been a tacky but cozy little home, I recognized a single object. Lying under a corner of the bed, almost hidden by mattress stuffing, was a gorilla head mask. Though it, too, had been partly torn open, it looked exactly like the ones Emile Legrand had bought at Monster Mash, the booth at the Western Toy Fair. I picked it up and examined it. A small tag on the inside of the neck, at the back, identified it as a product of Fantasy, Inc. It seemed an incongruous object in this room, totally out of sync

with the taste Marisa exhibited in her selection of
decorations, toys, and furniture, as if it had been left
behind by somebody else. Of course it might have been,
though I couldn't imagine why. Anyway, I decided I had
seen enough, so I dropped it on the bed and took one
last look around before turning out the light and quietly
easing myself back into the night.

Instead of heading for the border, I went back to the
Encanto where Victor was surprised to see me. The two
old men were still talking seriously where I had left
them, but the lonely working girl had departed, to be
replaced by two others, both younger and a little fatter.
They perked up visibly when I came in and smiled
brightly at me, as if I had arrived bearing myrrh and
frankincense. I went up to the far corner of the bar and
beckoned Victor over.

"Another beer, *señor?*"

"No, Victor. Listen, this is very important." I dug
into my pants pocket and came up with another ten-
dollar bill, which I dropped on the counter in front of
him. "If you see Marisa—" I hesitated, not knowing
exactly how far I could trust him.

"Yes, *señor?*"

"Tell her you saw me and that I asked for her," I
said. "Tell her I said to be very careful. It would be
better, in fact, if she stayed for a while with friends. You
understand, Victor?"

"If I see her, *señor.*" He picked up the ten and very
fastidiously folded it, then dropped it into his breast
pocket. "You wish to look for her yourself to tell her
this?"

"If I knew where to find her."

He hesitated, as if making a decision. "You know the
Rinoceronte, *señor?*" he asked at last.

"Yes, I do. Marisa took me there the other night."

"Ah." He smiled and his eyes twinkled, as if he now

knew for certain something about me he had previously only suspected. "Ah, *sí*. Well, you know Antonia?"

"I don't think so."

"He is tall, with blond hair."

I remembered the big girl at the bar with the sailor, the one who had spoken to Marisa on the way out. "I think I know the one you mean."

"He and Marisa, they are good friends. Maybe you go see him."

"Him?"

Victor shrugged and looked away. "You know, *señor*—"

"Yes, I know, Victor. How many are like that in there?"

"The ones at the bar, *señor*. It is that kind of place. His real name is Antonio."

"Thanks, I understand." I shook his hand. "Marisa may be in trouble, Victor. She could be . . . hurt."

He said nothing, but nodded, then again turned away from me and began suddenly to wash glasses. He had now heard a little too much and felt he had said enough, so I had been dismissed. I smiled wanly at the girls in the corner and walked out into the street.

The band had gone home at the Rinoceronte and the place was nearly empty of customers, except for a corner table of middle-aged American men and a scattering of young sailors and marines. Music was being raucously piped in from somewhere, and some other naked girl was dancing on the small raised stage, but she seemed exhausted and had the sort of drooping body that no Grecian sculptor would have bothered to immortalize. The perfervid atmosphere of rampant lubriciousness that had struck me on my first visit had been replaced by an air of utter desolation, as if these survivors of the weekend had been permanently consigned to one of the outer circles of hell. Nobody even approached me and I went straight to the bar, where a couple of raddled-looking transvestites were glumly sipping fizzy drinks. The bartender, a large man with a heavily pockmarked face, stared at me disinterestedly, as if I had wandered into the premises by mistake. I smiled brightly at him and ordered a beer. "I'm looking for Antonia," I said as he glumly set it in front of me.

"She not here," he answered, turning away.

"It's very important," I called after him. "I have a message for her from Marisa."

He ignored me so totally that I thought he might be retarded or deaf, but the creature nearest to me, a few stools away, turned to look, then spouted something in rapid-fire Spanish to the bartender. He folded his arms, leaned back against the wall, and shrugged, his eyes fixed on some faraway locale inside his head, perhaps his retirement flat in Acapulco. I swung around on my stool to face the person who had spoken up. "Please," I said, "if you know where Antonia is, it's very important."

He was small and dark, with black eyes over-whelmed by mascara and a tiny pug nose someone had long ago flattened, but he had a nice woman's body, with a full bosom two thirds exposed by a low-cut, shiny green cocktail dress. He moved from his stool, sat down next to me, and placed a hand on my thigh, just above the knee. "You want make love?" he asked. "My name is Felicia. I blow your top, okay?"

"That's a wondrous offer, but no thank you," I said. "I'm really looking for Antonia. It *is* important, really."

"Too bad." He sighed. "You got money?"

"Ten dollars if you tell me where I can find her."

"For twenty I tell you and give you nice hand job. Okay?"

"You're too generous with your favors," I said. "I just want to find Antonia. But here's ten. And I'll give you another ten if you find her for me or tell me where she is."

He took the ten, laughed, stuffed it into his bosom, then got up off his stool and walked out of the room toward the back. He returned a few minutes later, sat down again, and held out his hand. I put another ten-dollar bill into it and watched it disappear, like the first one, into his bosom. "So what about—"

"You go back there," Felicia said, indicating the direction he had come from. "She finished and she see you now."

I went out the back of the room, through a thick curtain that led into a corridor lined by small cubicles. A heavyset, gray-haired American man came out of one of them, gave me a quick, startled glance, and averted his eyes as he passed me, heading out toward the main room, probably to rejoin his party. Antonia, dressed only in a white silk robe, appeared in the doorway and looked at me expressionlessly. "Antonia, I'm looking for Marisa," I said to her. "I was here with her the other night and I was told you're old friends. Look, this is really important, I'm not kidding."

Wordlessly she ushered me inside and closed the door behind us. "You sit," she said, indicating the single chair in the tiny room, which also contained a sink, and a narrow cot covered by a single stained, worn-looking blanket. A picture of the Virgin of Guadalupe graced the wall above it and was the only decoration, the light coming from a single unshaded bulb dangling from the ceiling. I hadn't imagined that even commercial sex could get quite this dismal. "You speak English?" I asked as I sat down and she sank onto the cot, her robe falling partly open to reveal a long bony leg and the edge of her Jockey shorts.

"*Poco*," she said in her deep masculine voice, holding up a thumb and index finger to indicate exactly how little, "*ma comprendo muy bien. Qué pasa con Marisa?*"

I told Antonia a story that was partly made up, but which contained some important elements of truth. The crucial part of the message I was trying to get across was that she was in great physical danger and ought to stay out of sight for a while. "A man named Mellini is looking for her," I said. "I saw him and another man come out of her house about an hour ago. You must tell her to be very careful."

The creature on the bed looked at me blankly and I wasn't at all sure she had understood everything I had just told her. After a minute or two she sighed, sat up, reached into the pocket of her robe, and produced a long, thin cigarillo that she proceeded to light.

"Do you understand me, Antonia?" I continued. "Marisa mustn't go home for a while. Does she have any relatives, anyone she can stay with?"

Antonia looked at me in silence. *"Tiene un hermano,"* she said at last.

"She has a brother here? Maybe she could stay with him."

Antonia cocked her head back and blew a pungent column of tobacco smoke toward the ceiling. "God, I needed that," she said in perfect American English. She smiled at me. "You smoke?"

"No," I said. "Okay, Antonia—"

"Oh, call me Tony," he said. "I'm still pretty well hung, eight and a half live inches."

"I guess I really wanted to know that," I said. "You're American."

"No, no, sweetie. Mexican. But I grew up here. I'm a true *fronterizo*. My pop came from Patzcuaro, but all of us kids grew up on American TV and we go back and forth. I don't know what my family does anymore. I think they want me dead, you know?" He smiled. "I think they'd really like that."

"Why did you pretend not to speak English very well?"

"I don't know you, sweetie. I saw you with Marisa the other night, but that's about it. You got any money?"

"A little." I dug into my wallet again and found a twenty. "It's expensive having conversations here," I said, handing it to him.

"Tough," he said. "You think I do this for fun? I need bread, sweetie. We all have to live, right?"

"That's debatable," I answered. "Now, about Mellini—"

"Yeah, he's bad news, that guy," Tony agreed. "I warned Marisa about him when he came in here one night, a few weeks ago. You get so you recognize the bad ones, you know? I knew he'd beat her up and do all kinds of bad shit, but she went out with him. She said he paid her a lot, two or three hundred dollars sometimes. But it was bad. He does all kinds of scenes, you know?"

"Maybe she likes that."

"No way, José," Tony said. "Strictly for the money. Marisa needs the money more than most of us."

"Why's that?"

"She wants the operation, sweetie. She wants to be a woman real bad. I mean, she *is* a woman, only she has this little tiny thing hanging there. But it costs a lot of money. That's why most of us are here, sweetie. We all want to be just girls."

"You too?"

"Naw, I don't give a shit." He took another big puff from his cigarillo, but thoughtfully turned his head away so as not to blow the smoke into my face. "I like what I've got and so do a lot of the guys who come in here, you'd be surprised." He grinned wickedly at me. "You want to see?"

"No, thanks, I get the picture." I stood up. "Well, you will tell her? Maybe she could go and stay with this brother of hers."

"Wait a sec." He fished a crumpled piece of paper out of his pocket. "You got a pen?"

I handed him my racetrack ballpoint and he scribbled an address on the slip, then handed it to me. "Here," he said. "She's with me and that's where I live. You know where that is?"

"No."

"It's a street off Diaz Ordaz, behind the racetrack,"

he said. "It's my own place, a little house. It has a white
picket fence in front, like the one I once saw in a Doris
Day movie on TV. She'll be there. You want to see her
tonight?"

"No, I've got to go to L.A. tonight," I said. "I'll be
back by the weekend." I stood up. "Listen, Tony, you be
careful too."

"Oh, you bet," he said with a smile. "I know about
those guys. I got a nice big shotgun to blow them away,
sweetie, if they come around my place."

"What were they looking for, Tony? Did Marisa tell
you?"

"No, she didn't say nothing. It's just the way they
are, I guess," he said. "Bad *hombres*, you know?"

"I think they were looking for something. Is Marisa
into drugs? Are you?"

"What a question, sweetie," he answered. "A little
sniff now and then, what the hell, but nothing major.
That kind of shit can lead to a habit, you know? All I want
to do is make *dinero*, sweetie. *Comprende, señor?*" He
grinned wickedly at me and put his hands up under his
breasts, thrusting them at me. They looked hard and
rubbery, stuffed with silicone. "You want a little bit of
this, sweetie? You paid for it."

"A very generous offer, Tony, but we'll just be
friends, okay?"

"You and Marisa . . ." And he brought his index
fingers together and tapped them against each other.

"I didn't know, Tony."

He laughed. "Oh, sure, sweetie," he said, "that's
what they all say."

I hit the border well after midnight, but there was
still some traffic and I found myself in a line of cars,
several hundred yards from the booths. I picked up
some painless soft rock on the car radio to make the time
pass faster and rolled down the window. The air-
conditioning in the Datsun had long ago broken down

and I had never bothered to have it repaired. As my agent and friend, Happy Hal Mancuso, had once put it, I was not destined for a life of ease and wealth. "Shifty, you're a loser," he had said, with the kindly bonhomie that had endeared him to me. "Horses and magic, two ways to stay broke forever. You don't need an agent. You need a therapist."

"Don't worry about it, Hal," I had told him. "Someday I'll hit the carryover Pick-Nine and I'll be rich beyond my wildest fantasies."

"Why don't you play the lottery instead?" he had answered. "That way you can throw your money away without having to spend any time at it."

"Someday I'll be on *Lifestyles of the Rich and Famous*, Hal, and I'll tell them I owe it all to you."

"Yeah, sure," he had said, tilting himself back in his chair and glancing glumly up at the ceiling, as if I had just informed him I was working on a move that could turn water into champagne. "That's what I like about you, Shifty. You got a firm grip on reality."

The boys and girls in their little booths were slowing things down, as they often did on Sunday nights, and I had plenty of time to think about Hal and my life in general, as the line I was in moved slowly, in short bursts of ten or twelve feet at a time, toward the border. I sat there, awash in music, reminiscence, and idle speculation, only tangentially aware of the street action around me.

The usual complement of beggars and peddlers, many of them small children, was threading its way through the lines of cars, hustling for coins and selling clothes, hats, blankets, soft drinks, chewing gum, candies, plastic figurines, jugs, jars, plates, model boats, toys, baskets, all sorts of hideous curios, whatever could be unloaded at the last moment on the tourists going home. Suddenly, the face of Frankenstein's monster appeared at my window, on the passenger side. I jumped a bit in my seat, which must have made the vendor holding the mask in his hand think I could be turned into a customer. He was an old man, with a leathery, wrinkled face the color of burnished copper, and he came shuffling around the front of my car. He was a walking display case of toys and puppets, with several of the large head masks dangling from one shoulder, including the Frankenstein. He now waved it smilingly at me as he came. "*Señor*, you like? Twenty dollars, *señor*."

"Too much," I said.

"For you, *señor*, only for you—fifteen dollars."

"How about ten?"

"Fifteen, *señor*. I lose money for you, *señor*."

"No gorillas?" I asked.

"Gorillas, *señor*?" He shook his head. "No, I have no gorillas. Dracula? *Le gusta*? You like?" He started to reach for another of the masks. "Death, *señor*?"

"No, it's all right," I said hastily. "I'll take the Frankenstein." I gave him fifteen dollars and the old man retreated, counting his bills. I put the thing down on the front seat beside me and let it sit there, staring blindly at me, until I finally crossed the frontier. When I stopped for coffee an hour later at an all-night diner in San Juan Capistrano, about halfway to L.A., I picked up the mask and examined it. It had a small tag in the back exactly like the one on the gorilla mask in Marisa's house. When I got home, I threw it into my closet and forgot about it for a couple of days. I'm not even sure now why I bought it.

Fourteen

OUTTAKES

Max Silverman, the manager of my apartment house in West Hollywood, was glad to see me. He was sweeping up around the pool early the next morning, when I went out to get the papers. He was dressed in a ragged-looking, old blue jogging suit and basketball sneakers, with his familiar black beret clamped to his head like a bottle cap. Wisps of gray hair stuck out from under it and his glasses were perched, as usual, almost on the tip of his nose. He leaned on his broom and smiled, but without opening his lips; Max rarely put his teeth in in the morning, but he was embarrassed by their absence. "Well, Shifty, where have you been?" he asked. "It's been quiet here without you. Only two robberies, one mugging in the garage, and two days ago the police came and took Stella away."

"Who's Stella?"

"That little actress who rented 2F two months ago," he explained. "At least she said she was an actress. The police say she is a prostitute." He looked mildly distressed, as if he'd tasted something excessively salty. "And she seemed like such a nice girl. I rented to her because she knew who Leo Tolstoy was. It isn't often today, Shifty, that you meet a nice girl who knows that Leo Tolstoy isn't a rock band."

"Very true, Max. How are you?"

"How should I be? I'm alive. So where have you been?"

I told him I'd accepted a job in San Diego for a few

weeks, at a hotel on Mission Bay. Max disapproved of my horseplaying, and I didn't want to distress him unduly, especially because I liked him a lot. He was a retired musician who lived alone in a one-room ground-floor flat on a small pension and his Social Security payments. He paid no rent because he managed the building for the landlord, a retired actor who didn't believe in gouging his tenants, and he was a humane and civilized man. His favorite author was Fyodor Dostoievski, which was why he worried about me. According to Max, the Russian author had been a diseased gambler whose addiction had blighted his personal life. Max didn't want that to happen to me, so I usually tried to spare him the gaudier details of my adventures with the ponies.

"Why do I think you're not telling me everything?" he commented. "Somewhere in the vicinity there must be the sound of hooves."

"Agua Caliente, Max, across the border."

"Ah, of course, I knew it," he said sadly, his suspicions confirmed. He pushed his glasses back up on the bridge of his nose and began sweeping again. The pool looked abandoned, with leaves and brown palm fronds floating on the surface of the green water, and the battered aluminum patio furniture stacked to one side. I had grown fond of the place, because the rent on my tiny studio apartment in the back was relatively cheap and I had lived there for nearly ten years now, surrounded by the bits and pieces of my life—my decks of cards, boxes of props, magic books, and catalogues, stacks of old *Forms* and racing programs. My walls were decorated by framed posters of Houdini and other famed conjurors; Giuseppe Verdi, the magician of song; and blowups of legendary horses in moments of triumph. God knows it wasn't a room most people would have felt at home in, but it was mine; it summed up my small achievements and grand passions, and I cherished it.

When I came from the corner of Sunset with the *L.A. Times* under my arm, Max had disappeared. I made myself a cup of coffee and read the paper. Once again, this time in the "View" section, I came across a picture of Emile Legrand. It was in connection with the exhibit of his pre-Columbian artifacts in San Diego. Emile, the writer declared, was a somewhat mysterious person who reportedly invested in movie productions but who was reluctant to discuss either his personal or his professional life. He would talk about his art collection, however, one of the most extensive and valuable ones in private hands. The exhibit in San Diego marked the first time that it had been put on public display anywhere and perhaps the last. "It is a great nuisance for me, of course, and I don't know why I agreed to do it," Emile was quoted in the piece. "I have to submit to interviews, which I abhor." It was nothing personal, he assured the interviewer, apparently a rather solemn young woman the *Times* had dispatched to talk to him. It was simply that he valued his privacy. But such exhibits would greatly enhance the value of the collection, would they not, the young woman asked. "Oh, indeed," Monsieur Legrand had replied with a cold smile. "That was the entire purpose for doing it, as I am contemplating a possible dispersal sale of many of these items. I have too many of them, my dear young lady." These two people had clearly not hit it off, and it showed in the way the story had been written. The reporter had captured Emile as himself—a cold, self-serving, self-absorbed investor, whose only redeeming quality appeared to be an acquisitive interest in a particular kind of beautiful object. "I first became interested in these works when I was filming in Mexico many years ago," Emile declared. "It has become a passion, I'm afraid, and all passions must have an end."

On my way out of the building late that morning, I dropped off the paper in front of Max's flat. I knew that the old man couldn't afford a subscription because he had once told me so, and I always made sure he'd see my copy whenever I was in residence. I also knew that he had an interest in art. His most prized possession, apart from his ancient Italian violin, was a small original Degas drawing, a dancer at the bar, that graced the wall over his bed. He had acquired it in Paris back in the late thirties and would not have parted with it unless absolutely forced to. I put the "View" section on top of the heap and left.

Ed Hamner was surprised to see me. He came out of his office into the waiting room to greet me and personally ushered me inside. "Well, Shifty," he said, looking at me over his long nose. "I presume you're still going to the races."

"They haven't closed the track here, have they?" I asked.

"No, but I haven't been going much myself," he said, gazing at me sorrowfully. "Too busy."

"Yeah, I haven't seen much of you guys over the past year or so," I said. "What are you betting on now? Basketball?"

The doctor laughed. "No, no," he said, "it's just that Charlie and I bought a couple of horses two years ago, after you and Allyson split up, and we took a bath with both of them. So we decided to cool it for a while. Or, to be more accurate, our wives decided for us. I suppose you're on your way out there Wednesday," he added wistfully.

"Indeed. Want my best bet of the card?"

"Don't tell me," he said, gazing unhappily out the open window to the street below. "I might get the urge. It's harder than giving up cigarettes."

"Which you haven't done," I observed as he lit one up.

"No." He blew a cloud of smoke into the air above him. "And I still sneak out there occasionally. So does Charlie. But we lie about it."

I laughed. I liked these two men. They were both middle-aged doctors who shared a successful but unpretentious private practice in a small office building on Gardner, a not very fashionable section of Hollywood, about half a block north of Sunset. I had met them three years earlier, when I became involved with a woman who had been their head nurse. They were diseased horseplayers, which meant, as far as I was concerned, that they were on the side of the angels. "How's Allyson?" I asked as casually as I could manage it. I had really been in love with that woman, but in the end I hadn't been able to measure up to her high ethical standards and she had walked away from me.

"She doesn't work here anymore," Ed said.

"I know that."

"And you also know she got married."

"I heard. To that writer."

"Yeah. They're living in Del Mar. She's opened a nursery."

"A what?"

"A nursery. You know, where you raise and sell plants. She's big on roses. She calls herself the Queen of Mulch."

"No kidding? I kind of thought she'd have horses or something like that."

"No, she gave all that up, Shifty, after you two went your separate ways. Anyway, she couldn't win at the track anymore. You remember how she could dream winners?"

"I'll never forget."

"The dreams all stopped. Maybe because she doesn't need them anymore."

"Everyone needs dreams, Ed."

"She says you stole her soul."

"Me? Come on."

"She was kidding, Shifty. She's pretty happy with this guy. He writes tony stuff for all these Eastern magazines, books, stuff like that."

"I guess maybe I don't want to hear too much about it."

"No." He sighed, shrugged, and then suddenly stubbed his cigarette out and flicked it through the window into the street. "So what's going on in your life?" he asked. "You have a problem?"

"Not a medical one." I reached into my pocket and produced the little pill bottle I had taken from Hatch's tack room. "I'd very much like to know what's in this bottle."

Ed unscrewed the cap and delicately sniffed the contents. "Smells like sugar to me."

"I'd be willing to bet it isn't."

"What's up?"

"I think somebody I know is either doping horses or running drugs across the border from Mexico, maybe both," I explained. "I don't think you really want to know any more than that."

"You want me to run a toxic screen on this stuff?" Ed said. "My little lab here can't handle it. I'll have to send it out. And I'll have to bill you for it."

"How much?"

"Don't worry about it. I'll give you the horseplayer's discount. Whatever it costs us, that's all."

"I trust you."

"I wouldn't. Doctors are like most people and most people are shit."

"Your patients must adore you."

"Amazingly enough, most of them believe I can help them."

"So you're making money."

"Not a lot, Shifty," he said. "What we really need right now is a good epidemic."

I laughed and got up to go. "I really appreciate this," I said. "How long will it take?"

"Seventy-two hours," he answered. "Give me a call on Thursday."

I now recall those few days back in L.A. as a series of bright, crystal-clear vignettes, as if everything I did

and all the people I saw or talked to suddenly appeared
frozen for a few seconds in time, only to vanish as
abruptly as they had materialized. I thought of myself as
standing in a darkened room while a hidden projectionist
flashed what the movie people called outtakes at me,
quick fragments of scenes, bits of dialogue discarded on
the cutting-room floor from the making of some larger
epic I couldn't quite make out. It was both frustrating
and tantalizing, but by then I had determined simply to
let the mysterious projectionist have his way with me. I
sat back, alone in the dark, pushed buttons, and let the
scenes flash chaotically past me. In some ways, too, the
experience was like standing before an enormous abstract collage, waiting for a pattern to emerge from the
multitude of separate small images. An odd, not unre-
warding experience that reminded me of a remark the
poet Marianne Moore reportedly once made about
abstract art. "We all bring our own preoccupations to
such pictures," she was supposed to have said, "and out
of those preoccupations we derive some meaning."

   That same Monday afternoon, with the track closed,
I was lying by the pool, stretched out on one of the less
rickety lounge chairs and basking in the pale November
sunlight, when I heard Max's voice. I opened my eyes to
find him standing over me, holding the "View" section of
the *L.A. Times* in his hand and looking indignant. "You
know that many of these things have been stolen," he
said, rustling the paper at me.

   "What things, Max?"

   "The objects on display in this show." He thrust the
offending story under my eyes. "See this?" He pointed to
a paragraph that listed some of the artifacts Emile
Legrand had given the gallery. "The burial jars, the
Mayan cross, the figurines, the ornaments—all stolen."

   "How do you know that, Max?"

   He had his teeth in by this time and he clicked them
in disapproval, as if testing them for snapping power.
Max was the sort of man who could let the world slide

sadly past without eliciting even a whimper from him, but in matters literary and artistic he could be easily aroused. "Most of the art objects from the period in private collections have been stolen," he said. "This man Legrand should be arrested. He is a thief. Were you ever in the Anthropological Museum in Mexico City?"

"No, Max," I confessed, "I haven't."

"It is a magnificent building, full of wondrous objects," he said. "I was there, in Mexico, with the orchestra one year on a tour. We had three days in Mexico City. Every morning I went to this museum. Three or four years ago, during the Christmas holidays, someone broke in at night, while the guards were asleep or drunk, and stole many of the most beautiful objects. None were ever recovered."

"What are you telling me, Max? That this collection of Legrand's was stolen from the museum?"

"No, no, of course not. It simply reminded me of this event," Max explained. "But it is typical of everything having to do with the pre-Columbian period. Private collectors have been looting down there for years, and most of the great art objects have been stolen. By the time all these Latin-American governments came around to protecting their patrimony, it was too late. Our museums here, in this country, are full of purloined treasures. After my visit to Mexico, I became very interested in this art and I read about it. I've visited many museums, Shifty, so I know what I am talking about. This person in this story, this Frenchman, he could not have built up such an extensive collection without at least having bought some of it from thieves. So he is an accessory to crimes. That's what I meant."

"I know the guy," I said. "Maybe I'll ask him to comment on your assessment of his treasures. Why do you think he's showing his collection, Max?"

"To increase the value, of course," Max said, "as it hints in the story. This man sounds frightful."

"He's not one of your upstanding citizens."

"How do you know him?"

"From the track."

"Ah, of course, I should have realized." Max shook his head sadly.

"Now, Max, some of my very best friends are horseplayers."

Max did not react to that statement as I might have expected him to, with a sort of vast, worldly disdain and a sorrowful expression, indicating that he understood but could not condone the extent of my sinful self-indulgence; he seemed lost in thought, his eyes fixed on some long-lost view. "It was the most beautiful object I have ever seen."

"What, Max?"

"The mask."

"What mask?"

"It was in the basement of the Mayan exhibit in Mexico City," he said. "I knew nothing about it and had never even heard of it until I saw it. In the center of this large hall there is a staircase that led down to a tomb. They had found it in Palenque and it dated back to somewhere between 500 and 800 B.C. The tomb contained this mask, made entirely of gold inlaid with jade, a magnificent thing. There were other masks in the display down there, but nothing to match this one. It must have belonged to a king or a great warrior. It was the most beautiful thing I have ever seen."

"I'll have to have a look at it sometime," I said. "They have a racetrack in Mexico City, I understand. Maybe I can get Hal to book me into a hotel down there."

Max ignored me. "All the most beautiful things in life are destroyed or stolen," he said.

"The Palenque mask was stolen?"

"Oh, yes, an irreplaceable loss."

"But what could a thief do with such an object? Sell it to some private collector?"

"Precisely," Max said. "That is what happens to

most ancient artifacts and much great art. How do you think such great collections are acquired?"

"You could go down and dig for them."

"People do that, too, and then they sell what they have found to people like this man here." Max indignantly tapped the offending story. "It is shameful," he added, "shameful that people like this terrible friend of yours should be buying up the world's most beautiful things and hiding them away for themselves. I would like to see this exhibit, but I wish you had not shown me this story. It makes me physically ill to think about such things."

The old man dropped the paper on my lap and started back toward his room. "Max, what exactly could an object like this be worth, if you could put it on the market?" I asked.

"The Palenque mask?" Max answered, stopping just long enough to glance fiercely back at me. "No one can estimate the worth of such an object, Shifty. It is, quite simply, priceless."

I spent most of Tuesday morning on the phone, trying to find a firm called Fantasy, Inc. There was no listing in the directory and calls to various telephone information services all over the state proved fruitless. Finally, at about noon, I was able to track down Jeff Regan, the live wire who had hired me to entertain at the Western Toy Fair. He sounded just as dynamic and forceful as ever. "How're you doing, kid?" he asked, barking into my ear as if afraid the world at large might fail to take sufficient notice of him unless he shouted. "What's new in the magic business?"

"Everything's fine, Jeff. What I need to—"

"Great, great," he said. "Glad to hear it. We sold tons of toys, kid, tons. Biggest fair ever. We're going to add one in the spring. I'll call you about it."

"Jeff, listen—"

"What can I do for you, kid?"

I told him, loudly and rushing it, so he'd be sure to get it through the raging flow of facts and figures sweeping through his head like a flash flood full of minor debris. "Oh, sure, I know about that," he interrupted me. "The owner is a guy named Len Adelson, who works out of West L.A. He used to be in the rag business, but the INS raided him so many times for employing wetbacks that he threw in the towel a couple of years ago. He's a nice old guy, but he had a real sweatshop down there, people working twelve-hour days, seven days a week, making three or four bucks an hour, that kind of thing. So he went into the toy business."

"Where can I find him?"

"Him? Who knows, kid? Maybe in Beverly Hills or Bel Air. Lenny always liked to live well. But his factory's in Mexico. It's what they call a *maquiladora.*"

"What part of Mexico?"

"Tijuana, I'm sure, or somewhere along the border. Down there he can pay his workers five dollars a *day.* You see the advantages?"

"You mean he can make his toys very cheaply, ship them north, and charge American prices, is that it?"

"Basically, yeah," Jeff said. "What you do is you build a little factory on the Mexican side of the border, where they got a big unemployment problem, and you hire people real cheap without any bullshit about health insurance, Social Security, taxes, disability compensation, unions, profit sharing, all the shit that's strangling the American dream, right?"

"I hear you, Jeff, I hear you."

"Mexico just wants to get its people working. They allow you to bring in, duty free, all the components used to manufacture your product. You put the shit together and ship it back to the States. You pay only American duty on the value added by labor costs, which are minimal, and any foreign-made parts. It's a bonanza for a lot of American companies. We got toy factories down there and people making computer keyboards, carburetors, water beds, refrigerators, you name it. Since you only got to pay your people maybe one-sixth what workers make in Japan, say, the advantages are obvious, especially since they've got a big inflation problem down there and you can't even button your fly with the peso anymore."

"Sounds like a good deal," I said.

"The best," Jeff agreed. "They've got over a thousand of these *maquiladoras* down there, hundreds of them in Tijuana alone. But if you need to talk to Lenny, you won't find him down there, I'll bet you. Look him up in the L.A. phone book, on the west side of town. And say hello to him for me. I've been trying to get him to join our association, but he's a tight man with a dollar."

It took me only two more phone calls to track down Leonard Adelson, who didn't really want to talk to me, but who agreed to do so after I told him I was a free-lance magazine writer on assignment to write a story about the *maquiladoras* phenomenon. "After all, I suppose it's the only way many American firms can compete these days, isn't it?" I suggested. "I want to stress the positive side of this, Mr. Adelson." He warmed up a degree or two after that lie, and I made an appointment to see him at four o'clock that afternoon.

I found him seated behind a plain wooden desk in a small, barren corner office of an old four-story pink building on Little Santa Monica, in Beverly Hills. The directory in the lobby downstairs merely listed his name and he apparently operated with only a secretary, a thin, white-haired woman of about sixty, who looked as if she had been nibbling on lemon rinds most of her life. Adelson himself was in his seventies, a soft, plump old man with large hands and thick eyeglasses, who seemed to be slowly decomposing inside his rumpled brown suit. He squatted behind his desk like an old owl. Perhaps to keep himself from falling off his perch, he restricted his movements to simple hand gestures and nods of the head. When I sat down across from him in one of the two

plain wooden chairs that were the only other furnishings
in the room, I had the impression that his real life had
already been lived, far away, in some other time; he had
retired to a monastery and this was his cell. "So what can
I do for you, young man?" he asked in a dim echo of a
voice hoarse with overuse.

I repeated the story I had concocted about an
assignment from a magazine to write a piece on *maquiladoras*. "I covered the Western Toy Fair for the *Times*,"
I lied, "and Jeff Regan put me on to you."

The old man nodded slowly, his big hands folded
placidly on the desk in front of him. "Jeff Regan is one
big pain in the ass," he said, "a man who never knows
when to keep his mouth shut."

I agreed heartily.

"So you want to know about my operation in
Mexico?" he asked. "So I know you'll find something to
write about. So I don't care, you know that! So go ahead,
write what you want." The dim old eyes stared at me
through his thick lenses. "So I pay my workers the going
wage, so I import, so I make money, so what? Is that
bad?"

"No, no," I answered. "I just want to find out how it
all works, Mr. Adelson. For instance, those big head
masks you make down there, the Frankensteins and the
gorillas, I've seen them on both sides of the border—"

"So what about them? We design them here, we
buy the materials, we ship them south, and we make
them down there," he answered. "So it's perfectly
simple, so no big deal. Like all our toys. So what's so
bad?"

"Would you mind if I went down there and had a
look around?" I asked. "After you give me some facts and
figures. My piece is going to be about the smaller
operations."

"Sure I mind," he said, "but that isn't going to stop
you, is it?" He sighed from deep inside himself, then
pushed a button next to his telephone. The door behind

me opened and his secretary appeared, holding a steno pad as if she were about to stab someone with it. "Miss Folger, please take this down." He blinked sorrowfully at me. "I want to be quoted correctly. You newspaper guys always get everything wrong."

Miss Folger perched on the edge of the other chair next to me, her pencil poised like a dagger above her pad, and waited, her mouth drawn into a tight, disapproving line, as if she knew that nothing good could possibly come of this. Adelson slumped even lower in his chair, and I began to ask him questions about his business. He answered readily enough, without once hesitating or having to grope for a missing fact, and I realized after a few minutes, as Miss Folger scratched industriously away, that he had a facility for figures Einstein would have envied. Lenny Adelson had built a career on numbers, especially as they pertained to the relationship of costs to profits, and he had the figures stored away where only he could get at them, inside his head. The IRS must have had a hell of a time with him, and I realized that he'd have made a great handicapper.

After about fifteen minutes of this bravura performance, as the numbers continued to pour out of him, he suddenly paused. "You're not making notes," he observed. "So what kind of reporter are you?"

"This is not a piece about how many toys you make and sell and where, Mr. Adelson," I said. "This is a story about *how* it works. You've given me a story about profit and loss. I want the people story. I'd like to visit your factory."

He stared at me. Miss Folger made a little sucking sound in her chair next to me, as if she were clamped onto a moist surface. "So what do I care?" Adelson said. "Miss Folger, get him Tommy's phone number and the address of the plant. Then call Tommy and tell him this reporter will be in touch with him." He blinked at me. "So when do you want to go down?"

"Friday. That all right?"

"So why not? So write what you want. So knock me around, what do I care? Only you'll see I do a real good job. We make a nice product, all kinds of toys the kids love. So you'll knock it, so you do what they pay you for, you're a reporter, so go ahead and report."

Miss Folger and I stood up simultaneously. "Who's Tommy?"

"Tommy Sanchez Herrera," the old man said. "He's my plant manager. He speaks good English. So ask him anything you want, what do I care?"

Miss Folger walked quickly out of the room, her stubby flat heels pounding a dull tattoo on the bare tiles. I thanked the old man and reached across the desk to shake his hand. He allowed me to do so, but without moving an inch from his roost. "So go already," he said. "So what do I care?"

"Do you know a man named Legrand?" I asked. "Emile Legrand?"

"So who is he?" Adelson replied. "Is he in the toy business?"

"No, not that I know of. He makes pornographic movies and collects pre-Columbian art, that's all I really know about him," I explained. "I thought you might know him. He bought a whole bunch of your masks for one of his pictures."

"So why would I know him?" Adelson asked. "I don't care who buys the stuff, so long as it sells. So long as you don't write that I make toys for porn pictures. So what can you do to me? So go and write something."

On my way out, I thanked Miss Folger for her cooperation. "He's a sick man," she said, turning contemptuously away from me. "And he's a genius. It's people like you who hound him to death."

"I promise not to do that, Miss Folger," I said. "I'm just writing a story."

"You're not a reporter," she snapped. "You're from the IRS, aren't you?"

"No, actually I'm a prestidigitator," I said.

"You stink," she said, "you people stink."

She was entitled to her opinion, I suppose. We all stink it up sooner or later anyway.

Fifteen

TRACINGS

The Weasel was leaning up against a corner of the bar on the second floor of the clubhouse at Hollywood Park when I arrived about twenty minutes before post time for the first race that Wednesday. He wasn't surprised to see me, but he had noticed my absence from the scene and he chose to comment on it. "What's the matter, Shifty, haven't they been treating you good?"

"Not so well, Weasel," I said. "I thought maybe I ought to cool it for a while."

"Ain't seen the Fox around either. You guys must be hurting."

"It hasn't been a good meet, Weasel, let's put it that way."

The Weasel snorted with suppressed rage. "The fuckin' people that run this place, they write cards no one can beat," he said. "All they care about is the fuckin' carryovers, building up them pools in the Pick-Six and Pick-Nine, so the suckers come in here to chase the million-dollar pots. Ain't no way you can pick all them winners just handicapping. You might as well play phone numbers or your birthday. Racing's become a fuckin' numbers racket, like the lottery. I hate this fuckin' place."

"So what are you doing here, Weasel?"

"Same thing you are, Shifty. Every now and then they run an honest race, where the right horse wins legit. I wait for those and I'm in action, you understand what I'm saying?"

"If I felt the way you do about the races, Weasel, I'd never come here at all."

"Ah, it's the only game in town. I mean, if they was ever to throw me out of here, I wouldn't come back even if they let me back in, you know what I'm saying?"

"I guess so, Weasel, though I find your logic a little quirky. You like anything in the first?"

"Ten-thousand-dollar cripples sprinting, what's to like?" he answered. "It all depends whose turn it is. Let me buy you a drink."

"You must be in the chips."

"I hit a real good Exacta Sunday," he admitted. "They put up the inquiry sign on me, these fuckin' gangsters, but the stewards had bet it the other way, so they let the order of finish stand. It was a jockey claim anyway, and they don't allow but one of those a year, on account of the stewards have to admit in them cases that they blew one and that don't make 'em look good, you understand what I'm saying? So I got to cash a good ticket for a change. Here, what are you having?"

I ordered a Coke with a slice of lime and lingered for a while to get caught up on the local action. The Weasel, with his paranoid view of the world as a place in which every game is always fixed and every human being is on the take, was nevertheless a good source of information. He knew all the local hard knockers and kept a body count in his head. Year after year, despite a stream of reverses, he lingered on, always in action. His real first name was Mort and he must have had a last name, though I never heard it. To everyone at the track he was known as the Weasel, a mean, fast-moving, underhanded survivor of the racing wars. You couldn't like the Weasel or trust him, but you had to admire his perversity. He refused to be broken by a process he knew was rigged against him. He was a modern Sisyphus, never over the top, always scrambling up for more every time he was knocked down. He had the guts of a club fighter.

We chatted about this and that, with the Weasel giving me a detailed rundown of all the atrocities perpetrated against him over the past several weeks by the management, the jockeys, the trainers, and the IRS, which had had the effrontery, as the Weasel saw it, to withhold taxes from his big Sunday payoff. "It's not enough these bastards cut over twenty percent out of the combination pools," he said, "they get to cut twenty more out when you win a big one. Fuckin' thieves!"

I commiserated with him and then we watched the first race together on the nearest TV monitor. It was won by a twelve-to-one shot no one had picked. "See what I mean?" the Weasel commented. "That fuckin' dog had no more business winning the race than a lame goat. It was his turn, you understand what I'm saying? Fuckin' crooks!"

"Tell me, Weasel," I asked after he finally calmed down again, "have you seen Fingers anywhere?"

"No, he ain't been around," he answered. "Just dropped out of sight, like you and the Fox." The Weasel snickered. "A lot of guys come and go over the years, you understand? They can only take so much of this shit and then they throw it in. You stand a better chance in Vegas, you know what I mean? Fingers, though, I figured he'd always be around, but you never know, do you? You stay out here long enough, these cocksuckers beat your fuckin' brains out. Of course Fingers didn't have no brains, but he was always like around, you know what I'm saying? No, I didn't figure he'd disappear, but what the hell—" And he shrugged his shoulders, shifting the weight of his corrupt world to make it slightly more bearable. "But a lot of guys have dropped out over the years—Duke, Al Bananas, Jack the Plumber, Charlie the Baker, Bernie Rivers, Moonshine, all gone. A couple of 'em are dead, I guess. The fuckin' vigorish killed 'em."

"You mentioned a guy named Rivers. Who's he?"

"Bernie? He used to go to the track every day too. I knew him for twenty years, a real sickie. He played the

horses, football, basketball, baseball, you name it,
Bernie bet on it. He was a big player too. Used to bet
five, six hundred dollars a pop. He was in the costume
jewelry business and blew it all out here. You never
knew him? Everybody knew Bernie. They used to call
him Bunch, because he always used to say, when he
really liked something, 'I'm goin' to bet a bunch.' How
come you didn't know him? He was always around till
maybe three, four years ago."

"I never met him," I confessed. "What happened to
him?"

"Ah, who knows?" the Weasel answered. "I heard
he was Tap City in Vegas and he jumped. He probably
bet on it. He'd have bet on snot if they'd have let him.
When he won, he won big, but he must have lost a
whole lot of money over the years and I heard he was
into the bookies for a bundle."

"You know Rico Mellini?"

"A scumbag. Stay away from him, Shifty."

"I wonder if he had anything to do with Rivers."

"Bunch knew him, that's for sure. He could have
borrowed off of him, maybe. But you got to pay guys like
Mellini back, and with interest, or they break your arms.
By the way, he ain't been around either and that's not
like him. It must be this fuckin' track. Nobody can pick
a winner here."

"You did last Sunday, didn't you? Why don't you
cool it for a while, Weasel, and enjoy your success."

"Listen, Shifty, if I don't come to the track, what am
I going to do? Stay home and watch TV? I don't bet on
nothin' else. I got to hold out till Santa Anita, that's all.
Now, that's a racetrack, Shifty. This place, you might as
well run your money through a fuckin' shredder."

I left the Weasel after the third race and wandered
out into the grandstand area. The scene, I have to
confess, depressed me. Hollywood Park is an ugly track.
It used to have a certain funky charm, when the infield
was dotted with lakes and flower beds and was presided

over by an annually elected Goose Girl, a pretty young thing in an absurd costume set off by a conical white hat, whose task it was to stroll about among the geese and ducks cavorting over the lawns and around the lakes. Today the Goose Girl is no more, most of the lakes and lawns have been paved over, and the infield is dominated by a huge screen that feeds information and images to the betting public, while also effectively shutting off a section of the backstretch from the view of people in the grandstand. The whole place, in fact, has been reconstructed, including the track itself, so as to make it almost impossible for anyone to see a race complete from start to finish. It has acquired all the charm of a garishly decorated gambling casino, in which the only purpose seems to be separating the public from its money, while also depriving it of the aesthetic pleasure to be derived from the spectacle of magnificent animals competing against each other in a beautiful setting. Hollywood Park, as a whole, I decided, had become simply another manifestation of the peculiarly American impulse to stamp out traditions and charm wherever they can be identified. Nothing must be allowed to interfere with the making of money, I reflected as I strolled about between the grandstand boxes.

It was already growing dark on this late November afternoon, and the lights had been turned on so that I suddenly had the impression I was walking down the aisles of an enormous supermarket. The horses now heading for the starting gate on the track below me looked unreal in the orange glow, an irrelevancy. Someday, I told myself, they'd find a way to computerize these images so as to eliminate the live racing altogether. Who needed real horses and riders when all that mattered was the making of money?

I watched the next race from an empty box over the sixteenth pole, near where Jay used to hang out, but I couldn't make myself become interested in it. The small crowd in the stands around me also seemed subdued and indifferent, but then, that may have been because the contest itself was devoid of interest, a mile gallop for cheap maidens in which an odds-on favorite romped in by ten lengths. When it was over, I got up to leave. The only race on the card that interested me at all was the feature, in which a handful of talented fillies and mares were going to compete against one another at a mile and one-eighth on the turf course, but I didn't feel like waiting another two hours in this setting for it to go off. I decided to make a bet on my selection, the second or third choice in the race, and depart. I could watch the rerun of it that night at home, on a TV cable channel, and cash my ticket some other time, if I won. I didn't even know why I had come, except on the off chance of running into Fingers or someone who might have seen him. I now had so many more questions I wanted to ask him that I felt like a fool for having allowed him simply to slip away on me. Knowing of his addiction to the racing scene, I had hoped he might have sneaked back into town. In fact, I had begun to wonder if he'd ever made it all the way up to his brother's place in Oakland.

On my way out, I looked down toward the winner's circle, where the owners and the trainer of the victor were having their picture taken next to their horse, and I spotted a familiar figure. He was sitting alone in a front-row box, gazing down at the action below. I came up behind him. "Hello, Emile," I said, "who's picking winners for you these days?"

He looked around, the small, pale eyes focused expressionlessly on me. "I pick my own winners, of course," he said.

"Really? Since when?"

"Since I decided I do not like to be cheated."

"How's the movie business?"

"I am always in production, my friend."

"Emile, I guess I really don't care to be your friend."

"That is heartbreaking news to me."

"I want you to know that I don't appreciate having your hired goon chase me around the streets of Tijuana at night," I told him, but kept it light and airy. "First you sic him on Jay, then on me, for some reason. What's going on?"

"I haven't the faintest idea what you are talking about. Would you please leave, or shall I call an usher and tell him I do not wish to be bothered while I am trying to amuse myself? You are being obnoxious."

"Am I? I tried to explain to you, Emile, that Jay is doing his best to get your money to you. Having one or both of us stomped on is not going to speed the process. Call off your dog."

Emile stood up and waved for an usher, who was standing at the head of the aisle above us. The man started down toward us. "It's okay, I'm going," I said. "By the way, I didn't know you were an art collector. You should learn to be nice to reporters."

I left before the usher reached the scene and retreated back through the clubhouse. The Weasel was still perched at his corner of the bar. "You know what, Shifty?" he said as I passed him. "I saw you talking to that guy Legrand. You know about him, don't you?"

"No, what?"

"If you look up the word *asshole* in the dictionary, it's got his picture right there next to it."

It took me about half an hour, after I got home that afternoon, to track down Fingers's brother in Oakland. Frank Pendleton turned out to be the owner of a used car dealership called Good Wheels in one of the dingier parts of town and he sounded on the phone like a man whose business was in trouble. "Look, I don't know where the bum is," he said. "He was supposed to show up here two weeks ago, only he never made it and I never heard from him. What, does he owe you money?"

"Well, sort of," I said. "We're in a deal together."

"God help you, mister," Frank Pendleton said. "You

ain't never going to see any part of your money. Why would you do a dumb thing like that?"

"I didn't have a choice," I said. "It just sort of happened."

"Well, good luck to you. I hope he never shows up here."

"If he does, would you please have him call me? Or at least let me know he's there."

"I'm not doing anything, mister," Frank Pendleton said. "The less I know about Johnny's doings, the better off I am. When he called me and said he was coming up here, I asked if he was on the run. He said no, but then, he lies all the time, so I figured he was, probably 'cause he owes some bookie money. You a bookie?"

"No, just a fellow horseplayer."

"Then you're a bust-out, just like him."

"Not quite, Frank."

"Horseplayers are all bust-outs and losers. Anyway, every time Johnny comes up here, somebody shows up looking for him. I don't need the aggravation right now."

"I understand. Just tell me one more thing, has he ever not showed up when he said he was going to?"

"No, he usually makes it and he sticks it out maybe two, three weeks. Then he's back at the track up here a couple of days a week, then every day, and then I throw him out and he disappears again. I'd like to see him disappear for good, mister. I don't need this right now. I ain't moving any cars this month and Johnny ain't going to be any help, that's for sure. Look, I'll tell him you called, okay?"

"I'd really appreciate it. Does he have any other family? Anywhere else he might go?"

"No, I'm all he's got. I promised Pop I'd take care of him 'cause he's always been in trouble. But I can't handle it anymore. Aw hell, if he shows up, I'll let him stick around for a few days. You know, he could help me, if he wanted to. But the bum only wants to bet on horses. He's a bum and a bust-out. And I guess all of his friends are the same. You sound like a nice guy, but you probably ain't no different."

"There are varying degrees of success, Frank, in every enterprise," I assured him, "even in horse racing."

"Yeah? Well, success is one word Johnny don't even know about," Frank Pendleton said. "He's the world's biggest loser, mister. If he wasn't my brother, I wouldn't even know him."

Twenty minutes after this depressing conversation, I got hold of Larry Sturm in Las Vegas. He was a lieutenant of detectives in the police department there, whom I'd met during the course of a stint in that town not too long ago. I'd been mugged in a parking lot and robbed of three thousand dollars. Later Larry had helped me unravel a complicated mess I'd become involved in during the few months I was hanging around as a sort of paid gambling consultant and walking good-luck charm to Fulvio Gasparini, the opera star. Larry had a cop's-eye view of the world as a toxic dump inhabited largely by vermin, which made him a gloomy dinner companion, but I had learned to appreciate his utter dedication to his self-assigned role of exterminator. He was a short, strongly built citizen in his early forties, as square as his Whitey Herzog haircut, and the last man in the world I'd have wanted to run up against in a confrontation of any kind. I think he rather liked me, because I had proved to be minor comedy relief for him, and I knew I could trust him to be completely honest with me. "What's that?" he said when I asked him about Bernie Rivers. "Out a window? It's hard to do that in this town. You can't open windows in most of these hotels here, on account of fresh air is bad for gamblers, don't you know that? Who is this guy and why are you asking?"

I told him what little I knew, but without speculating too much on connections I hadn't quite made in my own mind. "I just think the guy might have been pushed, Larry," I concluded. "This acquaintance of mine is missing and he may have gone the same way."

"I'll get back to you," he said, and he did, about half an hour later. "Okay, this guy Rivers did jump" were his opening words. "From a downtown parking structure, on October 24, 1985. But there's no evidence it was anything but a suicide. There were no signs of a struggle, no other marks on the body except the injuries from the fall that killed him. He went off the roof late that night. We checked around and found out he'd been losing big. He was staying at the Riviera and must have jumped on impulse, when he went to get his car."

"You don't find that a little odd, Larry?"

"What do you mean, odd?"

"What was he doing downtown, when he was staying on the Strip?"

"What are you, a detective? What are you telling me, Anderson, that he was killed? By whom? Why?"

"He owed people money, especially this guy Rico Mellini."

"Maybe so, but that's not enough to go on. And usually these loan sharks and bookies don't kill the guys they're into. It wouldn't make sense. They rough them up and try to scare them, sure. But terminating them, that's a little too final. How do you get your money out of them?"

"You checked all this out, I gather."

"Not personally, Anderson, no. Who's got time? There was an investigation and a report. There were no clues, there was nothing except this guy's body, okay? So you come to a reasonable conclusion, you file a report, and that's it. Are you suggesting I reopen the case? What kind of evidence have you got?"

"Not very much to go on," I admitted. "But you've been helpful, Larry."

"Anderson, a lot of people get into trouble in this town and can't get out," the detective said. "So they put an end to all their troubles. They don't usually jump, that's true. This guy Rivers was the only jumper we had that month. Usually it's a gun or pills. But what does it matter, so long as it's final? Anything else I can do for you?"

"No, thanks, Larry. I really appreciate your help."

"You don't want to be too involved with these losers," Larry said. "Why don't you just stick to what you know, Anderson?"

"I keep trying to do that, Larry, but events always seem to overwhelm me," I explained. "Maybe there's just something about me that attracts trouble."

"Try becoming a police officer," he advised me. "You'll get all the aggravation you need, Anderson, and then some."

That night I had dinner with my agent, Happy Hal Mancuso, who took me to Chasen's, an old Hollywood hangout I had only been to once before in my whole life, after a huge winning day at Santa Anita five or six years earlier. The place had a history that dated back to the golden age of the movie business in the thirties and forties, and I had always wanted to go there, but had never been able to afford it except that one time. I also knew that it wasn't the sort of oasis Happy Hal frequented, so I was surprised when he suggested that we meet there. Then I figured out that he probably had some bad news to tell me, though I couldn't tell by his appearance, of course. He was sitting in a booth, slumped in his seat and looking as if he expected the world to end at any minute. Hal smiled, on an average, two or three times a week, and then only at the sort of news other people might consider a calamity. I had heard him laugh only once, on the day Reagan went on the air to tell the American people that he knew nothing about the Iran-Contra scandal. "I could book this act," he had said. "All I got to do is keep him talking and we can watch his nose grow."

"Hello, Hal," I said, sliding into the seat opposite him, "what's the big occasion? Why are we celebrating? Did somebody drop a nuclear device somewhere?"

He refused to tell me right away. Instead, he ordered drinks, then a very expensive bottle of French Bordeaux to go with our venison steaks. He didn't seem to want to talk, so I kept up a lighthearted chitchat about recent events in the news and waited for him to come out with it. I had been with Hal long enough by this time, nearly six years, to know that he could not be rushed and also that what he had on his mind had to be important to our relationship. Hal was not given to squandering money on expensive meals for his clients, especially one like me, whom he kept on simply, I think, because, in his own perverse and gloomy way, he liked me. I was an antidote to his daily diet of Vegas lounge comics, rock stars, and TV talk show personalities.

"Shifty," he finally said, over a second cup of coffee, "where the hell have you been?"

"In Tijuana, mostly," I answered. "Don't ask me why. You don't want to know."

"Six times I tried to reach you last week."

"I'm sorry, Hal, I forgot to put my answering machine on," I explained. "I'd have called you right away, you know that."

He slumped even lower in his seat, looking like a grumpy frog on a lily pad. "I had a very good part for you in a pilot for a new series," he said. "I kept lying to the casting director about how you were out on a cruise job somewhere and trying to get him to keep the role open till you got back. And all the time, goddammit, you're fucking around in Tijuana, probably catching an incurable disease while you lose money gambling on the horses. You're hopeless, Shifty. You're a loser and you're beginning to depress me."

"It doesn't take much to depress you, Hal. You're a walking low-pressure zone. I gather I lost the part?"

"Almost certainly. I might be able to get you one shot at it, but only if the guy they think they've got for the role fucks up at the reading." He lapsed into silence, his eyes glumly focused on an adjoining table where the aging star of a defunct medical TV series was chewing out his girlfriend, who was red-faced and in tears. "Look at that bum," he mumbled. "She probably forgot to bring his dope."

"That's the Actor," I informed him. "He's a losing horseplayer and he's probably beating on her because he had his usual terrible day."

"I should have known," Hal said, reaching for his wineglass.

"Hal, you want to tell me a little more?"

He took a swallow of his wine, then turned the sour gaze my way again. "It's a new show called *The Works*, about a kooky broad who owns a bookstore in a college town right next to an espresso bar in a shopping center, somewhere in the Midwest. Basically, it's a ripoff of *Cheers*, okay? Everything in Hollywood is a ripoff. But it's written and produced by a couple of guys with a good track record and it might go. You could have actually had a legitimate job for real money, but you blew it because you're a fucking addict."

"Hal, what's the part?"

"The waiter in the espresso bar is an out-of-work magician who has a thing for one of the girls in the bookstore," Hal explained. "It's a nice little comedy bit and you get to do your number with a lot of funny patter, the kind of bullshit I hear you spout all the time. You also figure in the plot twist. And, best of all, you don't have to be Larry Olivier to play this part. It's you, Shifty, every cheap, funny bit you do."

"So get me a shot at it."

"I told you, you blew it by not being around. They got a guy in from Vegas to read for it. If he works out, that's it."

"Who's the guy?"

"Somebody named Garry Williams."

I laughed. "He knows about six moves, Hal, and that's it."

"Yeah? Well, he looks okay, and if he can act, he's got it."

"And if not, you'll get me a shot at it."

Hal leaned toward me, his round face dark with anger. "You're hopeless, you know that? You're a goddamn degenerate, wasting your life on cards and horses. Let me tell you, Shifty, I've had enough. If you blow this one, I'm through with you, you understand? You call my office at nine o'clock on Monday morning. If there's a reading, you go to it. And if, by some miracle, you don't fuck it up and you get the part, I'll think about renewing our contract. Otherwise I'm through with you."

"What if Williams works out and I don't get the part?"

"I told you, I'm through with you. I can't take the aggravation. I even had you paged at the fucking racetrack."

"You take the aggravation from everybody else."

"But they earn me commissions, Shifty," he said. "They make money. Even this bum over here, chewing out his girlfriend, he makes money. You—you're just—just a goddamn horseplayer who does card tricks. What do you think I am? A charity?"

"I'd never mistake you for one, Hal," I said, reaching for the check. "And now I'd like to pay for my own dinner, if you don't mind."

He snatched the bill angrily out of my hand. "What are you, nuts? You can't afford this dump."

"I've become the king of the nightcap, Hal," I said. "I win the last race on the card every day."

"You're crazy, you know that?" he said, slamming a credit card down on the check and shoving it toward the corner of the table for the waiter to pick up. "You're fucking nuts. Even if you get this part, you'll blow the money on the horses."

"What does it pay, Hal?"

"I can maybe get you four thousand," he said. "If it goes into a series, you can make twenty-five hundred, three thou a week."

"That's nice money," I said. "I could buy a good two-year-old with that kind of income." I flashed Hal a grin. "Relax, Hal, I'm kidding."

"Sure you are," he said. "So was Hitler, when he said he was going to start World War Two."

Ed Hamner's voice on my answering machine sounded gruff and tired when I got home that night at about ten-thirty. "What have you been up to?" it said. "I have the lab result. You can call me at home until midnight." And it concluded by leaving me the number of his private line, somewhere in West L.A.

"Well?" I asked when he picked up the receiver. "Was I right?"

"About what?"

"It *was* some kind of drug, right?"

"It's sucrose, Shifty, prepared in this case as a crystalline substance."

"How about telling me in English?"

"Sugar, pure sugar."

"You're kidding."

"Why would I kid you?"

"I feel like a fool," I said. "I'm sorry I wasted your time and my money. What's it going to cost me?"

"Two hundred dollars."

"Shit. I'll send you a check in the morning. Good night, Ed."

"Wait a minute," he said, "I haven't finished. There's something else."

"In the sugar?"

"No. When the lab called back the same day with its result, I had them check out the little bottle you had the sugar in. That has turned out to be a little more interesting. The lab found traces of a drug called Nubain."

"What's that?"

"It's a synthetic narcotic, one of dozens that have been showing up all over the place recently."

"What kind of narcotic?"

"Essentially, it's a painkiller, but it acts as a stimulant in horses. Have you heard of buprenorphine?"

"No."

"That showed up around here last year. Its trade name is Buprenex. These drugs are all related, and they're about thirty times as powerful as morphine. Some horse trainers began using the stuff in New Mexico and were caught. They got five-year suspensions. You didn't read about it?"

"Somehow I missed it."

"Okay, the basic fact about all these drugs is that they're used to bring a sore horse back to life," Ed continued. "You shoot a horse with this stuff and he'll run his eyeballs out for you. Of course, the drug doesn't cure whatever's ailing the animal, so you can do him some real damage, break him down for good."

"Maybe kill him?"

"If you overdose him, sure. It takes less than half a drop of buprenorphine, for instance, to affect a horse. The usual dose will last anywhere from fifteen minutes to six hours, but apparently its peak effect is about an hour after it's given. You'd want to administer it maybe an hour before the race."

"How did I miss all this in the papers?" I asked.

"I don't know, Shifty. There was a big scandal last fall. After the news broke in New Mexico, there were all kinds of stories about trainers using this stuff at Santa Anita too."

"Did they catch anybody?"

"Not that I remember," Ed answered. "But some guys who had been winning a lot of races, trainers who had been around for years as just so-so performers, suddenly stopped winning again when the story broke and they started a lot of testing. And there are guys at the New York tracks who, according to a friend of mine back East, ought to be given the Nobel Prize in chemistry for what they're doing to their horses."

"This is wonderful news for racing."

"Isn't it? They should have set these guys down for life, not just five years."

"It makes the old cheating tricks, like battery devices, look a little out-of-date. Why goad your horse with a little electricity when you can shoot him full of juice?"

"You got it, Shifty," Ed said. "You know, there are all sorts of synthetic heroin substitutes on the market right now, these so-called fentonyl variations that are a lot more powerful than the real thing and they can be made in your kitchen chem lab. We're seeing them in our practice now, with street addicts. Know what the worst part is about all these drugs?"

"What?"

"Most of them can't be detected by standard blood and urine tests," Ed said. "You could put enough of some of these new drugs on a postage stamp and literally kill thousands of people. We're just lucky more people haven't died, let alone the poor horses. Up until a few months ago, you had to send samples to the state lab in Illinois to test for buprenorphine. Nobody else could identify it. God knows what else the miracles of chemistry are going to provide for us, Shifty. Now, you want to tell me what you're up to?"

"Not yet, Ed. I don't want anybody involved in this but me," I said. "It's something going on south of the border."

"Down there? In Tijuana? Hey, good luck, Shifty. If they cheat up here, where the purses are big enough, imagine what goes on at Caliente! Watch yourself. I know about Mexico, Shifty. They shoot people down there."

"They shoot people everywhere, Ed," I said. "I'll send you a check in the morning."

"You know, Shifty, I wouldn't play any favorites down there if I were you," he said. "Strictly longshots."

Sixteen

PIECE WORK

"There is someone waiting for you, *señor*," the young clerk at the Conquistador informed me as I stepped up to the counter that Friday night to register. He grinned hugely, displaying a bright gold tooth shining like a small beacon out of his dark Mayan face. "Is very nice."

"Where is he?" I asked, looking around for my visitor.

"Is a she, *señor*," the clerk said, still grinning. "Very nice."

"Where is she?"

"In the café, *señor*."

"Thanks." I finished checking in, left my bag in the car, then walked across the driveway to the restaurant. It was dark inside and I paused by the entrance to get my bearings. Because it was early by Mexican standards, only seven-thirty, the room appeared to be empty. I didn't see anyone at first, except for a couple of American families having dinner to my left. I began to walk across the room when I heard Marisa's voice. She was sitting in the darkest corner, behind a pillar and near an exit door leading into the street. I couldn't see her very well, as she seemed to be hunched back against the wall, obviously eager to avoid being seen.

"Shifty! Over here!"

I sat down across from her, and her face, pale and drawn in the dusky light, thrust itself toward me. "Shifty," she said, "you must help me! Please!"

She was clearly terrified. She was wearing a black

shawl over her head and a plain black dress, as if she were in mourning; her features, devoid of makeup, looked young and very vulnerable, exactly like those of the boy whose picture I had seen in her house. I went around the table to sit beside her and put my arm around her shoulders. She was trembling, as if in the grip of a rising fever. "You need a drink," I said. "Let me get you one."

"No, is all right," she answered. "Is only I am so afraid."

"What happened? What's going on? Did you get my message?"

"*Sí, sí*," she said, leaning into me as if she really thought I could protect her from whatever was out there in pursuit of her. "You are a good person, Shifty. You help me, please."

"Come on," I said, "I have a room here. You can stay with me for now."

"No, I have to go soon. Is bad if they find me."

"Then what do you want me to do?"

She reached under the table and picked up a plain square cardboard box wrapped in brown paper and tied with string. "You take this and keep it for me, Shifty," she said. "You take it away."

"And then what?"

"You take it home, Shifty. You give me your address and I come and find you."

"In L.A.?"

"*Sí*, in L.A."

"How will you get there, Marisa?"

"I know *coyotes*," she said. "I pay them and they take me to the States. You don't believe me? I do that before one time. Is not so hard. I pay the *coyotes* money and they take me. You wait for me, Shifty."

"I'm not sure I can do that, Marisa. What's in the box?"

"If I tell you, you don't believe me."

"If I get caught with this going across, Marisa, what's going to happen?"

"You don't get caught, Shifty. I know. They don't check you at the *frontera*, no, I know that. You cross late tonight or tomorrow, after the races. Nobody check you, I know that. And even if they do, they find nothing."

"Nothing? What's in the box, Marisa?"

She didn't answer, but continued to lean into me, clinging to me inside the shelter of my arm. "I be nice to you, Shifty," she said. "I make love to you. Please help me."

"Why shouldn't I open the box, Marisa?" I asked. "I mean, what makes you think I won't open it?"

"You open it, Shifty. Is nothing for you. Is nothing. Is only something for me." She reached up and turned my face toward hers. "I love you, Shifty," she said. "You help me, please. You don't do nothing, but you keep this box for me and one day I pay you much money. I see the doctor, Shifty, and then I come to you. I be for you one day. Is not long, Shifty. You help me, please, this one time."

"Okay, Marisa, I'll take the box," I said. "Only I'm not going back to L.A. until late tomorrow night, maybe not till Sunday. It depends."

"Depends? On what it depends?"

"On my horse, Fred's Folly," I explained. "He's running either tomorrow or Sunday, I haven't seen the entries yet."

"You go tonight, Shifty," she said. "Is safer. Then you come back tomorrow." She suddenly sat up and her face became alive with hope. "No, is better I go with you! I come with you—tonight!"

"How, Marisa?"

"You put me in the back."

"In the back? In the trunk?"

She nodded. "*Sí*, the trunk," she said in a fierce whisper. "No one look for me there, Shifty. That way we go to L.A. together."

"No, Marisa, I'm not going to do that."

"Why not? Why not, Shifty? Please." Again she leaned into me, one arm now going up around my neck. "Please. I'm good to you. I make love to you. You like that, Shifty. I know you like that. And soon I be a real woman for you, Shifty."

I gently removed her arm from around my neck and forced her to pull away from me. I took her hands and placed them in her lap. "Now listen to me, Marisa," I said. "First, I'm not going to sneak you across the border tonight or any other time. It's a felony and I'm not about to be arrested, have my car confiscated, and maybe have to go to prison for turning myself into a gringo *coyote*, okay? Even if we made it across here, there's another checkpoint at San Onofre, between Oceanside and San Clemente. I'm not going to take the chance and break the law, plus I could be arrested as a smuggler. I know what's in the box, Marisa. At least I think I know."

"You know? What you know?" Her face looked alarmed again, on the edge of panic. "What you know?"

"Why didn't you tell me about your brother, Marisa?"

"You don't ask. I tell you if you ask."

"Where are you now? Are you with him?"

She nodded. "We go away tonight," she said. "We go away because is not safe here. They look for me, Shifty."

"Where are you going, Marisa? Where is it safe?"

"Vicente say he know a place near Rosarito where we can stay two, maybe three nights. Monday we come back."

"Because if he didn't show up at work, they'd miss him, right? And maybe begin to ask questions?"

"Yes."

"Do they know about him? About you and him?"

She shook her head. "No, they know nothing about us. They kill him if they know. They kill me too. I find out about this thing one night when I am with them and

I get Vicente to take it for me. Vicente, he know nothing, only that we make much money, I tell him. So he help me. Shifty, please . . ." Her arms went up around my neck again. "Shifty, you help me. I come to you in L.A. Next week I pay the *coyotes* and I come to you."

"Marisa," I said, "what makes you sure I won't keep what's in the box? I mean, how can you trust me?"

She looked suddenly stricken and shrank away from me, as if I had suddenly spat in her face. "You don't do that," she said. "No, you don't do that."

"Mr. Good Guy, the gringo nerd," I said. "Give him a little head, promise him a world of flesh, and you walk off into the sunset to an angel choir singing up a rainbow with a big pot of gold at the end of it. Whose idea was this? You or your brother's?"

She didn't answer me right away, but sat there staring at me in the soft, dusky light, her eyes looking suddenly enormous and full of pain. "What you know, Shifty?" she finally answered. "What you know about anything? You always got money, so what you know? You don't live in a place where there is nothing, where no one do nothing for you. You don't grow up with dirt on the floor and a hole in the ground where you shit and a house that is made of *cartón* with a roof that lets in the rain and there is nothing to eat. No, you don't know nothing, Shifty, about what it's like. How you know anything, gringo? I am fourteen when I begin to sell my body to the men in the streets and they stick their cocks up my ass, okay? And I am the only one bringing in money and my mother cry all the time and my father, he look at me like I am nothing, like I am dead. But I am lucky, Shifty. I live with one man for three years, a *político,* and he teach me a few things and he pay for music lessons and he pay my family some money and he send Vicente to school. He bring Vicente and me here, to Tijuana, and is okay. Only, when he die two years ago, I am alone again and I go to work in the bars and I sing good, like *un estrella,* a real star, only nobody give a shit about that, is my body they want. And I send my family money and I give money to Vicente and my father, he tells everyone at home, in Los Mochis, that I am dead. Nice, huh? You like this story, Shifty? Is okay, gringo? Maybe one day you make a movie about my life, huh?" Holding the box with both hands, she began to slide away from me and stood up. "So long, Shifty. I thought you was *un honorable, un hombre digno de confianza.* I was wrong."

I took her by the hand and pulled her back toward me. "Wait a minute, Marisa," I said. "Wait just one goddamn minute, okay?"

She sat down again, her face averted from me. "What you want, Shifty?" she asked. "Half the money? You got it."

"I don't want the money, Marisa, even assuming you can sell this thing. I want to know why you aren't at Tony's."

"I was there," she said. "I was there when they came for me. I hear them and I go out the back. There is a little narrow path there and I run. I go first to Vicente's house and then I come here." She started to leave again. "Is okay, I find someone else, Shifty."

I kept my grip on her hand and pulled her down again. "And what about your friend Tony? What's happened to him?"

She groaned, in real distress again, and her eyes once more turned toward mine. "Tony don't know nothing, Shifty," she said. "I tell him nothing. Is bad for him, maybe, right now, but he don't know nothing to tell them."

"So maybe they won't kill him, is that what you're saying?"

She didn't answer, but she began to cry, soundlessly there in the dusky half-light of the nearly empty restaurant, her hands still clutching the box now resting on her lap. I leaned over and took it from her. "The trouble with medicine in general and surgery in particular," I declared, "is that it costs too much. Somehow we have to take the profit motive out of it and then you could have an operation without getting your friend Tony and your brother and me and God knows who else into such a rotten mess." I put the box down on the table, took my wallet out of my pocket, and fished out one of my business cards. *Shifty Lou Anderson*, it read, *the Poor Man's Houdini*. It listed Hal's name and telephone number as well as mine. I handed it to Marisa, picked up the box again, and looked down at her. "You can call me next week in L.A.," I said. "I'll wait to hear from you. I'll wait for thirty days, which should be enough time, I assume, for you to get up there. If I don't hear from you, I'm going to turn this over to the Mexican consulate in L.A."

"No, Shifty, you don't—"

I leaned over toward her to cut off her protest. "That's it, Marisa," I said. "I promise you I'll do the best I can for you, but that's all I can promise. I'll try to hang on to this and I also promise you I won't open it, because, frankly, I don't want to know for certain what's inside. I can't guarantee you more than that. Take it or leave it, Marisa."

She hesitated, but only for a matter of seconds, the tears still running down her face. "You go now," she said. "You go. I wait here for Vicente. He come for me here."

I left her and went back to the front desk. The clerk was surprised to see me, but confirmed my hope that Harry had arrived for the weekend. "Twenty minutes ago," he said, and gave me the old man's room number on the second floor, above the courtyard. Harry answered the door in his underwear, which consisted of a T-shirt and a set of baggy white drawers with red ants crawling all over them. "Well, hello there, Shifty," he said, obviously happy to see me. "Come on in. We can talk about horses and I'll get you a drink. You got a *Form*?"

"Not yet, Harry," I said. "Listen, I can't stay.

There's someone I have to see. But I have to ask you a favor."

"Shoot."

I handed him the box. "I want you to keep this for me till you hear from me, okay?"

"Sure. What the hell is it?"

"I think it's a gorilla head."

"A what?"

I explained it to him. "It's got a valuable object hidden inside it, Harry. Somebody stole it and is trying to smuggle it over the border. It's a long story and maybe it's better you don't know too much about it. All I want you to do is keep it for me. I'll take it back from you sometime over the weekend."

Harry set the box down on his bed. "I'll lock it up in the trunk of my car," he said. "That way it'll be safe. What are you, a cop, Shifty?"

"Not exactly, Harry, but I'm trying to keep somebody I know out of trouble with this thing."

"You want me to cross with it? Ain't nobody goin' to question me, Shifty, on account of I been comin' down here so long they all know me at the border. It ain't some kind of drugs, is it?"

"No, Harry, I promise you, it isn't. But I don't need you to take it to the States. If by some chance you don't hear from me or see me again this weekend, drop it off at the American consulate here. You know where that is?"

"Sure do. It's about a block from the track."

"They'll know what to do with it. You can just drop it off. Don't put a return address on it, unless you want to answer a lot of questions."

The old man looked at me and grinned. "Goddamn, Shifty," he said, "but you got more tricks up your sleeve than any magician I ever saw before. Hey, don't you worry about a thing. Ain't nobody gets this box away from me but you or the *judiciales*, and those bastards would have to arrest me for it."

"Thanks, Harry, I appreciate it," I said. "I'm just trying to help one good person out. Marge here?"

"Not this trip," he said. "I can't do that to poor old Walter two weekends in a row; he'd have nothin' to do with me no more. He'll be down tomorrow for the racin'. I came down today on account of I had to get away from them damn widder women, always tryin' to get me to go picnickin' or some damn thing or other. You ain't goin' tomorrow?"

"Oh, I guess I'll be there, Harry, if I possibly can."

"I guess I know that," he said. "Ain't no way you keep a good horseplayer from gettin' to the races. If you ain't there tomorrow, I'll figure they killed you."

"A comforting thought, Harry," I said, "but maybe an accurate one."

They don't make them like Humphrey Bogart anymore and I am no exception. This is why I chose to go to my room and lie down instead of getting right into my car and driving off to confront Marisa's pursuers. But the longer I lay there, fully dressed on my motel bed and staring at the ceiling, the more I realized that I had almost no other choice. Eventually, I knew, they would begin to look for me too. I stood a better chance of confronting them successfully at a time and in a place of my own choosing than just sitting back and waiting for them to find me. That was my rational brain at work, but I had more urgent concerns. My main one in all of this was coming out intact. It would be just like Mellini to want to break my fingers. And Castle, Emile's hired playmate, would also welcome the opportunity to even his score with me by beating a rattling tattoo on my helpless carcass. As I lay there, paralyzed by my fear and wondering how in the hell I had gotten myself into this mess, I could almost hear my bones snapping like dried celery stalks. How did I get myself into these messes? All I wanted out of life was a little magic, an occasional good woman, and a few winning horses. Was that too

much to ask? Of course, I had maneuvered myself into
the middle of this game, as usual, I realized. I could have
ignored enough of what had been going on to stay in the
clear, but no, I had to ask questions, I had to go and talk
to people, I had to jump right into this sleazy arena and
now I couldn't get out. Why me? Is there just something
about me that pisses the wrong people off? I sat up and
tried once again to think recent events through, to place
them all into a comprehensible perspective. Because, if
I turned out to be wrong, I might be paying too high a
price for the error of my ways. I went into the bathroom,
splashed water on my face, and sat down again. What,
exactly, had Neal Brown revealed to me that morning?

During most of our conversation he had passed the
time rearranging his pompadour. He was a tall, willowy
young man with the face of a ruined evangelist, who
smiled frequently and overflowed with enthusiasm for
the collection of pieces on display in his gallery. The
Ferrara consisted mainly of a single, very large room on
the main floor of what had once been a box factory in
downtown San Diego. It specialized as a showcase for
large private collections of art that the owners wanted to
sell without having to subject themselves to the spot-
lighted procedures of the auction houses. "Most of our
clients are publicity shy, at least about money matters,"
Neal Brown informed me. "We offer them an alternative
way. We publicize the collections and put them on
display, with all the appropriate fanfare, but we don't
reveal to anyone the prices paid for any of the objects or
works sold here." The current show, he did admit, would
undoubtedly become the most successful venture in the
gallery's short history. "We're only four years old," he
explained. "We've done rather well, but this exhibit has
been a tremendous coup for us. What publication did
you say you were with?"

I had invented a new magazine purportedly published in Seattle. Luckily Brown had not asked to see my
credentials, but I hadn't expected him to. His job, as he

saw it, was to publicize the exhibition, thus stimulating bids for and sales of the various objects on display. He was happy to give me a tour of the show and would provide photographs if I needed any. "Of course, by the time your article appears," he said, smiling broadly as we strolled about, "most of these pieces will have been sold. There's been a fantastic response. This is the most remarkable private sale of pre-Columbian artifacts in a decade or more. Many of the buyers here, especially during the first week, came from museums all over the world. All of the most important pieces, in fact, are accounted for. I can't imagine why Monsieur Legrand would wish to sell this collection."

"Maybe he likes money," I said.

Neal Brown laughed, a high-pitched giggly sound way at the back of his throat. "Well, of course, to be sure," he said. "But it does seem a shame."

"How would a private individual acquire such a collection?" I asked. "And from so many different countries?"

"Oh, well, yes, we never ask *that* kind of question, Mr. Anderson," Neal Brown answered. "That's not any of our business. But it was once quite easy to acquire this kind of art, as late as the nineteen-fifties and even into the sixties. Anyone with the right connections and enough money, of course, could rather quickly put together a very decent grouping. Most of the objects here, perhaps eighty percent of them, are Mexican. I would imagine that Monsieur Legrand began acquiring them during that period, before it became almost impossible and quite illegal to export such art out of its country of origin."

"I suppose that with the collapse of the Latin-American economies and the high inflation rates down there," I said, casually, "some of this art must have begun to appear again on the market."

"Oh, I wouldn't know about that," Neal Brown replied. "Look, let me show you my favorite pieces here." And he led me over to a corner of the room where a large glass-enclosed case contained three small stone statues of seated, bare-breasted women with hawklike noses and elaborate headdresses. "Aren't they exquisite?" he said, clasping his hands in delight. "Classic Mayan art, dating back to several hundred years B.C. These pieces sold on the very first day."

"Probably stolen from somewhere," I observed. "Right?"

"Oh, originally, I suppose," he said. "All ancient art everywhere was originally looted from some tomb or palace or temple somewhere. Nobody used to bother then about where things came from. If we had, no museum in the world would have anything to display except for things from its own country. Now, wouldn't that be a bore?"

I admitted that it would and allowed him to complete the tour. "Well, thanks," I said when it was over. "I don't suppose you want to give me some sort of rough figure on what the whole collection is going to sell for?"

The curator giggled again. "Oh, dear, no, that would be a betrayal of the agreement we make with our clients," he said. "I'm awfully sorry, but you do understand."

"But if I say well over a million dollars, that wouldn't be inaccurate, would it?"

That giggle again and then: "Oh, my, yes, you can say *that*. Oh, yes, you can say *that*, all right."

He had walked me to the door. "It was *so* nice of you to take an interest," he said. "Please send us a copy of your article and you *will* mention the gallery by name, of course."

"Of course. By the way, Neal, what about the Palenque mask?"

"The Palenque mask? You mean the one from the museum in Mexico City?"

"Yes, that one. I don't imagine you'd be able to sell that one if it showed up, would you?"

"Oh, dear, no," he said. "At least, not publicly."

"Ah. But you *could* sell it, right?"

"Why do you ask?"

"Just curious."

"We couldn't put it on display, you see."

"No, of course not. But you could sell it."

"My dear man, the Palenque mask is one of the most exquisite pieces of ancient art in the whole world," he said. "It's a tragedy that it was stolen and never recovered. If somebody brought it here, though I can't imagine that anyone would, well"—and here he seemed to hesitate, as if pondering an alternative course—"we'd have to notify the Mexican authorities, of course."

"Oh, of course. You wouldn't want that kind of notoriety, would you? But if it could be sold, you could find a buyer for it. I mean, there are people who would buy it, regardless."

"Well, of course it's all hypothetical, my dear man," he said, his hands again engaged with his soaring hairdo. "The Palenque mask is a masterpiece. There are people who would probably kill for it."

I got as far as my car and then sat there, unable to make myself turn on the ignition. What if, somewhere along the line here, I had miscalculated or guessed wrong? And what was the missing piece in this odd little puzzle? Because I was sure there was one, at least one. I felt like a climber groping in the dark for a foothold while clinging by one hand to a slick wall; one misstep and I was gone. I had to be absolutely sure of myself before taking that step, because this was one proposition, unlike any horse race I had ever bet on, that I could not afford to lose. I did a little more thinking.

I had been surprised, I remember, by the modest dimensions of Lenny Adelson's toy factory. It was a small, square, white adobe building standing alone on a flat lot no more than a couple of hundred yards from the Mesa de Otay border crossing. A chain-link fence topped by a single strand of barbed wire enclosed the area, and a one-lane driveway, barely wide enough to accommodate a medium-sized truck, connected the property to the main highway, where a line of about twenty vehicles was waiting to cross into the U.S. A couple of dozen shabbily dressed Mexicans, most of them women, were outside in the dusty courtyard, smoking and talking quietly to each other, under a faded sign proclaiming the presence of "Fantasy, Inc., Industria Internacional de Juguetes." I had arrived during a break, I guessed, but nobody seemed in the least curious about my presence. I parked in the lot beside the building and walked in the front door. The reception desk was unoccupied, so I kept on going. I proceeded down a narrow corridor past several empty, cubicle-sized offices, then pushed through a set of swinging doors and found myself in a neon-lit, windowless rectangular room containing half a dozen assembly lines for all sorts of cheap-looking toys, mainly dolls and stuffed animals, the sort of garish junk that graces the game booths of carnival midways. The air was oppressive, almost stifling, with only one large fan stirring up a lethargic breeze. Five or six workers had chosen to linger by their machines instead of going outside, and their faces seemed wan, prematurely aged in the artificial light. I felt I had somehow blundered into a scene out of Dickens, as if a tiny corner of one of his mid-Victorian sweatshops had been transported intact from a London slum and dropped into place in this arid, semitropical mesa. It was a setting devoid of joy and laughter, mocked by the blankly benevolent expressions frozen permanently onto the faces of the crude objects being manufactured on the premises. *"Buenos días,"* I called out to the person nearest to me, a plump, middle-aged woman in a ragged-looking blue smock, who looked as if she would have welcomed the end of the world, *"busco el Señor Sanchez Herrera."*

She looked at me blankly, then seemed to be peering beyond my left shoulder. I turned and found myself confronted by a short, chunky young man dressed in a pair of tight gray slacks and an open-necked blue shirt. A heavy gold coin, suspended from a thick gold chain, nestled inside his black chest hairs, and he exuded a perfumed air of arrogant affluence. He had black, cunning eyes, a thin sliver of a mustache, and thick lips, but he clearly imagined himself to be irresistible. "Yes?" he said. "I'm Sanchez."

I introduced myself and he nodded, but without noticeable enthusiasm, then offered me his hand as if I might want to kiss it. "I just need sort of a quick tour and a few facts," I explained, "and Mr. Adelson said you'd provide both. I'm doing a piece about the *maquiladoras* phenomenon—"

"Sure, sure," he said, interrupting me, "I know. Mr. Adelson called me." He looked at me as if he had a question he wanted to ask me, but thought better of it. "Okay, I'll give you the quick tour."

It took less than twenty minutes, mainly because there wasn't much to see. "We have forty-eight full-time employees here, but we get up to sixty-four during certain peak months and depending on orders," he said in his fluent border American as we strolled past the long counters where the toys were being put together. The workers had come back off their break and were seated in rows, each employee with a single, small task to perform as the toys moved slowly past them along the assembly lines. "We pay good, about six dollars a day in your money, plus food and transportation allowances," he continued. "Everybody's very happy here. We had a couple of malcontents, but we got rid of them. But we don't mistreat anybody and everyone works hard."

"You have mostly women, I notice."

"Sure, they work better than the men. It's pretty dull stuff, see, just sitting there and doing the same thing over and over, day after day. Women do better at this kind of work. The guys, they get fed up with it. Shit, I would too, man." He smiled. "The guys, they got better things to do, like spending the money the women make for them."

"Sounds like women's lib would have a tough time down here," I observed.

"Women's lib? You got to be kidding, man," he said. "We don't put up with that shit down here. So is there anything else?" We had reached the end of the main workroom and he was obviously eager to unload me. I had a feeling I was interfering not so much with his professional as with his social life. I imagined that young Tommy Sanchez probably cut a sizable swath at night through the town's fancier restaurants and discos. If you make good money in a Third World country, and Tommy Sanchez looked every inch a moneymaker, you live a lot higher on the hog than the average wage earner anywhere else.

"What about the masks?" I asked.

"The masks?"

"Yeah, the head masks you guys make. I've seen some of them."

"Oh, those. We've stopped making them for a while. They went good, but we've got a backlog and orders have tailed off since Halloween," he explained. "So we'll probably start up again on them in a couple of months. They're fairly expensive to make because the cloth we use for the neck pieces comes from Guadalajara and there's a duty to pay on that in the States. It's more profitable right now to make the dolls and the animals. The plastic is shipped down from L.A. And they're always in demand. We sell them by the truckload and move them out of here as fast as we can make them. Big turnover, big bucks."

"I'd like to see some of the masks. You got any around?"

He looked at me a little strangely. "We got some in storage back there," he said, gesturing toward the rear of the building, "but there's nothing to see."

"I like the gorilla ones."

"Gorillas? We don't make no gorillas," he said. "Just the standard monster stuff. Where'd you come up with the gorillas?"

"I've seen them, with the Fantasy, Inc., label on them."

He shook his head. "No, you got it wrong. Maybe we made a few one time, but they didn't sell too good, so we stopped making them," he said. "These masks, they cost maybe five, six dollars in materials alone. You got to sell them for three times that to make a profit. Any item that don't go, you stop on it real quick. That must be what happened on the gorillas. What you saw was something maybe we made last year or at the time of *King Kong*. I've only been here about eight months, see. But we don't make them now, that's for sure." He took my arm and started to lead me out toward the front. "Anyway, I guess you've noticed we're pretty busy. I haven't got time to pull any stuff out of our storage bins for you. You want an animal or something?"

"No, thanks. I was just curious. By the way, how's Luis?"

"My dad? You know him?"

"I've got a horse with Sandy Hatch."

"No shit? That's nice. Yeah, Dad's doing okay, I guess. He likes the horses. Me, I can't stand them. It's real boring."

"Well, you either love racing or you don't. You must have grown up around the track, right?"

"No. He and my mom split up when I was maybe eight years old. He wasn't around much till I got older. We get along okay now."

We had reached the front of the building by this time, with Sanchez ushering me out as quickly as he could manage it without making it too obvious that he was dying to unload me. As we passed the administrative offices, a young man came out of a room at the end of the corridor and started toward us. He had a beard, but otherwise he was the image of the youth I had seen in the snapshot of Marisa's family, the one I had assumed was Marisa herself before she became a transsexual. He was dressed like Sanchez, in slacks and an open-necked shirt, and I guessed that he worked in some sort of clerical job. As he passed me, he realized I had been staring at him and he shot me a quick, startled look, like that of a wary wild animal, before hurrying past us toward the factory floor. I started to say something, but caught myself. Instead, I allowed Tommy Sanchez Herrera to lead me out into the dusty courtyard beyond the front door. The reception desk was now staffed, I noticed, by an extraordinarily pretty girl of about twenty, who flashed us a huge smile as we swept past. "Pretty," I observed as we stepped into the sunlight.

Sanchez grinned. "Juanita? You bet. You know what? I get to hire and fire in this job. Not bad, huh?"

"Nice work if you can get it. Thanks for your help."

Again he allowed me to hold his hand. "It's okay, man," he said. "No sweat. But, you know, about this reporter shit, you guys sure write a lot of dumb stories. Where do you get all that shit you write about?"

"We make it all up, Tommy," I admitted with a grin. "Real life isn't interesting enough."

"Yeah, well, I'm sure glad I don't do what you do," he said. "Here in Mexico, somebody writes that shit, we blow them away, man."

"Killing the messenger who brings the bad news is an old western tradition," I said.

"Yeah, man," he said, turning his back on me and walking away toward the front entrance, "who needs bad news?"

Seventeen

BINDING ARBITRATIONS

I had no trouble finding Tony's house. It was a small beige-colored one-story structure set far back from the street behind an anomalous white picket fence. The neighborhood was one of the better ones in Tijuana, with a number of large new villas hidden behind high walls. His place must have been one of the original dwellings, a survivor from a more modest era, before the city had begun to expand so rapidly in the seventies and the rich had started to move away from the old districts around Revolución to build themselves *palacios* in the newer, more spacious neighborhoods. I noted that Tony's house was sandwiched between two of these mansions, whose high walls towered over it, effectively isolating it. I drove past it and parked at the corner of Diaz Ordaz, the main avenue that was an extension of Boulevard Agua Caliente, then walked back toward it.

The gray Lincoln Continental was parked across the street. I took a deep breath and walked up to it on the passenger side. Larry Youkoumian was asleep behind the wheel, his head slumped back against the headrest and his mouth open. I tapped on the window. He sat up with a start, then looked at me in amazement before scrambling out into the street. "Even the wicked sleep," I said. "Hello, Larry. I thought I'd get you in good with your boss if I let you usher me in. Otherwise he might wonder how I got past you."

"Fuck you," Larry said, fumbling clumsily under his jacket.

"Don't pull a gun on me, Larry. I want to see Mellini. I've got something he's been looking for. But I'm not letting you take me in there with a gun in your hand."

"You'll do what I tell you, asshole," he said, finally producing what looked to my untrained eye like a .38.

"No, I won't. Put the gun away, Larry. Firearms make me nervous."

"Get your ass over there." He indicated the house. "Move."

"Put the gun away, Larry," I said quietly, as if addressing a demented child. "I'm not going to play fugitive to your bounty hunter. Besides, it might go off. You're the kind of moron who'd shoot himself in the foot." I smiled at him, hoping that he wouldn't hear my knees knocking together.

He did, however, do as I asked, and we walked together up to the front door of the house. It was in darkness and seemed to be empty, but Larry Youkoumian's soft double knock on a wooden panel was soon answered. The front door opened and I found myself confronted by the blond hulk who had attacked me in the street. "Mr. Castle, I presume," I said.

He reached out a large hand, grabbed me by my shirt and pulled me into the hallway. Youkoumian followed me in and closed the door behind him. Castle flung me back against the wall, then grabbed me a second time and hurled me forward into the living room. I fell over a chair, then raised myself to my hands and knees. The monster came up beside me and kicked me in the stomach, knocking the wind out of me and leaving me gasping against the wall, unable for a moment to utter a sound. He started for me again, perhaps to finish killing me, but was stopped by Mellini's voice: "Knock it off, Bert. You can have him later. We got business first."

I sat against the wall, fighting for air. Gradually, as

I became able to breathe again, I took in the situation in
the room, which was illuminated only by a single floor
lamp in one corner. It did not look promising. Jay Fox
was sitting in an upright chair they must have brought in
from the kitchen. His hands were tied to it behind his
back and blood was dripping down the front of his shirt
from his nose. He was only dimly aware of what was
going on. His face was a mass of bruises and contusions,
both eyes were nearly closed, and his lips were blue
welts. They must have been working him over for quite
a while. Mellini was sitting across from him, on the sofa.
He was dressed in pants and an undershirt and he was
sweating at having had to work so hard. A set of brass
knuckles lay on the coffee table between them, along
with a soda bottle and a bowl of red chili powder.

"Why don't you leave him alone, Rico," Castle said.
"This guy probably knows more anyway." He cocked a
thumb in my direction. "Only I get to do this one. I got
my own way."

"You want me here or outside, Rico?" the ferret
asked.

"What do you think, dummy? Outside."

"Okay, okay, just asking." Youkoumian grimaced,
undoubtedly disappointed at being shut out of the
action. He quickly let himself out of the room.

Somebody groaned and I looked around. Tony,
naked, his hands tied behind his back, lay huddled in a
corner of the room to my right. His mouth had been
taped shut and his eyes were wild with terror. He looked
unmarked and I assumed that his time had not yet come.
Mellini obviously was in no hurry, undoubtedly because
he so clearly enjoyed his work.

Castle leaned over and hauled me to my feet. "My
turn," he said, spinning me around toward the center of
the room.

"Wait a minute," I gasped, able at last to speak.
"Wait one goddamn minute. I've got the mask, okay?"

Time seemed momentarily frozen. Mellini stared at

me in amazement and Castle smiled broadly, as if I had just handed him a million dollars. Jay gazed dimly at me through the slits in his blue-black swollen face. He was obviously trying to say something, but the sound he made was an unintelligible mumble. Castle now pushed me back into the sofa and I sat down hard. He started to move toward me again. "Get away from me," I said. "You lay a finger on me and you'll never see it, ever. I guarantee it."

Castle paused, but only for a second or two. Then he reached over and pulled me up again. "Listen, fella," he said directly into my face, "you aren't exactly in a position to make deals, do you know what I'm talking about?"

"Why don't you ask Emile, or even Rico over here?" I said. "You guys are running around all over town, trashing people's houses, beating people up, God knows what else, and I'm in a position to give you what you want with a minimum of fuss. So why don't you listen for a change, instead of smashing up everything you touch?"

"Let him go," Mellini said.

Castle dropped me again and I sat down. My stomach hurt, but I was fairly sure nothing was broken. I looked at Castle. His face in repose had the smooth, polished look of a semiprecious stone, as if his bland, scarred features had been molded to disguise the beast inside. Unlike Rico Mellini, whose brutality and sadism were etched indelibly on his coarse features, Castle could have passed as a corporate executive, the business-man as hired thug. He sat down across from me, relaxed, happily in charge, content now to await the success he felt he so richly deserved. He even managed to smile at me. "Okay, let's hear it, magician," he said. "Let's have it."

Luis Sanchez Gomez walked into the room, zipping up his fly; he must have been in a bathroom down the hall and unaware of my arrival. He was clearly surprised and not especially pleased to see me. He paused by the entrance to the rear of the house and leaned against the wall, his small black eyes flickering from one area of the room to the other, as if sizing up the situation, estimating odds.

"Okay," I said, "I want to know first when Fred's Folly is running."

Castle's face darkened. "Listen, fella—"

"First things first," I said. "You want the Palenque mask, that's your business. My business is the horse, okay? I want to know when he's running." I looked at Sanchez. "Well?"

The fat Mexican wasn't sure what was expected of him. He looked first at Mellini, then at me, then at Castle, then back to Mellini. The loan shark nodded his head. "Sunday," Sanchez said, "he run Sunday."

"And it's a go, right?"

Sanchez nodded.

"This is a waste of time," Castle said, looking at Mellini. "I'm running out of patience."

"What the fuck do you care?" Mellini answered. "You'll get yours. He ain't going anywhere."

"Well, actually, you're wrong about that, Bones," I said, mustering up as much bravado as I could manage under the circumstances. "You see, I know where the mask is. And I know what it's worth."

Castle smiled. "All right, fella, and now you're going to tell us where it is."

"No, I'm not."

Castle's smile broadened and he flexed his huge hands, as if warming up for the mayhem he was obviously eager to perform on me. It was as if I had played deliciously into his hands. He stood up.

"Sit down, Bert, I'm not through," I said, turning again to Mellini. "You want to blow this deal? I don't care about the mask, okay? You can have it. What I do care about is my life and the health of my friends. So here's the deal. You're going to turn Tony loose, he doesn't know anything anyway, and Jay and I are going to walk out of here tonight. On Sunday, after old Fred runs, we'll meet in the open out in the parking lot, right next to the Foreign Book, where there'll be a lot of people around and you won't pull any shit, and I'll give you what you're looking for."

Castle laughed. "You have to be kidding," he said. "You expect us to agree to something as dumb as this?"

"Why not?" I answered. "You want what I've got and you're not going to get it unless we do this my way. If I don't come through, you aren't going to have any trouble finding me, are you?" I looked at Mellini, who seemed now to be made of stone. Only his eyes were alive, with the glittery, watchful menace of a predator suddenly unsure of his prey but still on the watch. "Let me see if I can convince you, Bones. Just so you know I've got it, Marisa gave it to me, okay? She's on the run from you and scared out of her wits. And I've turned it over for safekeeping to a friend I can trust. He's under firm instructions from me. If I don't show up again tonight, the package will be turned over to the Mexican consulate in L.A. However, I guarantee I'll have it for you on Sunday, as I just said I would. I've also written up a complete account of this transaction, with lots of fascinatingly pertinent details, that will be immediately turned over to the L.A. police if anything ever happens to me. I couldn't really trust you guys to leave me alone, now, could I, once you have what you want? So that's it. If you want to get your rocks off beating up on and torturing citizens, that's your problem. But I assume I'm dealing with businessmen. I'm proposing a deal."

"You want in, don't you?" Mellini said. "You want in, right?"

"Wrong, Bones, absolutely incorrect," I assured him. "I'm just a little guy trying to get along, all right? If it were up to me, I'd turn the mask over to the Mexican government and blow the whistle on the whole bunch of you. But I know I'd be writing my own death warrant, so I'm not going to do that. Basically I want out. I want my money, which I can recoup from the race on Sunday, if it's on the up-and-up. The rest of it I don't care about. You want to smuggle art objects across the border and split the profits with Legrand, that's up to you. I'll just go along my own way, doing a little magic, betting a few horses. Basically you've got a good deal, Rico. I'm sorry to deprive you of a little added pleasure, but you won't have any trouble finding other poor slobs to do your numbers on." I stood up, a little shakily, because my stomach was still sore from Castle's kick, and pointed to Tony. "Let him go, Rico. He doesn't know anything."

The shark stared at me, then he looked at Castle and nodded. The hulk walked over to the corner and hauled Tony to his feet. He tore the tape viciously off his mouth, causing him to cry out in pain, and flung him onto the sofa next to me. Tony gasped and began to cry, his mouth a red welt where the tape had torn off his skin. He looked pathetic and obscenely vulnerable in his nakedness. I leaned over and began to untie his hands.

"How about a little more *Tehuacanazo* on him?" Castle suggested with a smile. "Maybe he does know something. It's worth a try."

So they had already tortured him, I realized, but must have been saving him for a second go-round, perhaps because Jay had arrived on the scene or been brought in during the middle of it. They had taped Tony's mouth shut and poured Agua Tehuacán, Mexico's favorite carbonated mineral water, laced with chili powder, up his nose. It was a favorite torture of Mexico's judicial police and, of course, Luis Sanchez Gomez would have known all about it and probably recommended it. But what could Tony have told him? Nothing. I imagined that Mellini also had other delights in store for himself with Tony, which was why he was naked. Bones was clearly a man not averse to combining pleasure with business.

"Leave him alone," I said as I freed his hands. "He's just Marisa's friend. I tell you he doesn't know anything and he had nothing to do with this." I turned to Tony, who sat huddled up beside me, his hands on his sore mouth. "Go on, Tony. Go on inside, put something on. It's over, it's okay." I looked at Mellini. "It's okay, isn't it?"

The shark didn't say anything, so I helped Tony to his feet and walked him into his bedroom, a dark red womb featuring a wall-to-wall king-sized bed. He sank onto it with a groan and pulled a blanket up over himself, his eyes alive with fear and pain. I went back into the living room, closing the door behind me. Jay still sat in place, dripping blood over himself, his head slumped forward on his chest.

"Okay, Rico," I said, "we're getting out of here now."

"No," Castle objected. "This is nuts."

"Yes or no, Rico? You want to blow maybe a million or two just to get a little personal satisfaction?" I turned to Castle. "And what about you, Bert? How are you going to explain to Emile that you had the mask in your hands and you blew it? Is he going to like that, maybe give you a bonus because you've done such a brilliant job of it?"

The seconds ticked away in silence, each one sounding a small message of doom. "Get the fuck out of here," Mellini finally growled. "Beat it. You better be there on Sunday or you're history."

"I'm planning to cash a big ticket on that day, Rico," I said. I walked over to Jay and, using the small pocketknife on my key ring, I began to cut him loose. "Jay?" The handicapper's head rose and he grunted unintelligibly. "Come on, let's go. We're getting out of here. Can you walk?"

"Yeah," he whispered.

I looked at Sanchez. The Mexican had not stirred from his post by the kitchen door, but he was on the alert, up on the balls of his feet like a dancer, ready to move in any direction. "Oh, Luis," I said, smiling affably, "don't pull any of that stuff with our horse, okay?"

"What you talking about, man?"

"The drugs. I know what you do. Come on, Jay." I got the handicapper to his feet. He put his hand on my shoulder to steady himself and I gave him a handkerchief to press against his nose to slow the bleeding. We walked slowly toward the door.

"Hey," Mellini said.

I looked back at him. He had risen to his feet and was standing in the middle of the room.

"Hey, what's this shit about the horse?"

"You mean you don't know? Come on, Rico," I said. "These guys are using all sorts of stuff on their horses. They pumped that speedball El Gato so full of Nubain he ran himself to death. You mean you don't know that?"

"Nubain?"

"Like morphine, Rico, only stronger. They overdosed him. You didn't bet on El Gato, did you?"

He didn't answer. He simply stood there, in the center of the room, like a cornered beast in a forest glade, his eyes alive with suspicious malice in the orange glow.

"Let me explain it to you, Bones," I continued. "Hatch wasn't in on it. He expected El Gato to win and he gave him the usual dosage to keep him running, so the horse wouldn't know how sore he was, but Luis here had other ideas. He cashed a real nice ticket on the mare. Did you know she was trained and partly owned by Lupe Camacho's brother? I looked it up. I think his name is Andrés. He's also one of the owners of Quadra Esmeralda. Hey, Rico, I thought you were in on the deal. How big was your ticket, Luis?"

The Mexican didn't have time to answer because Mellini had whirled to confront him. "You fat cocksucker," he said. "I'll cut your fucking heart out."

Sanchez looked alarmed, but not because he was being threatened; his eyes were focused beyond Mellini, on the entrance to the bedroom, where Tony, dressed only in a tattered blue bathrobe, now stood holding a shotgun. *"Madre de Dios!"* the Mexican said, crouching down low and scrambling like a fat toad on ice through the door to the rear of the house. Mellini turned, but Castle, from his position to the left of the bedroom door, moved faster. His idea, I'm sure, had been to take Tony from the side, but it didn't work. The boy heard him coming and swung the gun toward him, firing one barrel into him at point-blank range.

The shot blew Castle back across the room. He hit the wall and stood there for a moment, an expression of amazement on the smooth, bland face, while his shirt-front turned dark red, then, clutching himself with both hands, he began to sink toward the floor.

I didn't wait to see any more. With Jay stumbling along beside me, I got the front door open and we made it out into the street. The ferret saw us coming down the walk and emerged from his car, gun in hand, on the mistaken assumption, I'm sure, that we had shot his boss and were making a getaway. "Hold it," he said. "You guys just hold it right there." And he came running up to us.

"You better get in there, Larry," I said. "Tony's got a shotgun. Didn't you hear the blast?"

"What the fuck—" he began, but was interrupted by several more shots, one of them a roar from the second barrel of the shotgun. With the front door open it sounded like a cannon going off. "Jesus!" the ferret exclaimed, paralyzed by the sound, his eyes staring at the open door.

My first kick caught him knee-high, slightly from the side, and sent him sprawling; my second one, a heel kick delivered full force on his face, broke his nose. Jay, meanwhile, had grabbed his wrist to keep the gun pointed away from us and was hanging on to him with whatever strength he had left.

Mellini appeared in the doorway, whitefaced and

clutching his bleeding left arm. "Larry!" he barked hoarsely. "Let 'em go!"

"Let go of the gun, Larry, or I'll give you some more," I said.

The ferret's fingers loosened and Jay wrested the weapon out of his hand. We staggered down the street toward our car. When we reached it, I took the gun from Jay and dropped it into the gutter. Then I helped the Fox into the car. I got in, did a quick U-turn, and drove back up the street past Tony's house. Youkoumian was dragging Mellini, who could barely walk, toward their car. I didn't wait to see what would happen, but kept on going up into the maze of streets behind the racetrack, then began to nose my way up into the hillside. My idea was to make my way back toward the border as quickly as possible.

I had no idea exactly what happened after Jay and I had gotten out of there, but I had no intention at that point of hanging around long enough to find out. The shots must have been heard all over the neighborhood, even behind the thick walls of the villas next door, and someone would surely have called the police. I would read about it later, I surmised. Meanwhile, my immediate task, as I saw it, was to get us out of there and Jay into a hospital.

We had no trouble getting across the border. The lines were short at that time of the evening, each one containing no more than ten or twelve cars, but I chose not to wait. I drove up a closed lane to the left, parked by the next open booth, and went to see the INS officer inside. He was about to query the driver of a van full of cheerful-looking American teenagers coming back from a night on the town, but my appearance got his immediate attention; my shirt was spotted with bloodstains. "Excuse me, officer," I said. "I have a badly injured man in my car and I need to get him to a hospital."

He looked mildly saddened by this information. He

was about fifty, a little overweight, with a lined, soft-looking face under a bristly shock of gray hair and he had obviously been at his job long enough not to be surprised by the news. He waved the teenagers through, held up the next car in line, and walked over to the Datsun.

Jay was sitting in the front seat, which I had tilted as far back as it could go, so that he was three-quarters prone. His nose had stopped bleeding, but the handkerchief still pressed to it was bright red and his face as a whole looked as if it had been slammed through a wall.

"What happened?" the officer asked.

"He got into a fight in a bar," I said. "They really worked him over."

"Who is he?"

"His name's Fox, he's a friend of mine," I said. "He lives in L.A."

"American?"

"Yes, sir."

"And you?"

"Me, too, I'm also from L.A."

"Come down for the weekend for a little fun?"

"That was the original idea," I said. "It hasn't been a lot of laughs."

The man sighed. "I guess I don't need to ask you if you're bringing anything back to declare."

"Hardly. We just want to get the hell out of here and I need to get him to an emergency room."

"The nearest one is two exits up 805," the officer said. "Turn left, go under the freeway, then back one block and you'll see it. It's a new private clinic with a big electric blue sign and a cross out over the avenue. They're open all night. Otherwise you'll have to go up to Physicians and Surgeons in southeast San Diego."

"Thanks."

He turned back to the waiting line of cars and held it up until I could maneuver past the front of it and across the border toward the freeway entrances. I waved appreciatively back at him, but he had already forgotten about us. To him we were just another couple of citizens too dumb to be allowed out of the country, I guess, and, judging by what had been happening to us, who was to say he was wrong?

Jay had a badly smashed nose that would probably require corrective surgery, and a possible concussion, I was informed an hour and a half later by the insanely cheerful young female doctor who examined him. She had cropped blond hair, a round, freckled face, and the sturdy build of a field-hockey star; no beauty, but she inspired confidence. "Where are you headed?" she asked.

"I guess to the nearest motel."

"I wouldn't do that," she said. "He needs X rays and he should be hospitalized for at least forty-eight hours. Then he'll need to consult a surgeon. I presume he has insurance."

"Yes, sure. If not, I've got cash."

"Fine. Making a buck is what good medicine is all about."

"It's what the country's all about."

"Ah," she exclaimed, and laughed. "Now, what hospital do you want to check him into? And I think we'll need an ambulance."

"You tell me."

"I'll call Mercy in San Diego," she said. "I have a connection there. Then I'll arrange for an ambulance. You want to go along?"

"No, I don't think so. Should I?"

She shrugged. "It's up to you. He might want his hand held."

"He's a big boy," I said.

"Not big enough, apparently. How did you manage to stay out of it?"

"I wasn't there."

"Well, that would explain it." She laughed again. "Okay, you can go in and see him if you want. I've got a couple of other little trouble spots to attend to." And she bounced briskly away from me back toward her office. "I'll call the hospital. It may be an hour or more, since it obviously isn't life and death and they can be busy."

I followed her down the corridor and found Jay. He was stretched out on an examination table with a couple of pillows under his head. Cotton had been stuffed into his nostrils and his face had been bandaged, so that only his puffed-up eyes and swollen lips were visible. I sat down on a stool and looked at him. "Okay, Jay, I'm going back across tonight," I said. "I'll look you up at the hospital tomorrow and we'll figure out what the play is. How are you feeling?"

"Shitty," he said, growling it from the back of his throat. "Headache."

"Yeah, that sadistic son of a bitch really worked you over. Where'd they find you?"

"Track. Followed me. Motel."

"And Jill?"

"Don't know. Had date. Late. Don't know."

"Why, Jay? Why you? What did they want from you?"

"Got me." His head stirred slightly on his pillows and his gaze flickered toward the wall. "Figured knew something. Bastards." He looked up at me. "Careful, Shifty."

I headed for the door with every intention of taking his advice. "Hey," he said hoarsely, "good kicking, Shifty."

"Yeah, the women's movement has made me a terror," I said. "I'm becoming a regular martial arts phenomenon."

Eighteen

BLOOD

Jill Thorne was still pretty angry. She saw me standing by the rail that morning at seven-thirty when she came back toward the gap from having just galloped some-body's animal around the track. "So where in the hell is that no-good friend of yours?" she asked, reining in her mount and looking furiously down at me, as if I person-ally had betrayed her. "We was supposed to have dinner last night. He left me settin' there in the damn lobby like a damn hooker for an hour. I'm goin' to kill that sucker."

"He's in the hospital, Jill, up in San Diego," I told her. "He got into a fight with a couple of guys in the parking lot and they beat the hell out of him. I had to drive him up last night. There wasn't any way to let you know anything."

"Aw, Jesus, he goin' to be all right?" she asked, her eyes now wide with alarm. "Who did it?"

"We don't know who did it," I lied. "But listen, he'll be okay. I just wanted to let you know."

"Damn, well, I'll get up to see him too," she said. "Where is he?"

"We'll talk about all that later, Jill," I said. "You have some horses to ride this weekend."

"I got two mounts today, but I ain't up on nothin' tomorrow," she said. "I could go see him then."

"You're going to have a horse in the nightcap," I said. "Fred's Folly is running. You want to ride him?"

"Hatch ain't goin' to put me up on that horse," she said. "Lupe's ridin' him. Ain't you seen the entries?"

"Yes. But I'm going to give the horse to Jimmy Felton and tell him to ride you."

"You're kiddin'. You can't do that."

"Why not? I own him."

She looked at me in complete disbelief, her mouth slightly open. The animal under her, a frisky little filly, suddenly reared up, then swung around in a circle, impatient at having suddenly to stand still after her workout. Jill got her quickly back under control and turned her head my way again. "You're serious, ain't you?"

"You bet. Think you can win with him?"

"I sure as hell can try," she said, grinning broadly. "Hey, I better get this filly back to the barn before she hurts herself. You goin' racin'?"

"Maybe the early ones," I said. "Felton knows how to get hold of you?"

"Sure. Anyways, I'm goin' around there later. Boy, Sandy's sure goin' to be mad at you."

"I'm used to that," I said. "He hasn't spoken one civil word to me since we met."

She clucked to her horse and they moved quickly away through the gap back toward the barn area. I followed her on foot, then stopped by the stable superintendent's office to find out where Felton was.

The trainer was sitting alone outside his tack room in Barn 38 when I showed up there ten minutes later. He was wearing his long gray overcoat and brown cap and quietly smoking a pipe. His stocky young Mexican groom was hot-walking a horse around the shedrow, but otherwise nothing was going on. The old man didn't seem surprised to see me, but I introduced myself to him again, in case he had forgotten me, and told him exactly what I had on my mind. "And I want you to train the horse, Mr. Felton," I concluded, "just so long as you promise to ride Jill on him in the race tomorrow."

He leaned back against the wall of the barn, shoved his cap up off his forehead, and looked at me out of his old brown eyes. "Does Hatch know about this yet?" he asked.

"Not yet. I wanted to make sure you'd take the horse first," I explained. "And I want you to ride Jill."

The old man sucked on his pipe and blew a cloud of pungent smoke into the air around his lined, leathery face. "Camacho's the best rider here," he said, "and you don't want him."

"He's a crook. He stiffs horses and you know it," I said. "I saw him do it last week, when he was on a favorite for Hatch, so his brother and the Quadra Esmeralda could win the race and they could all cash a nice ticket. They didn't even let Hatch in on it and they killed his horse. I'll get on Fred's Folly myself before I let Camacho up on him, Mr. Felton. I want to win this race tomorrow."

The old man chuckled. "It's getting so in this business you can't fool the owners like we used to," he said. "How'd you figure this one out?"

"I really haven't time to explain it all to you right now, Mr. Felton—"

"My name's Jim. My friends call me Jimmy, mostly."

"Jimmy, yes or no? I'm under a little pressure. A lot of pressure if you don't take him."

"You tell Hatch what you're doing and then I'll send my groom over to get the horse," he said. "You got the papers on him?"

"Hatch does, I'm sure. I'll get them from him."

"Okay. One more thing now—if I don't like the way the horse is going or I find something wrong with him, I won't run him tomorrow," he said. "I'll run him if I think he's ready to run."

"Well, you know he's bowed—"

Felton chuckled again. "Aw hell, I could tell that," he said. "We got a lot of horses in this place that run on bows, mister. No, I mean if I find something else, that's what I mean. Some of these horses here have a lot of things wrong with them."

"You're the boss, Jimmy," I said. "Obviously I don't want the horse to run if he's really hurting or he isn't ready and he can't win. But I sure could use the win and an honest ride to get it."

The old man stood up and put out his hand. "You got a deal," he said. "You let me know when I can send Francisco for the horse. And I'll put the girl up on him for you. She can ride better than most of these jocks they got down here anyways."

"She gave you a good one with Troubador."

He smiled. "Not bad," he said. "Not bad for a girl rider."

I started to leave and then remembered that I hadn't told him quite everything. "By the way, Jimmy," I said, "you don't want to pony this horse out onto the track. He'll try to mount him. He loves ponies."

The old man laughed. "I had another horse like that once, but he was a gelding," he said. "For some reason he was scared of the mares after they cut him. This one's a horse, ain't he?"

"Yes."

"Well, I'll be darned. I guess if you hang around the racetrack long enough, you get to see about everything there is in life."

I walked back to Barn 15, where I had left my car, and the first person I came upon there was Hatch. Looking, as usual, like a figure out of Hogarth, he was standing by the haypile, chewing out Miguel. The little Mexican, rake in hand, stood quietly in front of him, head bowed and accepting the abuse. He was used to it and was merely riding it out, waiting for the trainer to spend himself and unload his poisons so he could get back to work. The spectacle made me want to kick Hatch in my finest, newly acquired female defense style, but instead I leaned up against the corner of the barn behind the trainer and allowed the scene to play itself out. It took about three minutes more for Hatch to exhaust his fund of Spanish expletives, after which Miguel went back to work around the shedrow. There was plenty of activity going on because the trainer had three horses running that afternoon and he had a sizable string of animals anyway. I hadn't counted Jimmy Felton's horses, but I had seen only one being walked and I guessed that he couldn't have had more than three or four stalls. As usual in life, I surmised, it was a case of virtue going unrewarded, but I intended to even up the score by at least a point or two.

"Fuck off" were Hatch's first words to me, as he turned to go back to his tack room and spotted me.

"And good morning to you too, Sandy," I said. "No, I need to talk to you."

He stormed past me into his office and slammed the door in my face. I opened it and stuck my head into the room. "Do you want to talk to me now," I asked, "or shall I just go directly to the stewards with what I know about you?"

He stood in the center of his dismal little world, in this trash heap of a room that symbolized the state of his life, and glared at me. "What the fuck are you talking about?"

I walked in and shut the door behind me. "Let's get right to the heart of the matter, Sandy," I said. "I know you've been using what they call elephant juice on your horses and exactly what kind. I took a bottle of stuff out of here one night and had it analyzed. I know what happened to El Gato and I also know that Sanchez double-crossed you on that one and killed your horse. I figure maybe that's why he isn't around here anymore, right?"

He didn't say anything. His eyes, red and slightly yellow in the gray morning light, looked like those of a minor demon, something conjured up by the illustrator of a mildly nasty Victorian children's book, a figure designed to amuse as well as to frighten.

"If it's any consolation to you," I continued, "he also stiffed Mellini, and that one, I'm sure, has him worried. I imagine he won't be around much for a while."

"Beat it," Hatch said, but without conviction. He looked suddenly old and sick. He seemed to be on the verge of disintegrating before my eyes and propped himself with one hand against the corner of his desk, his complexion an unhealthy shade of orange and gray.

"You're sick, Sandy," I said. "You're dying and you don't even know it. Or maybe you do know it and you don't care. I don't think anybody else cares either. You sold out. You were once a decent horseman, I guess, but you're a wreck. Whatever happens to you, you deserve it. Where are the papers on Fred's Folly?"

His head jerked up in surprise. "What?"

"I'm taking the horse out of here," I said. "I don't want any part of you or your operation. I'm giving him to Jimmy Felton. He's sending his boy around for him just as soon as I tell him to. Where are the papers?"

"You don't own the fucking horse," he said hoarsely. "Get out of here."

"You're wrong, I do own him," I said. "I'm listed as the sole owner and you know it. My wonderful partners are both convicted criminals, with, I would guess, nice long records. They can't be licensed here or anywhere. That's why they need me, Sandy. You want me to go to the stewards? I don't know exactly how it works out in the end down here in Mexico, but the rules are basically the same as in California, whether it's elephant juice or hoods muscling in on what is supposed to be a legitimate game. Whatever happens, there will be an investigation and you'll be out of action, at least for a while. You ought to be suspended for life. You ought to go to jail, but you probably won't. But I can certainly cause you some serious trouble and I'd be only too happy to do that, you little shit. Now, where are the papers, or do you want me to go to the frontside right this minute?"

He waved toward the filing cabinet by the desk, to my left. "They'll take care of you," he said.

"Well, maybe, but right now they have other business on their minds," I said, "and I don't think Rico's feeling very well this morning." I pulled open the top drawer of the cabinet and found old Fred's file, tucked among those of Hatch's other animals. I took it out, checked its contents, and put it under my arm. "It's been wonderful knowing you, no, it hasn't," I said, heading for the door. "You do one more stupid thing while I'm around, Hatch, and I will go to the stewards. I'd love to see you drown in your own little cesspool."

This time I had the pleasure of slamming the door on him.

I had a lot of time during my drive back across the border to San Diego that afternoon to think the whole sordid business over. There had been nothing in the L.A. papers, which I had perused in the lobby of the Fiesta Americana, but the Tijuana dailies had given the story a good play. One of them, *El Mexicano*, had splashed it on the front page with a photograph of the premises where the murders had occurred. My racetrack Spanish wasn't good enough to get all the details, but the outline of the event emerged clearly enough.

The municipal police had answered two alarm calls reporting the sound of gunfire in a small house on Avenida de las Americas, at about nine-thirty on Friday night. The officers answering the calls had found the front door open and two corpses inside, in the living room. One was the body of an American businessman named Wilberton Castle, who had been shot at point-blank range in the chest and stomach, almost certainly by the other dead man in the room, Antonio Morales de Melinda. The weapon used had been a Model 500 Mariner twelve-gauge shotgun, a weapon powerful enough to blow a man's head off. It had been found, with both barrels emptied, on the floor between the bodies.

Morales had been shot in the neck and head, probably by a pistol, also at close range. The weapon that had killed him had not been located, although the police had picked up another gun, a Beretta .38, from the gutter near the house. It had not been fired, but had presumably been dropped there by someone leaving the scene in a great hurry.

The police were questioning the neighbors and calling for possible witnesses to come forward, but, the reporter speculated, the act of violence had undoubtedly been triggered by a confrontation over drugs and sex. A stash of cocaine had been found on the premises, in a bedroom closet, and Morales was well known to the authorities as a user and possible dealer. He was a notorious male prostitute and transvestite, who had been in trouble with the law before. The reporter surmised that Morales had probably picked up Castle at the bar the *travestito* frequented, the infamous Rinoceronte on Avenida Revolución, and lured him to his home, perhaps without revealing to him the truth about his sex. An altercation had broken out and Morales, perhaps to defend himself from his angry client, had shot him. Their tryst had been interrupted by the entrance of a third party or parties, who had come to the house to settle some sort of disagreement over a drug deal gone wrong. Morales had again attempted to defend himself and had fired a second time. Shotgun pellets had been found embedded in the wall by the kitchen door, a direction at right angles to the blast that had felled Castle. Morales, however, had in turn been shot by the unknown third party, who had then fled the scene. Neighbors reported seeing a large American limousine, either a Cadillac or a Lincoln Continental, parked earlier in the street directly across from the house. This would also account for the open front door and the presence of the Beretta in the street, although there must have been still a third weapon, the one used to kill Morales. And the story concluded with a somber exhortation to the authorities to look into, once again, the illegal activities of the nightclubs catering to illicit sex, which threatened the well-being of the tourist industry and, therefore, the overall health of the local economy. "Whoever killed these two pathetic individuals," the reporter concluded with a flourish of moral trumpets, "the true intellectual authors of the crime are the people in positions of public authority who continue to allow such sordid behavior to occur."

No one, in any of the stories I had read, I noted with relief, mentioned the presence of a battered-looking beige-colored Datsun 310 with California plates. Nor had anyone seen Jay and me leave the premises or our struggle with Youkoumian on the sidewalk. Luckily streets are not well illuminated in Tijuana, and it had been dark. Mexicans, who have become as used as we have to the sounds of violence in their streets, tend to hole up behind locked doors and drawn blinds when it happens. I stopped worrying about having been seen. I did wonder what had become of Bones and the ferret, but I imagined they would surface again soon enough in my life. I still had what they wanted and I intended to keep my appointment with them in the parking lot at Agua Caliente after the nightcap on Sunday, even though I couldn't begin to guess who, if anybody, would show up.

Jay did not seem the picture of health to me. He was propped halfway up in bed when I arrived, his eyes focused on an overhead television screen showing an old John Wayne western, but he still looked as if he had been in a major car accident. His nose had been packed and bandaged and his eyes and mouth were still swollen, his skin a deep purple-blue. He raised a hand in greeting and turned off the set as I walked in, but said nothing. It was evidently going to be difficult for him to talk much. "You're looking grand," I said. "Here." I dropped his notebooks and the *Form* on the bed and he grunted with satisfaction.

I looked around. They had installed him in a third-floor double room, but the other bed in it was empty, so we'd have a chance to do a little talking in private. I walked over to the window and gazed down over a parking lot to a main avenue beyond, where a sludge of cars moved slowly in both directions under a hazy, darkening sky. When I turned back to look at him, Jay was staring at me, his eyes full of questions. "So how are you feeling?" I asked.

"Better. Nothing broken but my nose," he answered in a harsh voice from the very back of his throat. "Fun, huh?"

"Yeah." I sat down facing him in the only chair in the room, at the foot of the bed. "We're in luck," I said. "There's nothing in the American papers. The Mexican dailies are full of it, but nobody saw us leave or drive away. They think it's a sex and drugs crime. In a way, I suppose, that's what it was. Castle's dead, so is Tony Morales. I didn't even know his last name. Mellini was wounded. Badly, I hope."

Jay stared at me in silence. I waited for him to say something. "You got it?" he finally asked. "Shifty, you got it?"

"The Palenque mask?" I nodded. "Yes, I think so." And I told him about my meeting with Marisa. "I haven't opened the box to make sure," I concluded. "And I don't think I'm going to."

"Worth millions," he muttered. "Millions, Shifty."

"It's worth nothing to us if we're dead," I observed. "Who's got it? You?"

"A friend of mine." I stood up and walked over to the window again, mainly because I was too agitated to go on sitting. I was trying to sort the whole thing out in my head, but the pattern had not quite taken complete shape yet. There were holes in it here and there and I was unhappy about it. "How much did you hear of what I said to them last night?"

"Most of it."

"I couldn't tell," I explained. "You were pretty groggy. They must have really worked you over. Mellini?"

He nodded, but his eyes were still full of questions, or perhaps only one question.

"Forget it, Jay," I said. "Forget about whatever it is you have in mind. I'm giving it to them. I'm going to show up tomorrow, in the parking lot by the Foreign Book, after the last race, just as I said I would, and I'm giving it to them, whoever it is who shows up. Youkoumian would be my guess. At least I'm giving them what I've got, which is the box Marisa gave me. Okay? That answer your question, Jay?"

He continued to look at me in silence, a question, perhaps another one now, still hanging in the air between us. Dusk began to press into the room through the window and it grew dark. Neither of us made a move to turn a light on. I think that instinctively we knew it would be easier to sort it out, to discuss the whole business in a half-light that might blur some of the harsher realities. I believe Jay must have sensed that I was angry, even though I wasn't sure myself about my exact state of mind.

I sat down again, on the bed itself this time, so I could keep a close eye on him. "I knew they were smuggling something across the border, Jay, but I didn't know what," I began. "I thought it was drugs. That's what everybody else is smuggling these days. I saw them moving horses back and forth and I figured they were doing it that way, maybe by putting the stuff in the saddles or the feed or somewhere in the vans. It struck me as a novel way to move the stuff and probably a safe one, since horses go back and forth all the time. And I'm pretty sure they are using the horses to move stuff over the border, and maybe it was drugs. Maybe it still is, I don't know. I don't much care. Everybody's in the drug traffic these days. Why else would Mellini and his crew be hanging around down there? They've got an operation set up to smuggle things across, that's for sure. None of Hatch's horses are winning races, or even doing much running at the California tracks, so there has to be some other reason they're shipping back and forth, right? Did you know about it?"

He nodded. "Figured," he said.

"Sure, that was easy enough," I continued. "And then I began to think about Legrand. He makes pornographic movies, but drugs? Well, why not? Of course I was only guessing. But if he's involved in the drug trade, then it would have to be a very recent development. I mean, he's rich and he's established. He'd have had his own network and distribution setup. What did he need Mellini for? Mellini's a punk, basically a small-time hood and loan shark. If he were in the drug traffic, then he'd be only a small cog in a very big wheel, just another soldier in the ranks. He wouldn't be in control of anything. Legrand is way out of his league. He'd use Mellini, sure, but he wouldn't be in partnership with him. Not in drugs, anyway."

I got up now and began to move around the room, working it out as I went along. Jay followed me only with his eyes, his damaged features indistinct now in the growing darkness. "And then I found out about Emile's art collection," I went on, "which dates back to the days, in the fifties, when he was making movies in Mexico. Somehow, it became clear to me, he'd made a connection to move a big shipment of very precious art objects over the border. Some of the pieces at least had been stolen from the National Museum of Anthropology in Mexico City. They have never surfaced. But the Mexican economy has collapsed in the last few years, with a massive inflation rate and the peso devaluations. It became urgent to sell these pieces, but obviously they couldn't be sold on the open market. So somebody contacted Emile, who is probably the world's largest private collector of pre-Columbian art. But not even Emile was wealthy enough to finance the purchase of this lot. So what does he do? He puts much of his own collection up for sale. Why? To raise the necessary capital to buy the Mexican shipment, and especially the Palenque mask, one of the most precious ancient artifacts in the world. Emile would sell everything he had to buy it and he has been selling his stuff. I checked it out. Now, he finds Mellini and figures out a way to move these pieces over the border. He and Mellini make a deal. They begin moving stuff across with the horses, but they hit some sort of snag."

"What?" Jay asked.

"I don't know," I admitted. "But I don't think it matters. Maybe they were moving too many horses back and forth and it began to look peculiar, I don't know. What I do know is that they decided at some point to make use of Lenny Adelson's *maquiladoras* operation. Luis put them onto that one. His son is the plant manager there. I don't think Adelson is in on it. I went to see him. If he'd been in on it, he would have kept me away from his factory. Strictly speaking, he's not a crook, just a scrambler in the toy trade. He's one of those upstanding American businessmen whose aim in life is to enrich himself at the expense of others, mainly by manufacturing shoddy goods, underpaying his workers, and cheating on his taxes. Just another pillar of the American community. But a crook? No."

Jay stirred restlessly on his bed, but I refused to rush myself. I was looking at it all as I assembled it for him and I needed to take my time. "The mask?" he finally asked. "What happened?"

I decided to approach the subject obliquely, mainly for my own benefit. "Jay, you don't have to be in Mexico very long or have too many dealings there before you begin to understand the central fact of Mexican life," I said. "Mexican society is a huge, tangled, dense web of

connections, and the binding tie, what holds the whole
delicate structure together, is blood. Everyone who is
anyone or wants to accomplish anything or make any
kind of score in Mexican life has to have his people in
place. As in any other poor society, what Mexicans count
on and fall back on in times of need or trouble is the
family unit. The only people you can trust completely
are your blood relations. Lupe Camacho stiffs the trainer
who puts him up on his horse in a race he is not
supposed to lose because he has a brother who is part
owner and the trainer of a rival stable. Luis Sanchez,
being a Mexican, sniffs that one out and cashes a big
ticket, but he doesn't inform Hatch or Mellini, why?
Because it's a blood connection. He and Camacho live by
it, they belong to the same culture, but they don't let the
gringos in on it. They wouldn't understand it anyway."

"So Sanchez's son is in the deal," Jay prodded me.
"They decide to smuggle the mask that way?"

"Yes. The one operation that mustn't go wrong is
the one involving the mask," I continued. "Getting hold
of the mask is what Legrand cares most about. By this
time I'm sure he's paid for it and paid a lot, at least a
million dollars, maybe more. He's selling off his own
collection to finance it. He's the one who probably also
hits on the seemingly weird idea of the gorilla heads. He
buys twenty of them at the Western Toy Fair and sends
them down to Tijuana, probably with Castle. Why
twenty? I really don't know. Maybe it's to move not only
the Palenque mask, but other artifacts as well. Each
gorilla head will contain something precious. They're
easily identifiable and there are only twenty of them.
The factory either doesn't make them at all or has
stopped making them. Castle's going to be around to
make sure nothing goes wrong. But something does go
wrong."

"Somebody stole it. Marisa?"

"Her brother," I said. "The blood connection again.
She finds out about the mask, directly or indirectly, from

Mellini. She's a lot smarter than he thinks she is. To him, she's just what he calls stick-pussy and she's become his favorite local sex toy. So he either tells her about it or she figures it out for herself. She also figures out that stealing it might solve all of her own problems—pay for the operation she wants, get herself and Vicente out of the country, get themselves set up somewhere. She had no idea how she'd go about cashing in, but she'll find a way, maybe by selling it back to the people who want it. She has to get hold of it first and she has the perfect instrument. Vicente, her twin brother, works at the factory."

"Twin?"

"Yes, identical. I saw his picture in her house the night Mellini and Castle wrecked it looking for the mask," I said. "I thought it was a photograph of her, with her family back in Los Mochis, before she became a woman. You know she's a transsexual, don't you?"

"Wasn't sure."

"Yeah. I found that out the hard way."

"Unfortunate choice of words."

I smiled. "I suppose. Anyway, that's one connection the boys haven't made, otherwise Vicente would be dead," I said. "Most gringos don't even know that a Mexican's last name is not his surname, but that of his mother's family. Tomás is Luis's son, even though his last name is Herrera, after his mother, and Luis's is Gomez, after *his* mother. Their surname is Sanchez, of course."

"Didn't know myself," Jay said.

"That's how the boys missed the Camacho connection," I said. "Anyway, Vicente has a beard, but if they were in the same room, you'd see the resemblance right away. I noticed him when I checked out the plant. No one else noticed it, because the only person who saw Vicente was Tommy Sanchez, his boss, and Tommy never met Marisa." I now proceeded to fill Jay in on the rest of my detective work, and he continued to lie there in silence, taking it all in, his puffy, battered face a blur in the dim light. "And so she came to me with it," I concluded my account. "She had to trust me."

"She know you're giving it back?"

"No, but I have no choice, do I? I mean, we do want to go on living and betting on horses, don't we, Jay? You don't think Legrand would let me get away with anything, do you? Goons like Castle are for hire, and there are plenty of them around. It's an overcrowded profession." I stood up and stretched. I was feeling suddenly tired, mainly because I hadn't been sleeping well and I felt like an old crippled plater carrying too much weight around on his back. "All I care about, Jay, is getting our money out on old Fred. If we hadn't come down here to do that, we wouldn't have become involved in this mess, would we?" He didn't answer, so I plunged on. "Funny, isn't it? We get out of town to get away from Legrand and Buddy and we blunder right into the middle of Emile's big operation. We'd have been safer if we'd stayed in L.A. I couldn't figure out why they were trying to beat our brains out for a few thousand dollars. You said it was because Legrand was a mean, vindictive son of a bitch and I'm sure you're correct, but it had to be something more. Right?"

"Right."

"So is there anything I've left out?"

"Don't think so."

"You sure?"

"Horse."

"Oh, yes, the horse." I sighed, trying to get my mind off Legrand and the rest of this mess. "Okay, here's where we stand." I filled Jay in on everything that had happened that morning. "So if he runs, he'll probably win," I concluded. "How do you want to bet?"

"You bet, Shifty. Up to you."

"Okay," I answered. "I've got six hundred dollars I can afford to lose. It's my net profit on my betting so far down there. How about you?"

He grunted. "You do it, Shifty. Up to a thousand, okay?"

"Okay." I stood up and stretched. "I'll see you tomorrow night," I said. "When are they letting you out of here?"

"Tuesday, they said. Concussion. Playing it safe."

"Good idea." I looked at him again. "Jay, is there anything I've left out? Or anything I should know that maybe I don't know?"

"Can't think of anything," he said. "Just be careful, Shifty."

I left him there a few minutes later when a nurse, all cheerful bustle and officiousness, opened the door, snapped on the light, and thrust a thermometer into his mouth. He waved to me as I left. I felt a little sick to my stomach, but I forced myself to smile and wave back.

Nineteen

LAST LAUGHS

"Why is Sunday the best day to drive the freeways?" Harry asked.

"How the hell should I know?" Walter answered.

"Because the Catholics are in church, the Jews are in Palm Springs, the blacks are in jail, and the Mexicans can't get their cars started," Harry said.

"That's the worst goddamn joke I've ever heard," Walter said, angrily snapping his *Form* open. "What's the matter with you today, Harry?"

"And like most jokes, a little racist," I observed from my post in the aisle.

"Aw hell," Harry replied, "all jokes are makin' fun of somethin'. If you can't have a laugh or two at life, what the hell's the point?"

"The point is picking winners," Walter said. "I don't come out here to listen to any damn jokes."

"You got to keep laughin', Walter," Harry said. "Laughs is what keeps you feelin' good. I know a man, he had this cancer, you know. Doctor told him he didn't have but about six months to live. Fella rented himself some old Laurel and Hardy movies and Marx Brothers and all like that and started watchin' 'em every day. He's still around, and that was five years ago now."

"I know who you're talkin' about," Walter said, "and he ain't cured."

"Godamighty, Walter, but you sure are a ray of sunshine," Harry said. "Bein' around you is like attendin'

282   **WILLIAM MURRAY**

some goddamn funeral. Don't you ever lighten up none?"

Walter stood up. "I'm going somewhere where I can think in peace," he declared. "I'll be back before the double." And he moved away from us, a look of icy disdain on his face.

Harry chuckled. "Thought I'd never get him to go," he said. "Sit down, Shifty. What's up?"

"Nothing but my pulse rate."

I joined him in the box. It was still nearly an hour before post time for the first race, but I had already been around the track all morning. I had no place else to go. I had spent the night in a cheap motel in San Ysidro, on the American side of the border, where I thought I'd be safer, and I had crossed into Tijuana early that morning. I had hung around Felton's barn and watched him work with his horses, including Fred's Folly, who stood stolidly in his stall, peering out at his new surroundings with the indifference of a passenger on a familiar bus ride. "Oh, he knows what's going on, all right," Felton had told me. "He's a pretty smart old horse, I guess, and he knows he's going to run, but it don't worry him none. He's okay."

The trainer hadn't found anything major wrong with old Fred, apart from his bowed tendons. "Might as well leave him run," he said. "Of course he ain't got but about three more races in him, the way his legs look. And he could go anytime. But we'll take a shot with him in here. On three legs he ought to beat the field he's in with today. I guess Sandy did all right with him."

"Sandy's a horseman," I said. "Even the fact that he's a crook can't take that away from him."

Felton grinned. "You got him pegged, mister," he said, "only don't tell him I agreed with you. He gave my boy Francisco a pretty hard time when he went over to get the horse yesterday. Cursing and shouting at him, calling him all kinds of names, and me too."

"He's not one of your great human beings," I said. "Can he do you any harm?"

"If I ever get a decent horse again and put him in a claiming race, he'll take him off me," the trainer said. "But I'll worry about that later." He smiled again. "Maybe I can unload a couple of my bums on him. Move them up in class and fool him into taking them."

"Unload Troubador on him."

Now Felton laughed. "Nobody wants that old sucker but me," he said. "He's kind of like my dog anyway. Don't do much, but he's always around."

I had begun to feel a little better about my life and things in general after an hour or so around Felton. I've always liked these old horsemen, with their tall tales and salty expressions, mainly because I admire people still in pursuit of a dream. And what bigger dream can an ordinary man have than latching on to a good horse and sharing in his glory? With horses you're always on the yellow brick road and the Emerald City is just around the far turn. It's a better way to live than playing careers in a corporate jungle. "If you think of what you do every day as work," Jay Fox, the Savonarola of the grandstand, had once declared, "then you're throwing your life away. For me every day out here is an adventure."

Jay Fox. The thought of him that morning had made me wince. I had a thousand dollars of his money in my pocket to bet on Fred's Folly and I was reminded of it when Jill showed up at the barn toward the end of the workouts. Even dressed in her boots, jeans, padded flight jacket, and helmet, she looked quintessentially adorable. She walked right over to old Fred, gave him a lump of sugar, patted him on the neck, then turned to look at me. "Jimmy around?" she asked.

"He went over to the stable office," I said. "He'll be right back."

"Old Fred looks pretty good," she declared. "Have any trouble with Sandy?"

"Some. Nothing major."

She looked at me a little oddly, as if I represented a small enigma for her, a problem she hadn't quite worked out. "You know, Shifty," she said, "there's somethin' about you I ain't quite figured out. You and Jay, you're so different. I can't figure it."

"We're united in our addiction," I explained. "We're both mainlining speed horses."

"You sure talk funny too," she said, and sat down on the bench beside me. "So what's goin' on, Shifty?"

"Nothing that you winning on old Fred can't cure," I said. "Someday, maybe, Jay or I will tell you a little more. Think you can win with him?"

"Sure. I ain't worried," she said. "I just got to stay out of trouble with him. He'll give you that one big run of his when you ask him. I'm goin' to wait on him till about the three-eighths pole and try to stay outside so nobody can shut him off. So if he holds together, he ought to win. Might pay good too."

"I'm betting fifty dollars on him for you, Jill. Just do your best."

"Jay ain't comin' down?"

"No. He's got a broken nose and a concussion. Nothing too serious, but he has to stay in bed another couple of days. He looks like hell too."

"They still don't know who did it?"

"A couple of soreheads, I guess, guys Jay put on a loser, maybe."

She didn't answer immediately, but stared out beyond me toward the track. "You live by bettin' real money on these suckers, you live dangerous," she said. "Got a lot of nuts runnin' loose around here."

"I know," I told her, "I've met some of them."

"And Jay's got a mouth on him, too, just like you." She slapped my knee and stood up. "Well, I got to get goin'. I got two more horses to gallop and then I'm goin' home to catch up on my sleep. This gettin' up so early and all ain't good for a growin' girl."

"You look pretty good to me, Jill."

"Aw hell," she said, smiling, "if I don't win the damn race for you, you'll think I'm a real dog. I know you guys better than you think. See you, Shifty." And she walked quickly away from me.

"So what do you want me to do with the damn box?" Harry asked, cutting into my reminiscences. "You got it in the car, right?"

"Sure, like I told you. You want me to take it home tonight?"

"I don't think so, Harry. I'll come and get it from you right after the last race, okay? You aren't in a terrific hurry, are you?"

"Walter will be, but he can wait," Harry said. "There's always a delay at the damn border on Sunday nights, it don't matter what time you get there. I'll just sit tight right here till after the race."

"No, Harry," I said. "Just go and get the box and bring it to me inside the Foreign Book, okay? I'll take it from you in there and then you and Walter can take off."

"Sure thing."

"I really appreciate this, Harry. You're a friend."

"Well, hell, you got your friends, you got your health, and you got good women and fast horses, what the hell else is there?" he said. "I ain't like old Walter. It's just pitiful what he does. He couldn't get no satisfaction out of winnin' the goddamn Kentucky Derby, that's how pitiful he is. Me, I'm here for the run to the roses in life." And he laughed and slapped himself on the thigh. "Damn, if I ain't the loudest old fart at the track. Guess I'm pretty crazy."

"Sure you are, Harry," I said. "Like an old coyote, that's how crazy you are. So who do you like in the double?"

He stopped laughing and reached for his *Form*. "Now you're talkin' like a grown man," he said. "We're goin' to pick us some winners here!"

* * *

I spent most of the afternoon with Harry and Walter. Several times I took a stroll through the stands, simply to make sure nothing else was going on I ought to know about, but I saw no one. Mellini, Youkoumian, and Sanchez seemed to have dropped off the face of the earth, which was fine with me. I knew that at least one of them would surface sometime during the course of the day, but I was in no hurry to deal with that problem. I made a few token bets, after discussing each race with my companions, but essentially I was waiting for the eleventh and final contest on the card. I managed to look cool about my action, but it didn't fool Walter. Along about the seventh race he began to get on me.

"So, Anderson, you're going to make a real killing here today, right?" he said at one point. "How are you planning to do that?"

"I think the horse will run well, Walter," I answered. "That's all I can tell you."

"I suppose that old fart Jimmy Felton told you he would," he said. "That old man doesn't win more than one or two races a meet. How can he know the horse will run well? Wasn't Hatch your trainer?"

"Yes, he was. I didn't like what he was doing, so I turned him over to Felton."

"Bad mistake," Walter said. "Hatch may be a bum, but at least he wins races. This guy Felton, he can't train goats."

"That's your opinion, Walter. You don't have to bet on the horse."

"Bet on him?" Walter said incredulously, as if I had suggested he take a dive from a cliff top into a teacup. "Bet on him? I'm going to get rich betting against him. Camacho's up on a horse in there that can't lose, stretching out from six for the first time, and he'll be three or four to one. Bet on your horse? I guess you're a nice guy, Anderson, but I don't bet on sure losers."

"Well, bein' a nice guy is somethin' no one can ever accuse you of," Harry said to him. "Goddamn, Walter, but you sure have become a mean-mouthed old son of a bitch."

"Wrong, Harry," Walter said cheerfully. "I was always a mean son of a bitch." He stood up, brandishing a winning ticket on the previous race. "And now, if you don't mind, I'm going to go and cash." It was his third consecutive winning bet of the day and he was reveling in his success.

"Don't that beat all?" Harry commented after he'd gone. "A couple of winners and Walter gets to thinkin' he's immortal. What about your horse, Shifty?"

"All I can tell you, Harry, is that we're betting on him," I said. "It's a Trifecta race. You could hook him up in there with three or four other horses and maybe make some money. The horse doesn't look like much and he's bowed, but he can run, believe me, and today's the day."

"I guess I don't need to know much else," Harry said. "Walter's goin' to pee in his pants when this horse comes in, Shifty."

"I'd enjoy that," I said. "This is a big race for us."

I went down to the paddock, of course, to watch Fred's Folly being saddled. Francisco, Jimmy Felton's stocky little groom, flashed me a big grin when he saw me, and Felton, in his old gray overcoat and cap, seemed calm enough. I was very nervous, and if I had been performing that day, I'd have botched every move. The trainer noticed it. "Take it easy," he said. "You'll wash out before the race."

Out in the walking ring I stood in the middle of the circle and watched Francisco lead our horse around and around while we waited for the jockeys to appear. It was a nine-horse field in which, except for his heavily bandaged legs, Fred's Folly stood out. His coat gleamed and he seemed to be bouncing in place, like a boxer waiting for the bell to ring. "I guess he knows he's going to run," I said.

Felton nodded calmly. "He's an old pro," he said. "They always know when it's a go. I just hope he holds together. With that big belly on him, he ain't going to have but about one move in him."

My nervousness suddenly gave way to a strange kind of euphoria. The horse looked unbeatable to me; I *knew* he was going to win. By the time Jill appeared, outfitted in a borrowed set of brown silks, I had become as confident about the outcome of the race as if I were betting on Secretariat going against a bunch of ten-thousand-dollar platers. "Don't win by too much, Jill," I said to her as we waited for the call to the post. "We don't want to embarrass anyone."

She looked at me a little strangely. "Maybe you ought to know that Camacho came over to me in the jocks' room," she said. "He didn't take kindly to bein' bumped off this horse. He said he was goin' to bury my ass."

"Stay clear of him," Felton warned her. "You're outside of him, so he can't pin you on the rail. When you make your move, make sure you don't come inside."

"You bet," she said. "I ain't about to get killed."

I smiled. "You could beat this bunch coming through the parking lot," I said. "Just win, Jill."

I had isolated the contenders in the race to a total of four horses, including ours. One of them was the sprinter stretching out, Don Gus, Lupe Camacho's mount, who had drawn the one hole, on the rail. He didn't figure to give us any trouble because Fred's Folly would break from the outside post and take back, waiting to make his one big run from the three-eighths pole. The other two contenders were also speed horses, who would be expected to press the pace while the rest of the field was composed of third-rate plodders, the sort of horses that almost never win and are used to fill up the fields in cheap races. One of them was the favorite, a lumbering old gelding named Cold Al. We were at the bottom of the racing barrel here, a thirty-two-hundred-dollar claiming race at a mile and a sixteenth for cripples, has-beens, and never-weres. I watched Jill move out onto the track and break old Fred into a slow canter with the ease of a veteran rider. I was as confident of a win by this time as Napoleon reviewing his troops at Austerlitz.

"I think there's a claim in for him," Felton said, his voice breaking through my reverie.

"What?"

"I said somebody put in a claim for him," the trainer repeated.

"You must be kidding. Can't they tell he's bowed?"

"There's a big outfit in here from Mexico City," Felton explained. "They're mainly looking for brood-mares, but Fred's got some breeding. He's out of a decent mare by an okay Irish stallion. They may want him for a stud."

"Should we tell them the horse only likes ponies?"

Felton smiled. "You want to lose him, don't you?" he said. "He can go anytime."

On our way back to the grandstand, I thought I caught a glimpse of Youkoumian hurrying away from the paddock area, but I could have been mistaken. I decided I wasn't going to worry about him or anything else until after the race, however, and I went back upstairs to make my final calculations. I was planning to bet our sixteen hundred dollars in Trifectas, using Fred's Folly as my key horse with the other three contenders in the race. The Trifecta is a so-called exotic wager in which the bettor has to pick three horses in the exact order of finish. This is extremely hard to do, and I wouldn't even have considered it, but a single wager of sixteen hundred dollars to win on our horse would have showed up at once in the tote and not only knocked the odds way down on him but would have led others to bet on him as well. The exotic money doesn't show up in the tote, and we needed to win at least ten or twelve thousand dollars to bail out of our situation with Buddy and Legrand.

When I headed for the parimutuel windows, Fred's Folly was twelve to one, down three points from his morning line. He'd have been down much more if he had shown up with Camacho on his back; with Jill in the saddle, the price figured not to drop more than another point or two, another way of profiting by the use of a woman in a male-dominated environment.

I spent the rest of the time before the race running our money through the windows in dribs and drabs. I never bet more than a couple of hundred dollars at any one location and I moved about, ultimately using eleven or twelve different windows in various sections. By the time I got back to our box with my wad of tickets safely tucked into the inside pocket of my jacket, the horses were at the gate, directly below us. "Well, I suppose you threw your money away on your horse," Walter said cheerfully.

"I'm afraid I did, Walter."

"I should have booked it," he said. "He can't win."

"Pitiful, Walter, just pitiful," Harry said, turning to me. "I bet twenty on him, Shifty. How's he look?"

I glanced at the board. "At ten to one, Harry," I said, "he looks wonderful."

"That's ridiculous," Walter said. "There's no way Camacho's horse can lose this race, unless he breaks a leg."

Ordinarily I would have agreed with Walter; Don Gus looked to be coming up to this race perfectly. He had the speed to get the lead, had the right post position for his style, and Camacho would not use him up too early. Let him win, I thought, just as long as Fred's Folly runs at least third, with one of my other two horses also in the money.

I had expected Camacho to put Don Gus on the lead, but no sooner had the gate opened than he tucked him in along the rail, content to be fourth or fifth around the first turn. The other two contenders, Tabasco and Macho Man, my other Trifecta horses, went to the front, running head and head in modest fractional times, while Fred's Folly dropped back, with Jill moving him over to the rail to save ground, ten or twelve lengths behind the leaders. At the half-mile pole, Camacho moved Don Gus up to third, in perfect striking position within two lengths of the leaders. Fred's Folly was now fifteen lengths back, still galloping lazily along in last place.

With three furlongs to go, however, Jill asked old Fred for his move and the horse responded. He swung to the outside and began picking up the field one by one, as if the other horses were running on a treadmill. Two thirds of the way around the turn, he was fourth, just behind Don Gus. Camacho heard him coming and asked his mount to run. He moved way out into the middle of the track, carrying Fred with him. At the head of the lane the two leaders on the inside were still about a length in front and running nose to nose, while Don Gus and Fred's Folly battled on the outside, Camacho whipping his horse left-handed to keep him leaning on old Fred, impeding him every step of the way, about half a length in front of him.

I stood up and began to scream for Jill to get away from him. I understood at last that Camacho was quite prepared to sacrifice his own chances in order to keep Jill from winning. But there was no way she could get away from him because she couldn't take back and then come on again; Fred's Folly only had one run in him that day, and he'd give up if his rider tried such a tactic. So I had to stand there and watch helplessly while all my hopes of a betting coup were being crushed. Tabasco and Macho Man would lumber in first and second, with Don Gus third and Fred's Folly out of the money. My only hope would be a foul claim, in which the odds are always against the victim, mainly because racing officials the world over are reluctant to change the actual order of finish in a race unless the foul committed is so flagrant they can't overlook it. In this case I wasn't even sure Don Gus had made contact with Fred's Folly; Camacho was too skillful a rider to do more than herd our animal out, carrying him ever wider. They would be practically at the outer rail by the time they crossed the finish line.

About twenty yards from the wire, however, just as I had given up all hope and had already begun to wonder how Jay and I would manage to survive this catastrophe, Don Gus suddenly swerved to the inside. He took two or three lurching steps and then went down, sending Camacho flying. Fred's Folly, with Jill still urging him on, barely finished third, still a length behind the tired leaders, but only about a neck in front of one of the plodders, the eight-to-five favorite in the race, who had had an easy trip and had kept on coming in his usual undistinguished, predictable late-running style.

I looked at Don Gus. The poor animal was struggling to regain its feet, but couldn't; his left foreleg had been shattered, held on only by skin and tissue. It made me nearly physically ill to look at it, even though I've seen many such accidents at the track over the years. People were running toward him to keep him down until the track van, already moving around the far turn, could reach him. A vet would kill him with a lethal injection and the horse would be swiftly carted away, to be packaged eventually into dog food. Fatal accidents are one of the brutal realities of horse racing, but not one I've ever been able to accept. I excused myself from the box and hurried off into the grandstand area, away from this scene of minor carnage. My last glimpse of it was of the horse, still on the ground and being held down by half a dozen men, while Lupe Camacho, unhurt and indifferent, walked calmly away toward the jockeys' quarters.

I didn't go down to the winner's circle and so I only found out later, from Jimmy Felton, that Fred's Folly had been claimed by the outfit from Mexico City. I waited inside for the race to be declared official and then went back to the box, where Harry and Walter still sat, awaiting my return. The Trifecta had paid a hundred and seventy-two dollars even for each two-dollar wager, so that our hundred winning tickets were worth seventeen thousand two hundred dollars. Our net profit came to fifteen thousand six hundred dollars, of which five thousand eight hundred and fifty belonged to me. "That's a low Trifecta payoff" was Walter's opening salvo as I rejoined them. "With the favorite out of the money, it should have paid a lot more than that. Somebody must have bet it heavy."

"I did," I said. "I have it a hundred times, Walter."

The old curmudgeon blinked at me, his mouth agape; I had finally succeeded in shocking him. "A hundred times?" he said, his voice reduced to a disbelieving croak.

"Yes. Our net profit on the race, Walter, is fifteen thousand six hundred dollars. How does that grab you?"

"You're crazy," Walter said. "Crazy. To bet that kind of money on cheap claimers. You're going to die broke."

"Maybe, but I'm going to have a lot of fun getting there, Walter. Having fun is what this is about, in case you haven't noticed." I was sticking it to him pretty hard, but he deserved it and I wasn't going to spare him a single detail of my hard-earned win.

Harry laughed, his face turning pink with merriment. "Goddamn, Shifty, if you ain't the king of the nightcap after all! Fifteen grand? Godamighty, ain't that a pisser!" He turned to Walter. "You called it, Walter. You told him the only way his horse could beat yours was if yours broke a leg. You're bettin' on the wrong propositions, boy! And you sure ain't lucky, like old Shifty here!"

Walter glared angrily at him and then marched out of the box. "I'm sorry, Harry," I said, "but I have to confess he got to me. I thought I'd let him nibble on a little humble pie." I handed Harry all the bills I had left in my pocket, about two hundred dollars. "Your cut of this is five hundred, Harry," I said. "Here's a down payment."

The old man looked at me in astonishment, then down at the money in his hands. "I can't take this," he said. "I ain't no charity case, Shifty."

"Harry, I couldn't have done this without you," I said. "I mean it. You don't know what a help you've been, also with that box I asked you to hold for me. All I want you to do with it is take Marge out for a big night on the town. I want you to dance the night away, just the two of you. Okay?"

He hesitated, then his face softened into a huge smile. "Goddamn, Shifty, I'll do it," he said. "That poor old woman has sure been neglected lately. Too many sore horses and not enough picnickin'. You got a deal, Shifty."

"We only have one more thing to do, Harry," I said. "I'm going to cash and then I need the box. You have it?"

"In the trunk of my car."

"Okay, meet me in the Foreign Book, by the newsstand," I instructed him. "Then do me one last favor if you don't mind. Button up your jacket and just stand by the door of the Foreign Book, on the parking-lot side. Try to look as serious as you can and not like a horse degenerate. Can you do that? It shouldn't take more than five minutes."

"What am I supposed to be, a cop?"

"That illusion will do very well," I said. "But be sure you don't have a *Racing Form* sticking out of your pocket."

"Oh, yeah, goddamn," he said, plucking the offending article from his jacket and dropping it on the floor. "Anyway, it's yesterday's losers. Hell, let's get goin' here!"

It took about twenty minutes to get my money because I wanted it all in hundreds and no one window had enough cash to pay me off. By the time I reached the parking lot entrance to the Foreign Book, it was dark, the whole area only dimly illuminated by the pale glow of streetlamps and reflected light from the track itself. No sooner had I appeared on the steps than a black Mercedes sedan began to thread its way through the lines of parked cars toward me. It stopped at the corner of the nearest lane, to my left, its headlights trained on me from about fifty feet away. I held up the box Harry had given me and waited. The headlights blinked once, then went off. A moment's pause. "You want me to come with you?" Harry whispered behind me.

"No," I said, "but don't go away. If anything happens, Harry, just stay out of it."

I don't know how I managed it, but I walked toward the now dark, silent car, the box tucked under my arm. Larry Youkoumian was sitting in the driver's seat, glaring out at me through the open window. His nose was bandaged and he had a couple of black eyes. I couldn't see into the rear of the car. I stopped about four feet from the door, on the passenger side. "Get in the back," Youkoumian said.

"No, thanks, Larry," I said. "I've been in your aerobics class. I've got the box, as you can see. Come and get it."

The rear window rolled down, revealing the pale, soft features of Emile Legrand. "If you do not get in, I will shoot you, Anderson," the Frenchman said.

"You see the man standing in the door of the Foreign Book?" I said. "His name's Valentino. He's the CIA agent at the consulate here and a friend of mine. If anything happens to me, you won't get across the border tonight. Do you want this or don't you?" I balanced the box lightly in my right hand, then tossed it to my left one. "I'm a magician. I could make it disappear and the two of you as well." I flipped the box back into my right hand. "Take it or leave it."

"How do we know what is in it?" Legrand asked.

"That's your problem," I said. "I haven't opened it. This is the way it was given to me and this is the way I'm delivering it. Frankly, I don't want to know what's in it."

Larry Youkoumian stepped out of the car and walked around the hood of the Mercedes toward me. "Give it to me," he said.

I handed him the box. He took it, thrust it through

the window to Legrand, then headed back toward his post at the wheel. I noticed that the rear window remained open. As the ferret started the engine, I fell flat on the ground and rolled toward the back of the car. The muzzle of a gun equipped with a silencer protruded from the window and fired twice. By this time I was on my feet again, behind the car, and running in a low crouch through the parking lot. I didn't see the Mercedes leave, but when I poked my head up a few seconds later from behind the cab of a pickup, it was gone.

"Jesus Christ, Shifty, what the hell was that?" Harry said when I rejoined him. "Was them real bullets they was shootin'?"

"Yes," I said. "Not everybody likes my act."

"Goddamn, this is like bein' in a goddamn movie!"

"Let's go rescue old Walter," I said. "The least I can do is buy us a hell of a good dinner somewhere before we go home. It's been an arduous day."

"Arduous? Don't know what that means," Harry said. "But you sure know some pitiful characters. I mean, old Walter, he's a mean old fart, but he's harmless. You got to get some new friends, Shifty. Guys shootin' at you, that can change your whole way of thinkin'."

"It already has, Harry, it already has."

Twenty

NIGHTCAP

It was after eleven o'clock when I reached the hospital, much too late for visiting hours, but I knew Jay would be awake and waiting for me. I walked briskly into the front lobby, trying to look as much like a doctor as possible, and went straight up to his room. Luckily he was still alone in it. When I opened the door, he was sitting up, watching the late news. The minute he saw me he popped off the set and stared at me. "Well?"

I took a fat roll of bills from the inside pocket of my jacket and dropped it in his lap. "Just under ten thousand dollars," I said. "That's your share, Jay."

He laughed as he picked up the money. "Hot damn," he said, "so he won!"

"No, he ran third." And I gave him a thorough account of my day, including a vivid rendering of my post-race encounter with Legrand.

"Christ," Jay said. "That bastard."

"Yeah. I certainly hope the mask was in that box," I said. "Otherwise we may not be out of this." I indicated the money on the bed. "This should get us out of the Pick-Six caper."

Jay looked at the roll of bills and sighed. "I suppose so," he said. "Too bad."

"Too bad? Too bad what?"

"About having to pay them the money."

"Oh, I thought you meant about the mask," I said. "What you do with the money is up to you, I guess. I think you should claim your usual commission."

"Yeah, I suppose. A couple of grand for me, the rest for Buddy and the foul Frenchman." He looked up at me. "So what now, Shifty? You going home tonight?"

I nodded. "Yes. I've had enough of Tijuana for a while," I said. "I think I need to go back to work. Hal may have a job for me." I started for the door. "It's late. I'd better get on the road."

He was now counting the bills. "Thanks, Shifty. I really appreciate it."

I got as far as the door and then I turned back. I had to have it out with him or I knew that our friendship was over. "Jay, you could have told me," I said.

"Told you what?"

"What the deal was. From the beginning."

He looked up from the money in his lap. The skin around his damaged eyes had begun to turn yellow as the bruises healed, and his lips were not as swollen, but he was still a living ruin behind his bandages. "What do you mean, Shifty? What deal?"

"Come on, Jay, it's a little late in the game for innocence," I said. "What I haven't figured out is whether you and Emile cooked up the scheme before Fingers showed up at the box to cash our ticket or after. I'd really like to know, because it's going to make a difference."

"A difference? Why should it make a difference? What kind of difference?"

I sat down on the other bed in the room and ran a hand over my eyes, trying to clear my head; I was bone tired, I suddenly realized, and depressed. Not even the bulge of the five thousand dollars in cash in my pocket was providing much comfort. I wanted to lie down somewhere and go to sleep for ten hours. "It makes a difference to me," I said. "Especially in relation to you. I thought we were friends."

"We are, Shifty. We *are* friends."

"Then I think you owe me the truth," I said. "You almost got me killed, Jay."

"I almost got both of us killed."

"Yes, but you knew what was going on and I didn't," I said. "I don't like being assaulted in the street. I don't like being shot at."

Jay sank back against his pillows and sighed. "I guess I screwed up, Shifty," he said in a low voice, still hoarse from the blows he had received on his neck. "When the Palenque mask disappeared, they naturally blamed me. When you showed up in TJ, they assumed we were in on it together. That's what happened, Shifty. The mask is worth a fortune, but you know that. Emile has been trying to find it for years, ever since it was first stolen. When it finally did surface a few months ago, he agreed to pay a million and a half dollars for it. It's worth several times that, but he didn't have the cash. He began to sell off his own collection, just as you had it figured, to finance the deal. He paid the money and then the mask disappeared the day after it arrived in Tijuana. You had it figured just right, Shifty. It was going across the border in one of the gorilla heads from Adelson's factory. Four of the heads disappeared on the same day. The mask was in one of them, probably in the box Marisa gave you to keep for her. You figured it out, Shifty. If you could handicap as well as that, you'd be unbeatable at the track."

I didn't smile; I wasn't amused. "When, Jay?"

"What? When what?"

"Before or after Fingers showed up?"

"Oh, Christ, Shifty, after, of course," Jay said. "You really think I set that all up?"

"I don't know, Jay. Why don't you tell me what happened?"

"Okay. When Fingers went down to cash our ticket," he explained, "Youkoumian put the muscle on him for the fifteen grand he owed Mellini, just as Fingers said. He didn't have all the money, so he agreed to front for them in Tijuana. Fingers doesn't have a criminal record and they needed someone to list as the owner of their horse. Fingers agreed, but then he got scared. He realized very quickly what was really going on with the movement of Hatch's horses back and forth across the border and he wanted out. Fingers is a small-time hustler and horseplayer, but not a crook, and certainly not a drug trafficker. He came to me and told me. Or, rather, he called me one night from TJ and told me. Could I help him? Well, I could. Emile was putting a lot of pressure on me."

"So you didn't tell me the truth about what happened that day, when Castle confronted you in the grandstand."

"Yes, I did, but that wasn't the end of it. I went to see Emile and I talked to him directly. I was trying to get the man off my back. Fingers had called me, I told him. I told him everything. And that's when Emile proposed I make the linkup between him and Mellini. They had a smuggling operation and Emile needed stuff moved across the border. That's how it all started, Shifty. It just got out of hand. It went wrong, that's all. I'm sorry."

"So when I showed up in Tijuana, was that before the deal had been made?"

"No, after. Everything you and I did together in regard to Fred's Folly, that was all on the up and up," Jay said. "Fingers just panicked."

"I can understand why," I said. "So he used me to get out."

"I guess."

"Of course they wouldn't let him out," I said. "He knew too much about this operation. They killed him or they had him killed."

"Do you know that for sure?"

"Pretty sure, Jay. Fingers hasn't surfaced anywhere. My guess is they shoved him out a window or off a rooftop somewhere in this big country of ours. He was a gambler and a loser, so it passes very nicely as a case of suicide. Not somebody important enough for the police to bother very much about. Poor bastard."

"Shifty, I wasn't in with Mellini on anything like that," Jay said. "Or the drugs. You don't think I was, do you?"

"No, Jay, I don't," I assured him. "I know you too well for that. Did Emile tell you about the Palenque mask?"

"Not specifically. He said there was one object he really wanted. If he got it, I was not only off the hook with him, but he'd pay us fifty thousand dollars."

"Us?"

"You and me, Shifty."

"You never mentioned it."

"I decided the less you knew about all this, the better," he said. "I didn't want to get you involved. And frankly, I wasn't sure you'd go for it. You're too much of a straight arrow. I tried to get you to go home, remember? But I'd have found a way to give you the money. You have to take that one on faith. But the fact is I felt bad about what was happening. I got you, as well as me, in a mess, and I couldn't tell you about it. It had gone too far."

"I wish you had told me."

He sighed and gazed unhappily toward the window. "I guess. I guess I should have. It was a real mess. I kept hoping the mask would show up and get us off the hook. They didn't believe me when I told them we didn't have it."

"No, they made that abundantly clear by their actions," I said. "I guess you paid a price too." I stood up to go. "Jay, why don't you concentrate on handicapping in the future? That's what you do best."

"I know that, Shifty, but it's a tough racket," he said. "A guy comes along and says he'll either beat your brains out or pay you fifty grand for making the right connection for him, it's tough to turn the proposition down."

"Stick to horses, please. You're really good at that." Again I reached the door and this time I opened it. "Did Jill call you or show up?"

"No," he said. "She's okay?"

"I think so," I said, "even though Camacho almost killed her out there. Maybe she's had enough of you, Jay. God knows I have. For a while at least."

I walked out of the room as depressed as I've ever been in my life. Jay and I would still be friends at the track, I knew, but I would never quite trust him fully again. And that, as they say, is the slow death of a relationship.

I didn't make it back to L.A. that night. I was too tired to drive, so I stopped a few hours in a motel in San Juan Capistrano and got back on the freeway at six A.M. I was home by eight, and at nine o'clock I called Hal's office. He was surprised to hear from me. "I didn't think you'd make it, Shifty," he said.

"You were wrong, Hal. So what's up?"

The agent sniffed gloomily. "You blew it," he said. "They're going with this guy Williams."

"Well, thanks for trying. And thanks for everything." I started to hang up.

"Shifty, hold on!" he barked into the phone. "I got you a guest shot on the *Tonight Show.*"

"You're kidding."

"You heard me," he said. "Carson's a nut about magic. You have to audition for it, but otherwise it's pretty well set. Christmas week. After that I got you two cruises and maybe a shot in Vegas. Your pal Vince Michaels called. He's going to Europe and he wants you to work for him at the Golden Nugget for four weeks."

"I thought you were going to drop me."

"If you hadn't called this morning, I would have. You okay?"

"Sure I'm okay. Only one thing, Hal."

"What?"

"I'm going to miss most of Santa Anita."

"I should have dropped you," Hal said. "You're diseased."

"Just kidding, Hal," I assured him. "I can handle it. Anyway, they run all year round."

"I'm going to hang up now."

"Thanks, Hal."

"For what? You're still a loser." And he did hang up on me.

That same morning Jill drove up to see Jay in the hospital, but it was a doomed reunion. They held hands and discussed the possibility of a future together that neither of them believed in. Jill was still fiercely committed to making a career for herself as a rider and she was going to go on trying to get live mounts at Agua Caliente, determined to build herself a reputation she could eventually take north with her. Jay was itching to get back to his safe little world of numbers, the tiny kingdom of his grandstand box where he reigned supreme and, in his head at least, the horses ran around the track in every race exactly as he had ordained they should. Surrounded by the helpless suppliants who depended on his calm expertise to rescue them from penury, he ruled supreme, an island of fact in a vast swamp of indecision, prevarication, and rumor. What chance did any woman have to compete with that level of ego gratification? I think he went back to Tijuana once or twice that winter to see her, but they broke it off for good in early February. She had begun to date a sharp young Mexican trainer, who adored her and put her up on some winners. She also went on riding for Jimmy Felton and brought in Troubador again. It was clear to me that she had the talent to win on almost any kind of horse, and I hoped that eventually she'd make it.

The day after Fred's Folly was claimed from us, Felton sent Francisco around to talk to the big outfit from Mexico City. It was a courtesy call, the sort of gratuitous kindly gesture horsemen sometimes make for each other. Francisco was under instructions to tell old Fred's new owners about the horse's predilection for escort ponies. The little Mexican tried, but he was thwarted by the hostile indifference of the tall Texan who trained for the string. "Beat it," he told the groom. "There ain't nothin' about horses we don't know. We'll take care of it."

A week later, when Fred's Folly ran again, he came out on the track escorted by an outrider on a honey-colored pony. And right there, in front of the stands, old Fred unseated his jockey, Lupe Camacho, and tried to mount the honey-colored pony. He had to be scratched from the race. He then ran one more time, two weeks later, and won easily, but he broke down past the finish line and was retired to stud. Maybe he turned out to be bisexual and managed to service some mares. I hope so, because otherwise I have to think he'd have been turned over to a killer for dog food. At the bottom of the scale in the world of Thoroughbred horse racing, the endings are brutal, the facts mostly sordid.

I don't know what happened to the Palenque mask. Perhaps it *was* in the box I turned over to Emile Legrand that afternoon. I've seen him several times at the track early this winter, but I stay away from him. Once, shortly after opening day at Santa Anita in late December, we came face-to-face near the betting windows and he gazed at me with such icy hatred that I froze in place. But he moved wordlessly past me and neither Jay nor I have been troubled by him since. I wrote an unsigned letter to the director of the Museum of Anthropology in Mexico City in January, suggesting they might look into Legrand's activities regarding their stolen treasures, and perhaps they have begun to do so. I would like to believe they have. I would like to be able to feel that at some future date these priceless antiquities will be restored to their rightful owners, as the patrimony of the Mexican people, but I'm just cynical enough about individual motives and private lusts not to want to make a bet on the possibility.

I also made a couple of calls from a public phone to the Border Patrol offices in San Ysidro. I didn't leave my name and I made it quick. I told them a few facts about Hatch and Mellini and Youkoumian. A week later they arrested Youkoumian and there's a warrant out for Mellini, who hasn't been seen since the shooting in Tony's house. I heard a rumor at the track that he was in hiding in the East somewhere, while also recovering from a bad wound that had shattered his shoulder and partly paralyzed him. It couldn't have happened to a more deserving fellow.

Hatch is dead. He was found in his tack room by the Mexican judicial police officers who came to arrest him. He was lying faceup on the floor, having apparently choked to death on his own vomit.

As for Marisa, I have no idea where she is. However, a friend of mine who spent a weekend in Tijuana in early February told me that he had been to a nightclub in the Zona Norte, where he heard a wonderful singer named Marisa. She was starring in a musical revue, modeled on a Las Vegas show, that was mostly inept, a lavish mishmash of poorly choreographed dancers, comedians, and strippers. "But this girl could really sing, Shifty," my friend said. "She had a great voice and what a figure! Man, a set of bazongas and this tiny little waist! She'd be a star anywhere. I went over to talk to her afterward and she was very nice, speaks good English. I was going to ask her out, but then she introduced me to her boyfriend, who turns out to be the guy who owns the club."

"Her boyfriend?"

"Yeah. Big fat guy with a mustache. Sanchez something or other."

"He owns the club?"

"He bought it, she told me. For her."

That night I called up Victor at the Encanto and asked him if he knew how to get in touch with Marisa.

"*Sí, señor,*" he said. "She is at the New York. It is a club in *La Zona Norte.*"

"Please tell her to call me," I said. "I have something for her. It's important." And I gave him my telephone number.

"Sure, I tell her," he said. "Hey, we don't see you for a while."

"I'll be back, Victor," I said. "I like Tijuana. Maybe when Hollywood Park opens."

"You take care, *señor.*"

"You too, Victor. *Suerte!*"

The next day I went to my bank and put two thousand dollars into a savings account I opened in her name at the branch office in San Ysidro. It wasn't enough to pay for an operation, of course, but I owed her something. After all, I hadn't been able to do what she'd asked me to and she must have felt cheated. She's probably still mad at me, because she hasn't called yet. I think she will and when she does, I'll try to explain it to her and tell her about the money. If she doesn't call, I'll find a way to get the loot to her, though I don't think I want to risk another encounter with Sanchez Gomez. I love the idea of staying alive.

I'm still wondering what was in the box she gave me that I turned over to Legrand. I'm not so curious, however, that I plan to pursue it actively anymore.

These days I'm safely back into my world of horses, magic, and good times. I was out at Santa Anita recently and doing well, just a couple of days after I got back from my stint in Las Vegas, when I bumped into the Weasel again. He'd obviously been having a rough day, but had heard a rumor, maybe from Jay, that I'd been on a tear. He accosted me under a TV monitor while I was watching the rerun of a race I had just won nearly six hundred dollars on. "Shifty, how you doing, man?" he asked.

"Okay, Weasel, what's up?"

"Shifty, are you holding?"

"I'm having a good day, Weasel."

"Look, I wouldn't ask you, you know that," he said, his eyes flickering nervously about, as if afraid he'd been overheard. "I mean, I know you don't like to lend money at the track, right?"

"Right, Weasel."

"Only I got to have two hundred, Shifty." He opened his mouth and thrust a finger toward a back molar. "See this bugger here? My dentist tells me it's got to come out. I got some kind of infection in there and it's killing me, you know what I mean? I mean, if it don't come out, I could get real sick from it. You understand what I'm saying? The fuckin' tooth is killing me. Only I ain't got insurance and this guy won't pull the fuckin' thing unless I pay cash up front. I mean, Shifty, I'm fuckin' desperate. I'll pay you back next week, honest."

"Look, Weasel, I'd like to help you," I said. "You don't know it, but you were a help to me some weeks ago."

"Yeah? Really?" His face lit up with a surge of hope that actually brought some color to his normally sallow cheeks. "I helped you? Great!"

"Yes, you did," I said. "And I believe you about the tooth, Weasel. Only you know what I'm afraid of?"

"What, Shifty, what?"

"We got three races to go today," I said. "If I give you this money now, Weasel, I know you're going to blow it on some horse."

"No, Shifty, you got it all wrong," he said, clutching my arm and thrusting his face toward mine with all the sincerity he could muster. "You don't understand. I got the betting money!"

Oh, God, I thought to myself, I love this game. I love even you, Weasel. What could I do? I gave him the two hundred.

Please turn the page for a preview of *The Getaway Blues* William Murray's new hardcover starring Shifty Lou Anderson.

I caught my first sight of Melinda Kennedy when she appeared in the walking ring that afternoon for Mad Margaret's first race. I was standing next to Charlie, watching the filly being led around in a circle. The horse was a little nervous and spooked by the crowd of watchers at the rail, but Eddie had a good hold on her and she looked wonderful. Her chestnut coat gleamed with health and she seemed to be full of herself, an athlete in form on the brink of competing. The more I looked at her, the better I liked her chances and I told Charlie so. "You never know with these young horses," the trainer said. "If she breaks good and don't get too much dirt in her face, she could do it. She's been working just fine."

"If she breaks *well*, Charles," Bedlington said, "and *doesn't* get much dirt kicked up. You are mutilating the English language, dear lad."

"You ain't paying me to talk English, Mr. Bedlington," Charlie answered. "All I know is, the inside ain't the best place to be for a maiden filly first time out."

"You are incorrigible," Bedlington said.

"Hi! I'm sorry I'm late, Lucius," I heard a breathless female voice say. "The traffic on the freeway was just awful and I got off at the wrong exit. Is this your horse? Oh, she's darling!"

I turned around to find myself looking at an authentic beauty. I had imagined from Bedlington's account of his first meeting with her that she would be very attractive, but not the minor miracle I now confronted. She was not very tall, no more than five-four or five-five, but she seemed to be perfectly proportioned, with lovely legs and arms, a slender waist, and the pale, creamy complexion of a Renaissance princess. A mane of black curls framed high cheekbones, full lips, and a pair of lustrous hazel eyes. And she was elegantly dressed in a tailored dark brown suit that showed off her figure without flaunting it. Even Charlie seemed stunned by her. By the time Bedlington had introduced her to us, the trainer's chin had sagged open in bewildered admiration. "Control yourself, Charles," Bedlington admonished him. "Haven't you ever seen an attractive woman before?"

Melinda laughed, a sound of cheerful bells in a distant meadow. "I've heard so much about you both," she said, taking Bedlington's arm, "and I'm so excited. I've never been to a horse race before."

"I told her it was a highly overrated spectacle," Bedlington said, "but she insisted on coming."

"Oh, he's always so negative about everything," she said. "But we're going to change all that. And I *know* she's going to win."

"I'm glad to hear that," Charlie said, "on account of I could use a sure thing. Ain't ever found one yet."

"My goodness, who is that?" Melinda asked, staring across the ring at a big, dark bay filly that had suddenly reared up and kicked out with both forelegs, nearly hitting her groom and sending the onlookers nearest to her in the paddock scurrying for safety.

"The Gantry filly," Charlie said gloomily. "She's crazy, but I hear she can run."

"She hasn't yet," I said, "but you never know with that guy."

We watched while the groom and Gantry himself, a tall, studious-looking man in dark gray slacks and a lemon yellow cashmere sports jacket, struggled to calm the animal down. It took a couple of minutes, by which time the filly had broken out into a sweat, a lather forming against her neck and inside her haunches. "She's washing out," I said. "She isn't going to run a step."

"Don't count on it, Shifty," Charlie warned me. "She's

an Icecapade and they're all a little crazy. But they can run."

"Not the kind I can hammer at the windows, when they look like that."

"They all got speed," Charlie said, "and sometimes the worse they look, the faster they run."

"I think it's just fascinating to hear you two talk," Melinda said. "I don't understand one word, but I love the sound of it."

"Horse people don't talk, Melinda," Bedlington explained, "they sing the siren songs composed by the muses of ruin."

"Honestly, I think it's so sweet," she said. "I'm going to find out what it all means. Shifty will help me, won't you?"

"Are you lucky?" I asked.

"Oh, yes," she said, "always."

"Then you don't need to know anything," I said. "In fact, you're better off *not* knowing."

"I think you're decidedly a very cute person," Melinda said. "Lucius was absolutely right about you."

"What did he say?"

"'Merely corroborative detail,'" Bedlington declaimed, "'intended to give artistic verisimilitude to an otherwise bald and unconvincing narrative.'"

"Oh, Lucius," she said, smiling sweetly. "Which one is it?"

"*The Mikado*, my dear."

"How funny!"

The byplay between them had already assumed a pattern of intimacy that surprised me, if only because they had known each other for such a short time, and I found myself unable to believe in it. But she had an aura about her that was authentically bewitching and, whatever her motives, I found myself rooting for her. If anybody was going to be able to dissuade our eccentric plutocrat from doing away with himself, it was obviously going to be this girl. Bedlington seemed mesmerized by her.

"Oh, look at those adorable little men!" Melinda exclaimed, clapping her hands together. "Have you ever seen anything quite so cute?"

She was referring to the jockeys, who had suddenly appeared in the paddock and were heading for their mounts. Tim Lang was among the last to arrive, but came trotting toward us, then stopped in his tracks at the sight of Melinda. His greedy little gunslinger's eyes undressed her from head to foot, but Melinda seemed either unaware of his lust or indifferent to it. "It's *so* nice to meet you," she said, when Bedlington introduced her to him. "You're so sweet to ride our horse. I just know you're going to win."

"Do try, Timothy," Bedlington said. "This is Miss Kennedy's first visit to the races."

The jockey nodded, but never took his eyes off her. Charlie leaned in over his shoulder. "Tim, this filly's got speed and she's worked fine out of the gate," he said, "but she may not like the inside. If she backs up when the dirt hits her, take a hold, don't rush her. If you get clear, she'll run for you."

The rider nodded and smiled at Melinda. "You need the money, right, Mr. Bedlington?"

"Oh, no, he doesn't," Melinda said, shaking her pretty curls, "but we do so want you to win. Please do your best, it would mean so much to us."

Lang seemed dazed by her and could only nod. Even after Charlie gave him a leg up into the saddle for the parade to the post, he continued to stare at her. Then, as the horses moved out through the gap toward the track, he smiled and waved at her. "He's such a sweet boy," Melinda said. "Does he ride all your horses, Lucius?"

"Most of them," Bedlington said. "Charles seems to think he can ride."

"Oh, I just know he can," Melinda said, "and he seems like such a nice young man."

"I don't know about nice," Charlie said.

"Well, bright."

"Bright? He'd get lost in a round room," the trainer

said, "but you don't hire a rider for his brains. He's got good hands and he can get you out of the gate. He could be one of the top riders here, like a McCarron or a Pincay, if he'd listen."

"Oh. Why won't he?"

"Like I told you, miss, because he's dumb. Most jockeys are dumb. It's hard to get a lot of brains inside a size-four hatband."

"My goodness, but you sound so cynical, Mr. Pickard," Melinda said. "You sound just like Lucius."

"You're very young, my dear," Bedlington said. "After you've seen a bit more of the world and grappled daily with mankind's lumbering imbecilities, I suspect you'll be more appreciative of the older generation's negative assessment of the human condition."

"Sounds right to me," Charlie said, "even if I didn't understand half of what you just said."

Melinda laughed and took Bedlington's arm as we headed toward the grandstand. I fell in behind them, next to Charlie, who glanced slyly at me as we trailed after them. "Where'd he meet this chippie?" he asked.

"She's the daughter of one of his ex-wives," I explained. "I met the mother and she's quite a lot like her. Lots of manic energy."

"She'd wear me out pretty fast."

"Maybe you just don't like women, Charlie."

"It ain't that I don't like them, I just don't understand them."

"Were you ever married?"

"Once, a long time ago," the trainer said. "The three worst years of my life. She spent most of her time shopping. You know how to paralyze a woman from the waist down, Shifty?"

"I give up."

"You marry her."

We all sat together for the race in Charlie's box, which was in the lower grandstand area, about halfway between the sixteenth pole and the finish line. I had bet fifty dollars to win on the filly, figuring that she would either run her race and win or finish out of the money, so I kept my binoculars trained on her all the way to the post. If she had misbehaved or washed out, I would have rushed back to the betting windows and sold my ticket, but she seemed to be perfectly calm and well within herself as Lang brought her to the starting gate. Gantry's filly, on the other hand, was all lathered up and tossing her head about, fighting the attempt of her rider, Gary Leavenworth, to control her and get her settled down. She was going off the favorite, at eight to five, with Mad Margaret the third choice, at seven to two. A couple of minutes before post time, I lowered my glasses and sat back in my seat to await the start of the race. "She looks fine," I said to Charlie, who was sitting quietly beside me, his arms folded across his chest. "Gantry's filly is a mess."

"Don't pay no attention to that," the trainer said. "She'll run this time, I guarantee it."

As we sat there, I realized that Melinda had not stopped talking since leaving the paddock. She had snuggled in next to Lucius in the front row, her arms entwined in his, while she commented ecstatically on everything she observed, from the bright emerald green of the infield and the majestic rocky slopes of the Sierra Madre mountains, against which Santa Anita nestled like an old art-deco jewel, to the beauty of the horses themselves, the colors of the silks the jockeys wore, the elegance of the women in the Turf Club boxes, the amusing-looking characters who swarmed about us. She chattered away about everything and nothing, interspersing her observations with questions to which she evidently expected no answers. But instead of being exasperated by her, as any serious horseplayer would have been, Bedlington appeared to be enchanted. He sat quietly in place, beaming, his left hand over one of hers, as the horses began filing into the gate.

When the race started and the animals burst out of their stalls, with the jockeys pumping them out of there to get position before they hit the turn, Melinda leaped to her feet directly in front of me and began to scream. "Oh! Oh! Come on, sweetie! Come on, Maggie, you can do it! Oh! Oh! Come on, come on!" she shouted, jumping up and down. "Hurry up, hurry up! Come on, Maggie! Please! Please! Oh! Oh!"

She had caused me to miss the start of the race and I had to stand up myself in order to see what was going on. Mad Margaret must have broken slowly, because, by the time I picked her out of the pack of eleven horses moving along the backstretch, she was next to last, along the rail about eight lengths out of it. "She got left," Charlie said. "The damn starter took too long to get them out of there and she went to sleep."

By the time they hit the turn, Gantry's filly, Hustling, had opened up two lengths. Mad Margaret had room and had begun to move strongly up on the inside, but was facing a hopeless task. Even if she handled the clods of dirt now showering up into her face, she would either have to run too fast too early to make up the ground lost at the start and she would tire or some other horse would move over in front of her on the turn and shut her off. I kissed my fifty dollars good-bye, but kept my glasses glued to her just to see how she would respond to the hopeless challenge she now faced. There would be a next time, as there always is in racing.

Nothing that had happened in the race made the slightest impression on Melinda, who continued to scream and bounce up and down as if the filly were dueling for the lead. I stepped out into the aisle behind our box to get away from her and so I could make out what was happening. Instead of allowing his mount to relax and settle down, Lang was now pumping hard, asking her to run. "Dumb jock," I heard Charlie say, as Mad Margaret moved up steadily on the inside, running with her head down and seemingly unfazed by the dirt in her face. Luckily, no one came over on her as they hit the turn and she continued to make up ground, so that by the head of the stretch she was third and still closing. "Oh, wow, where is she? Oh, there she is, there she is!

She's going to win, she's going to win!" Melinda shrieked.

There was no way she could have won. Gantry's sweaty speedball had opened up four lengths on the field by that time and she continued to run hard down the lane, stretching her lead to six lengths at the sixteenth pole. Mad Margaret was second by then, but the effect of rushing up against a fast pace finally took its toll. She tired in the last few yards and came in fourth, seven lengths behind the winner, but still trying hard as Lang urged her on along the rail. "Oh, that's so sad, so sad," Melinda said, falling back into her seat. "What happened, Lucius? I just *knew* she was going to win! What happened?"

Bedlington put his arm consolingly around her as he began to explain a few facts of racing life to her. Charlie stood up and said good-bye. "I'd better go down and make sure she came out of it okay, Mr. Bedlington," he said. "Nice to have met you, miss."

I followed him out into the aisle. "She ran a hell of a race, Charlie," I said, "all things considered."

"Yeah, only I don't know how much Lang took out of her, that dummy," he said. "All he had to do was wrap up and let her get a taste of it. Instead he goes all out when it's hopeless. You can ruin a green young horse like that. These damn jocks, Shifty, they can kill you, you better believe me."

"I believe you, Charlie," I answered, as the trainer headed down toward the track. He was right about Lang, of course, and by using the horse hard that way he had tipped her quality to every smart horseplayer in the stands. In her next race she'd go off the favorite, maybe at prohibitively low odds. And all just because Lang must have wanted to impress Melinda Kennedy. Oh, well, I thought, nobody ever said this was an easy game. I headed back toward Jay's box, a couple of aisles away, to see if he still felt positively about his hard knocker in the seventh. I'd have to bet about a hundred on it now to salvage my day and I wanted to make no mistakes.

"Hey, Shifty, who is she?" Jay asked, as I joined him. "We saw you in the paddock. That's a Rose Bowl queen."

"Yeah, what's the angle on that?" Beltrami echoed him. "I got a blue-veiner just from looking."

"I'll explain later," I said. "Right now, Jay, I need a little reassurance. I had fifty on Bedlington's filly and she ran a hell of a race. Next time."

"Right," the handicapper agreed, smiling. "Go For Broke will not blow, Shifty."

"I'm glad to see the priorities observed," Arnie said. "The trouble with women is that you can't put saddles on their backs and whip them down the stretch."

"I don't need no saddles," Angles declared. "All I need is half an hour and a nice motel room."

"Angles is strictly a sprinter," Jay said. "Quick out of the gate and quick to finish."

"In the cheap claiming ranks," Arnie observed, "where the losers flourish."

"Ah, what do you know, Wolfenden?" Angles said, turning on him. "You ain't been laid in twenty years, I bet. I bet you ain't even had a hard-on since then."

"I keep calm, Angles," Arnie said. "Excitement of any kind scrambles the brain cells and this is a place that rewards tranquil contemplation."

"Ah, what do you know? Nothing, that's what you know," Angles said. "You don't figure the angles, you don't weigh the options. You gotta have a broad from time to time."

"I rely on the beast with five fingers," Arnie said. "And you know what, Angles? It never looks up at you and says, 'I love you,' or wants to be taken out to dinner or go shopping. And the momentary pleasure is the same, without any of the timeconsuming, costly side effects."

I bet a hundred dollars to place on Go For Broke, but decided to watch the race from the rail up above the box seats. Risking money at the track is a serious matter to those of us who go to the races regularly, and the uninformed chatter of a neophyte on the scene can become a serious irritant, not to say hazard. Let Bedlington wallow in Melinda's charming ignorance, I said to myself; I'd watch the race alone and rejoin them afterward.

As I stood there, waiting for the horses to get to the post, I saw Melinda heading down the aisle to my right, perhaps on her way back from the ladies' room. Lonny Richards's girlfriend, the blonde with the wonderful legs, rose up out of a box near the finish line, waved excitedly, and came running toward her. They embraced and I could tell that the blonde was astonished to see her, though Melinda had her back to me and I couldn't make out her expression. They talked animatedly for a couple of minutes, then parted again and returned to their own seats. I was wondering idly where these two could possibly have known each other before, but in less than a minute the race went off and I focused my attention on the fate of my bet.

It was an easy win. Go For Broke got up by a nose and I was sure Jay had the Exacta, which paid over two hundred dollars for every five-dollar ticket. My own bet in the place hole returned a profit of a hundred and thirty, so I could go home a winner, and I said my thanks to Jay as I passed his happy box on my way to rejoin Melinda and Bedlington.

"Where have you been, dear boy?" he asked, as I showed up.

I told him about my minor coup and Melinda clapped her hands together in delight. "Oh, that's so great!" she exclaimed. "That's the horse I wanted to bet on, but Lucius wouldn't let me! It had the longest tail and I *loved* the way it bounced up and down! Oh, Lucius, you see? We should have listened to Shifty."

"He didn't tell us anything, Melinda," the plutocrat said. "You can't wager on these beasts on the strength of their looks, my dear. Someone has to explain the facts of life to you." He took her hand and stood up. "Shifty, we are on our way. Melinda will drive me home. I know you wish to linger here."

"Well, I might stay through the feature."

He reached into his wallet and handed me the usual crisp one-hundred-dollar bill. "Thank you, dear lad, it's been enlightening, if not exactly rewarding. I'll call you."

Melinda leaned forward and pecked me on the cheek. "Oh, Shifty, it's been such fun," she said. "I hope I didn't make a fool of myself. You were very sweet to put up with me. I get so excited. I think this is grand, really. Thank you, thank you!" She took Bedlington's hand to lead him out of the box.

"Melinda, who's that girl you were talking to?" I asked. "The one who came over to you just before the race. I was standing up there and I saw you."

She looked surprised, but covered it up quickly with a laugh. "Oh, Angel? That's Angel Price," she said. "Isn't that amazing? We knew each other in Milan two years ago. She was a model and I was modeling, too. We were staying in the same hotel. Isn't that wild? I mean, imagine seeing her here, of all places. She's an actress," she said. "Wow, it's weird! She was pretty crazy and went out with a lot of wild guys, but she was fun. Hey, it's really a tiny world, isn't it?"

"You want me to phone you tomorrow, Lucius?" I asked, as they headed out.

"Certainly, dear boy," he called back, with a languid wave, then turned to Melinda. "'Let's depart, dignified and stately.'"

"Oh, Lucius," she said, "you're wonderful."

"*Iolanthe*, Act One. A favorite of mine."

BANTAM MYSTERY COLLECTION

- 28479 **THE ART OF SURVIVAL** Maxwell $4.50
- 18507 **DEATH IN FASHION** Babson $2.25
- 27000 **DEAD ON ARRIVAL** Simpson $3.50
- 28175 **ELEMENT OF DOUBT** Simpson $3.50
- 28073 **JEMIMA SHORE'S FIRST CASE** Fraser $3.95
- 27773 **LAST SEEN ALIVE** Simpson $3.50
- 27723 **MURDER MYSTERY TOUR** Babson $3.50
- 27470 **MURDER, MURDER, LITTLE STAR** Babson ... $3.50
- 28096 **MURDER SAILS AT MIDNIGHT** Babson $3.50
- 27772 **NIGHT SHE DIED** Simpson $3.50
- 28070 **OXFORD BLOOD** Fraser $3.95
- 27774 **PUPPET FOR A CORPSE** Simpson $3.50
- 27663 **THE RAIN** Peterson $3.95
- 27361 **REEL MURDER** Babson $3.50
- 28297 **ROUGH JUSTICE** Peterson $3.95
- 28019 **YOUR ROYAL HOSTAGE** Fraser $3.95
- 18506 **SIX FEET UNDER** Simpson $2.25
- 28459 **SUSPICIOUS DEATH** Simpson $3.95

NERO WOLFE STEPS OUT

Every Wolfe Watcher knows that the world's largest detective wouldn't dream of leaving the brownstone on 35th street, with Fritz's three star meals, his beloved orchids and the only chair that actually suits him. But when an ultra-conservative college professor winds up dead and Archie winds up in jail, Wolfe is forced to brave the wilds of upstate New York to find a murderer.